big NATE

GREAT MINDS THINK ALIKE

More

big NATE

adventures from

LINCOLN PEIRCE

Big Nate From the Top

Big Nate Out Loud

Big Nate and Friends

Big Nate Makes the Grade

Big Nate All Work and No Play

Big Nate: Game On!

Big Nate: I Can't Take It!

Big Nate: The Crowd Goes Wild!

Big Nate: Say Good-bye to Dork City

Big Nate's Greatest Hits

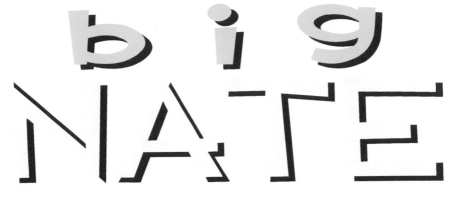

big NATE

GREAT MINDS THINK ALIKE

by LINCOLN PEIRCE

Andrews McMeel
Publishing®

Kansas City • Sydney • London

Big Nate is distributed internationally by Universal Uclick.

Andrews McMeel Publishing, LLC
an Andrews McMeel Universal company
1130 Walnut Street, Kansas City, Missouri 64106

www.andrewsmcmeel.com

ISBN: 978-1-4494-7399-0

Library of Congress Control Number: 2013944315

Big Nate can be viewed on the Internet at
www.gocomics.com/big_nate

ATTENTION: SCHOOLS AND BUSINESSES
Andrews McMeel books are available at quantity discounts with bulk purchase for educational, business, or sales promotional use. For information, please e-mail the Andrews McMeel Publishing Special Sales Department:
specialsales@amuniversal.com.

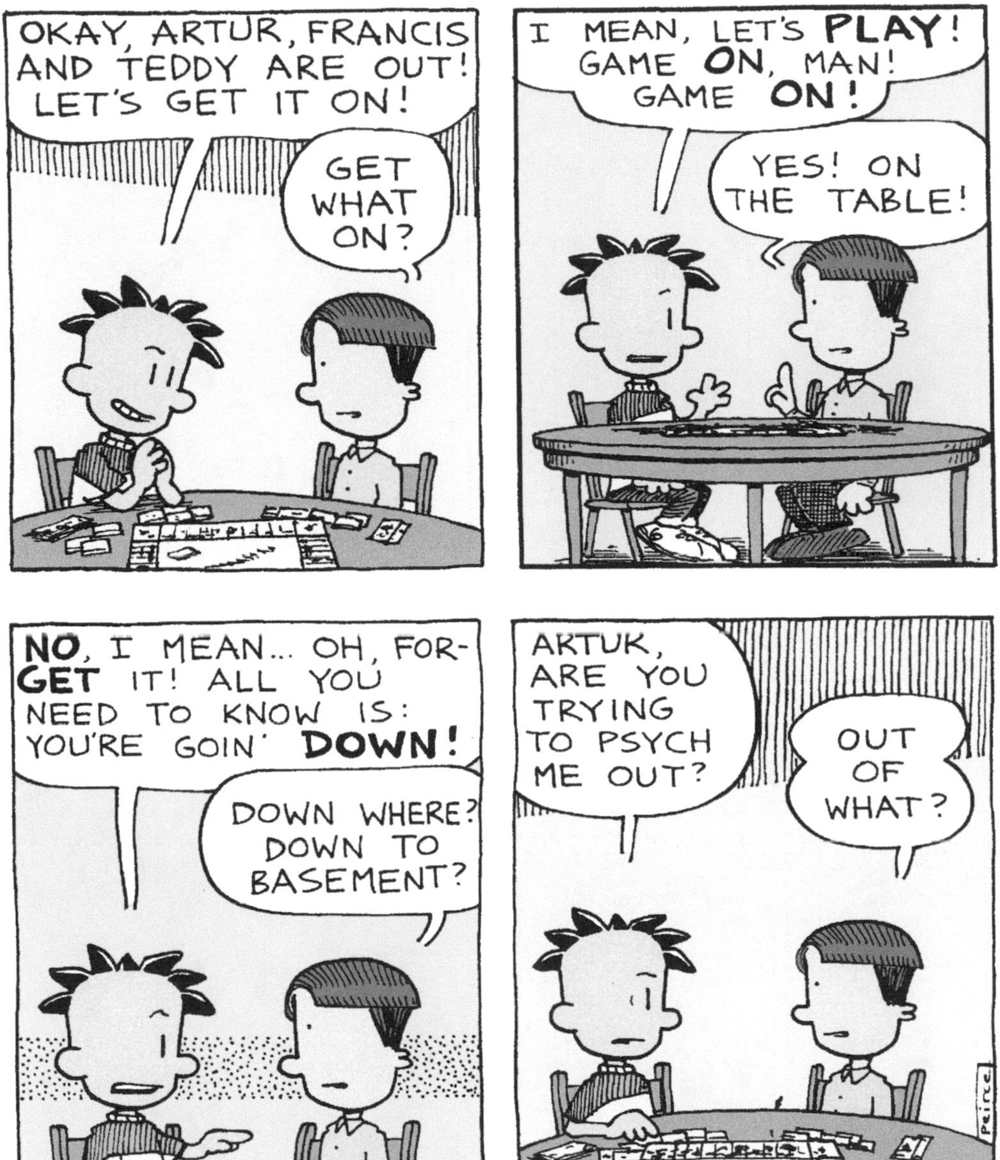
OKAY, ARTUR, FRANCIS AND TEDDY ARE OUT! LET'S GET IT ON!
GET WHAT ON?
I MEAN, LET'S **PLAY**! GAME **ON**, MAN! GAME **ON**!
YES! ON THE TABLE!
NO, I MEAN... OH, FOR-**GET** IT! ALL YOU NEED TO KNOW IS: YOU'RE GOIN' **DOWN**!
DOWN WHERE? DOWN TO BASEMENT?
ARTUR, ARE YOU TRYING TO PSYCH ME OUT?
OUT OF WHAT?
peirce

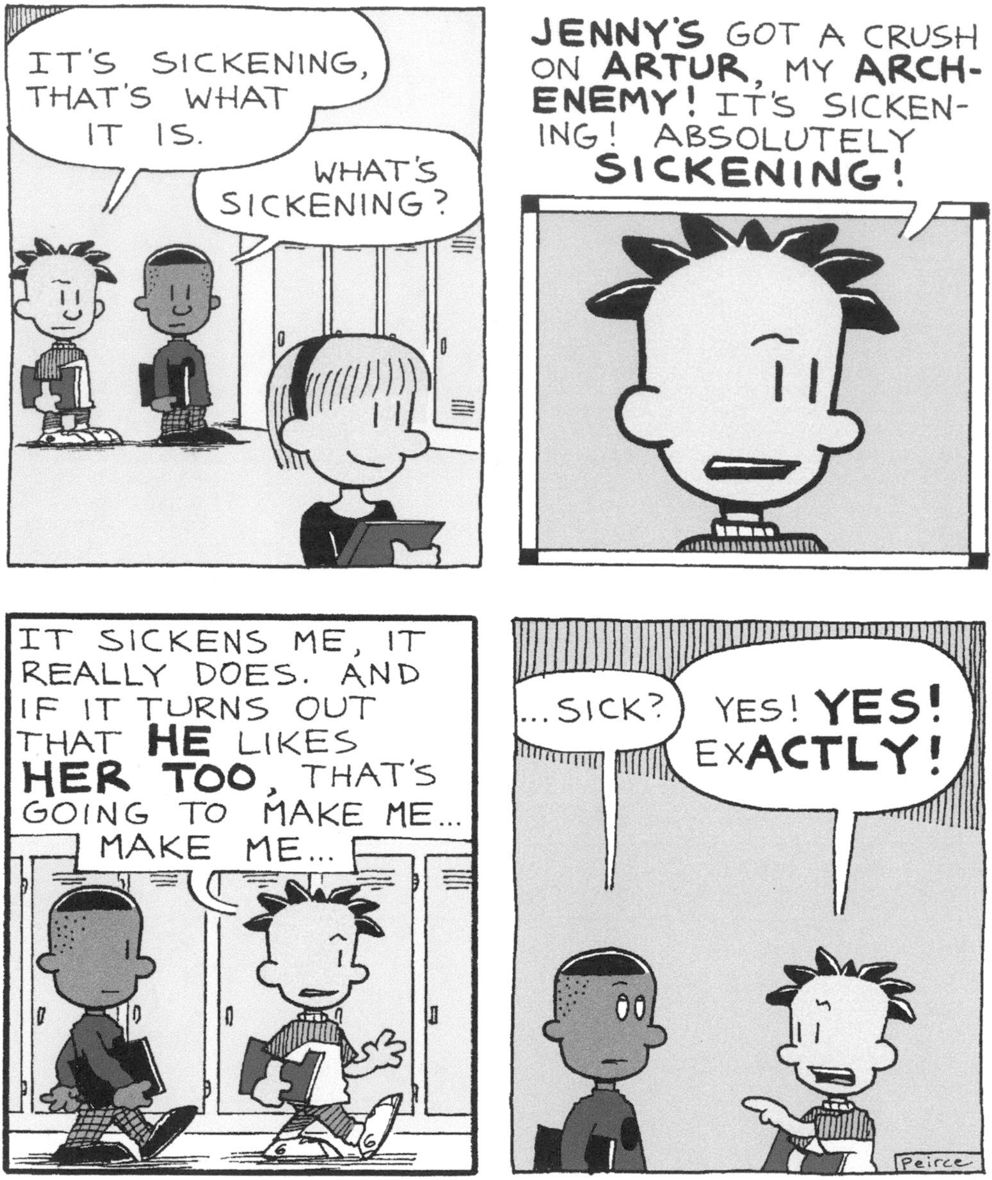
IT'S SICKENING, THAT'S WHAT IT IS.
WHAT'S SICKENING?
JENNY'S GOT A CRUSH ON ARTUR, MY ARCH-ENEMY! IT'S SICKENING! ABSOLUTELY SICKENING!
IT SICKENS ME, IT REALLY DOES. AND IF IT TURNS OUT THAT HE LIKES HER TOO, THAT'S GOING TO MAKE ME... MAKE ME...
...SICK?
YES! YES! EXACTLY!
Peirce

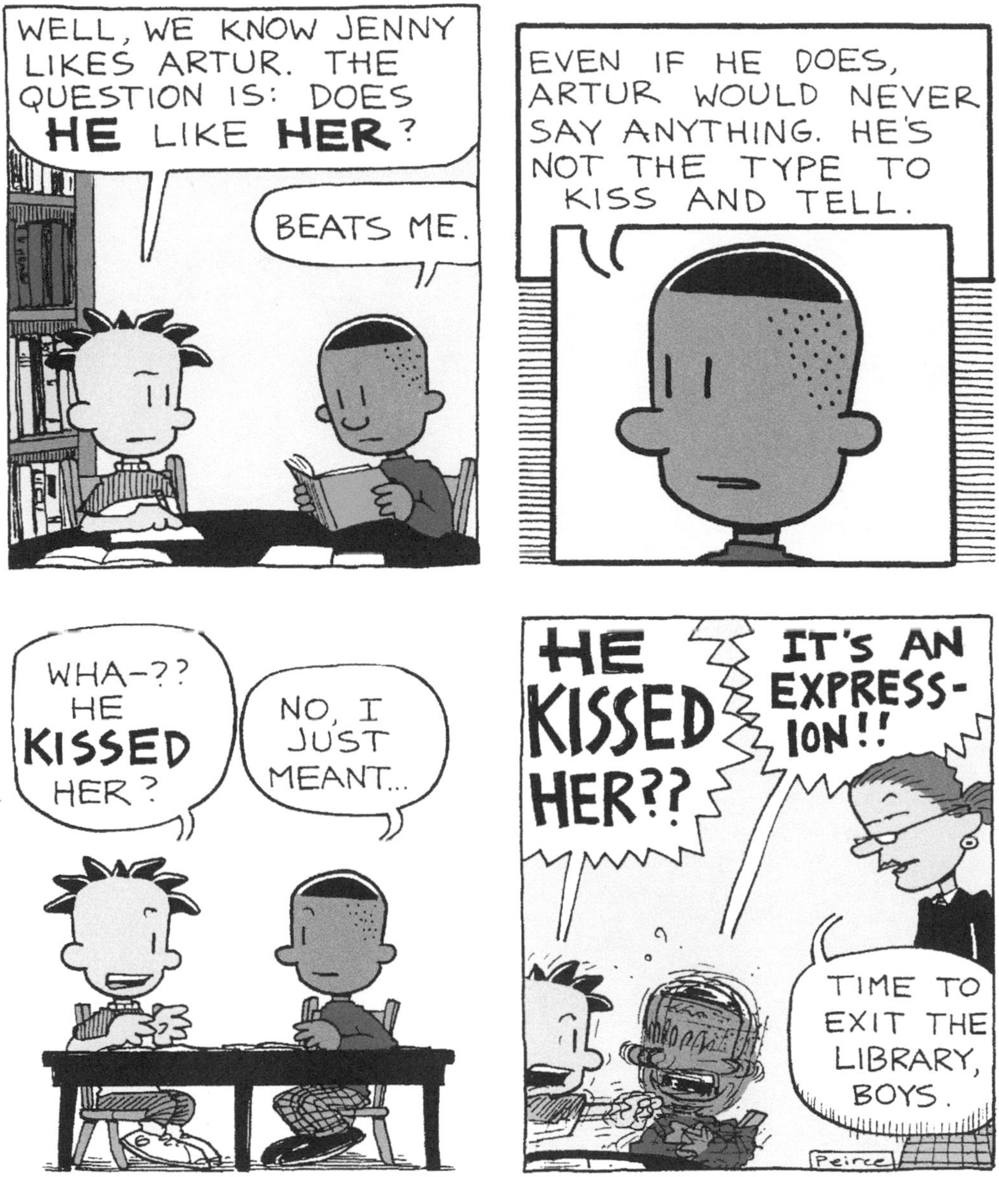
WELL, WE KNOW JENNY LIKES ARTUR. THE QUESTION IS: DOES HE LIKE HER?
BEATS ME.
EVEN IF HE DOES, ARTUR WOULD NEVER SAY ANYTHING. HE'S NOT THE TYPE TO KISS AND TELL.
WHA-?? HE KISSED HER?
NO, I JUST MEANT...
HE KISSED HER??
IT'S AN EXPRESS-ION!!
TIME TO EXIT THE LIBRARY, BOYS.
Peirce

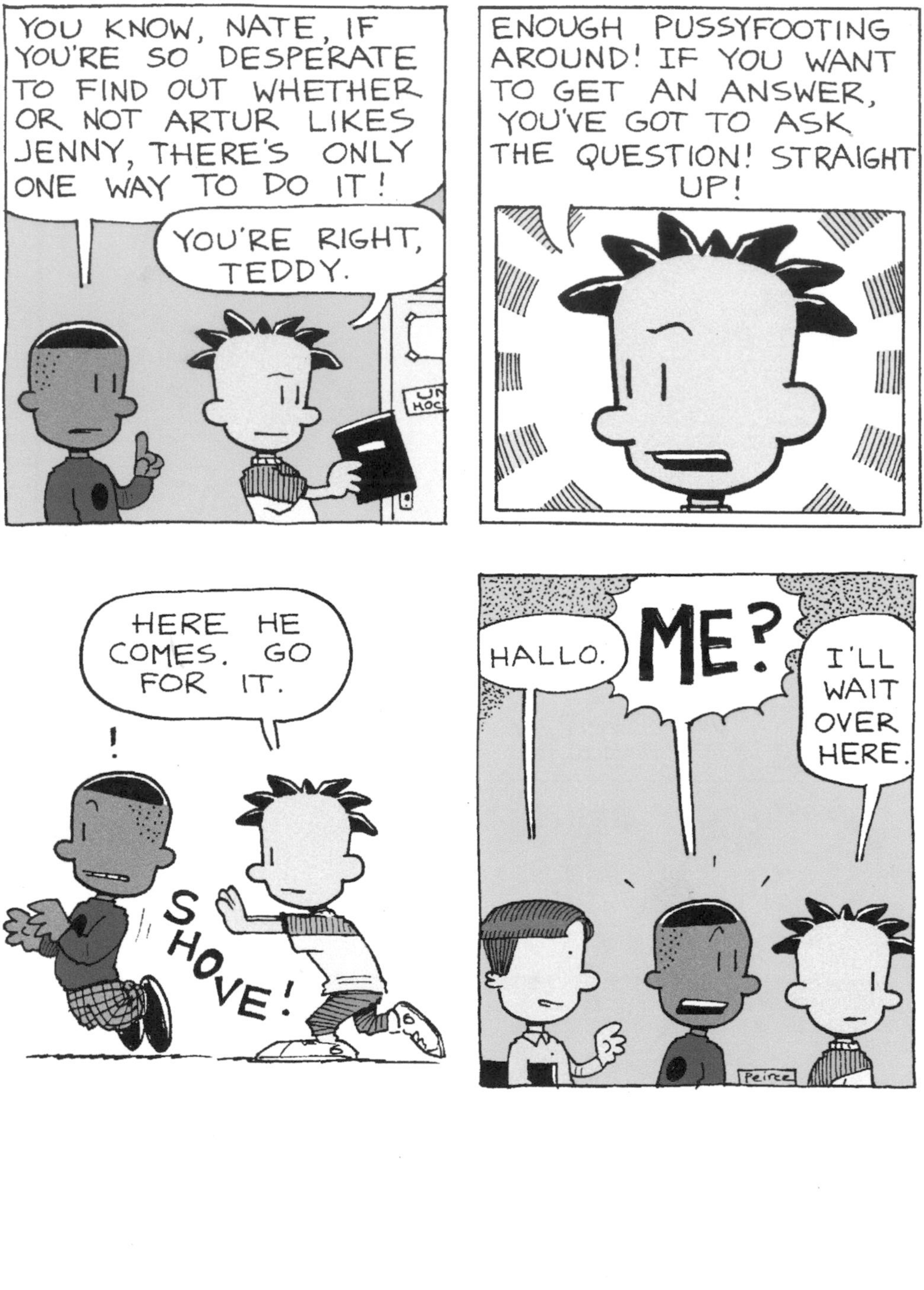
YOU KNOW, NATE, IF YOU'RE SO DESPERATE TO FIND OUT WHETHER OR NOT ARTUR LIKES JENNY, THERE'S ONLY ONE WAY TO DO IT!
YOU'RE RIGHT, TEDDY.
ENOUGH PUSSYFOOTING AROUND! IF YOU WANT TO GET AN ANSWER, YOU'VE GOT TO ASK THE QUESTION! STRAIGHT UP!
HERE HE COMES. GO FOR IT.
!
SHOVE!
HALLO.
ME?
I'LL WAIT OVER HERE.
Peirce

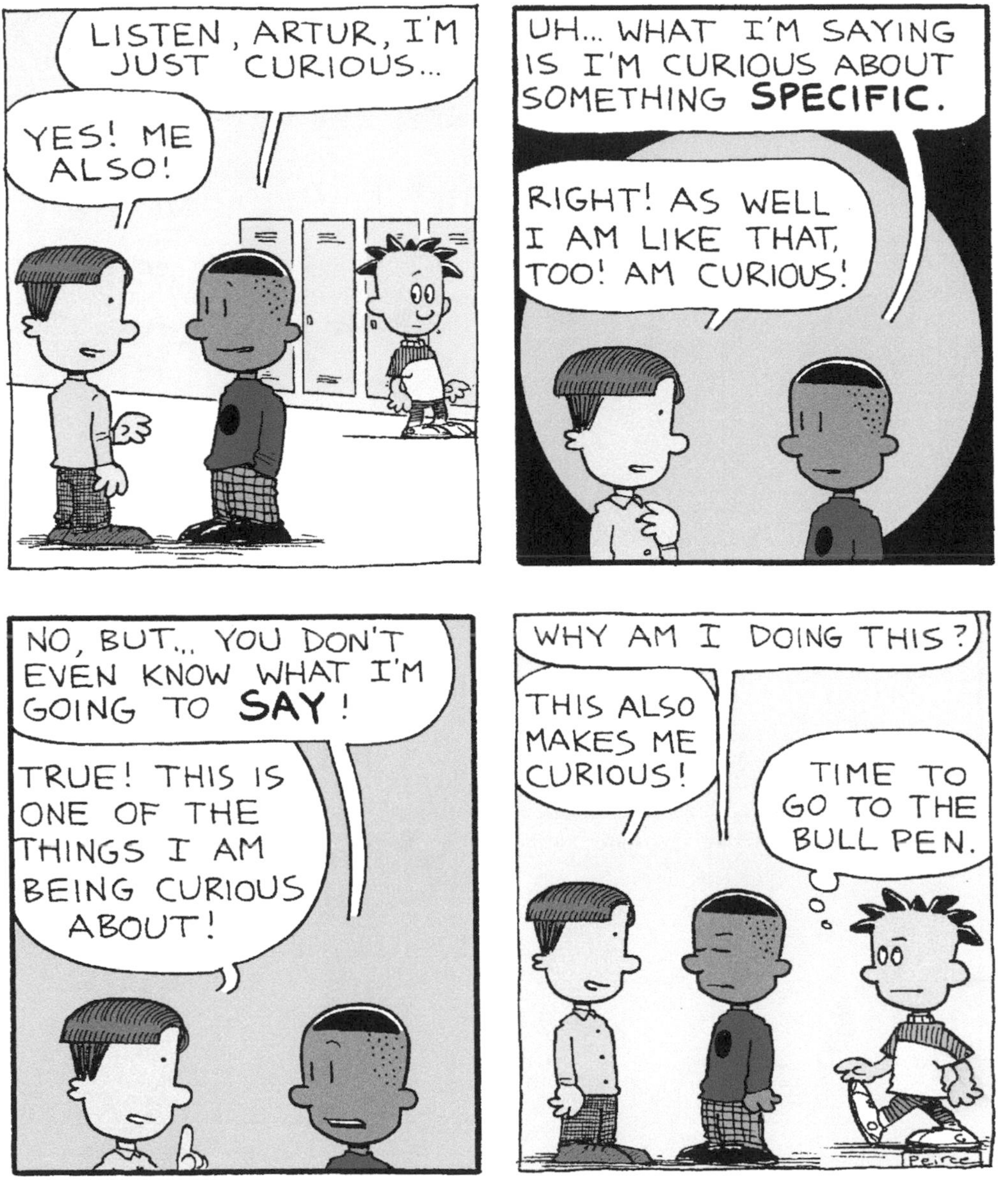

LISTEN, ARTUR, I'M JUST CURIOUS...
YES! ME ALSO!
UH... WHAT I'M SAYING IS I'M CURIOUS ABOUT SOMETHING **SPECIFIC**.
RIGHT! AS WELL I AM LIKE THAT, TOO! AM CURIOUS!
NO, BUT... YOU DON'T EVEN KNOW WHAT I'M GOING TO **SAY**!
TRUE! THIS IS ONE OF THE THINGS I AM BEING CURIOUS ABOUT!
WHY AM I DOING THIS?
THIS ALSO MAKES ME CURIOUS!
TIME TO GO TO THE BULL PEN.
Peirce

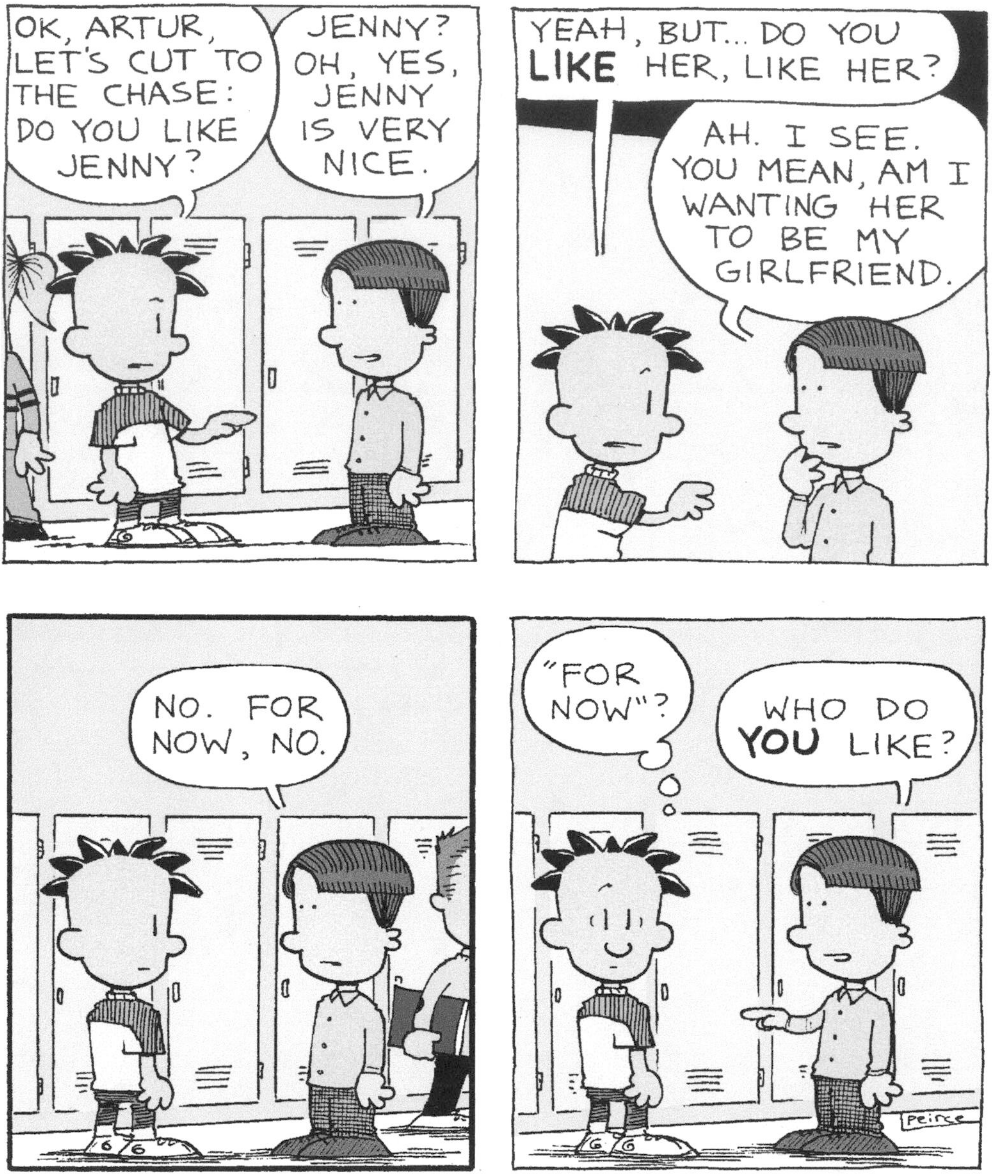
OK, ARTUR, LET'S CUT TO THE CHASE: DO YOU LIKE JENNY?
JENNY? OH, YES, JENNY IS VERY NICE.
YEAH, BUT... DO YOU **LIKE** HER, LIKE HER?
AH. I SEE. YOU MEAN, AM I WANTING HER TO BE MY GIRLFRIEND.
NO. FOR NOW, NO.
"FOR NOW"?
WHO DO **YOU** LIKE?
PEIRCE

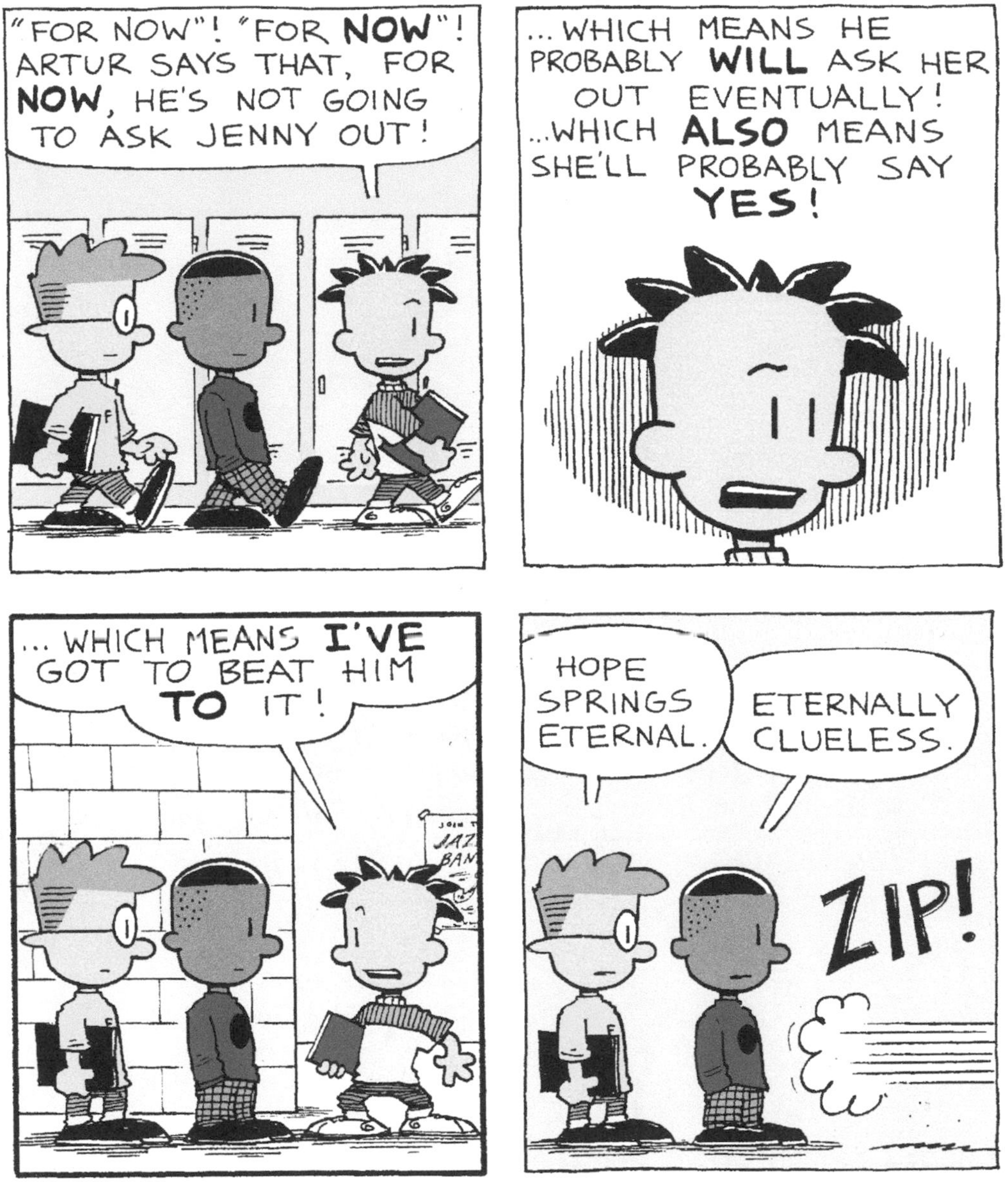
"FOR NOW"! "FOR NOW"! ARTUR SAYS THAT, FOR NOW, HE'S NOT GOING TO ASK JENNY OUT!
...WHICH MEANS HE PROBABLY WILL ASK HER OUT EVENTUALLY! ...WHICH ALSO MEANS SHE'LL PROBABLY SAY YES!
...WHICH MEANS I'VE GOT TO BEAT HIM TO IT!
HOPE SPRINGS ETERNAL.
ETERNALLY CLUELESS.
ZIP!

GORDIE! DID THE NEW ISSUE OF "FEMME FATALITY" COME IN YET?
IK
IX
DELIVERED JUST A HALF-MINUTE AGO!
THIS SIDE UP
LET'S TAKE A LOOK AT THE COVER AND SEE IF THIS ONE'S WORTH YOUR HARD-EARNED $2.95!
THIS SIDE UP
"WILL THE FABRIC-EATING MICROBOTS OF DOCTOR POX DEVOUR FEMME FATALITY'S MIDRIFF-BARING TANK TOP AND MINI-SHORTS?"
THIS SIDE UP
I THINK I SPEAK FOR EVERY RED-BLOODED AMERICAN BOY WHEN I SAY: RING IT UP!
POW!
KA-CHING!
Peirce

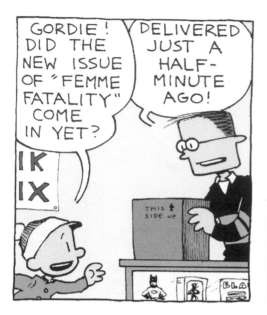

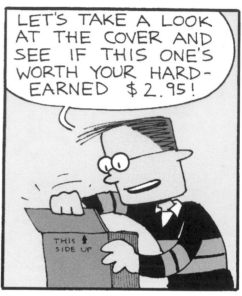

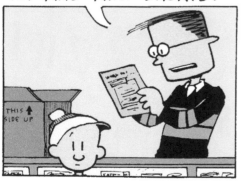

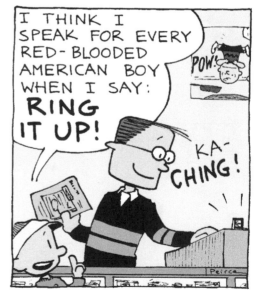

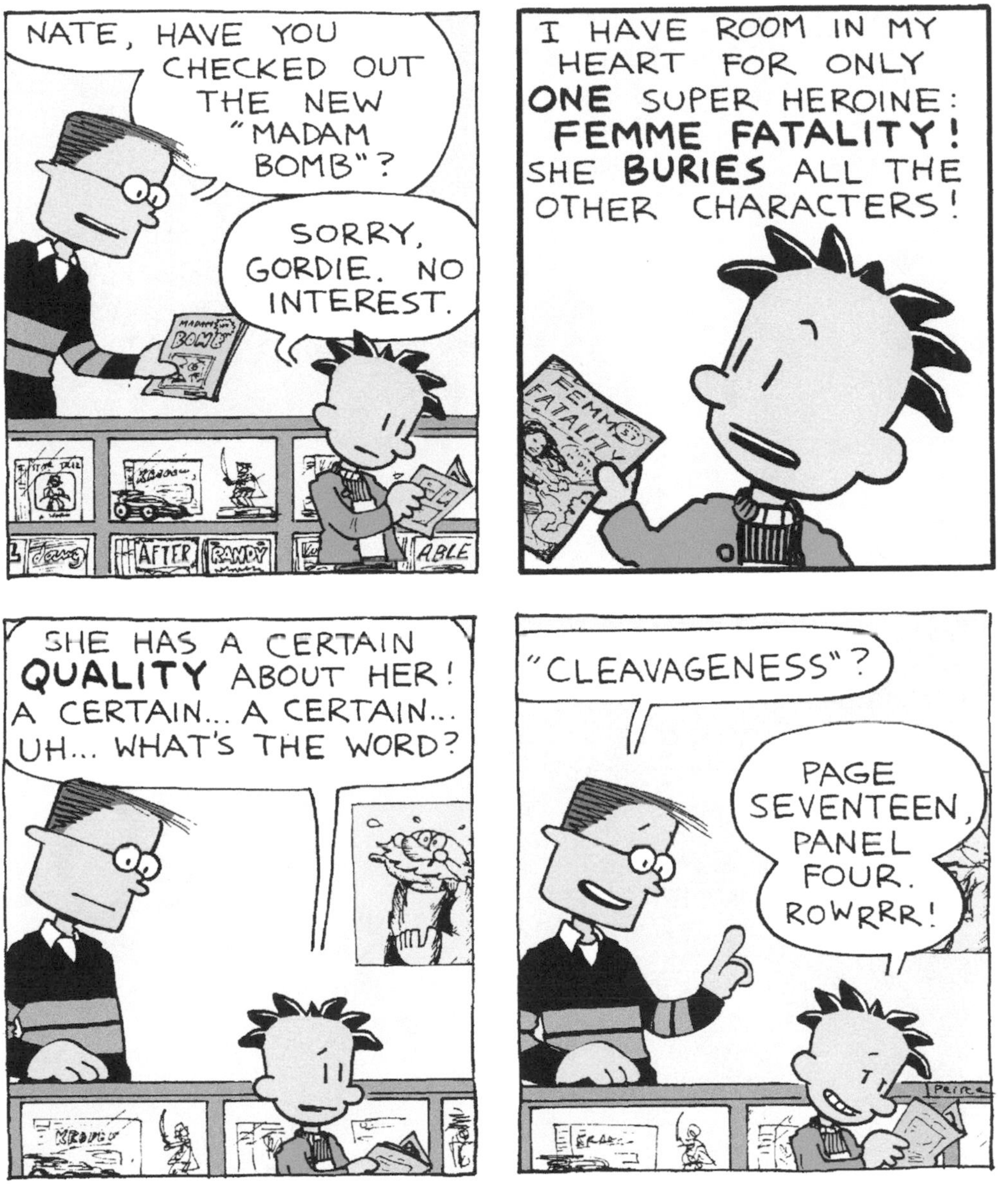
NATE, HAVE YOU CHECKED OUT THE NEW "MADAM BOMB"?
SORRY, GORDIE. NO INTEREST.
I HAVE ROOM IN MY HEART FOR ONLY ONE SUPER HEROINE: FEMME FATALITY! SHE BURIES ALL THE OTHER CHARACTERS!
SHE HAS A CERTAIN QUALITY ABOUT HER! A CERTAIN... A CERTAIN... UH... WHAT'S THE WORD?
"CLEAVAGENESS"?
PAGE SEVENTEEN, PANEL FOUR. ROWRRR!

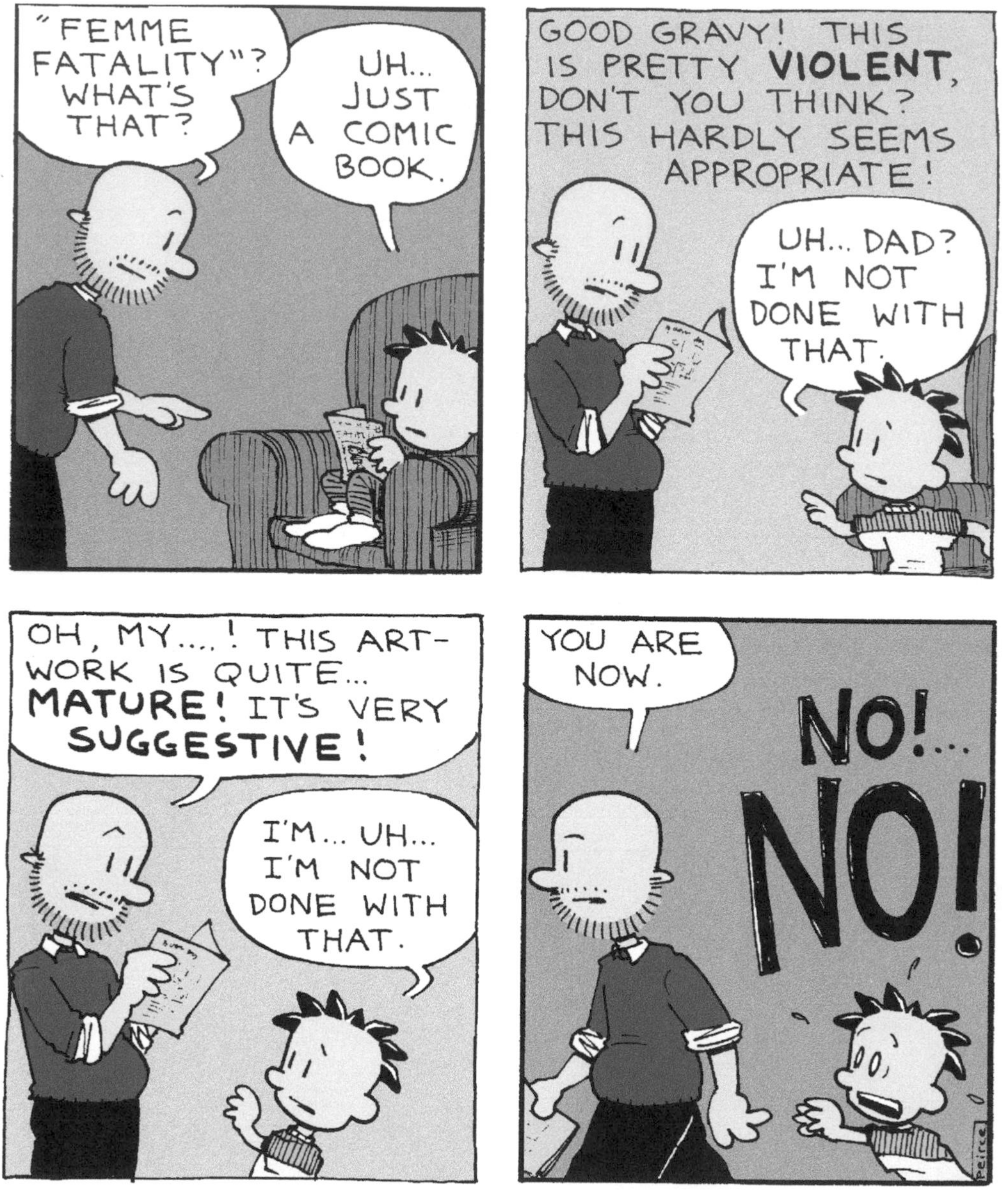
"FEMME FATALITY"? WHAT'S THAT?
UH... JUST A COMIC BOOK.
GOOD GRAVY! THIS IS PRETTY VIOLENT, DON'T YOU THINK? THIS HARDLY SEEMS APPROPRIATE!
UH... DAD? I'M NOT DONE WITH THAT.
OH, MY....! THIS ART-WORK IS QUITE... MATURE! IT'S VERY SUGGESTIVE!
I'M... UH... I'M NOT DONE WITH THAT.
YOU ARE NOW.
NO!...
NO!
Peirce

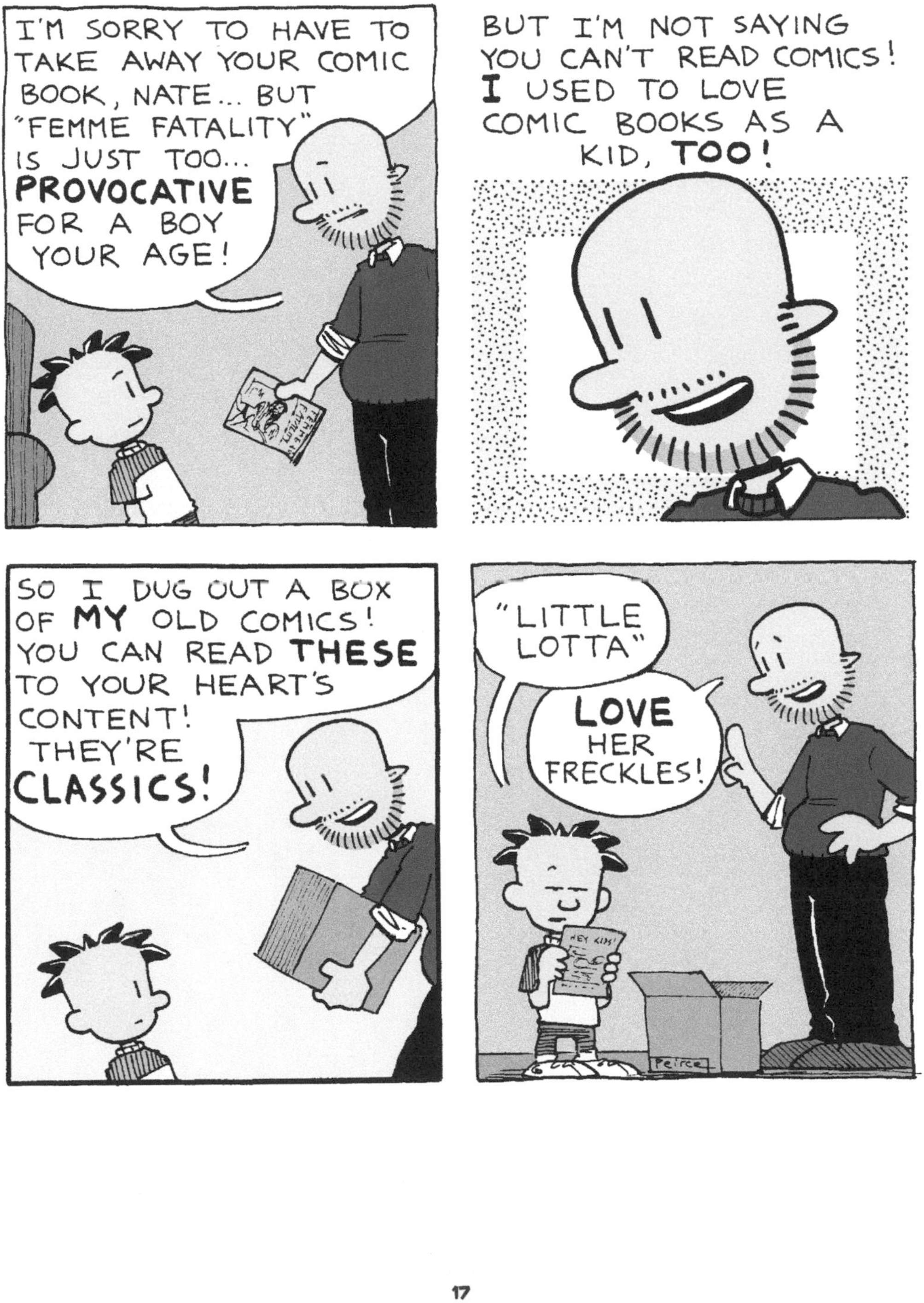
I'M SORRY TO HAVE TO TAKE AWAY YOUR COMIC BOOK, NATE... BUT "FEMME FATALITY" IS JUST TOO... **PROVOCATIVE** FOR A BOY YOUR AGE!
BUT I'M NOT SAYING YOU CAN'T READ COMICS! **I** USED TO LOVE COMIC BOOKS AS A KID, **TOO**!
SO I DUG OUT A BOX OF **MY** OLD COMICS! YOU CAN READ **THESE** TO YOUR HEART'S CONTENT! THEY'RE **CLASSICS**!
"LITTLE LOTTA"
LOVE HER FRECKLES!
Peirce

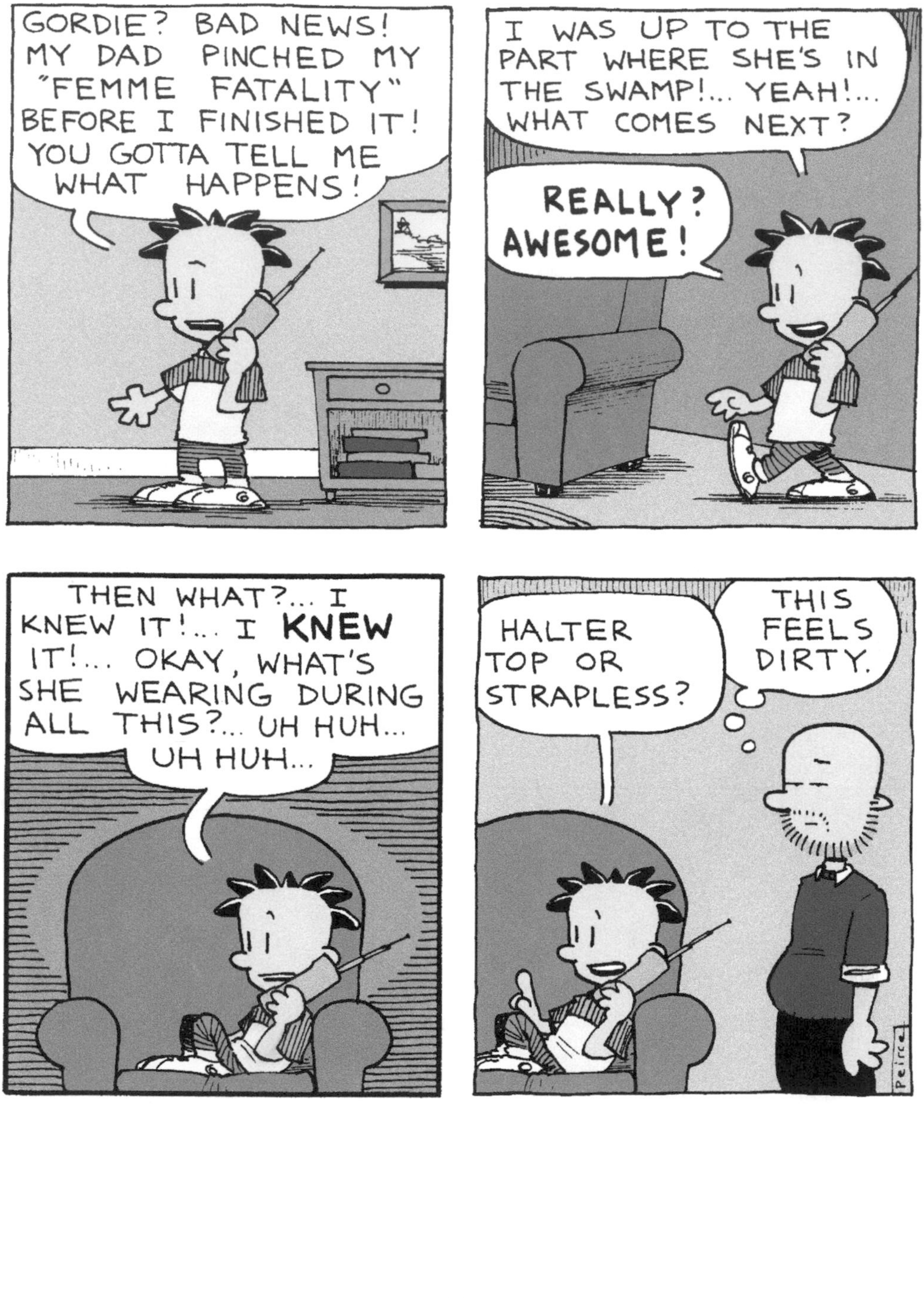
GORDIE? BAD NEWS! MY DAD PINCHED MY "FEMME FATALITY" BEFORE I FINISHED IT! YOU GOTTA TELL ME WHAT HAPPENS!
I WAS UP TO THE PART WHERE SHE'S IN THE SWAMP!... YEAH!... WHAT COMES NEXT?
REALLY? AWESOME!
THEN WHAT?... I KNEW IT!... I **KNEW** IT!... OKAY, WHAT'S SHE WEARING DURING ALL THIS?... UH HUH... UH HUH...
HALTER TOP OR STRAPLESS?
THIS FEELS DIRTY.
Peirce

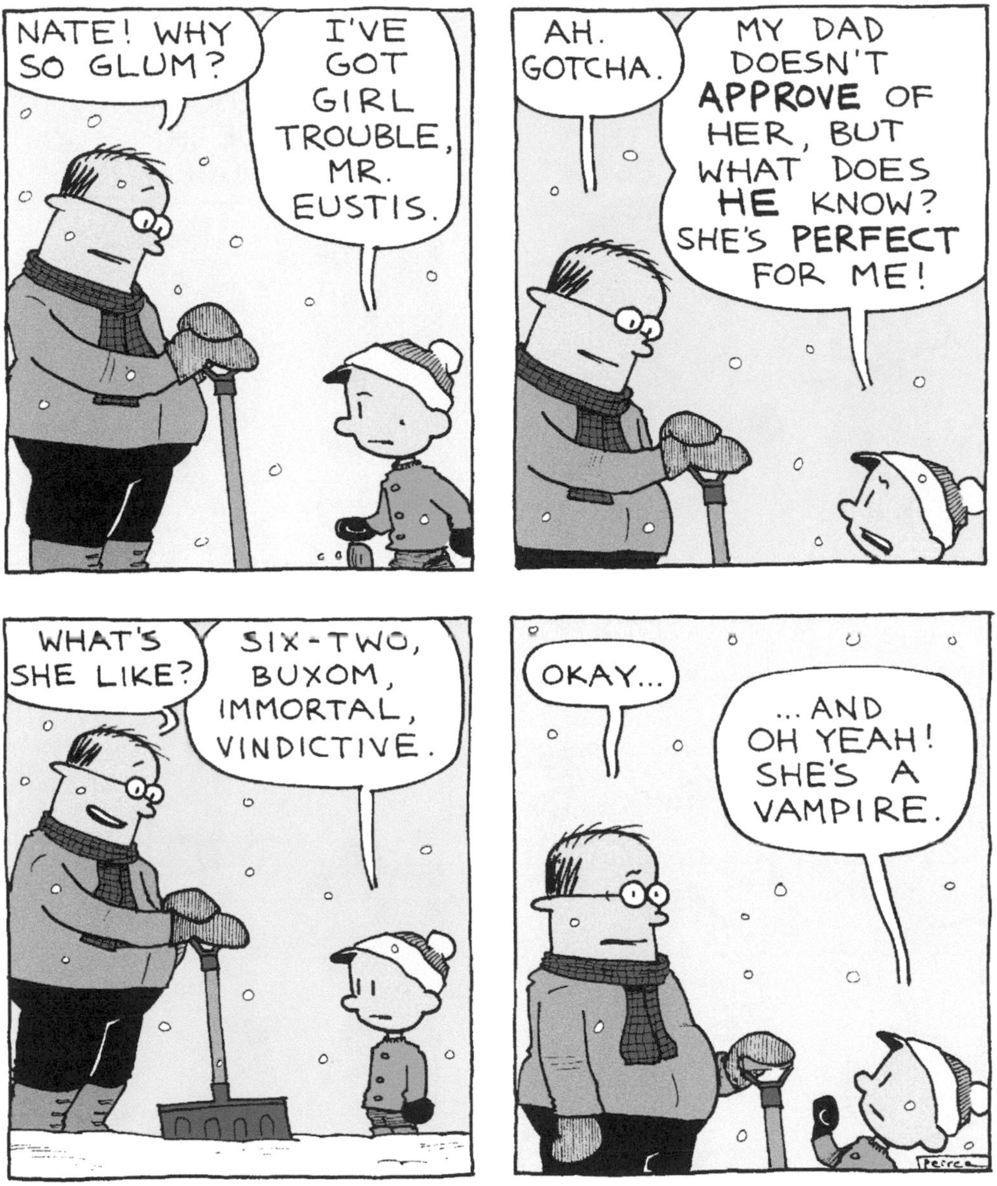
NATE! WHY SO GLUM?
I'VE GOT GIRL TROUBLE, MR. EUSTIS.
AH. GOTCHA.
MY DAD DOESN'T **APPROVE** OF HER, BUT WHAT DOES **HE** KNOW? SHE'S **PERFECT** FOR ME!
WHAT'S SHE LIKE?
SIX-TWO, BUXOM, IMMORTAL, VINDICTIVE.
OKAY...
...AND OH YEAH! SHE'S A VAMPIRE.
PEIRCE

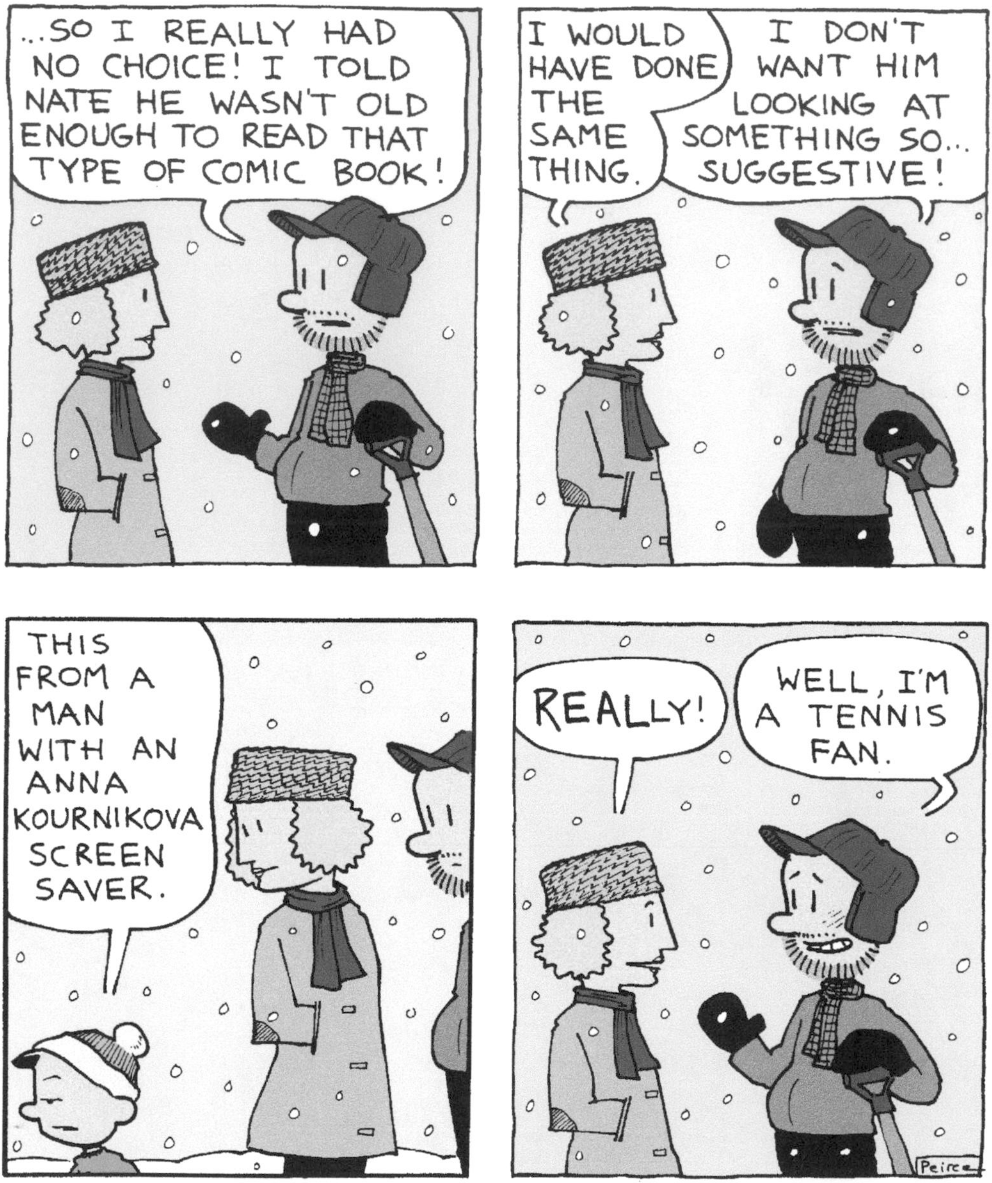
...SO I REALLY HAD NO CHOICE! I TOLD NATE HE WASN'T OLD ENOUGH TO READ THAT TYPE OF COMIC BOOK!
I WOULD HAVE DONE THE SAME THING.
I DON'T WANT HIM LOOKING AT SOMETHING SO... SUGGESTIVE!
THIS FROM A MAN WITH AN ANNA KOURNIKOVA SCREEN SAVER.
REALLY!
WELL, I'M A TENNIS FAN.
Peirce

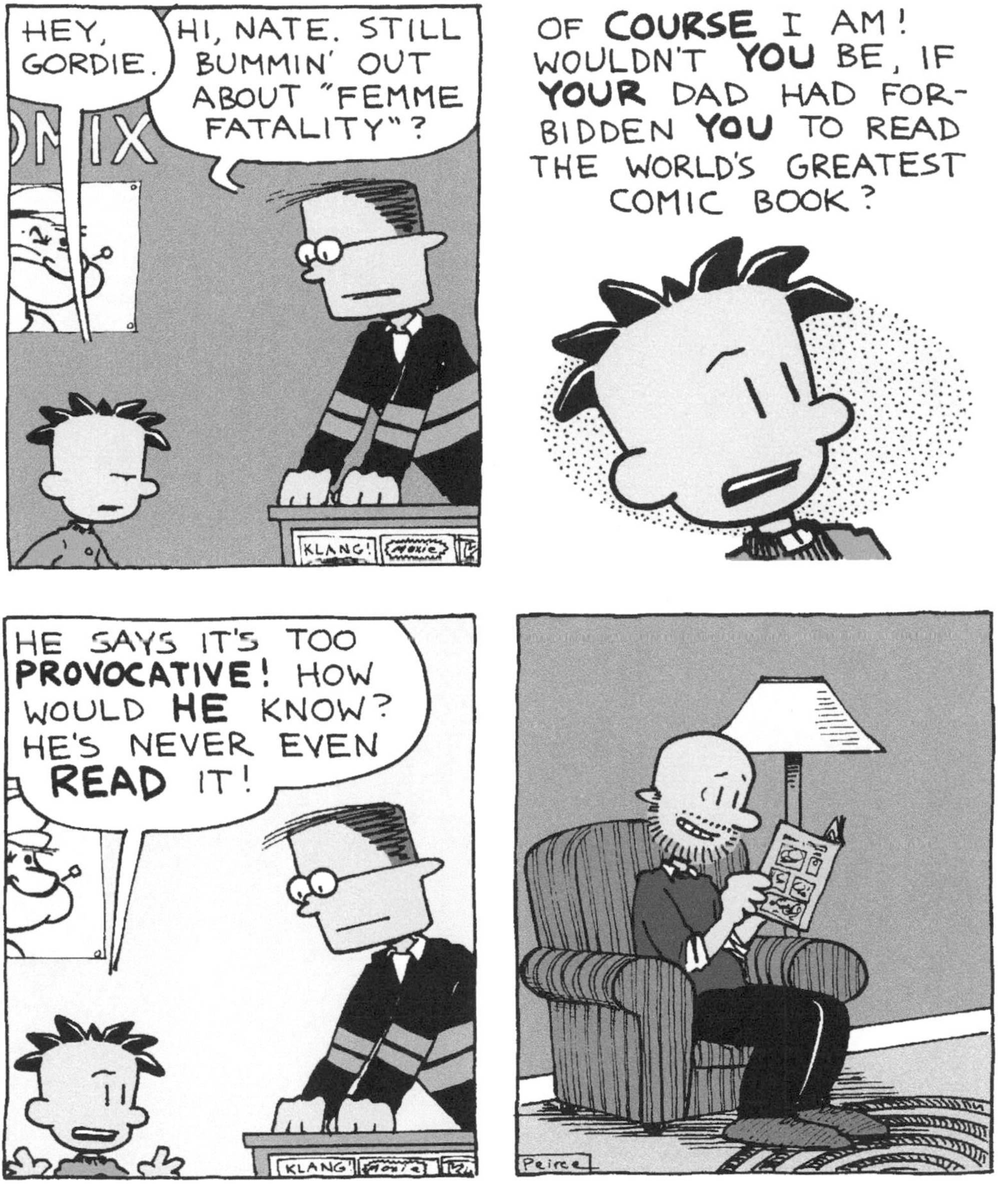
HEY, GORDIE.
HI, NATE. STILL BUMMIN' OUT ABOUT "FEMME FATALITY"?
OMIX
KLANG!
OF COURSE I AM! WOULDN'T YOU BE, IF YOUR DAD HAD FOR-BIDDEN YOU TO READ THE WORLD'S GREATEST COMIC BOOK?
HE SAYS IT'S TOO PROVOCATIVE! HOW WOULD HE KNOW? HE'S NEVER EVEN READ IT!
KLANG!
Peirce

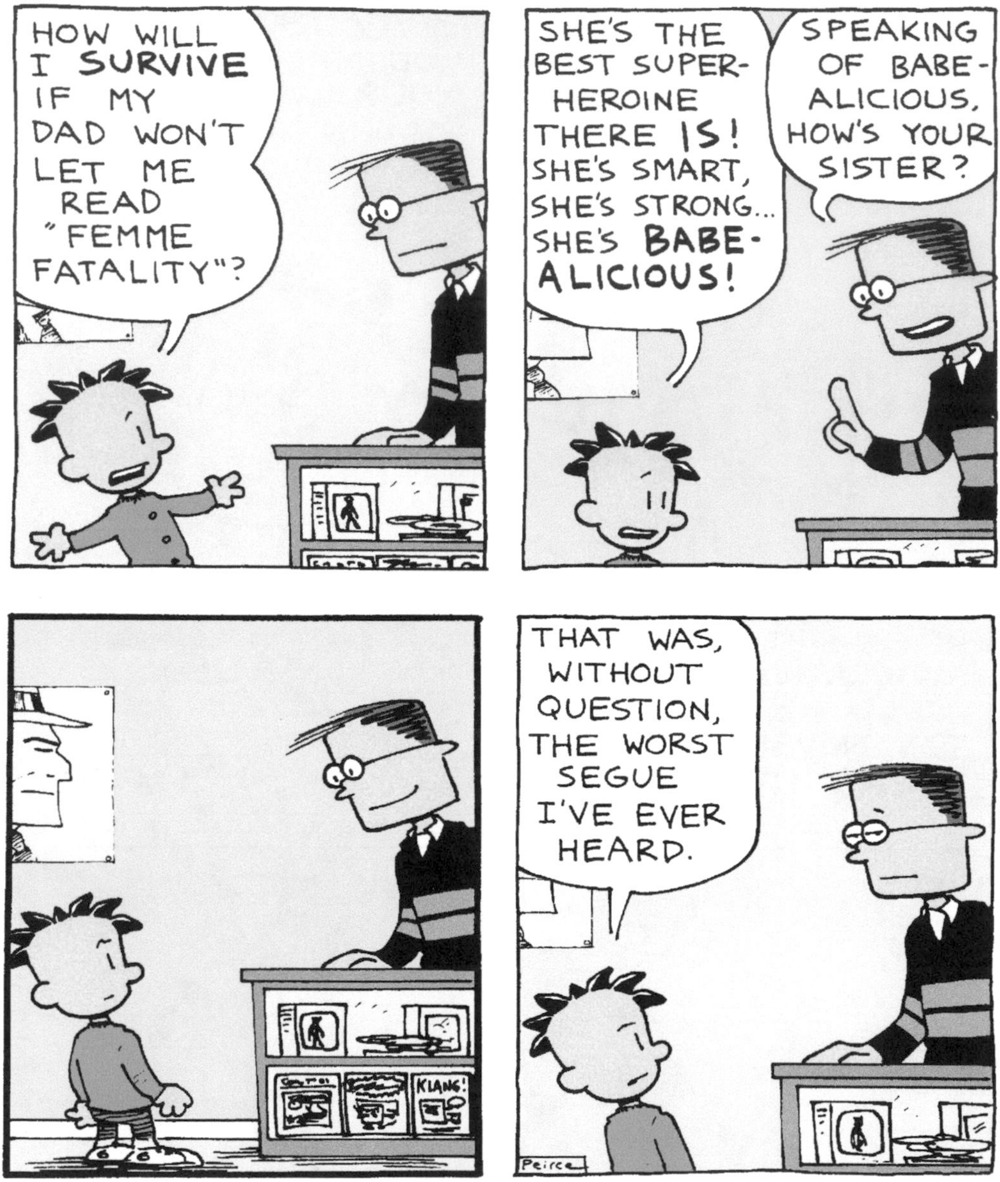
HOW WILL I SURVIVE IF MY DAD WON'T LET ME READ "FEMME FATALITY"?
SHE'S THE BEST SUPER-HEROINE THERE IS! SHE'S SMART, SHE'S STRONG... SHE'S BABE-ALICIOUS!
SPEAKING OF BABE-ALICIOUS, HOW'S YOUR SISTER?
KLANG!
THAT WAS, WITHOUT QUESTION, THE WORST SEGUE I'VE EVER HEARD.
Peirce

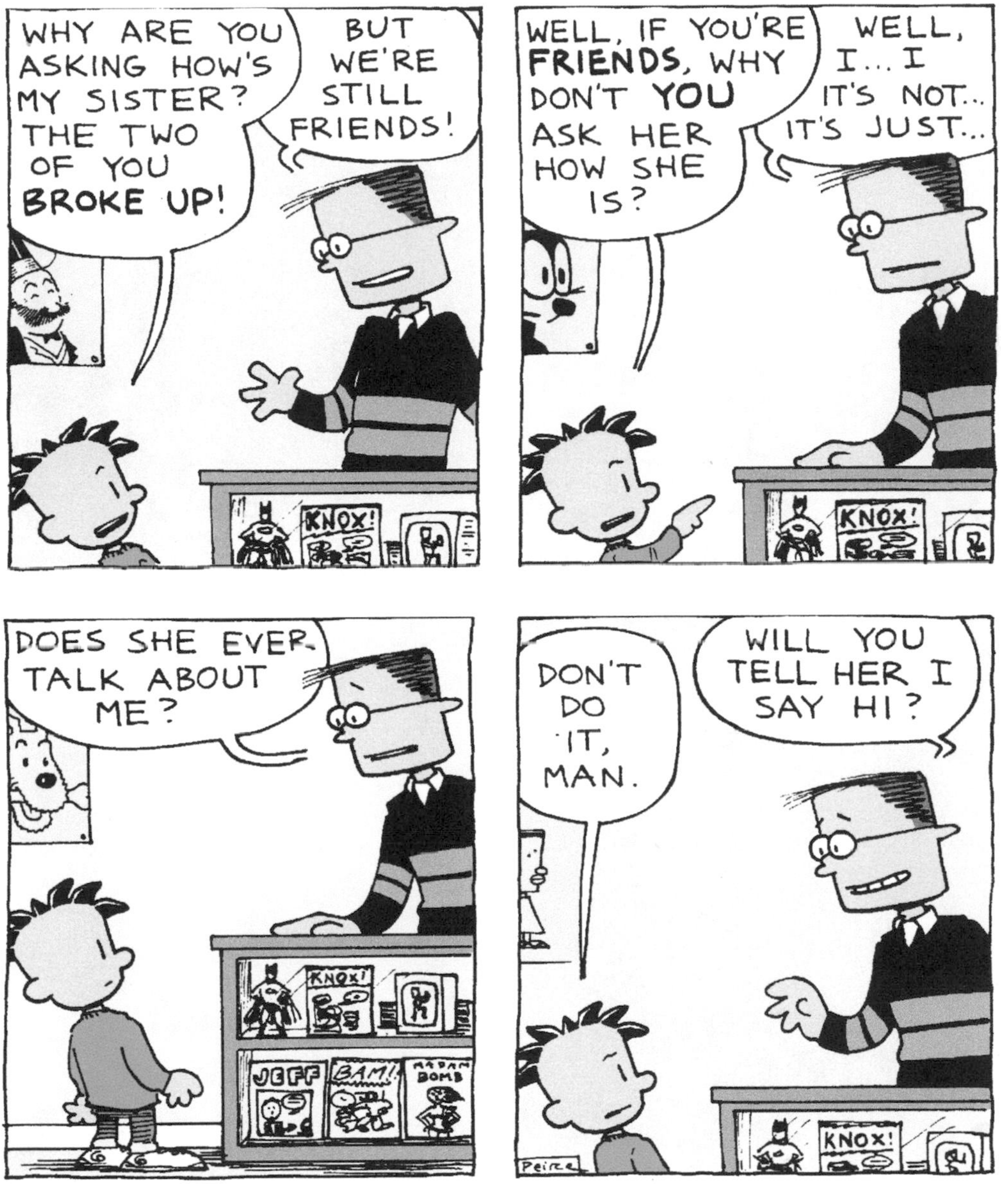

WHY ARE YOU ASKING HOW'S MY SISTER? THE TWO OF YOU **BROKE UP**!
BUT WE'RE STILL FRIENDS!
KNOX!
WELL, IF YOU'RE **FRIENDS**, WHY DON'T **YOU** ASK HER HOW SHE IS?
WELL, I... I IT'S NOT... IT'S JUST...
KNOX!
DOES SHE EVER TALK ABOUT ME?
KNOX!
JEFF
BAM!
MADAM BOMB
WILL YOU TELL HER I SAY HI?
DON'T DO IT, MAN.
KNOX!
Peirce

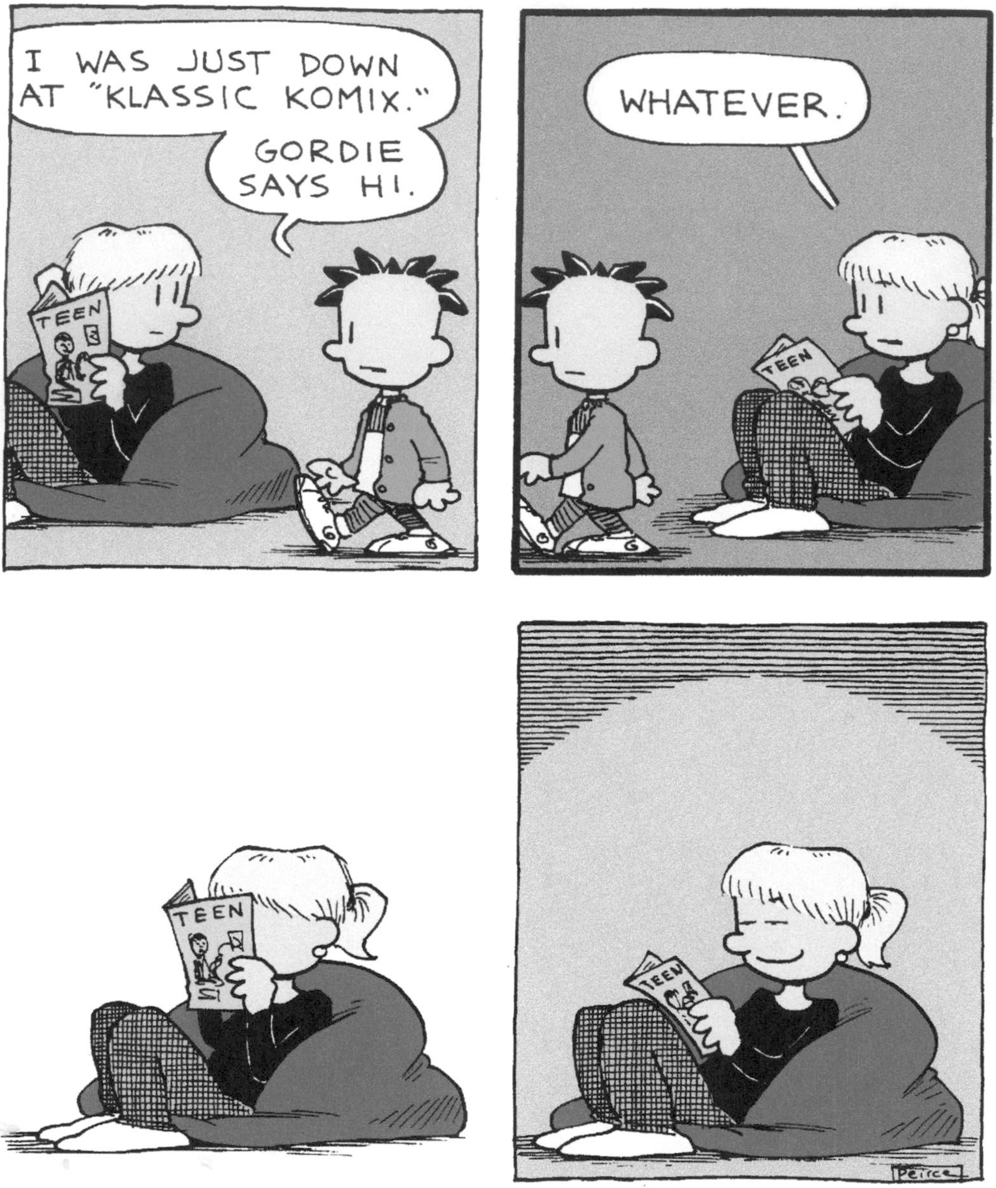
I WAS JUST DOWN AT "KLASSIC KOMIX."
GORDIE SAYS HI.
TEEN
WHATEVER.
TEEN
TEEN
TEEN
Peirce

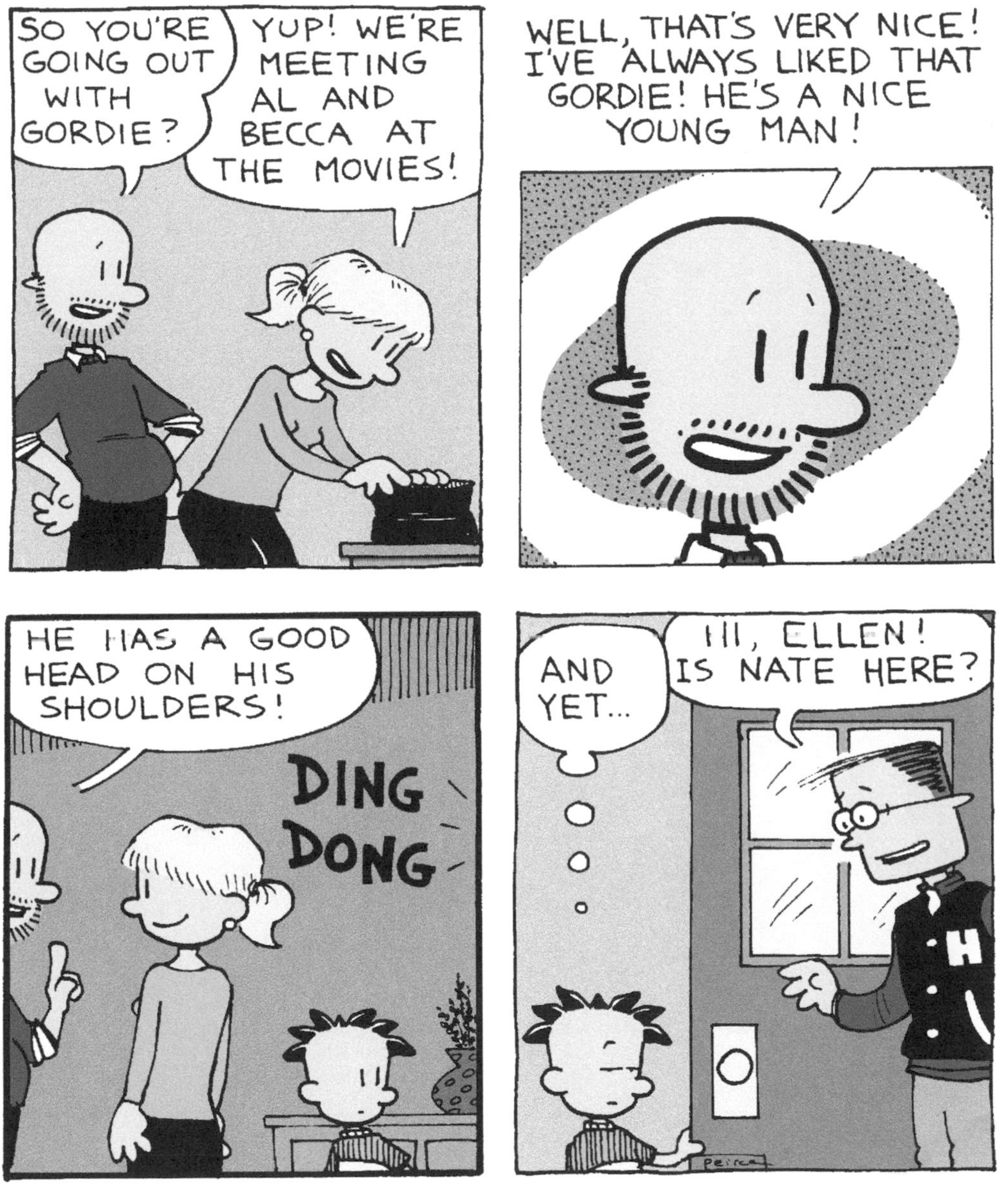
SO YOU'RE GOING OUT WITH GORDIE?
YUP! WE'RE MEETING AL AND BECCA AT THE MOVIES!
WELL, THAT'S VERY NICE! I'VE ALWAYS LIKED THAT GORDIE! HE'S A NICE YOUNG MAN!
HE HAS A GOOD HEAD ON HIS SHOULDERS!
DING DONG
AND YET...
HI, ELLEN! IS NATE HERE?
H
PEIRCE

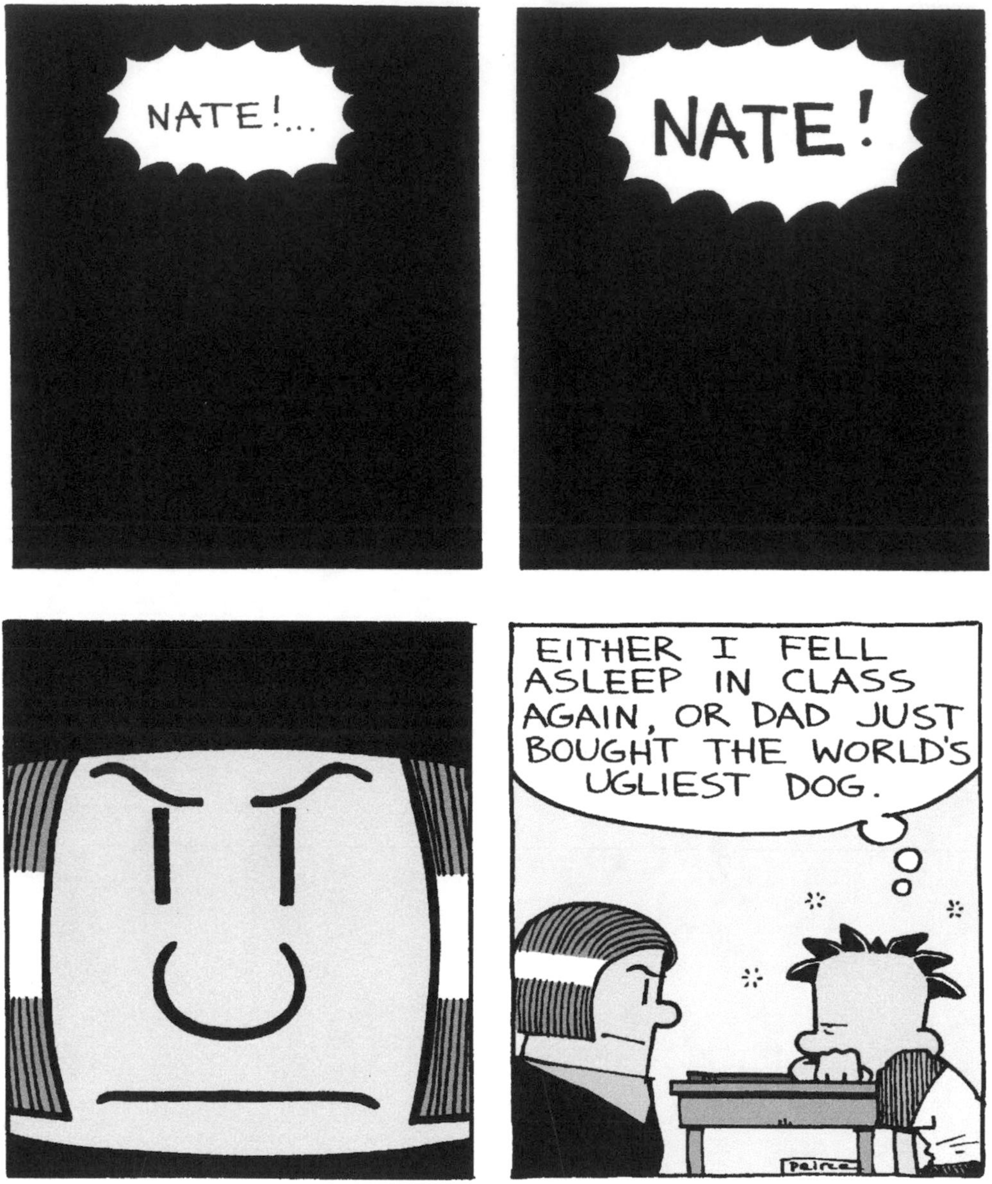
NATE!...
NATE!
EITHER I FELL ASLEEP IN CLASS AGAIN, OR DAD JUST BOUGHT THE WORLD'S UGLIEST DOG.
PEIRCE

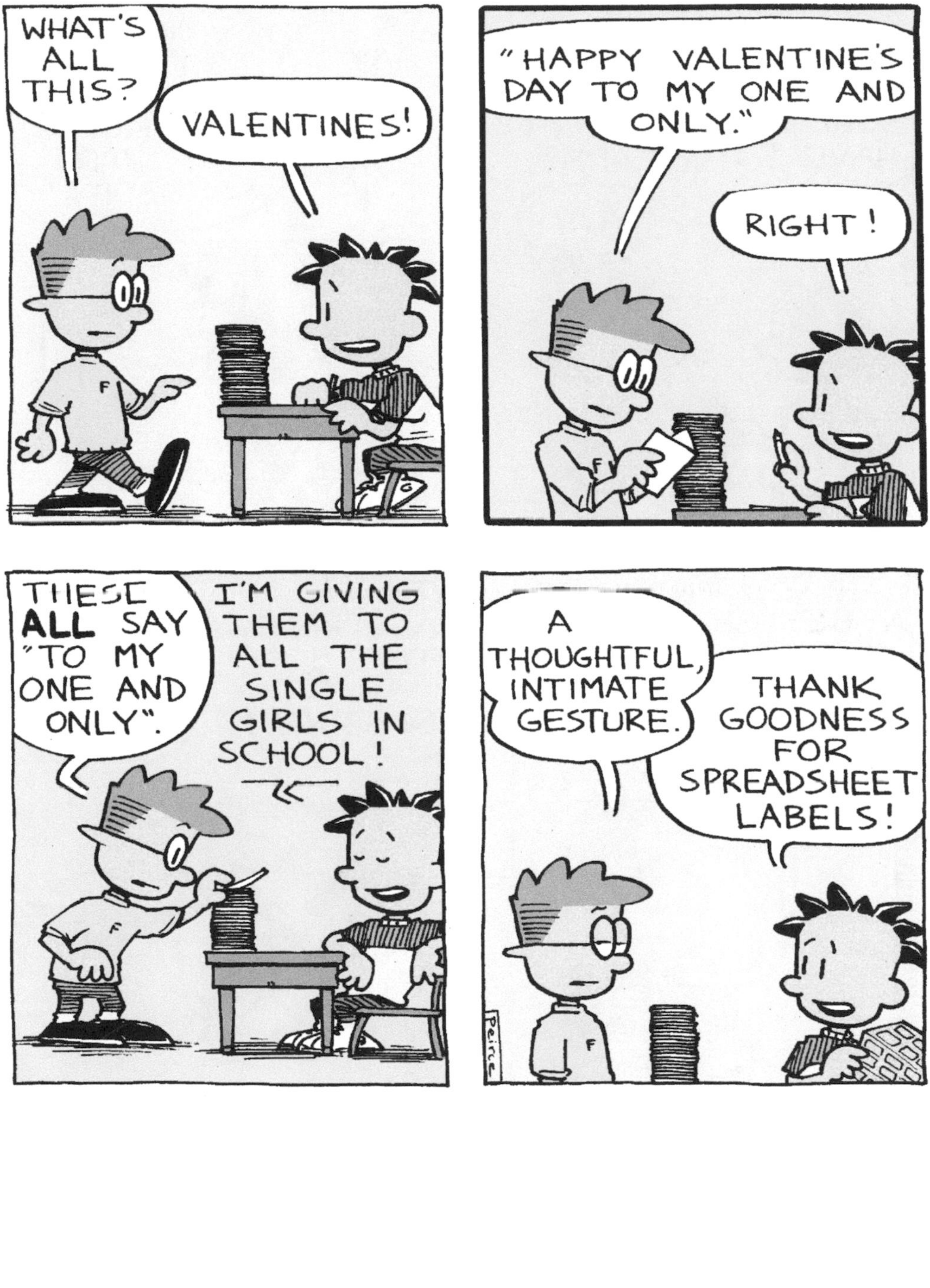
WHAT'S ALL THIS?
VALENTINES!
"HAPPY VALENTINE'S DAY TO MY ONE AND ONLY."
RIGHT!
THESE ALL SAY "TO MY ONE AND ONLY".
I'M GIVING THEM TO ALL THE SINGLE GIRLS IN SCHOOL!
A THOUGHTFUL, INTIMATE GESTURE.
THANK GOODNESS FOR SPREADSHEET LABELS!
Peirce

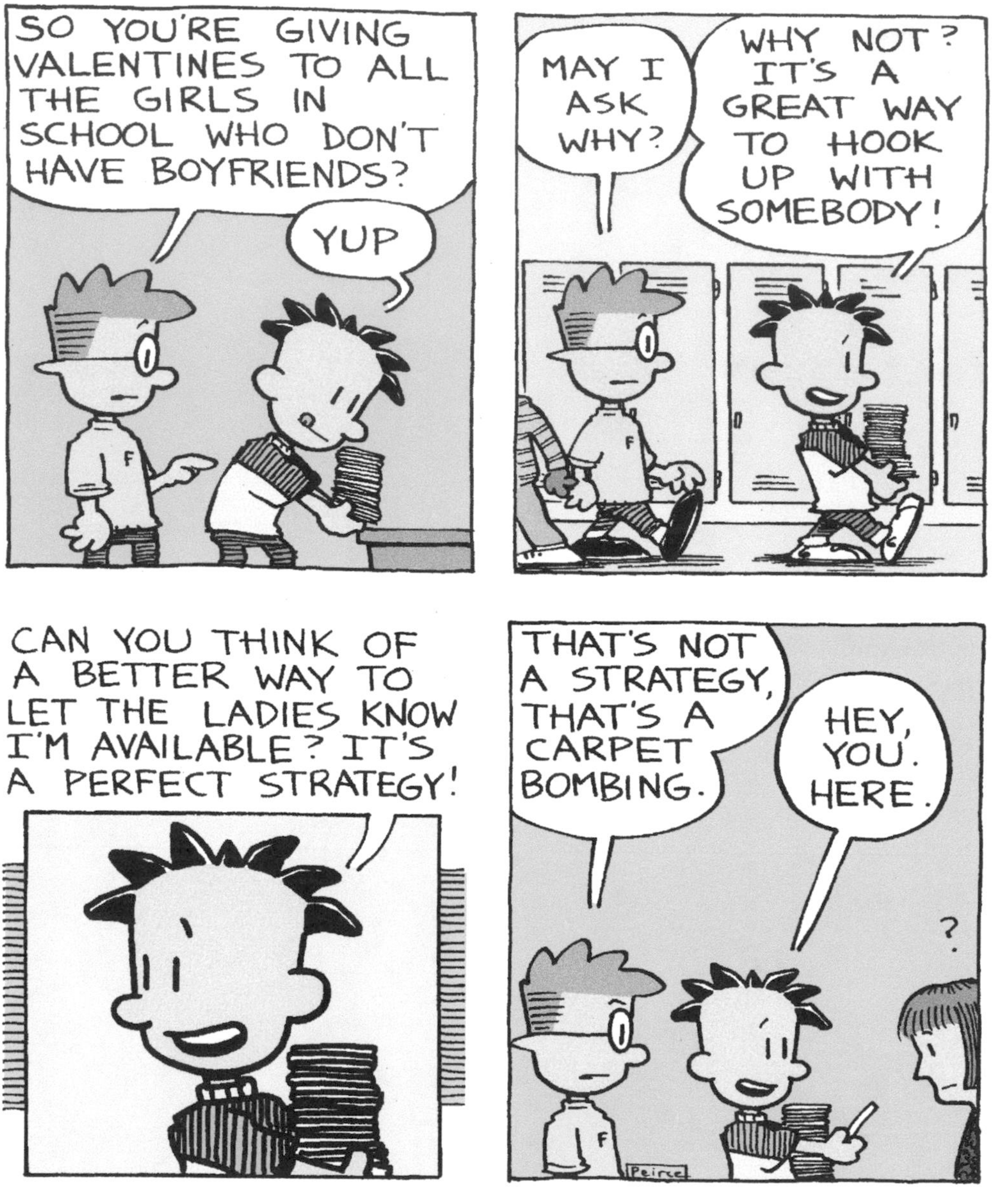
SO YOU'RE GIVING VALENTINES TO ALL THE GIRLS IN SCHOOL WHO DON'T HAVE BOYFRIENDS?
YUP
MAY I ASK WHY?
WHY NOT? IT'S A GREAT WAY TO HOOK UP WITH SOMEBODY!
CAN YOU THINK OF A BETTER WAY TO LET THE LADIES KNOW I'M AVAILABLE? IT'S A PERFECT STRATEGY!
THAT'S NOT A STRATEGY, THAT'S A CARPET BOMBING.
HEY, YOU. HERE.
?
Peirce

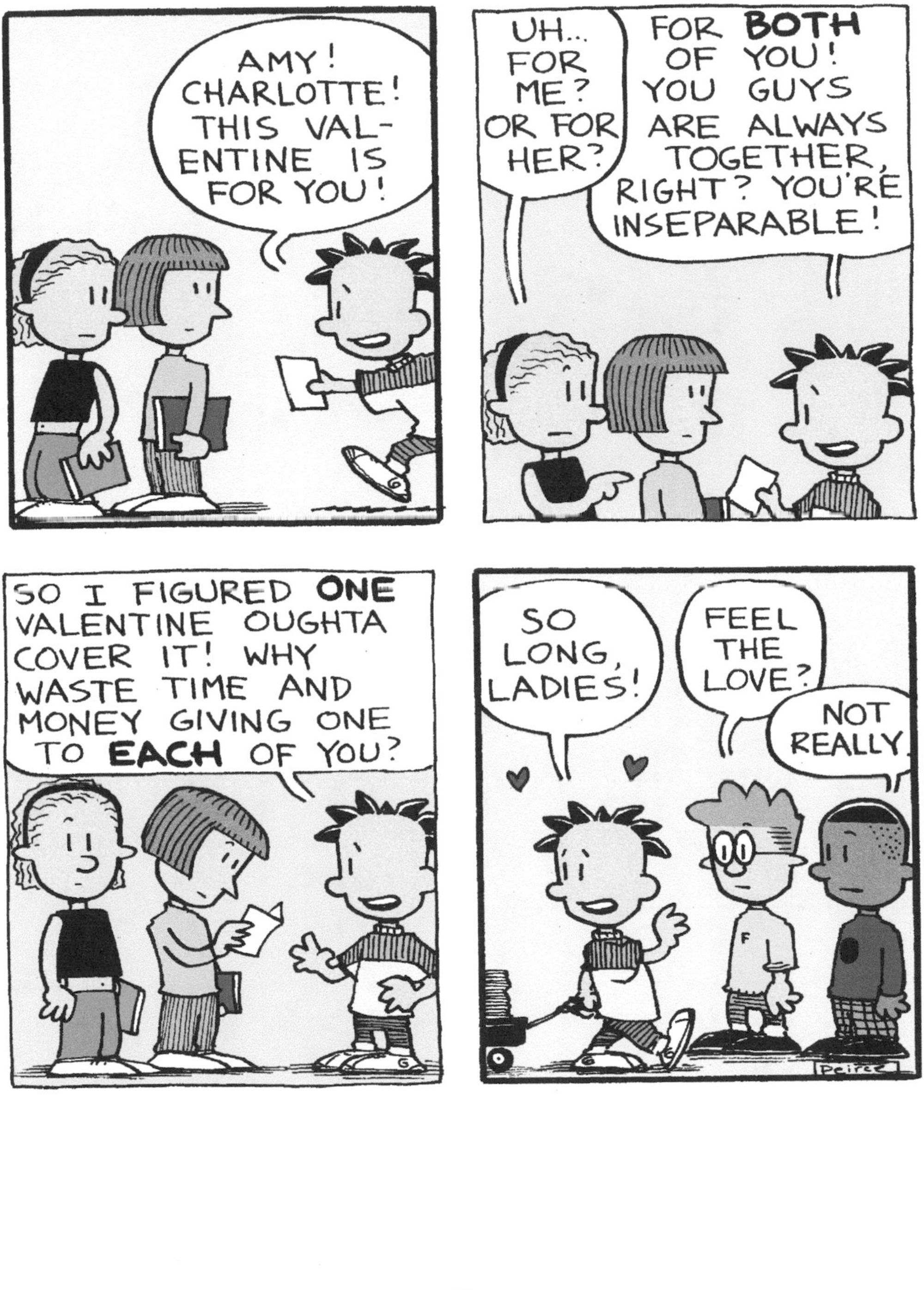
AMY! CHARLOTTE! THIS VALENTINE IS FOR YOU!
UH... FOR ME? OR FOR HER?
FOR **BOTH** OF YOU! YOU GUYS ARE ALWAYS TOGETHER, RIGHT? YOU'RE INSEPARABLE!
SO I FIGURED **ONE** VALENTINE OUGHTA COVER IT! WHY WASTE TIME AND MONEY GIVING ONE TO **EACH** OF YOU?
SO LONG, LADIES!
FEEL THE LOVE?
NOT REALLY.
Peirce

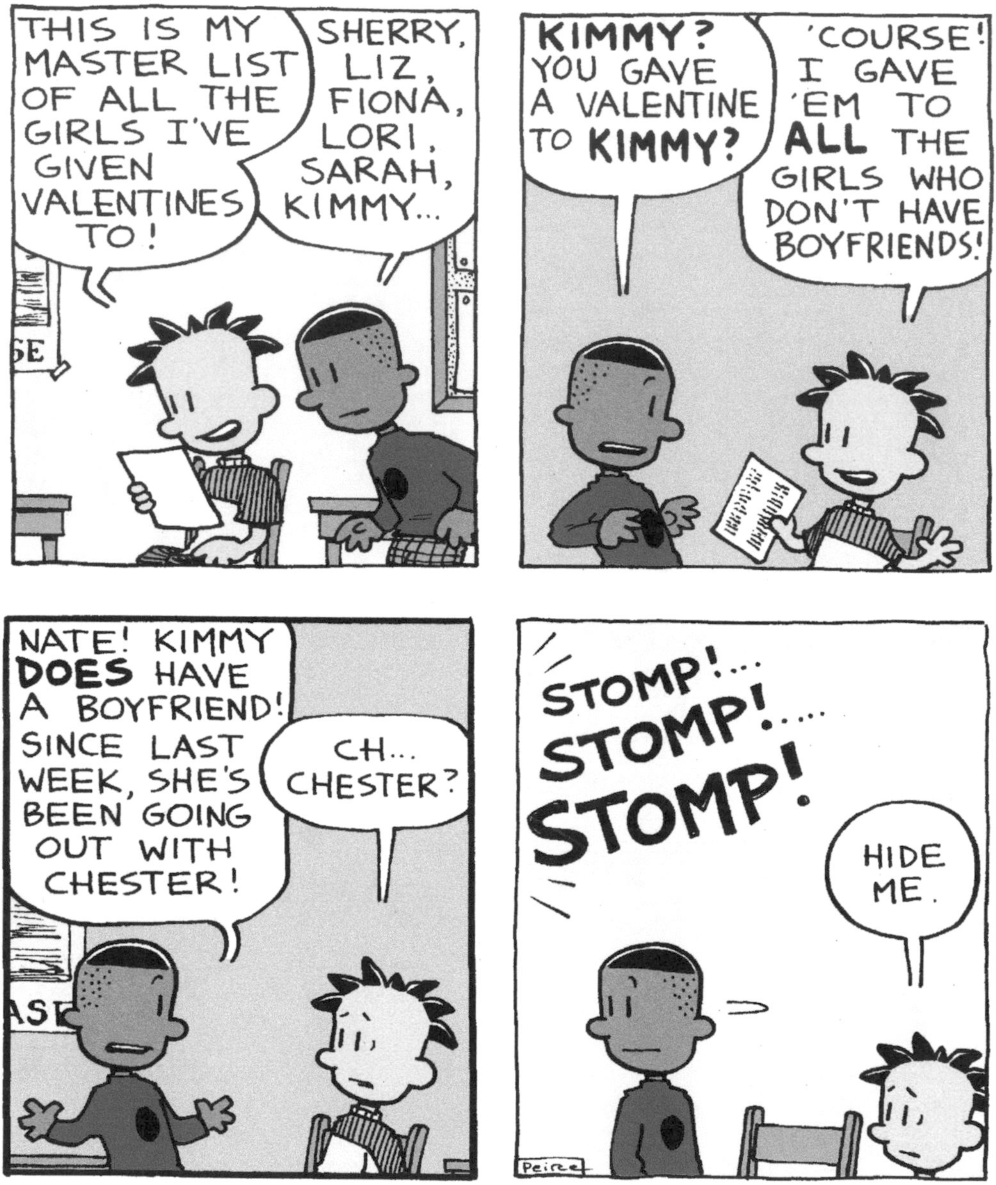
THIS IS MY MASTER LIST OF ALL THE GIRLS I'VE GIVEN VALENTINES TO!
SHERRY, LIZ, FIONA, LORI, SARAH, KIMMY...
KIMMY? YOU GAVE A VALENTINE TO KIMMY?
'COURSE! I GAVE 'EM TO ALL THE GIRLS WHO DON'T HAVE BOYFRIENDS!
NATE! KIMMY DOES HAVE A BOYFRIEND! SINCE LAST WEEK, SHE'S BEEN GOING OUT WITH CHESTER!
CH... CHESTER?
STOMP!...
STOMP!....
STOMP!
HIDE ME.
Peirce

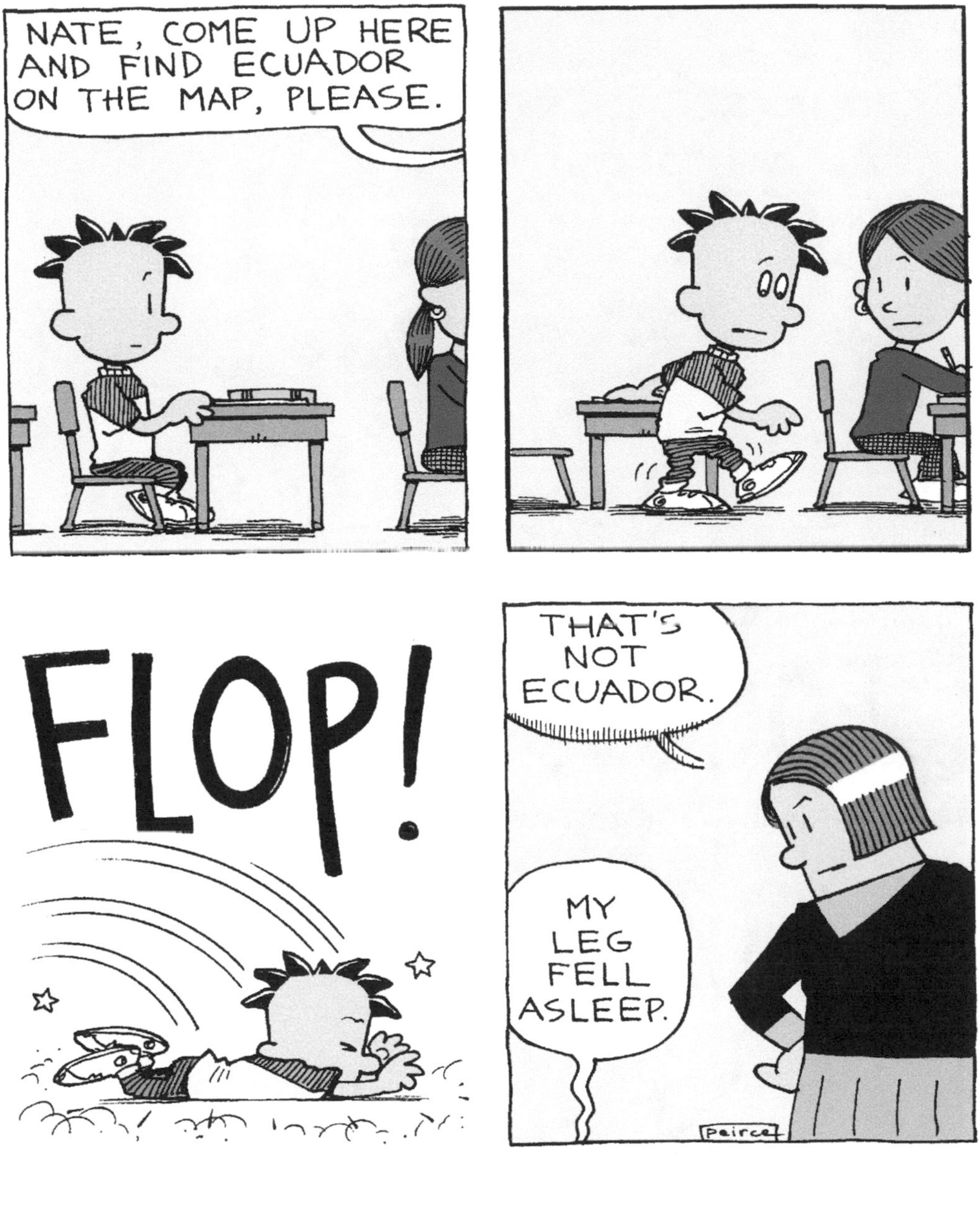
NATE, COME UP HERE AND FIND ECUADOR ON THE MAP, PLEASE.
FLOP!
THAT'S NOT ECUADOR.
MY LEG FELL ASLEEP.
Peirce

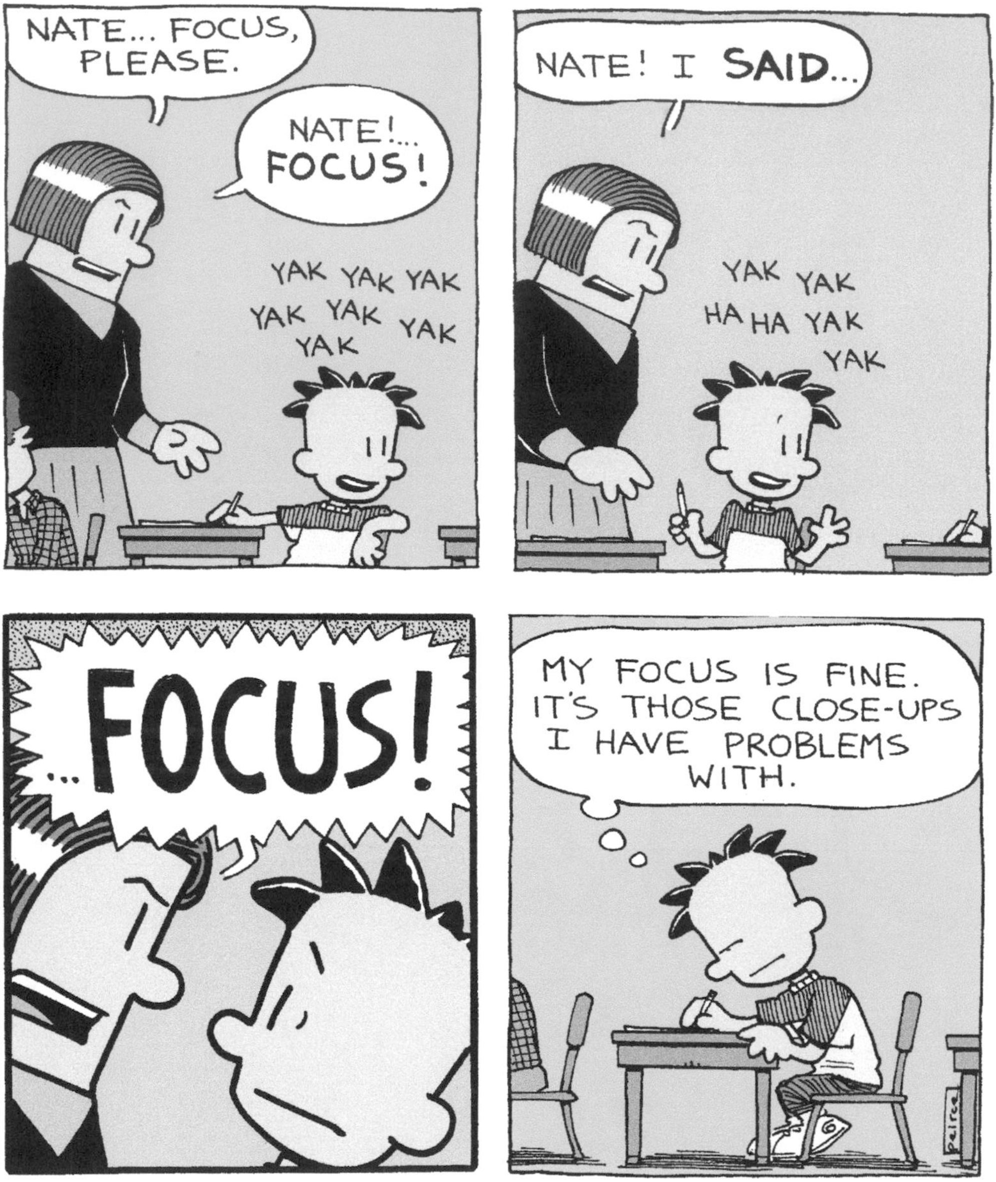
NATE... FOCUS, PLEASE.
NATE!... FOCUS!
YAK YAK YAK YAK YAK YAK YAK
NATE! I SAID...
YAK YAK HA HA YAK YAK
...FOCUS!
MY FOCUS IS FINE. IT'S THOSE CLOSE-UPS I HAVE PROBLEMS WITH.
peirce

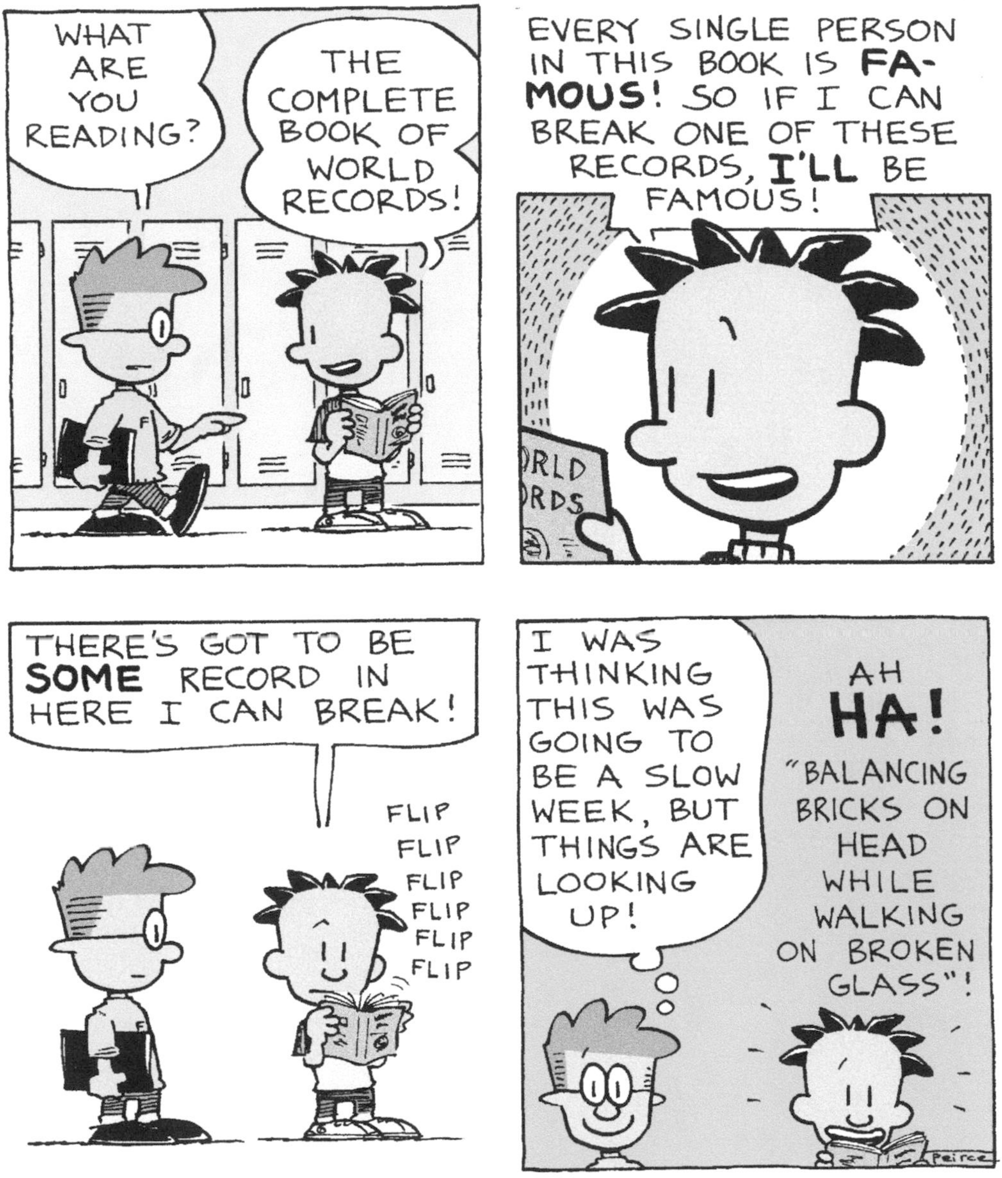
WHAT ARE YOU READING?
THE COMPLETE BOOK OF WORLD RECORDS!
EVERY SINGLE PERSON IN THIS BOOK IS **FAMOUS!** SO IF I CAN BREAK ONE OF THESE RECORDS, **I'LL** BE FAMOUS!
THERE'S GOT TO BE **SOME** RECORD IN HERE I CAN BREAK!
FLIP FLIP FLIP FLIP FLIP FLIP
I WAS THINKING THIS WAS GOING TO BE A SLOW WEEK, BUT THINGS ARE LOOKING UP!
AH **HA!** "BALANCING BRICKS ON HEAD WHILE WALKING ON BROKEN GLASS"!
Peirce

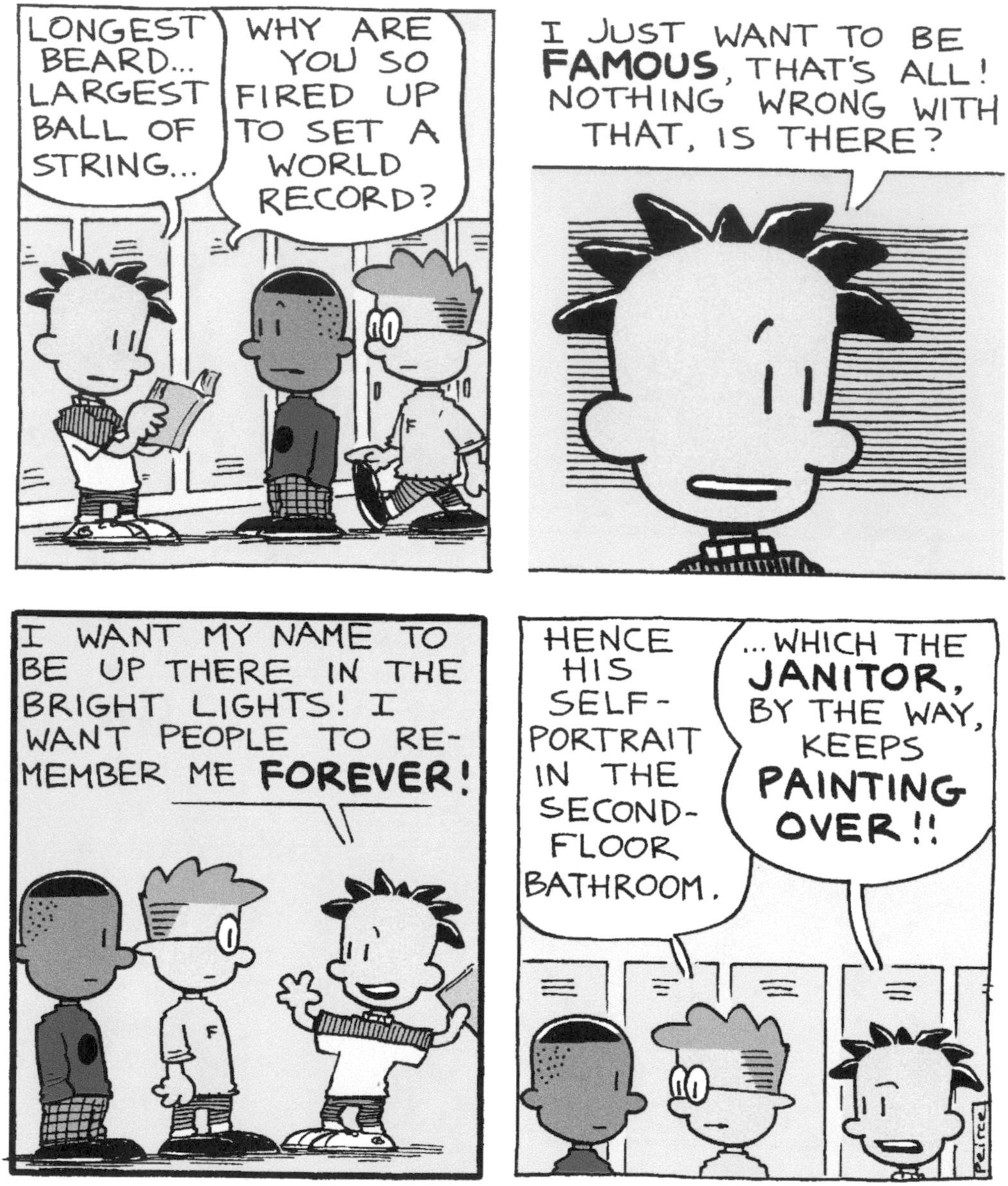
LONGEST BEARD... LARGEST BALL OF STRING...
WHY ARE YOU SO FIRED UP TO SET A WORLD RECORD?
I JUST WANT TO BE **FAMOUS**, THAT'S ALL! NOTHING WRONG WITH THAT, IS THERE?
I WANT MY NAME TO BE UP THERE IN THE BRIGHT LIGHTS! I WANT PEOPLE TO REMEMBER ME **FOREVER**!
HENCE HIS SELF-PORTRAIT IN THE SECOND-FLOOR BATHROOM.
...WHICH THE **JANITOR**, BY THE WAY, KEEPS **PAINTING OVER**!!
PEIRCE

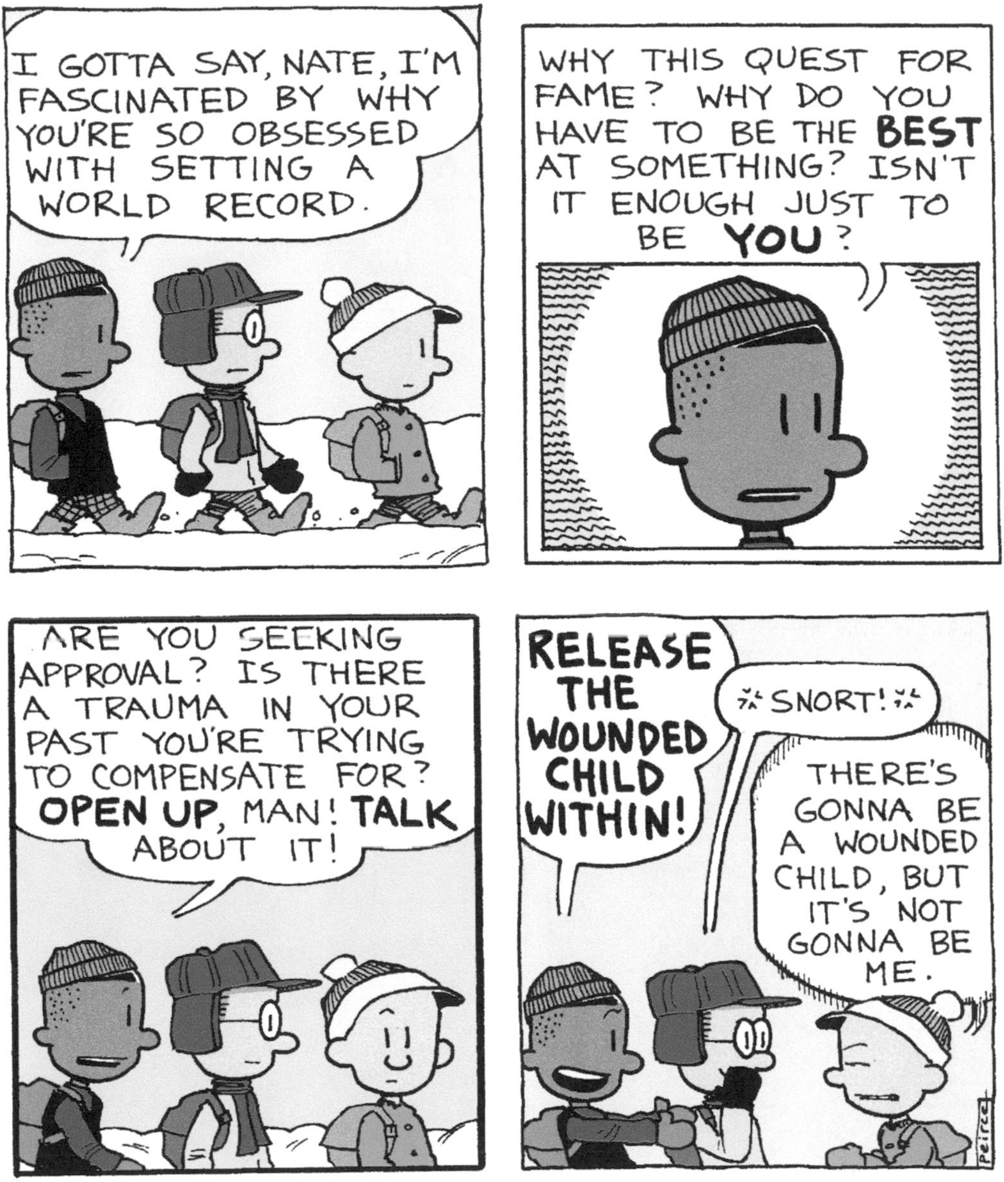
I GOTTA SAY, NATE, I'M FASCINATED BY WHY YOU'RE SO OBSESSED WITH SETTING A WORLD RECORD.
WHY THIS QUEST FOR FAME? WHY DO YOU HAVE TO BE THE BEST AT SOMETHING? ISN'T IT ENOUGH JUST TO BE YOU?
ARE YOU SEEKING APPROVAL? IS THERE A TRAUMA IN YOUR PAST YOU'RE TRYING TO COMPENSATE FOR? OPEN UP, MAN! TALK ABOUT IT!
RELEASE THE WOUNDED CHILD WITHIN!
SNORT!
THERE'S GONNA BE A WOUNDED CHILD, BUT IT'S NOT GONNA BE ME.
peirce

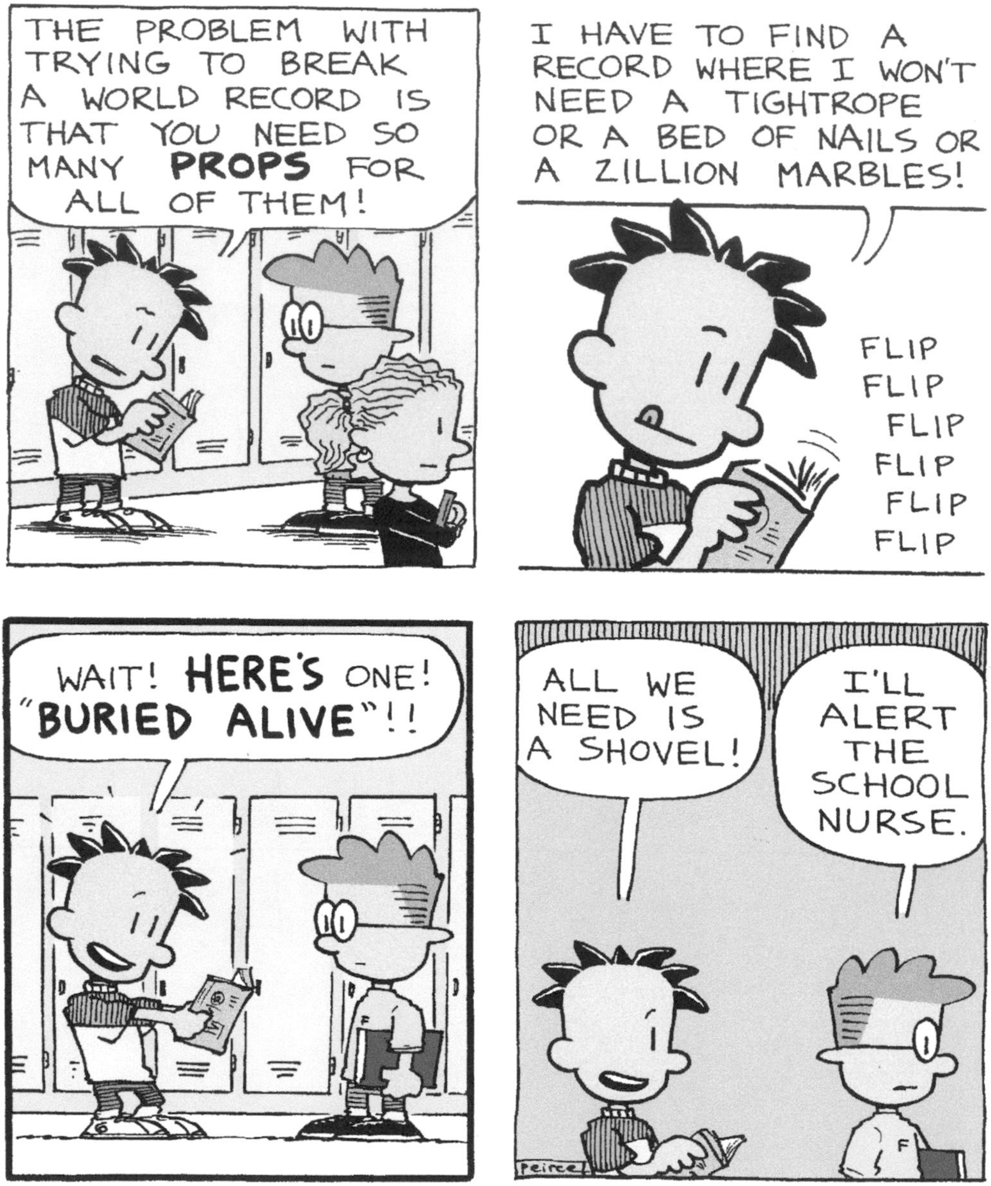
THE PROBLEM WITH TRYING TO BREAK A WORLD RECORD IS THAT YOU NEED SO MANY PROPS FOR ALL OF THEM!
I HAVE TO FIND A RECORD WHERE I WON'T NEED A TIGHTROPE OR A BED OF NAILS OR A ZILLION MARBLES!
FLIP FLIP FLIP FLIP FLIP FLIP
WAIT! HERE'S ONE! "BURIED ALIVE"!!
ALL WE NEED IS A SHOVEL!
I'LL ALERT THE SCHOOL NURSE.
peirce

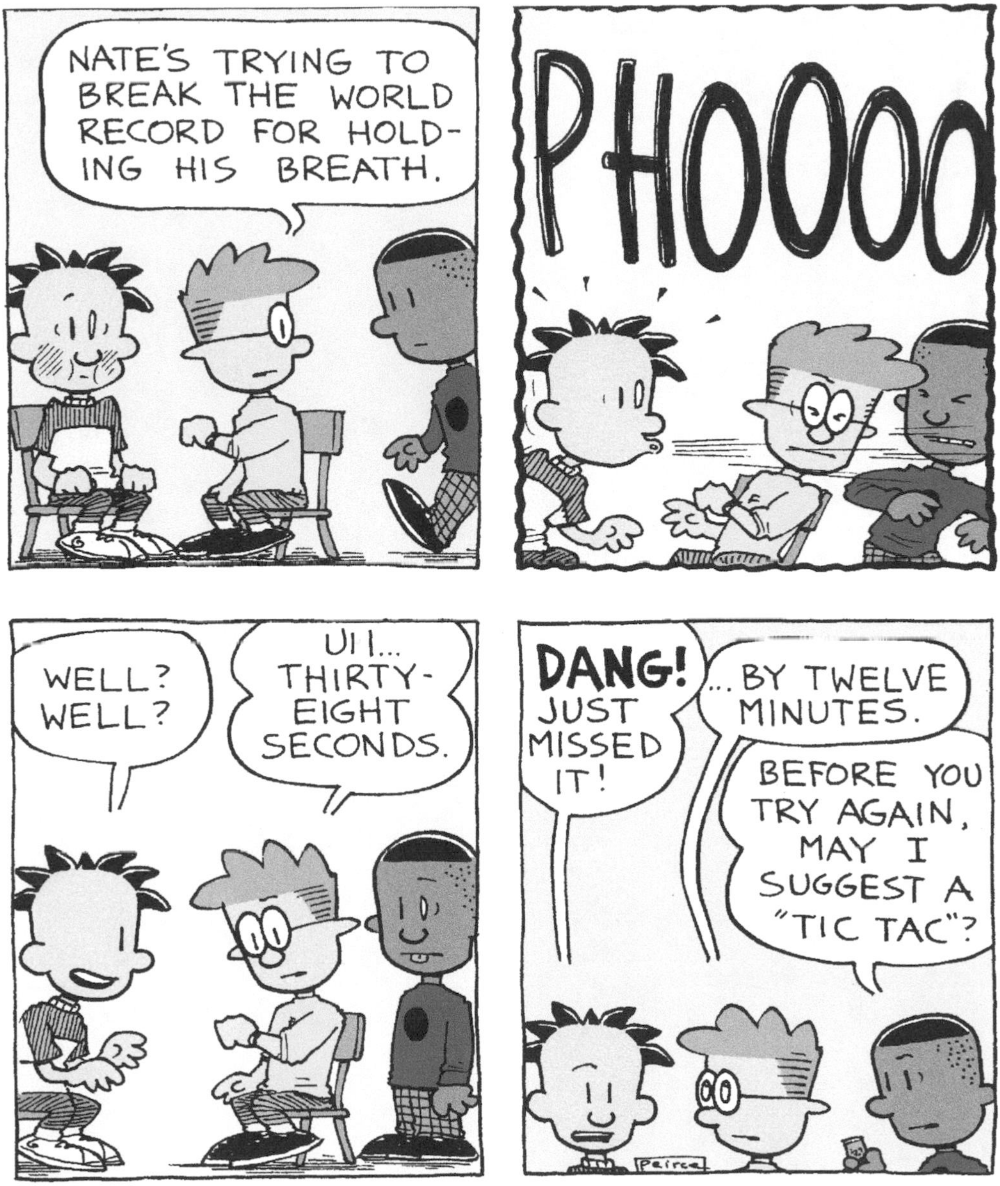
NATE'S TRYING TO BREAK THE WORLD RECORD FOR HOLD-ING HIS BREATH.
PHOOOO
WELL? WELL?
UH... THIRTY-EIGHT SECONDS.
DANG! JUST MISSED IT!
...BY TWELVE MINUTES.
BEFORE YOU TRY AGAIN, MAY I SUGGEST A "TIC TAC"?
Peirce

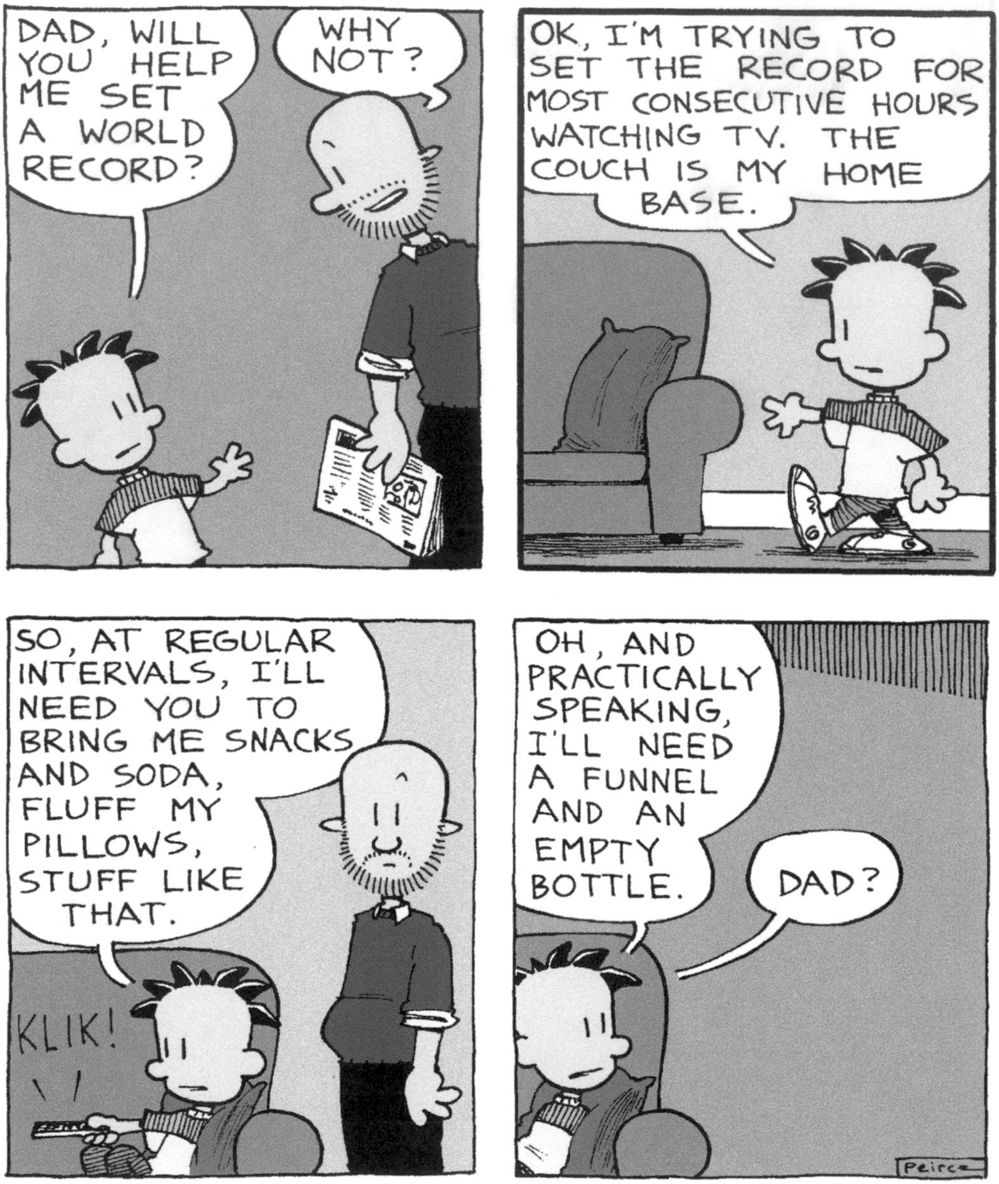
DAD, WILL YOU HELP ME SET A WORLD RECORD?
WHY NOT?
OK, I'M TRYING TO SET THE RECORD FOR MOST CONSECUTIVE HOURS WATCHING TV. THE COUCH IS MY HOME BASE.
SO, AT REGULAR INTERVALS, I'LL NEED YOU TO BRING ME SNACKS AND SODA, FLUFF MY PILLOWS, STUFF LIKE THAT.
KLIK!
OH, AND PRACTICALLY SPEAKING, I'LL NEED A FUNNEL AND AN EMPTY BOTTLE.
DAD?
Peirce

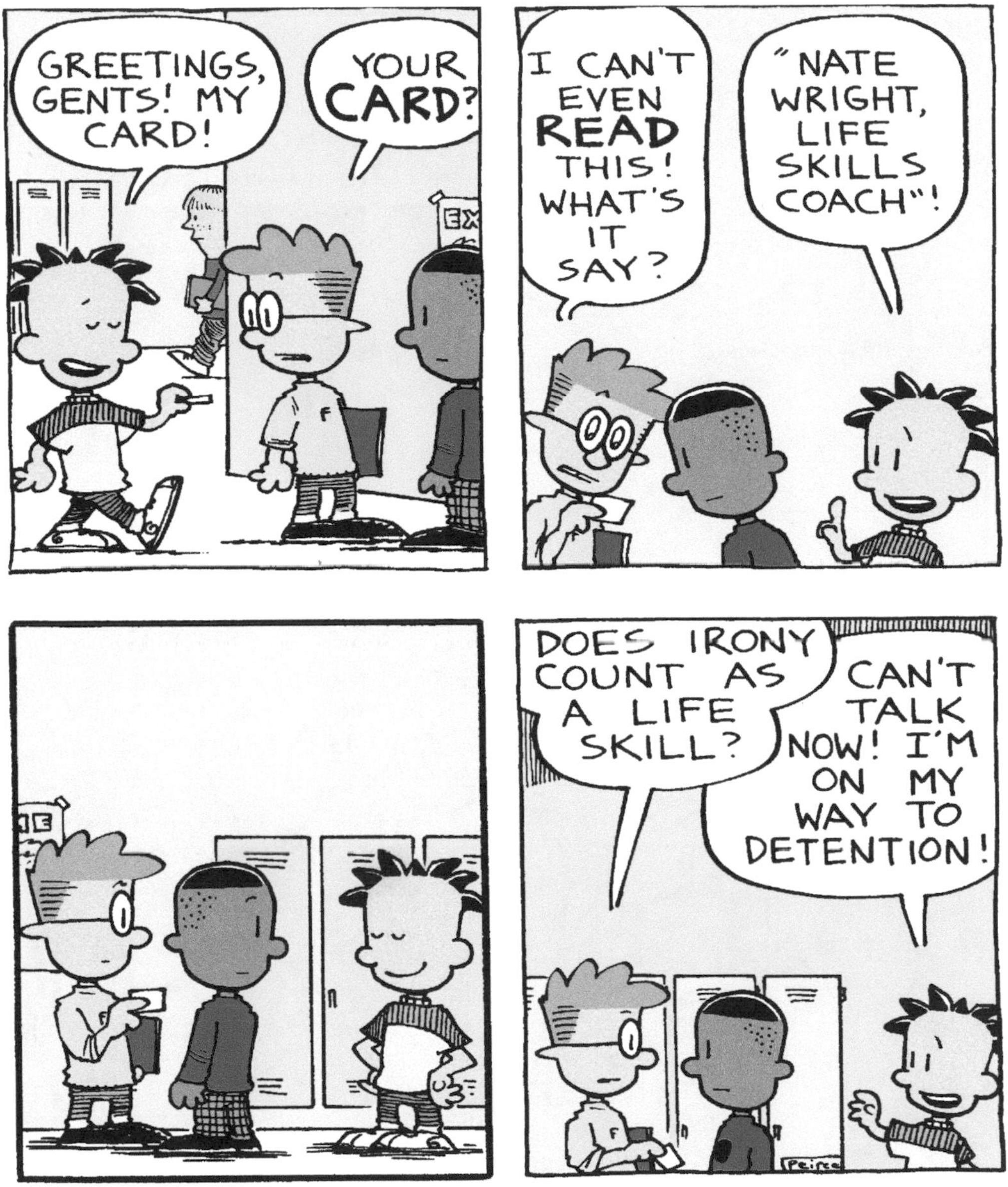
GREETINGS, GENTS! MY CARD!
YOUR CARD?
I CAN'T EVEN READ THIS! WHAT'S IT SAY?
"NATE WRIGHT, LIFE SKILLS COACH"!
DOES IRONY COUNT AS A LIFE SKILL?
CAN'T TALK NOW! I'M ON MY WAY TO DETENTION!
Peirce

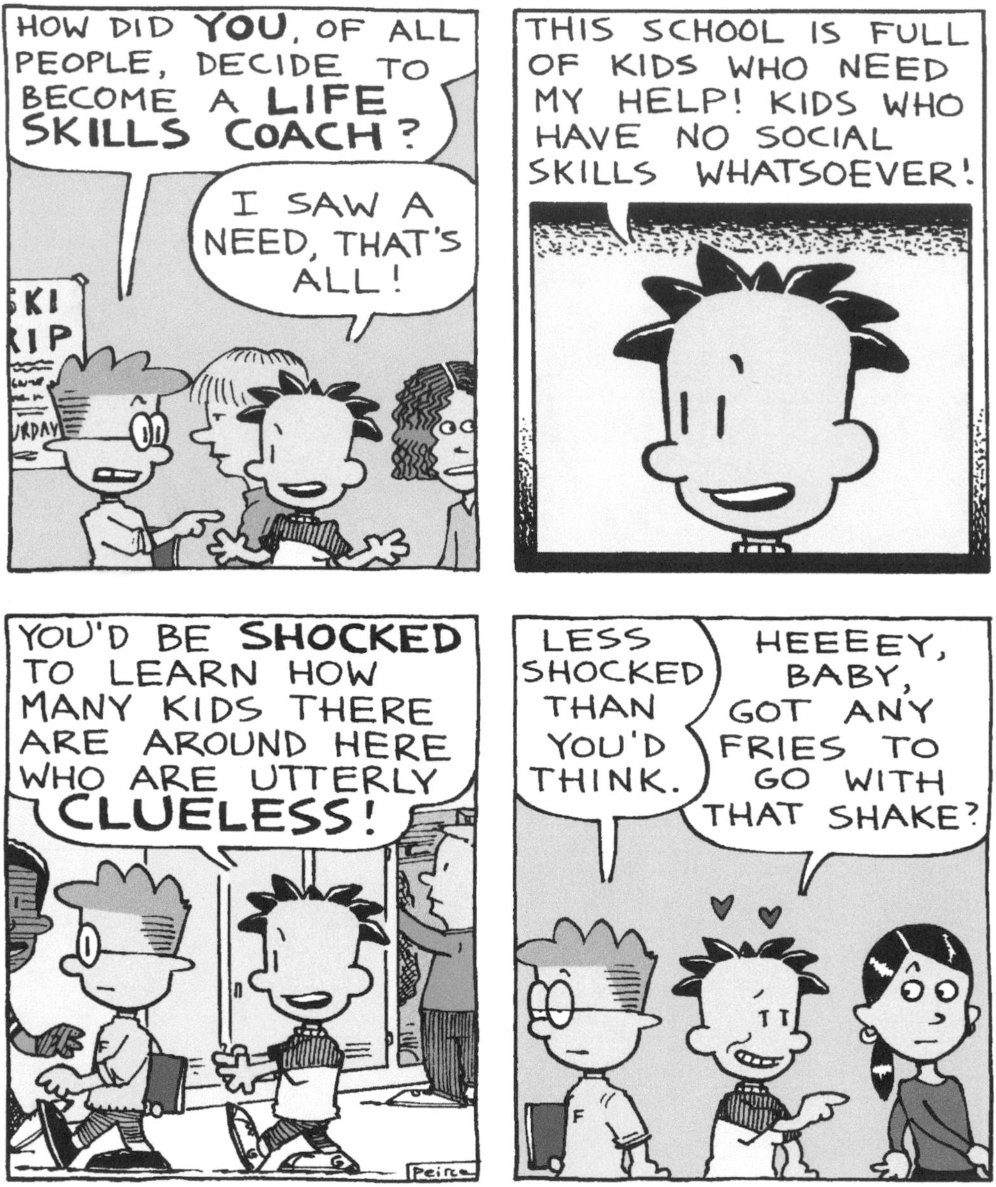
HOW DID YOU, OF ALL PEOPLE, DECIDE TO BECOME A LIFE SKILLS COACH?
I SAW A NEED, THAT'S ALL!
SKI TRIP
URDAY
THIS SCHOOL IS FULL OF KIDS WHO NEED MY HELP! KIDS WHO HAVE NO SOCIAL SKILLS WHATSOEVER!
YOU'D BE SHOCKED TO LEARN HOW MANY KIDS THERE ARE AROUND HERE WHO ARE UTTERLY CLUELESS!
LESS SHOCKED THAN YOU'D THINK.
HEEEEY, BABY, GOT ANY FRIES TO GO WITH THAT SHAKE?

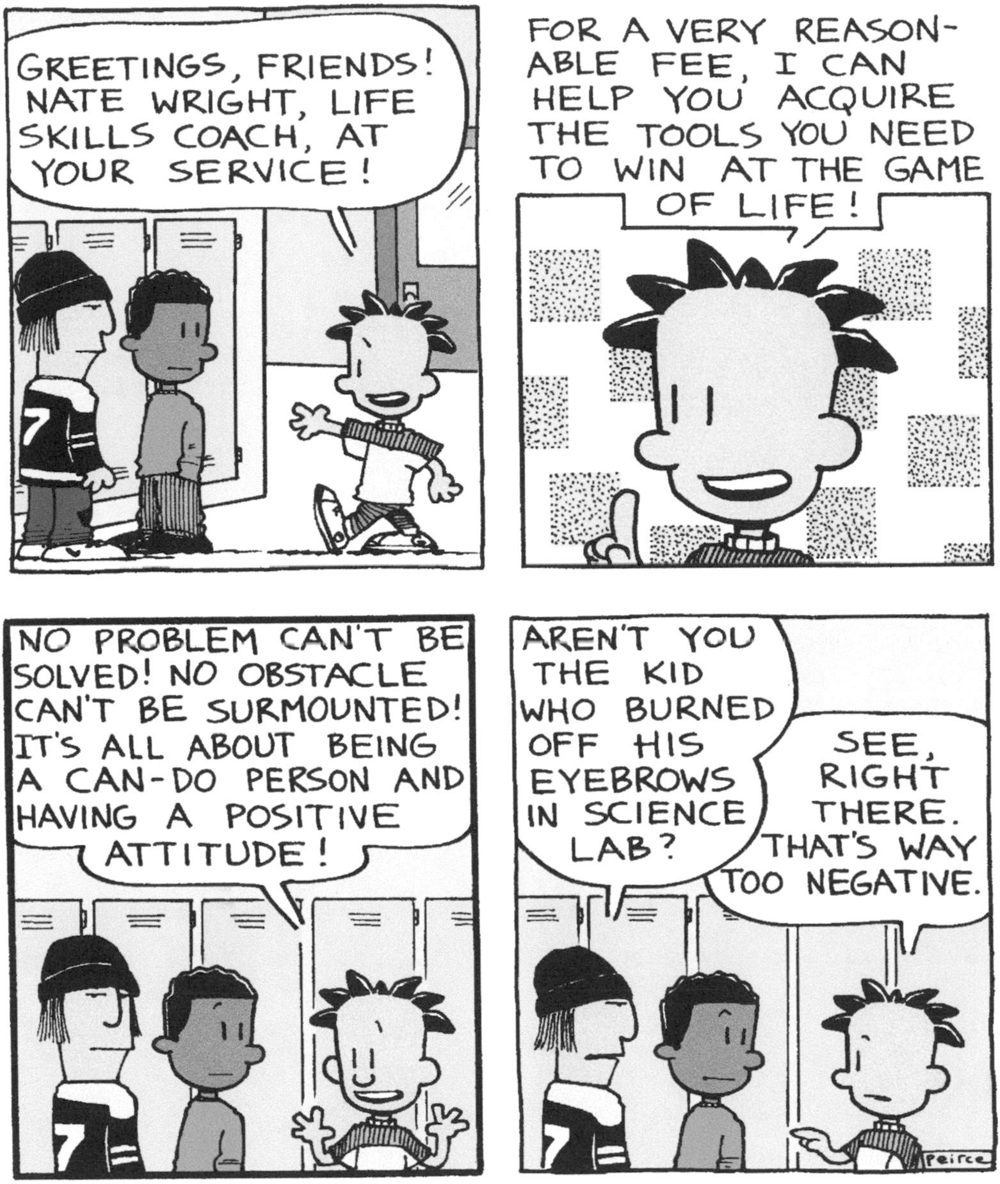
GREETINGS, FRIENDS! NATE WRIGHT, LIFE SKILLS COACH, AT YOUR SERVICE!
FOR A VERY REASON-ABLE FEE, I CAN HELP YOU ACQUIRE THE TOOLS YOU NEED TO WIN AT THE GAME OF LIFE!
NO PROBLEM CAN'T BE SOLVED! NO OBSTACLE CAN'T BE SURMOUNTED! IT'S ALL ABOUT BEING A CAN-DO PERSON AND HAVING A POSITIVE ATTITUDE!
AREN'T YOU THE KID WHO BURNED OFF HIS EYEBROWS IN SCIENCE LAB?
SEE, RIGHT THERE. THAT'S WAY TOO NEGATIVE.
Peirce

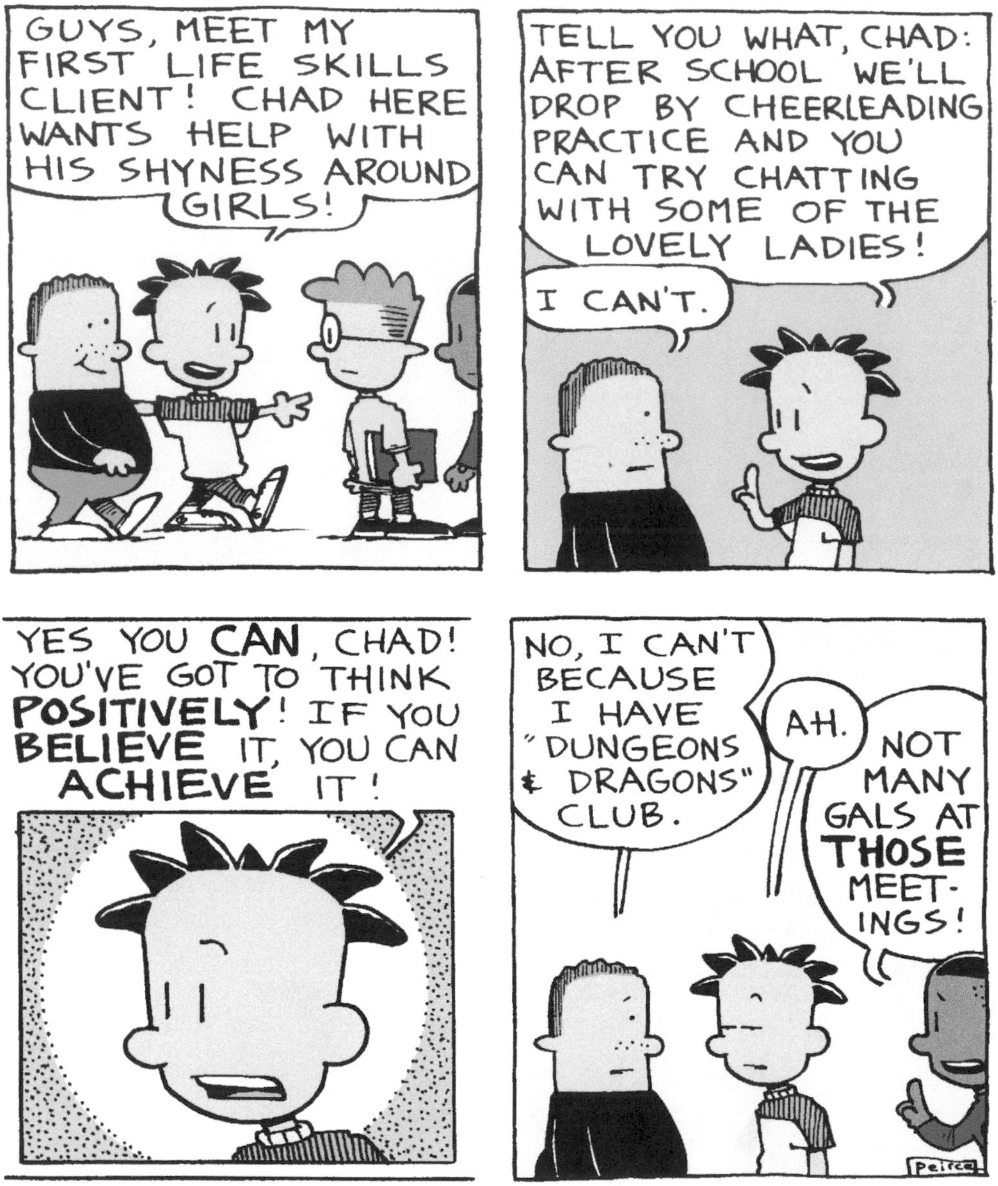
GUYS, MEET MY FIRST LIFE SKILLS CLIENT! CHAD HERE WANTS HELP WITH HIS SHYNESS AROUND GIRLS!
TELL YOU WHAT, CHAD: AFTER SCHOOL WE'LL DROP BY CHEERLEADING PRACTICE AND YOU CAN TRY CHATTING WITH SOME OF THE LOVELY LADIES!
I CAN'T.
YES YOU **CAN**, CHAD! YOU'VE GOT TO THINK **POSITIVELY**! IF YOU **BELIEVE** IT, YOU CAN **ACHIEVE** IT!
NO, I CAN'T BECAUSE I HAVE "DUNGEONS & DRAGONS" CLUB.
AH.
NOT MANY GALS AT **THOSE** MEETINGS!
Peirce

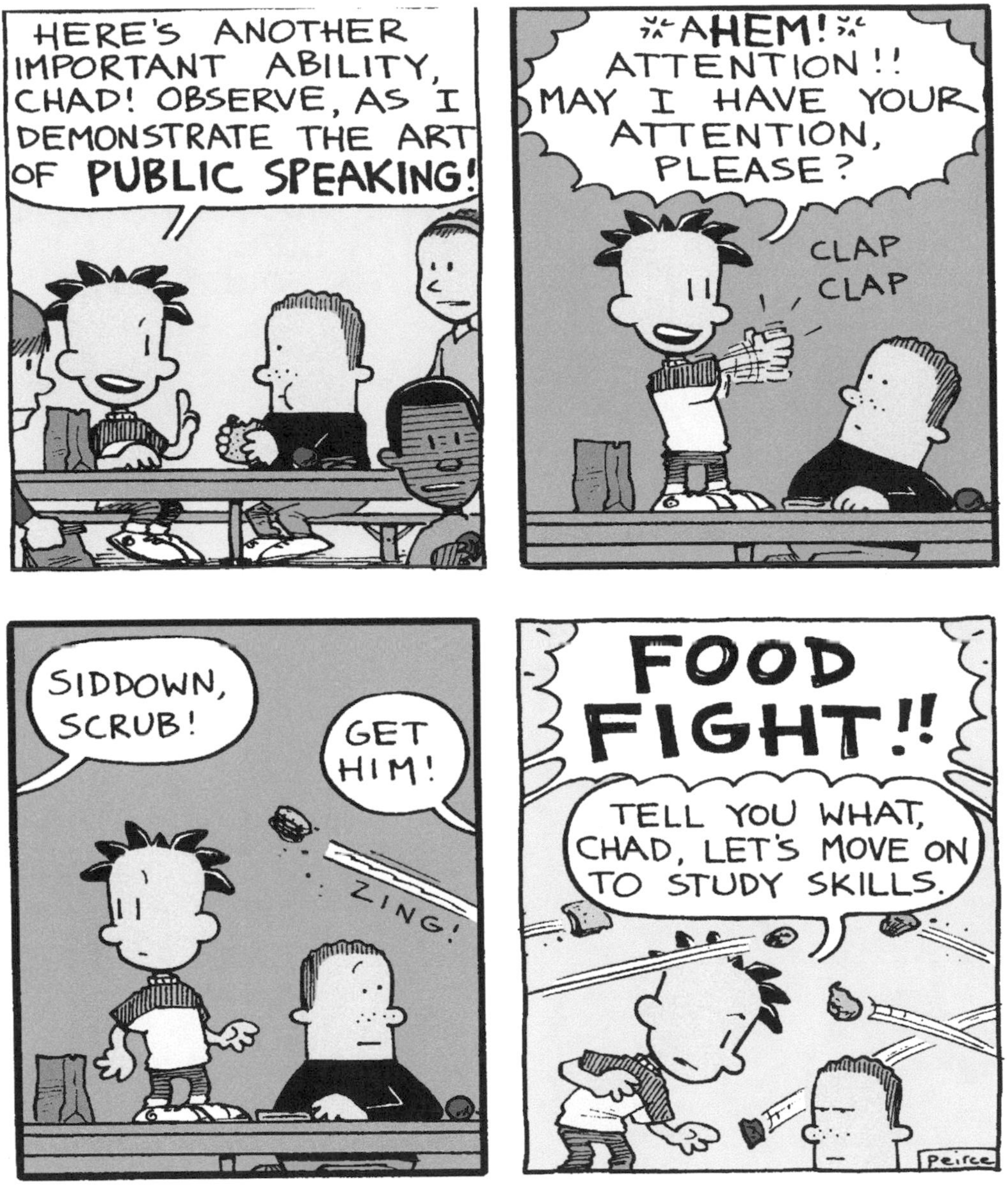
HERE'S ANOTHER IMPORTANT ABILITY, CHAD! OBSERVE, AS I DEMONSTRATE THE ART OF PUBLIC SPEAKING!
AHEM! ATTENTION!! MAY I HAVE YOUR ATTENTION, PLEASE?
CLAP CLAP
SIDDOWN, SCRUB!
GET HIM!
ZING!
FOOD FIGHT!!
TELL YOU WHAT, CHAD, LET'S MOVE ON TO STUDY SKILLS.
Peirce

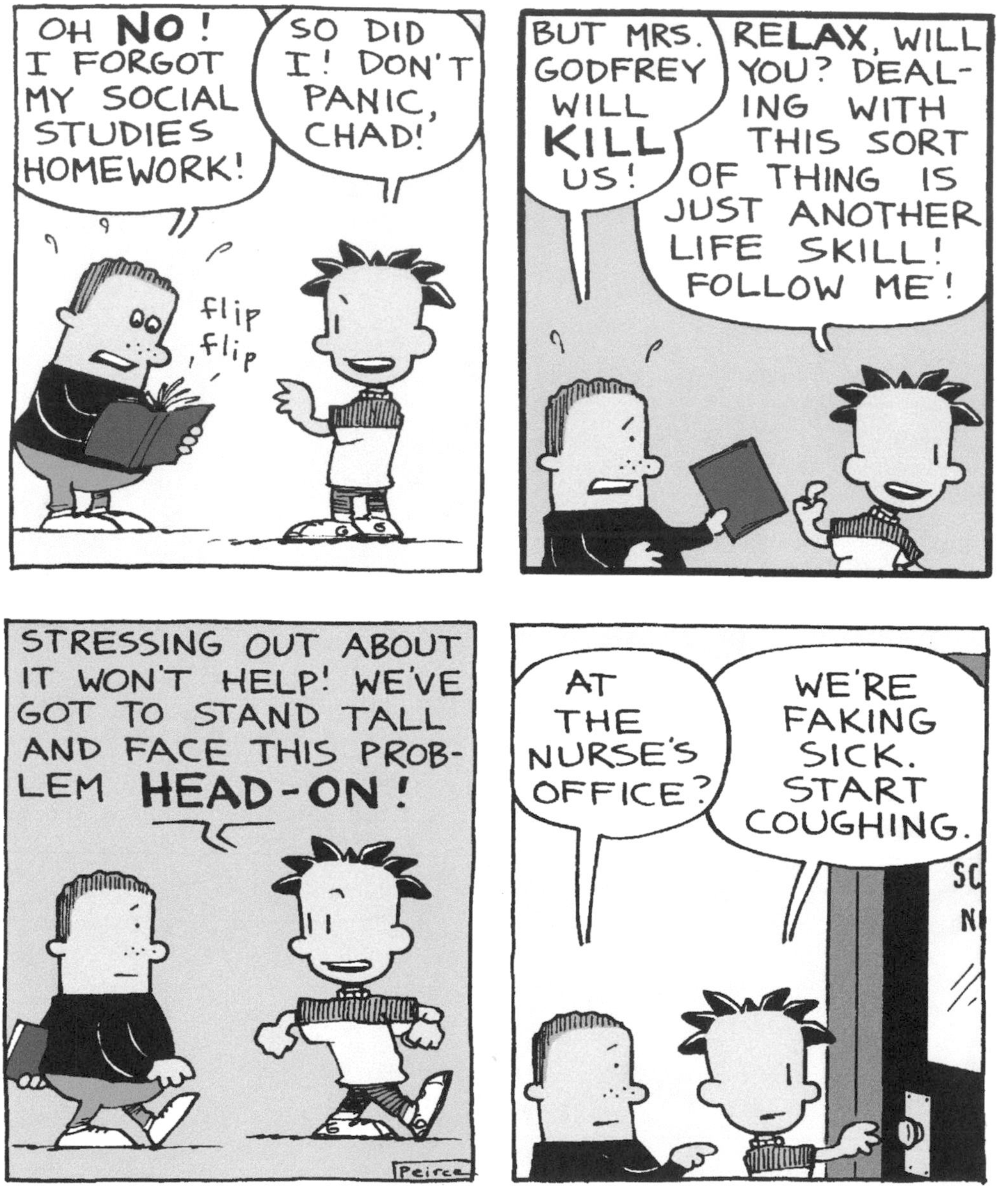
OH NO! I FORGOT MY SOCIAL STUDIES HOMEWORK!
flip flip
SO DID I! DON'T PANIC, CHAD!
BUT MRS. GODFREY WILL KILL US!
RELAX, WILL YOU? DEALING WITH THIS SORT OF THING IS JUST ANOTHER LIFE SKILL! FOLLOW ME!
STRESSING OUT ABOUT IT WON'T HELP! WE'VE GOT TO STAND TALL AND FACE THIS PROBLEM HEAD-ON!
Peirce
AT THE NURSE'S OFFICE?
WE'RE FAKING SICK. START COUGHING.

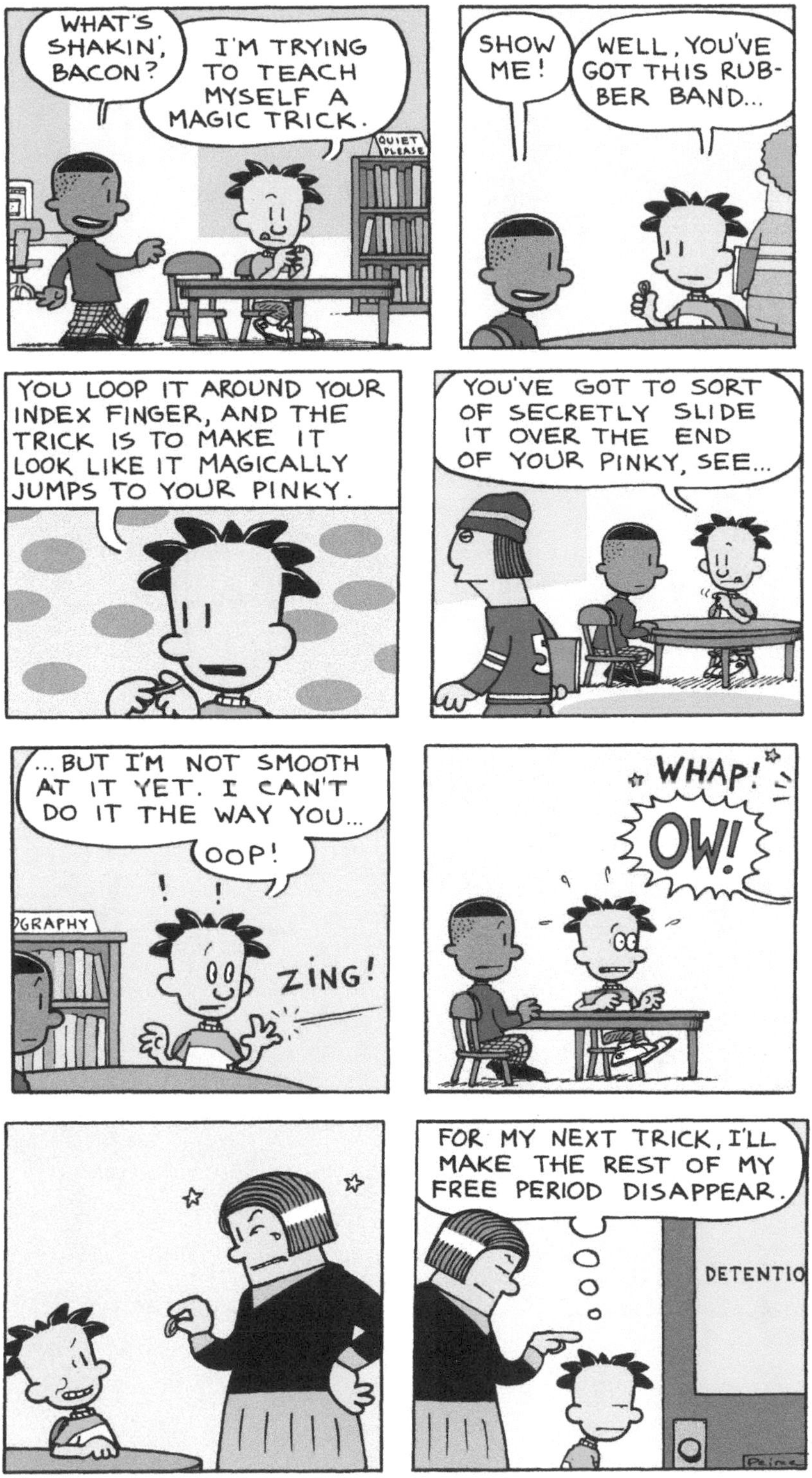
WHAT'S SHAKIN', BACON?
I'M TRYING TO TEACH MYSELF A MAGIC TRICK.
QUIET PLEASE
SHOW ME!
WELL, YOU'VE GOT THIS RUBBER BAND...
YOU LOOP IT AROUND YOUR INDEX FINGER, AND THE TRICK IS TO MAKE IT LOOK LIKE IT MAGICALLY JUMPS TO YOUR PINKY.
YOU'VE GOT TO SORT OF SECRETLY SLIDE IT OVER THE END OF YOUR PINKY, SEE...
...BUT I'M NOT SMOOTH AT IT YET. I CAN'T DO IT THE WAY YOU...
OOP!
ZING!
WHAP!
OW!
FOR MY NEXT TRICK, I'LL MAKE THE REST OF MY FREE PERIOD DISAPPEAR.
DETENTIO

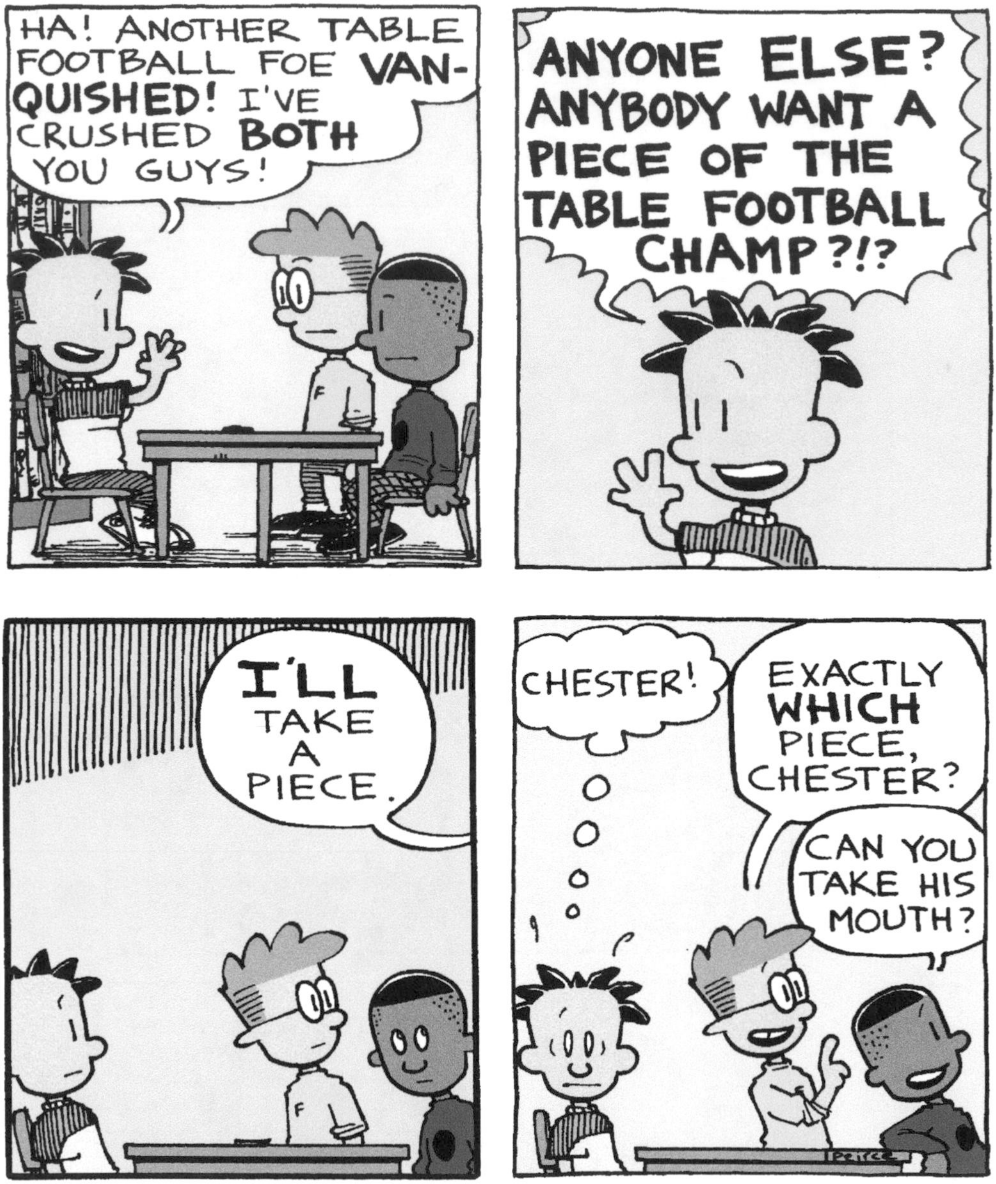
HA! ANOTHER TABLE FOOTBALL FOE VAN-QUISHED! I'VE CRUSHED BOTH YOU GUYS!
ANYONE ELSE? ANYBODY WANT A PIECE OF THE TABLE FOOTBALL CHAMP?!?
I'LL TAKE A PIECE.
CHESTER!
EXACTLY WHICH PIECE, CHESTER?
CAN YOU TAKE HIS MOUTH?

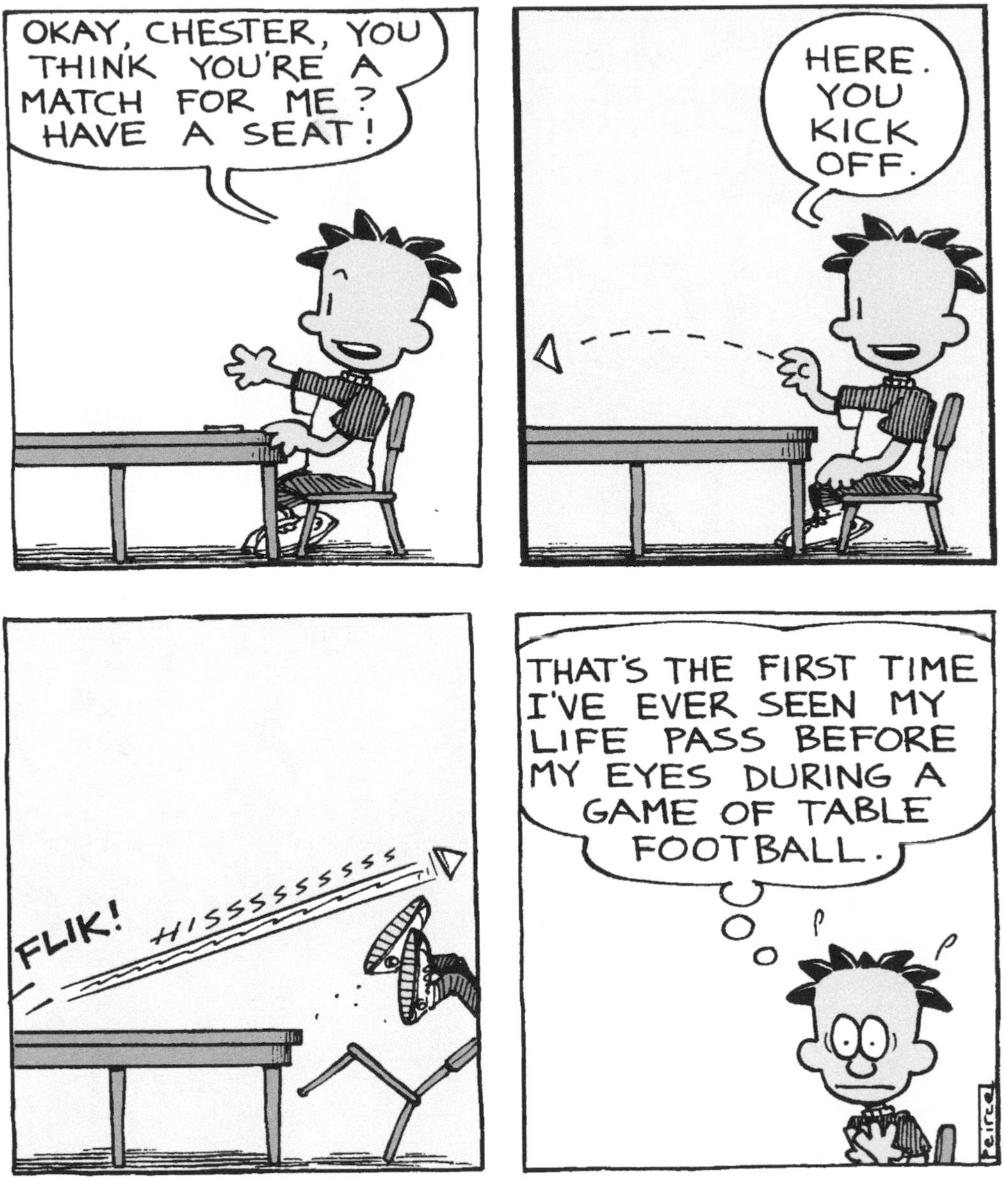
OKAY, CHESTER, YOU THINK YOU'RE A MATCH FOR ME? HAVE A SEAT!
HERE. YOU KICK OFF.
FLIK!
HISSSSSSSSSS
THAT'S THE FIRST TIME I'VE EVER SEEN MY LIFE PASS BEFORE MY EYES DURING A GAME OF TABLE FOOTBALL.
peirce

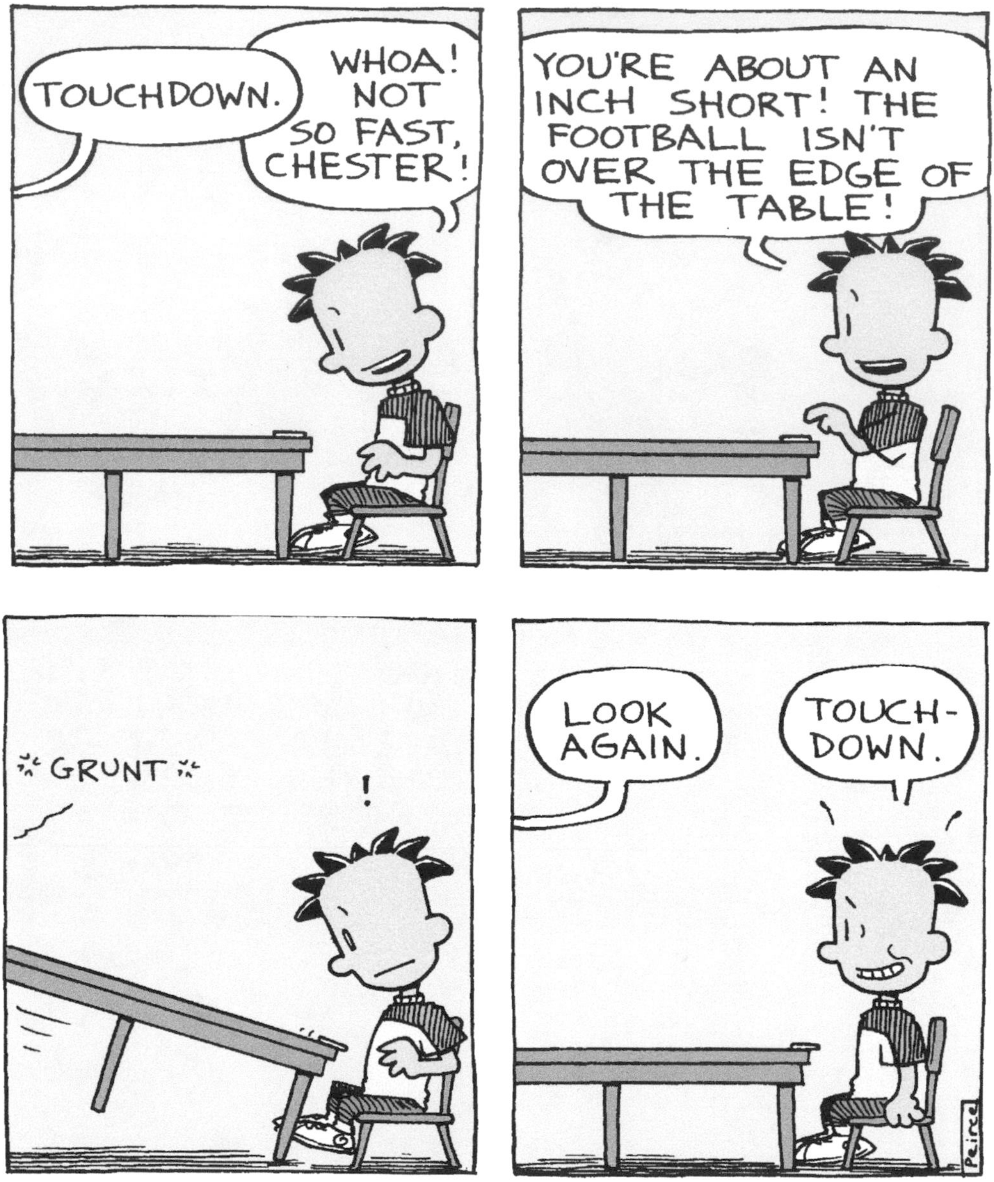
TOUCHDOWN.
WHOA! NOT SO FAST, CHESTER!
YOU'RE ABOUT AN INCH SHORT! THE FOOTBALL ISN'T OVER THE EDGE OF THE TABLE!
GRUNT
!
LOOK AGAIN.
TOUCH-DOWN.
Peirce

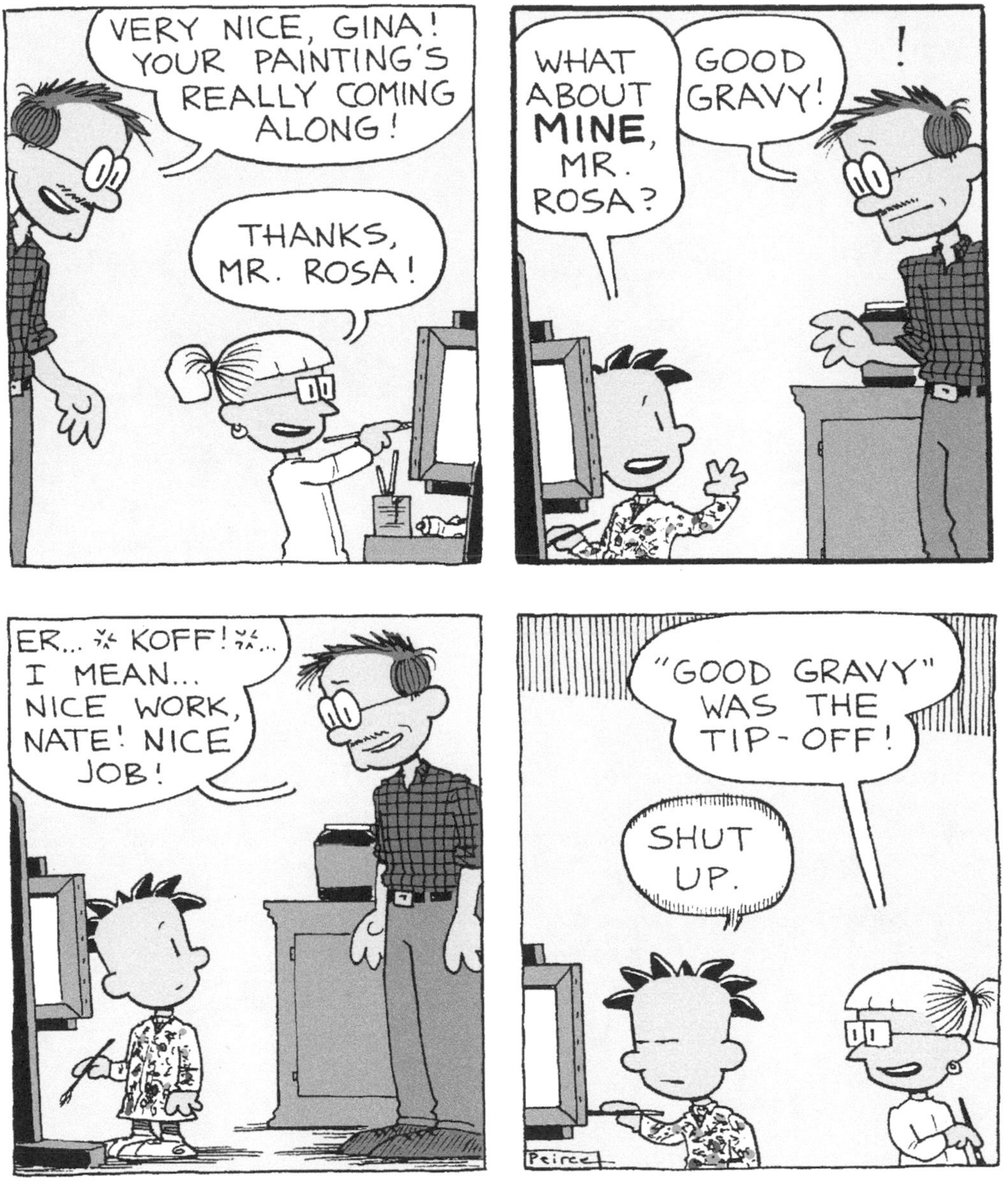
VERY NICE, GINA! YOUR PAINTING'S REALLY COMING ALONG!
THANKS, MR. ROSA!
WHAT ABOUT **MINE**, MR. ROSA?
GOOD GRAVY!
!
ER... KOFF!... I MEAN... NICE WORK, NATE! NICE JOB!
"GOOD GRAVY" WAS THE TIP-OFF!
SHUT UP.
Peirce

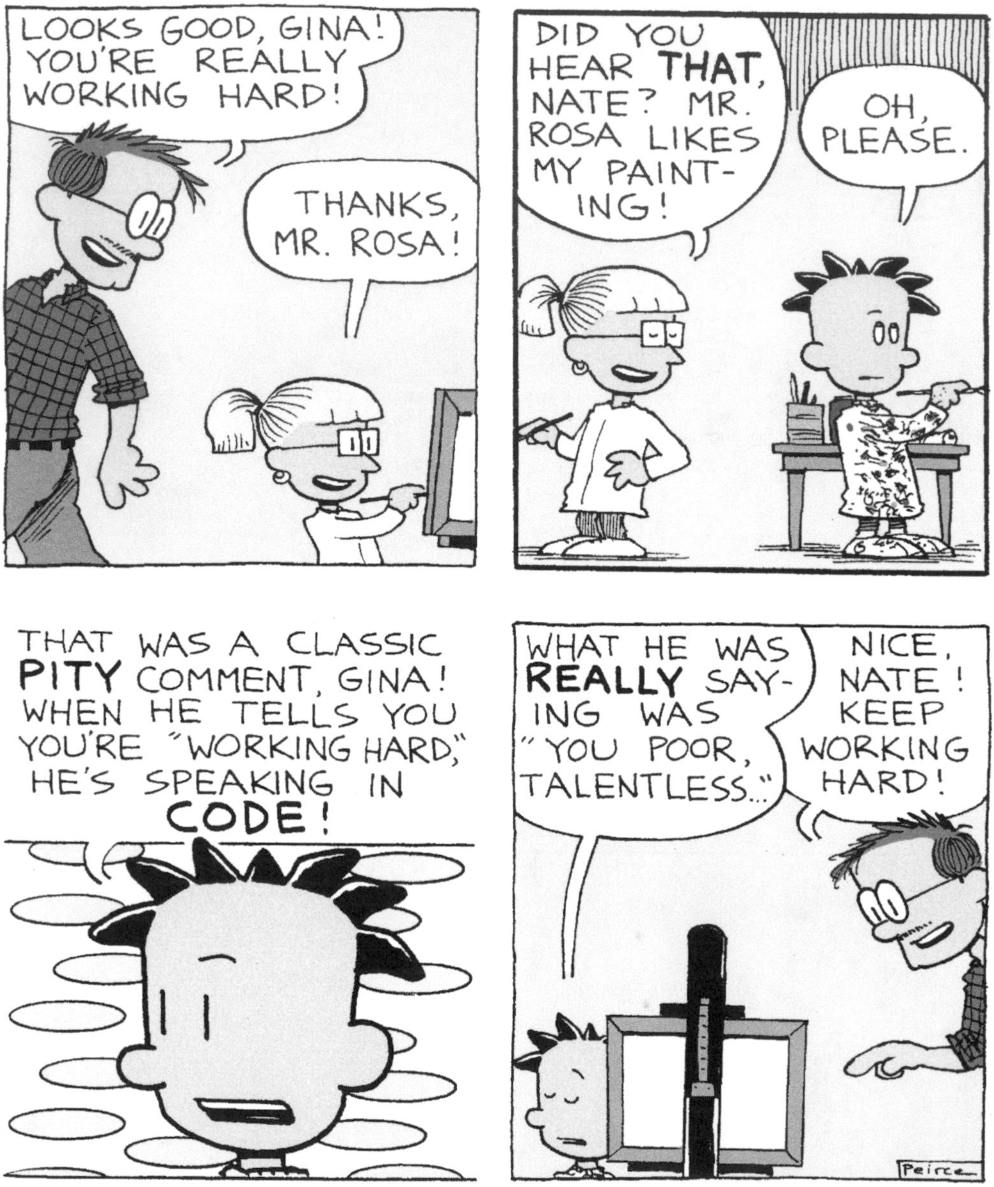
LOOKS GOOD, GINA! YOU'RE REALLY WORKING HARD!
THANKS, MR. ROSA!
DID YOU HEAR **THAT**, NATE? MR. ROSA LIKES MY PAINTING!
OH, PLEASE.
THAT WAS A CLASSIC **PITY** COMMENT, GINA! WHEN HE TELLS YOU YOU'RE "WORKING HARD," HE'S SPEAKING IN **CODE**!
WHAT HE WAS **REALLY** SAYING WAS "YOU POOR, TALENTLESS..."
NICE, NATE! KEEP WORKING HARD!
Peirce

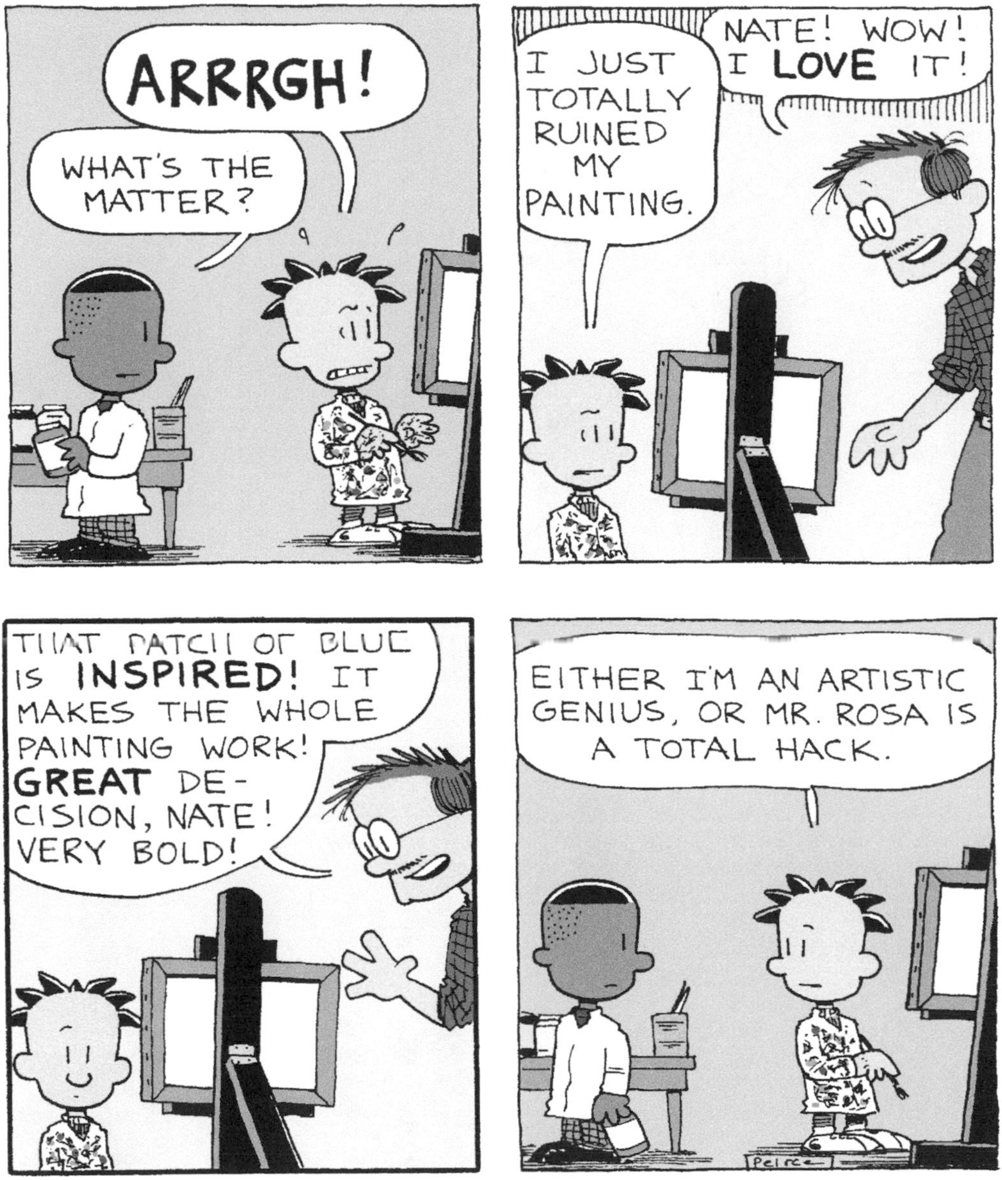
ARRRGH!
WHAT'S THE MATTER?
I JUST TOTALLY RUINED MY PAINTING.
NATE! WOW! I LOVE IT!
THAT PATCH OF BLUE IS INSPIRED! IT MAKES THE WHOLE PAINTING WORK! GREAT DECISION, NATE! VERY BOLD!
EITHER I'M AN ARTISTIC GENIUS, OR MR. ROSA IS A TOTAL HACK.
Peirce

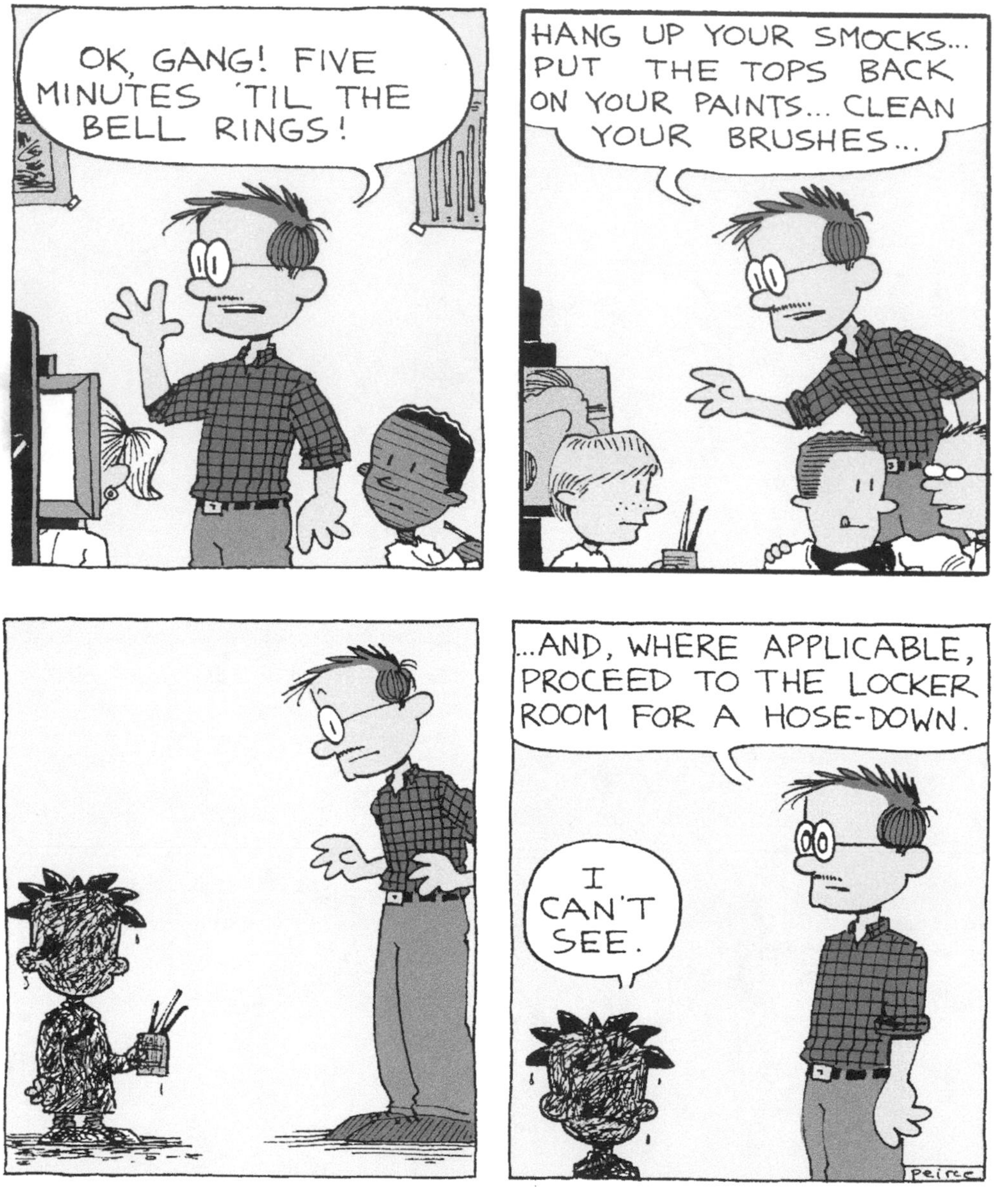
OK, GANG! FIVE MINUTES 'TIL THE BELL RINGS!
HANG UP YOUR SMOCKS... PUT THE TOPS BACK ON YOUR PAINTS... CLEAN YOUR BRUSHES...
...AND, WHERE APPLICABLE, PROCEED TO THE LOCKER ROOM FOR A HOSE-DOWN.
I CAN'T SEE.
Peirce

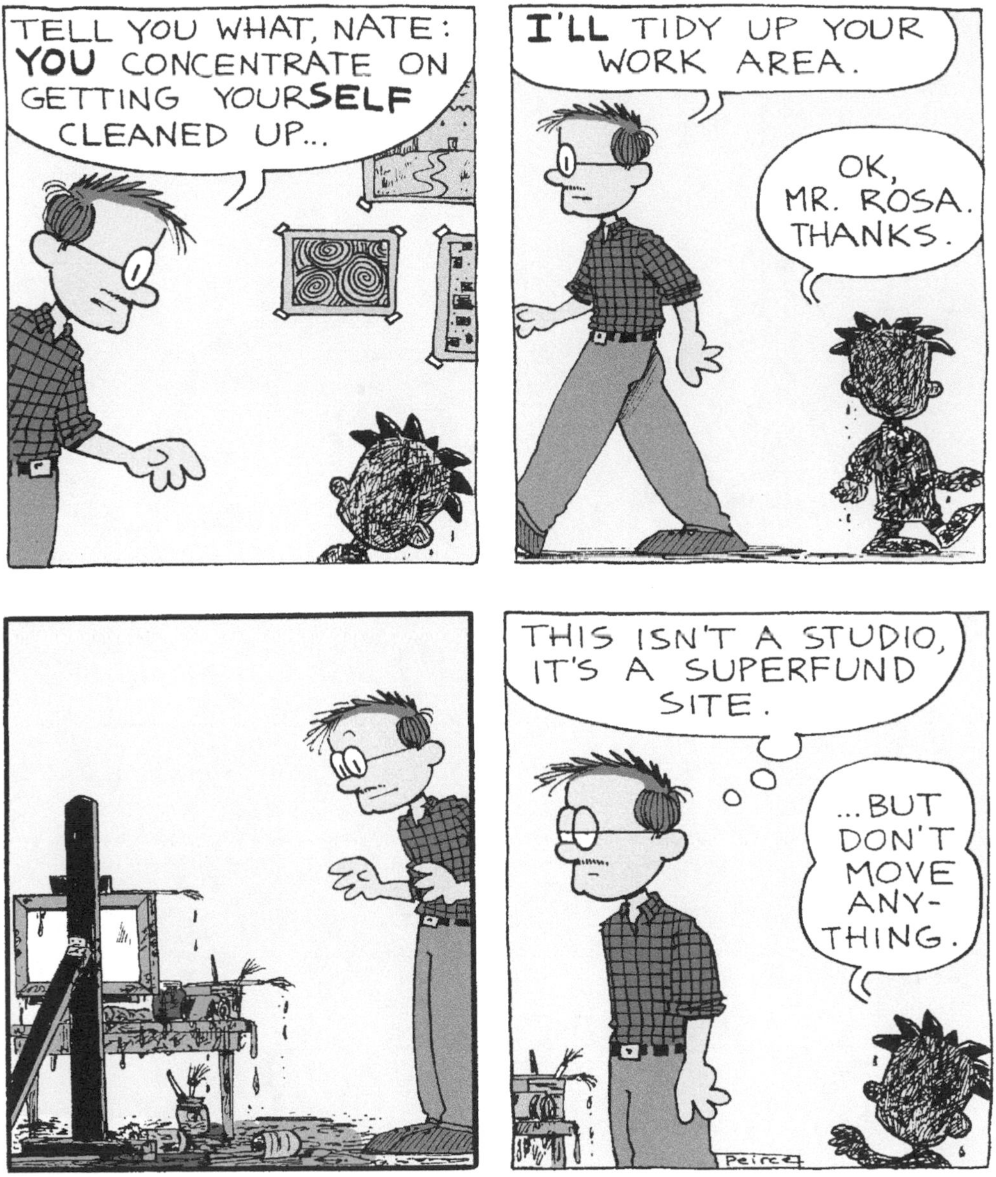
TELL YOU WHAT, NATE: **YOU** CONCENTRATE ON GETTING YOUR**SELF** CLEANED UP...
I'LL TIDY UP YOUR WORK AREA.
OK, MR. ROSA. THANKS.
THIS ISN'T A STUDIO, IT'S A SUPERFUND SITE.
...BUT DON'T MOVE ANY-THING.
Peirce

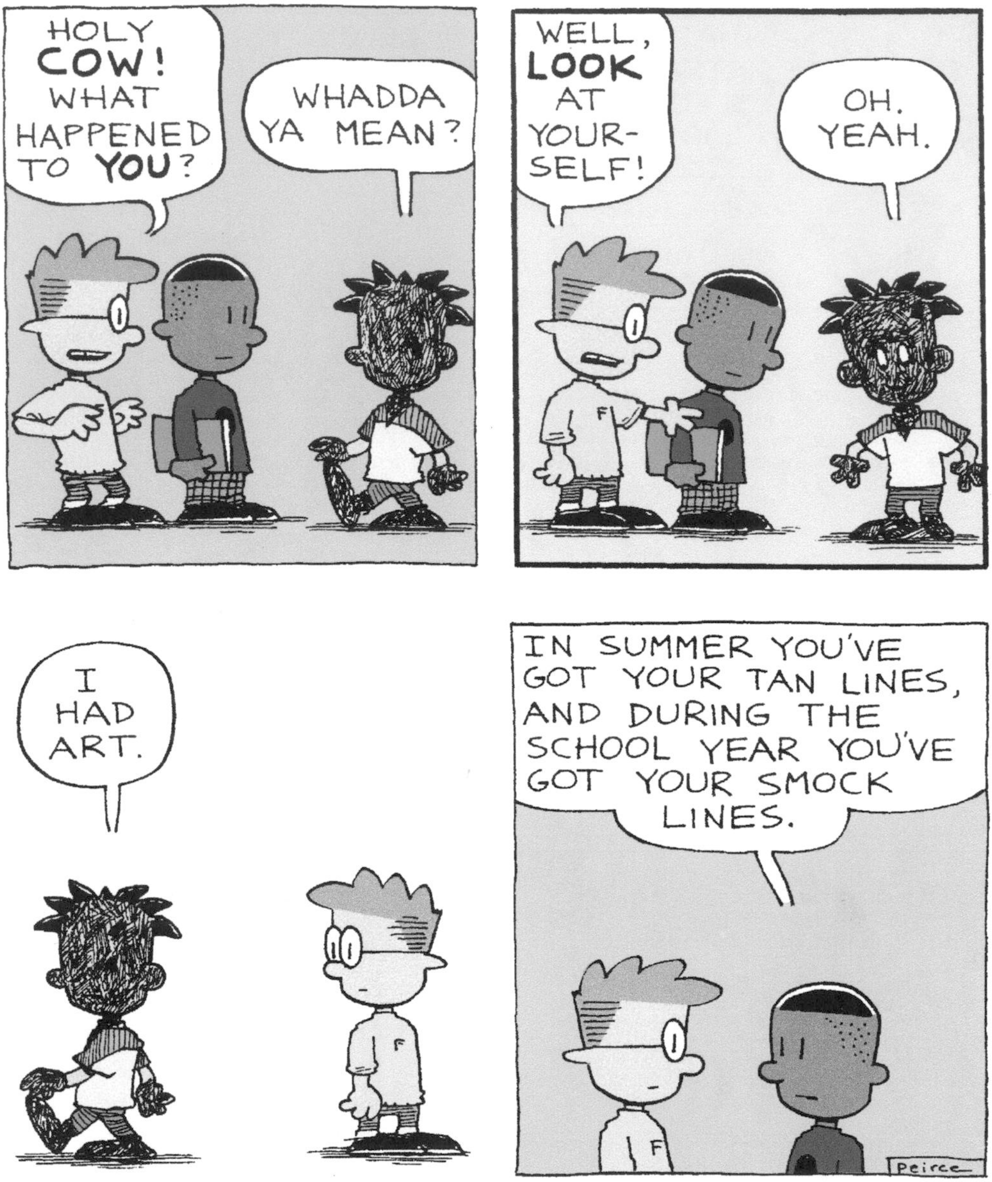
HOLY COW! WHAT HAPPENED TO YOU?
WHADDA YA MEAN?
WELL, LOOK AT YOUR-SELF!
OH. YEAH.
I HAD ART.
IN SUMMER YOU'VE GOT YOUR TAN LINES, AND DURING THE SCHOOL YEAR YOU'VE GOT YOUR SMOCK LINES.
Peirce

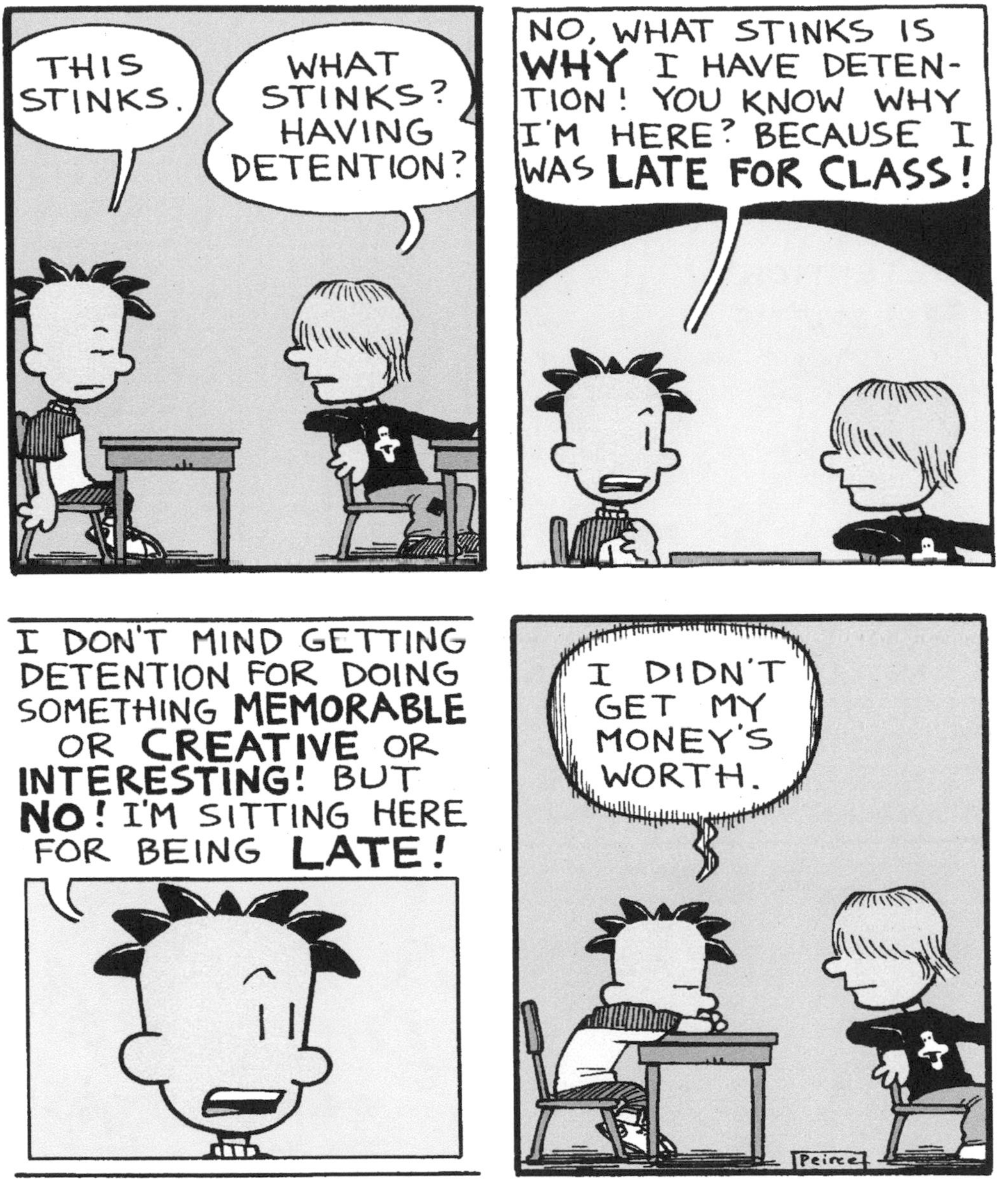
THIS STINKS.
WHAT STINKS? HAVING DETENTION?
NO, WHAT STINKS IS **WHY** I HAVE DETENTION! YOU KNOW WHY I'M HERE? BECAUSE I WAS **LATE FOR CLASS!**
I DON'T MIND GETTING DETENTION FOR DOING SOMETHING **MEMORABLE** OR **CREATIVE** OR **INTERESTING!** BUT **NO!** I'M SITTING HERE FOR BEING **LATE!**
I DIDN'T GET MY MONEY'S WORTH.
Peirce

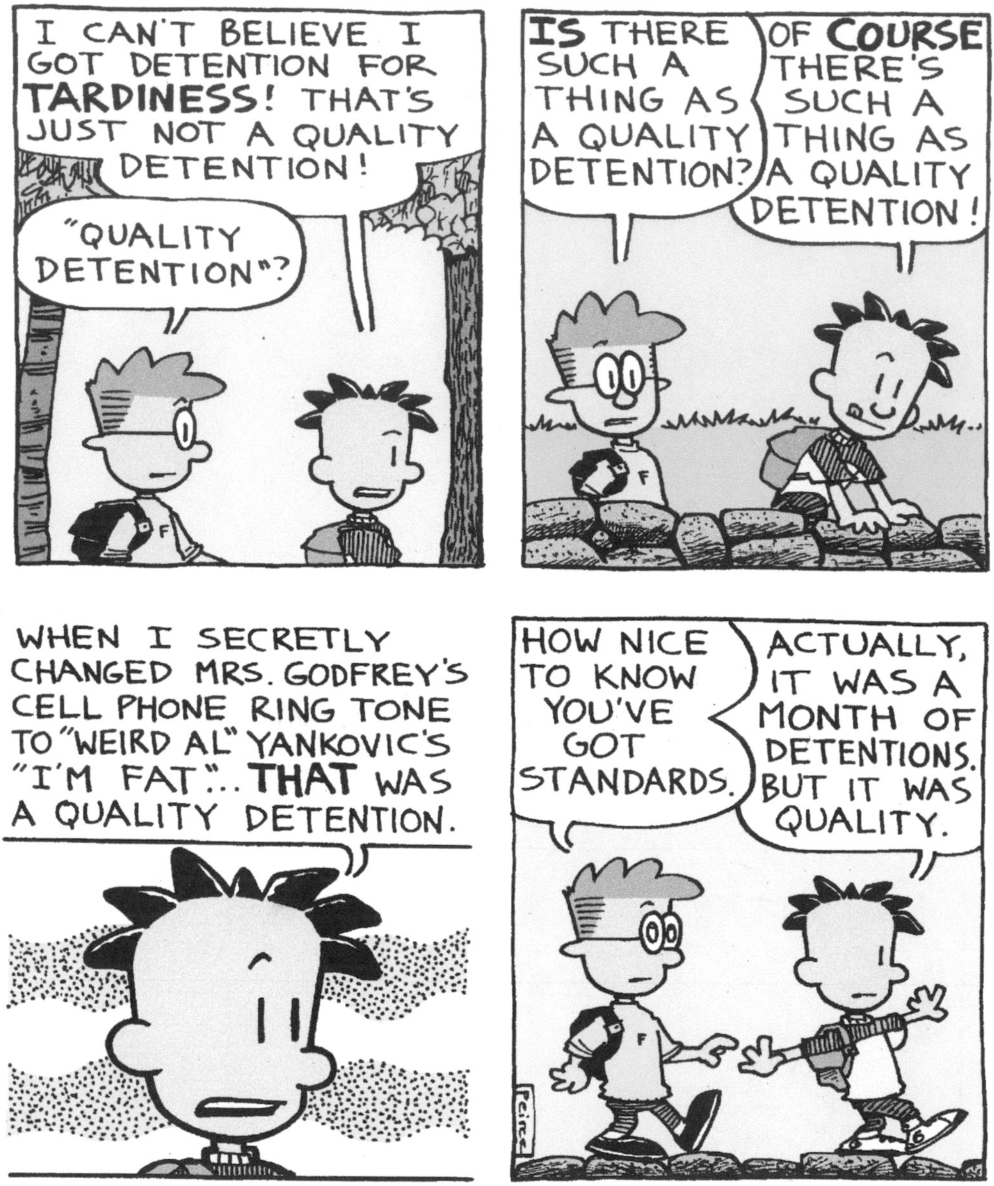
I CAN'T BELIEVE I GOT DETENTION FOR TARDINESS! THAT'S JUST NOT A QUALITY DETENTION!
"QUALITY DETENTION"?
IS THERE SUCH A THING AS A QUALITY DETENTION?
OF COURSE THERE'S SUCH A THING AS A QUALITY DETENTION!
WHEN I SECRETLY CHANGED MRS. GODFREY'S CELL PHONE RING TONE TO "WEIRD AL" YANKOVIC'S "I'M FAT"... THAT WAS A QUALITY DETENTION.
HOW NICE TO KNOW YOU'VE GOT STANDARDS.
ACTUALLY, IT WAS A MONTH OF DETENTIONS. BUT IT WAS QUALITY.
PEIRCE

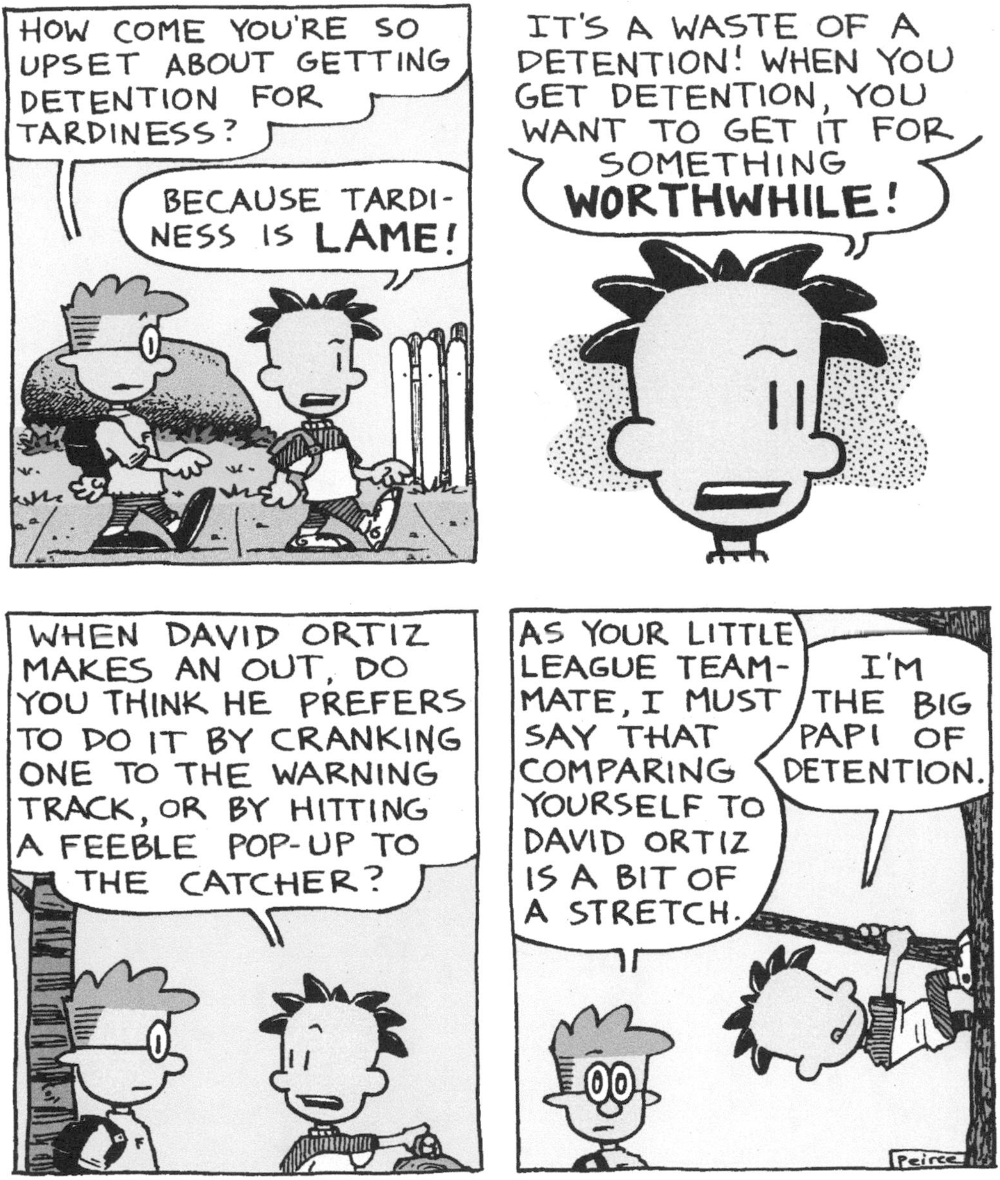
HOW COME YOU'RE SO UPSET ABOUT GETTING DETENTION FOR TARDINESS?
BECAUSE TARDINESS IS **LAME**!
IT'S A WASTE OF A DETENTION! WHEN YOU GET DETENTION, YOU WANT TO GET IT FOR SOMETHING **WORTHWHILE**!
WHEN DAVID ORTIZ MAKES AN OUT, DO YOU THINK HE PREFERS TO DO IT BY CRANKING ONE TO THE WARNING TRACK, OR BY HITTING A FEEBLE POP-UP TO THE CATCHER?
I'M THE BIG PAPI OF DETENTION.
AS YOUR LITTLE LEAGUE TEAMMATE, I MUST SAY THAT COMPARING YOURSELF TO DAVID ORTIZ IS A BIT OF A STRETCH.
Peirce

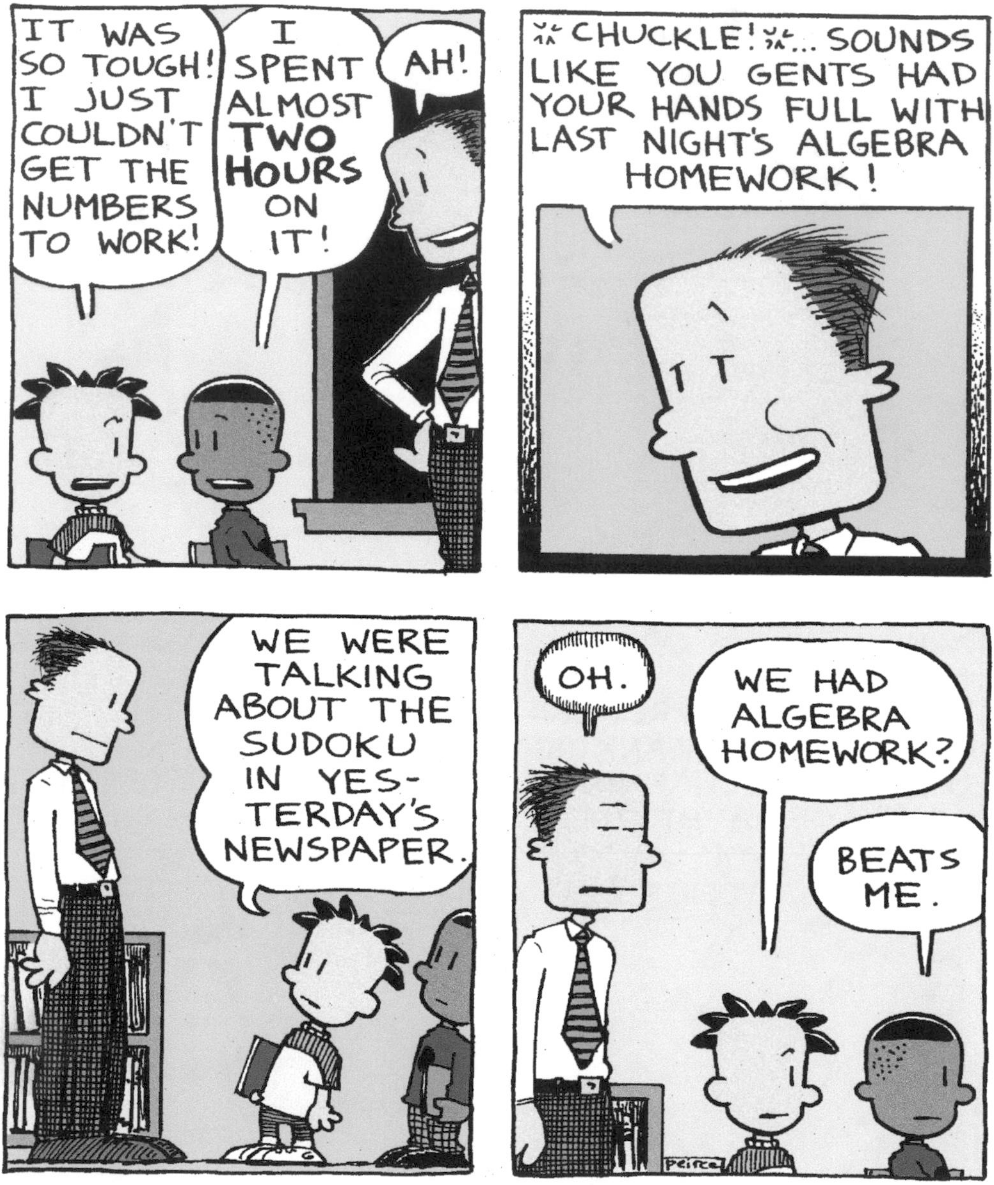
IT WAS SO TOUGH! I JUST COULDN'T GET THE NUMBERS TO WORK!
I SPENT ALMOST TWO HOURS ON IT!
AH!
CHUCKLE! ... SOUNDS LIKE YOU GENTS HAD YOUR HANDS FULL WITH LAST NIGHT'S ALGEBRA HOMEWORK!
WE WERE TALKING ABOUT THE SUDOKU IN YESTERDAY'S NEWSPAPER.
OH.
WE HAD ALGEBRA HOMEWORK?
BEATS ME.
PEIRCE

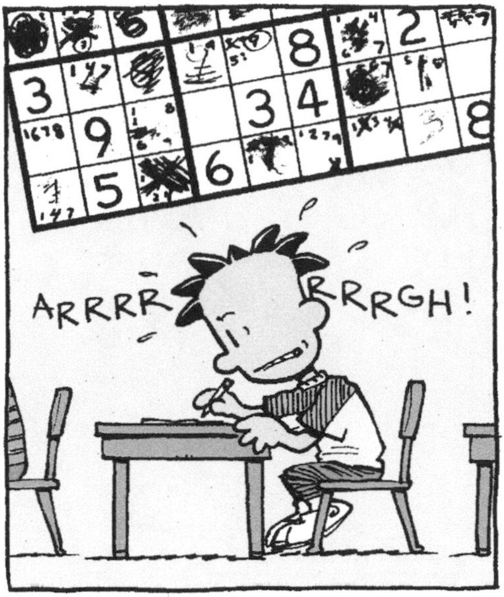
ARRRRRRRRGH!
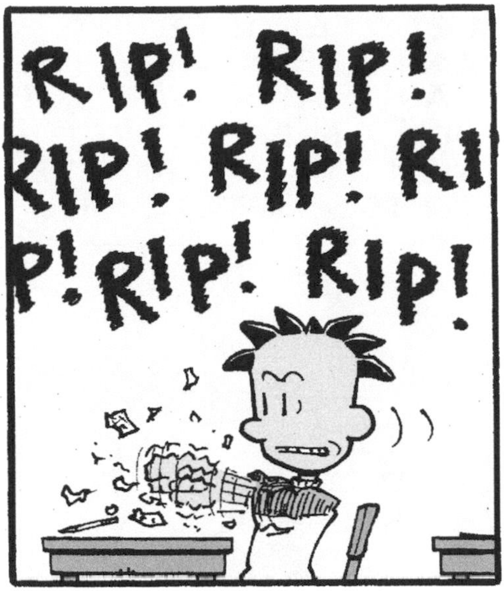
RIP! RIP!
RIP! RIP! RI
P! RIP! RIP!
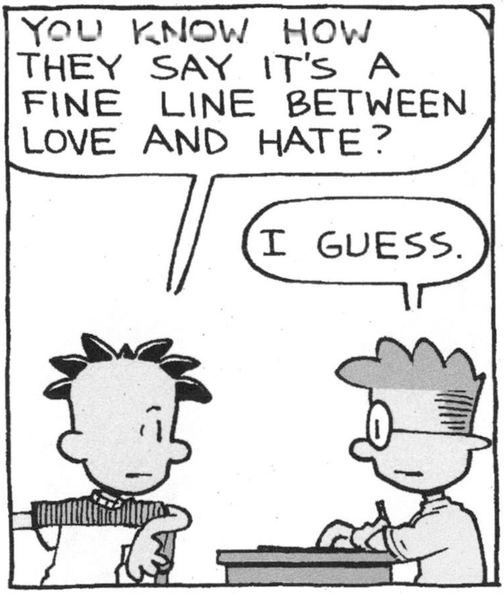
YOU KNOW HOW THEY SAY IT'S A FINE LINE BETWEEN LOVE AND HATE?
I GUESS.
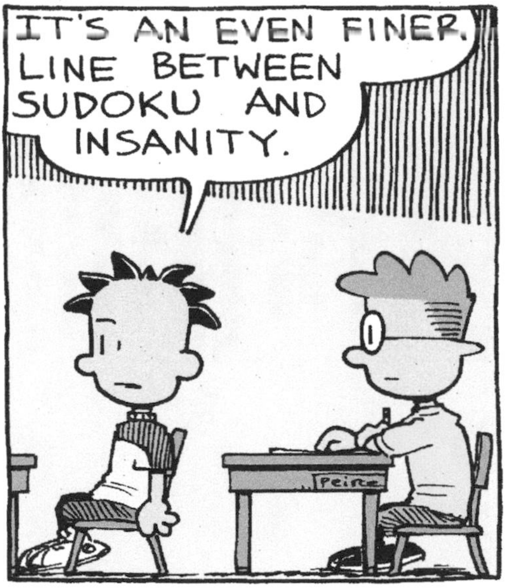
IT'S AN EVEN FINER LINE BETWEEN SUDOKU AND INSANITY.
PEIRCE

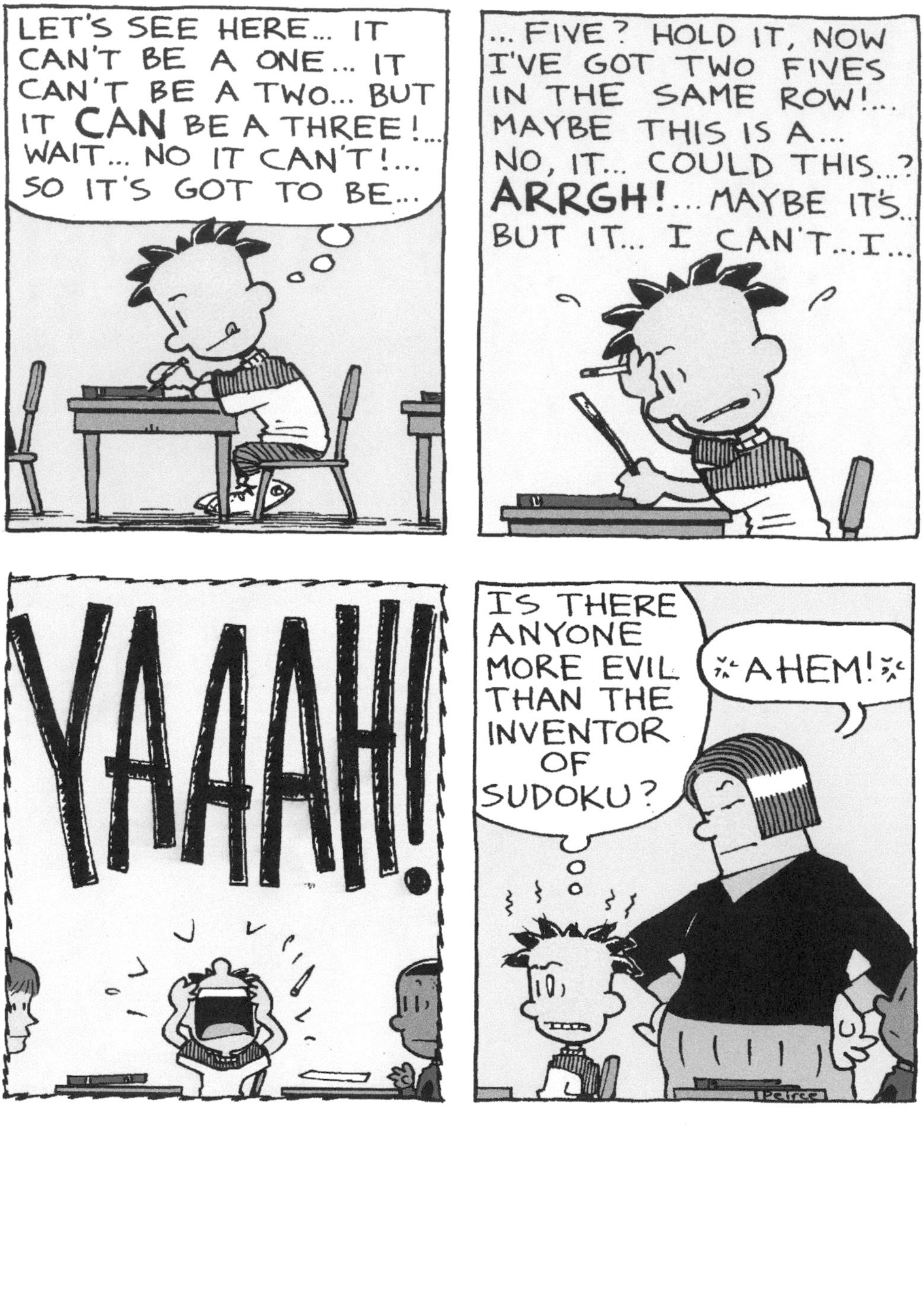
LET'S SEE HERE... IT CAN'T BE A ONE... IT CAN'T BE A TWO... BUT IT CAN BE A THREE!... WAIT... NO IT CAN'T!... SO IT'S GOT TO BE...
... FIVE? HOLD IT, NOW I'VE GOT TWO FIVES IN THE SAME ROW!... MAYBE THIS IS A... NO, IT... COULD THIS...? ARRGH!... MAYBE IT'S... BUT IT... I CAN'T... I...
YAAAH!
IS THERE ANYONE MORE EVIL THAN THE INVENTOR OF SUDOKU?
AHEM!
Peirce

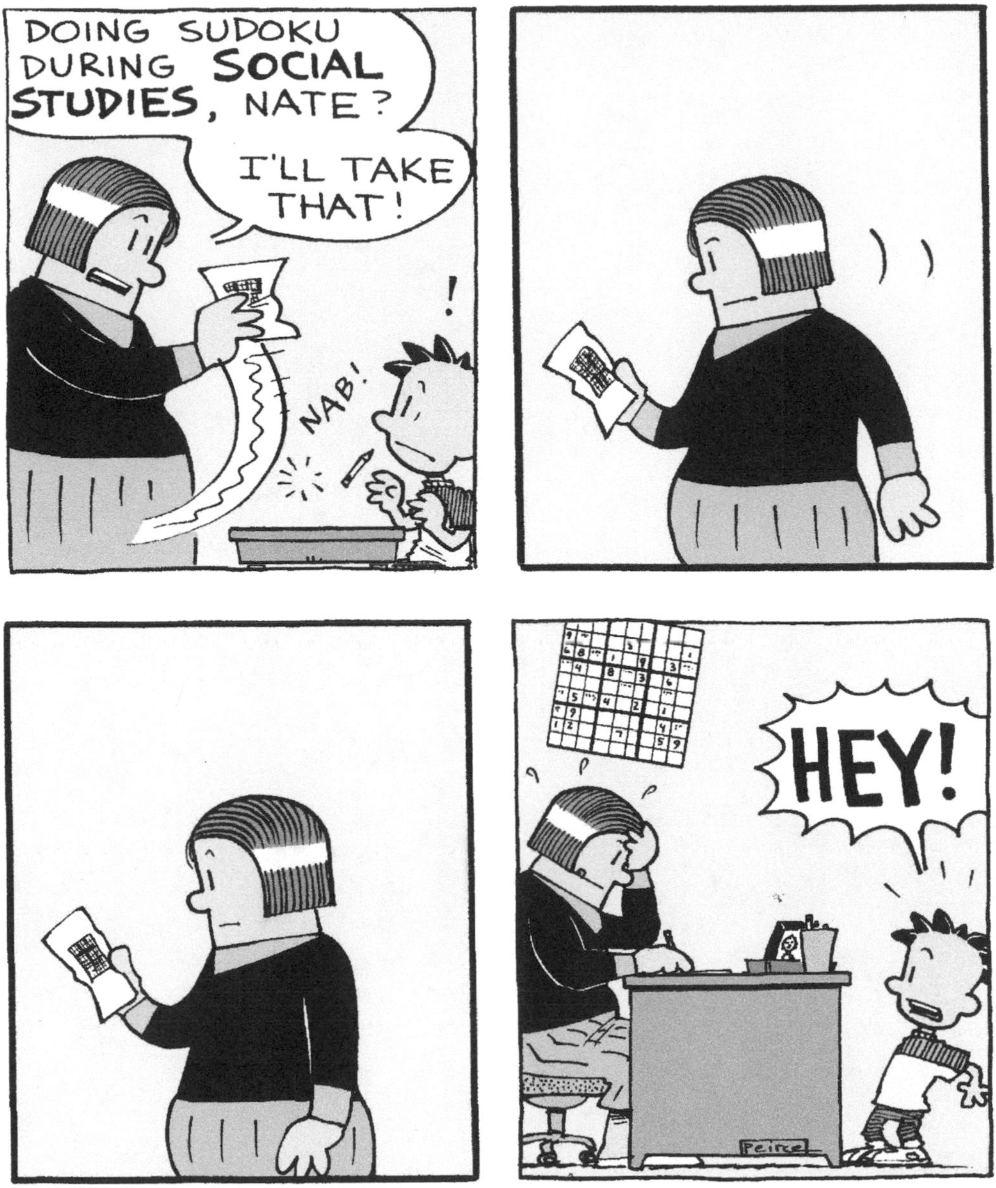
DOING SUDOKU DURING SOCIAL STUDIES, NATE?
I'LL TAKE THAT!
!
NAB!
HEY!

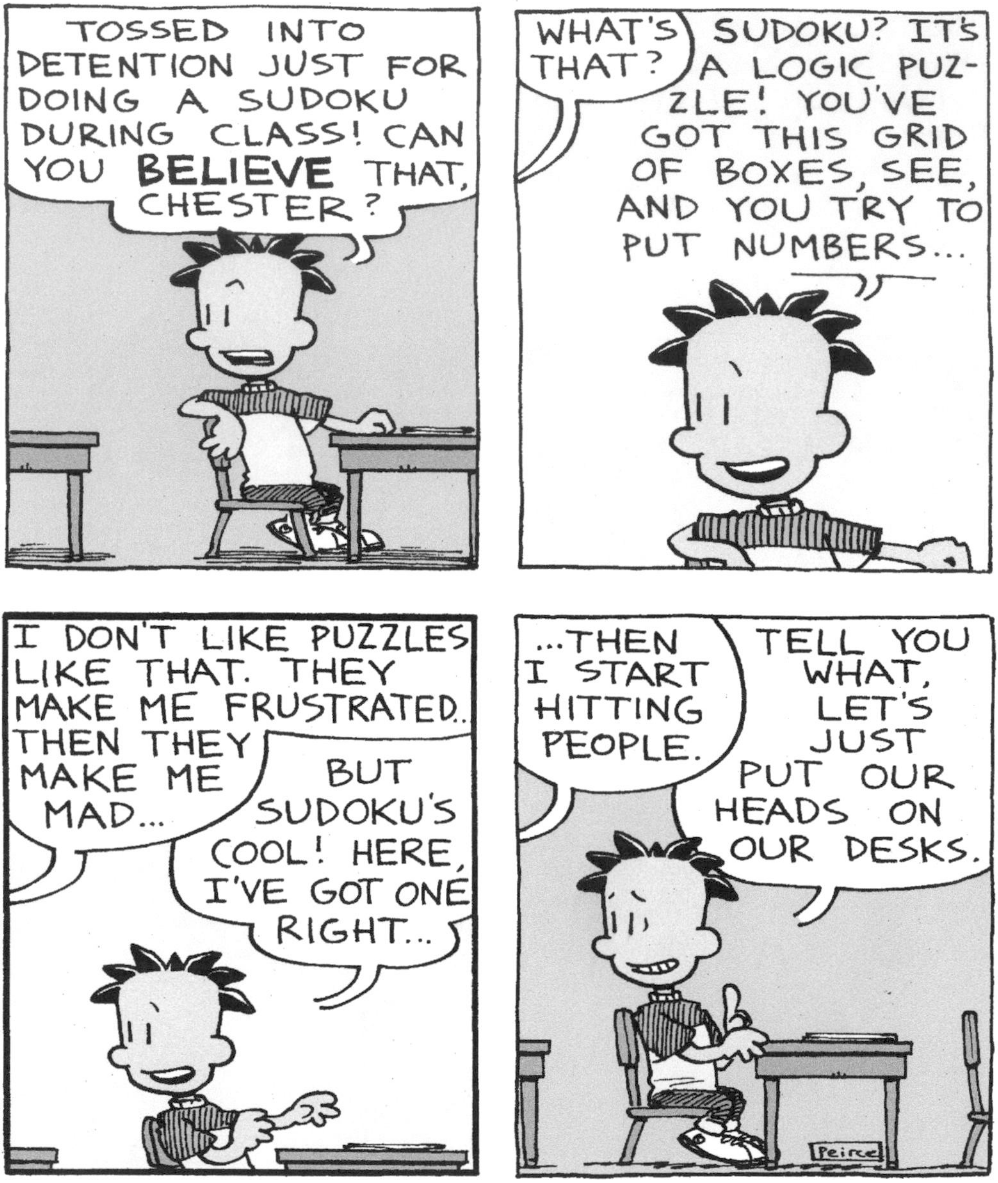
TOSSED INTO DETENTION JUST FOR DOING A SUDOKU DURING CLASS! CAN YOU **BELIEVE** THAT, CHESTER?
WHAT'S THAT?
SUDOKU? IT'S A LOGIC PUZZLE! YOU'VE GOT THIS GRID OF BOXES, SEE, AND YOU TRY TO PUT NUMBERS...
I DON'T LIKE PUZZLES LIKE THAT. THEY MAKE ME FRUSTRATED.. THEN THEY MAKE ME MAD...
BUT SUDOKU'S COOL! HERE, I'VE GOT ONE RIGHT...
...THEN I START HITTING PEOPLE.
TELL YOU WHAT, LET'S JUST PUT OUR HEADS ON OUR DESKS.
Peirce

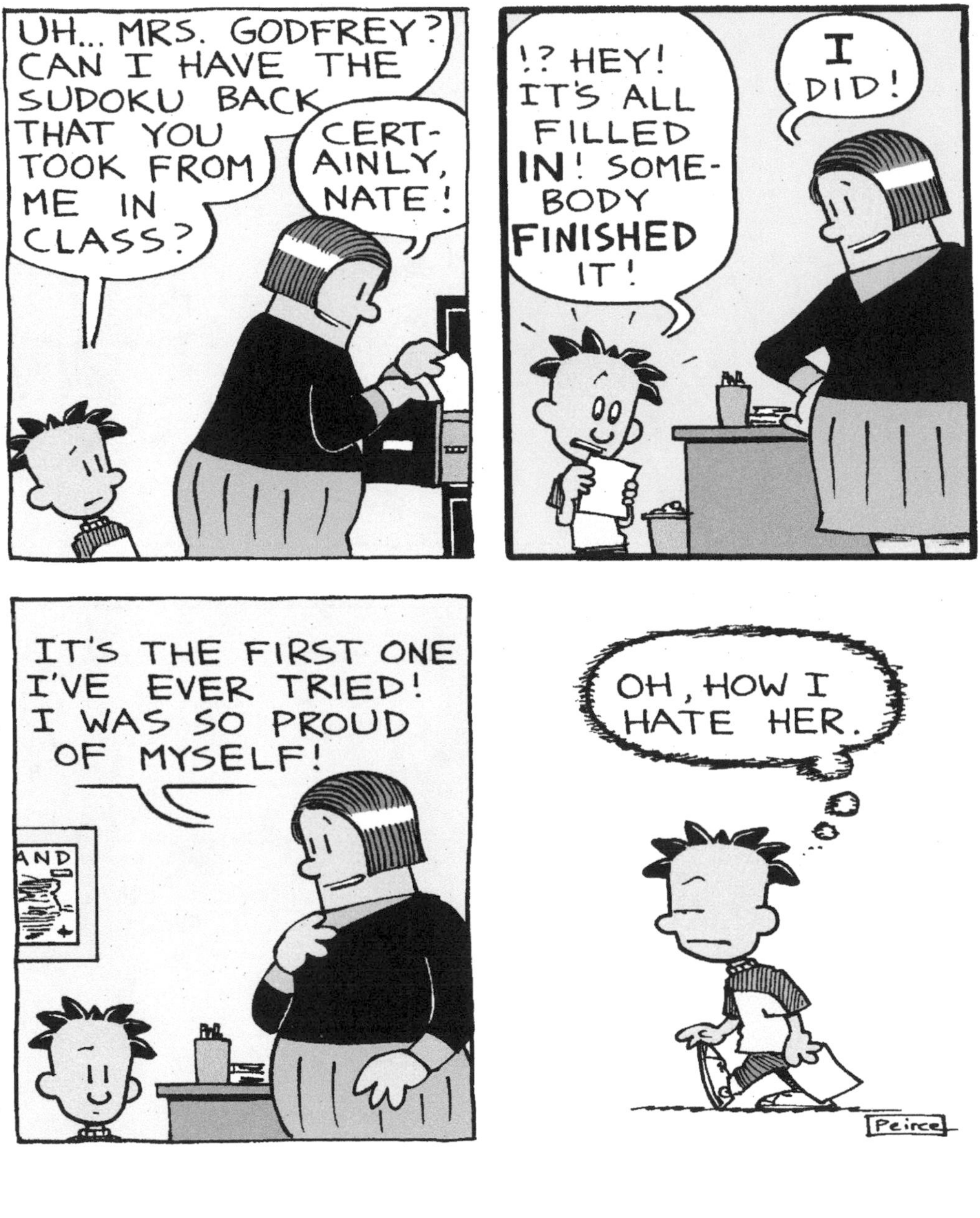
UH... MRS. GODFREY? CAN I HAVE THE SUDOKU BACK THAT YOU TOOK FROM ME IN CLASS?
CERT-AINLY, NATE!
!? HEY! IT'S ALL FILLED IN! SOME-BODY FINISHED IT!
I DID!
IT'S THE FIRST ONE I'VE EVER TRIED! I WAS SO PROUD OF MYSELF!
AND
OH, HOW I HATE HER.
Peirce

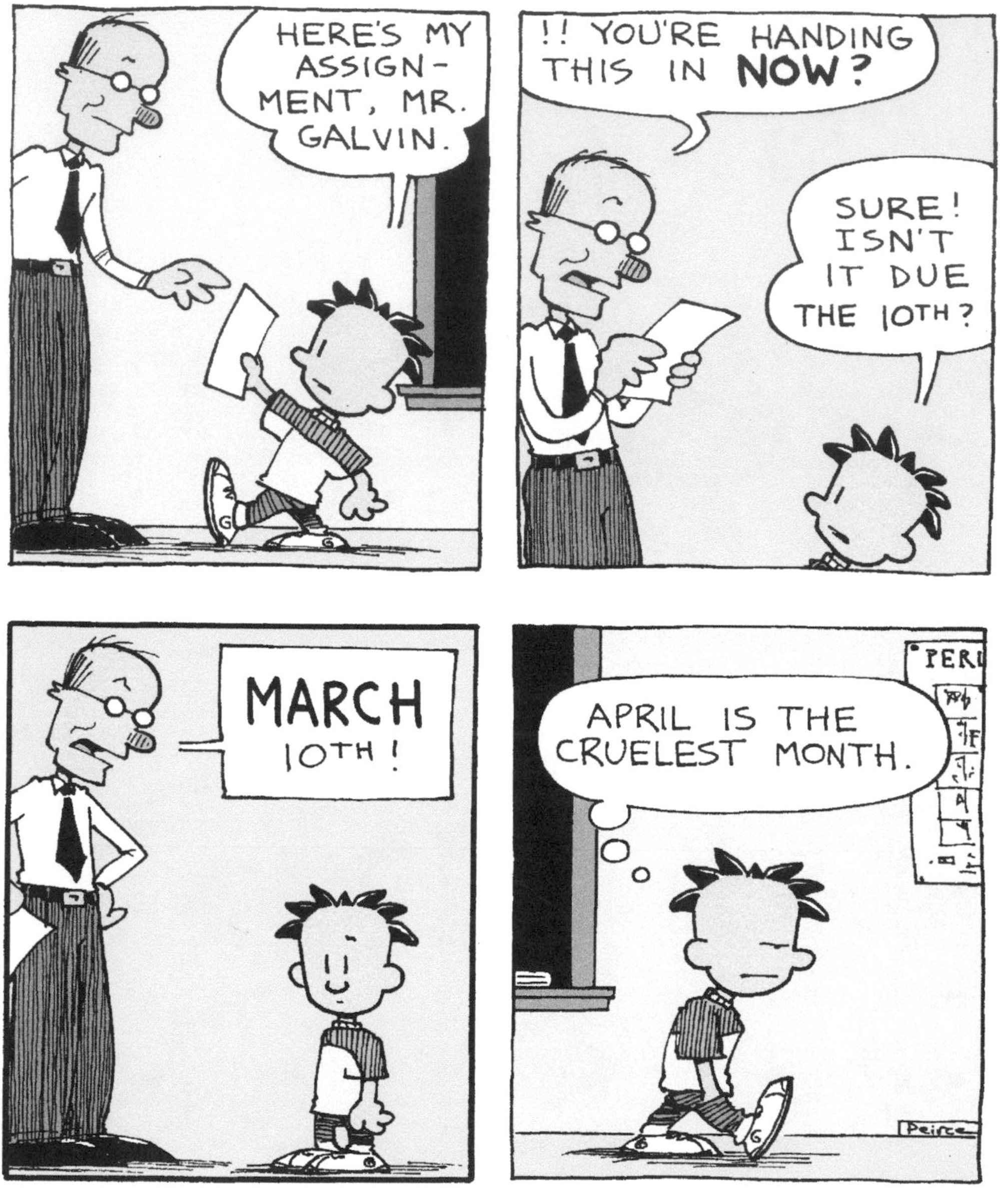
HERE'S MY ASSIGN-MENT, MR. GALVIN.
!! YOU'RE HANDING THIS IN NOW?
SURE! ISN'T IT DUE THE 10TH?
MARCH 10TH!
APRIL IS THE CRUELEST MONTH.
Peirce

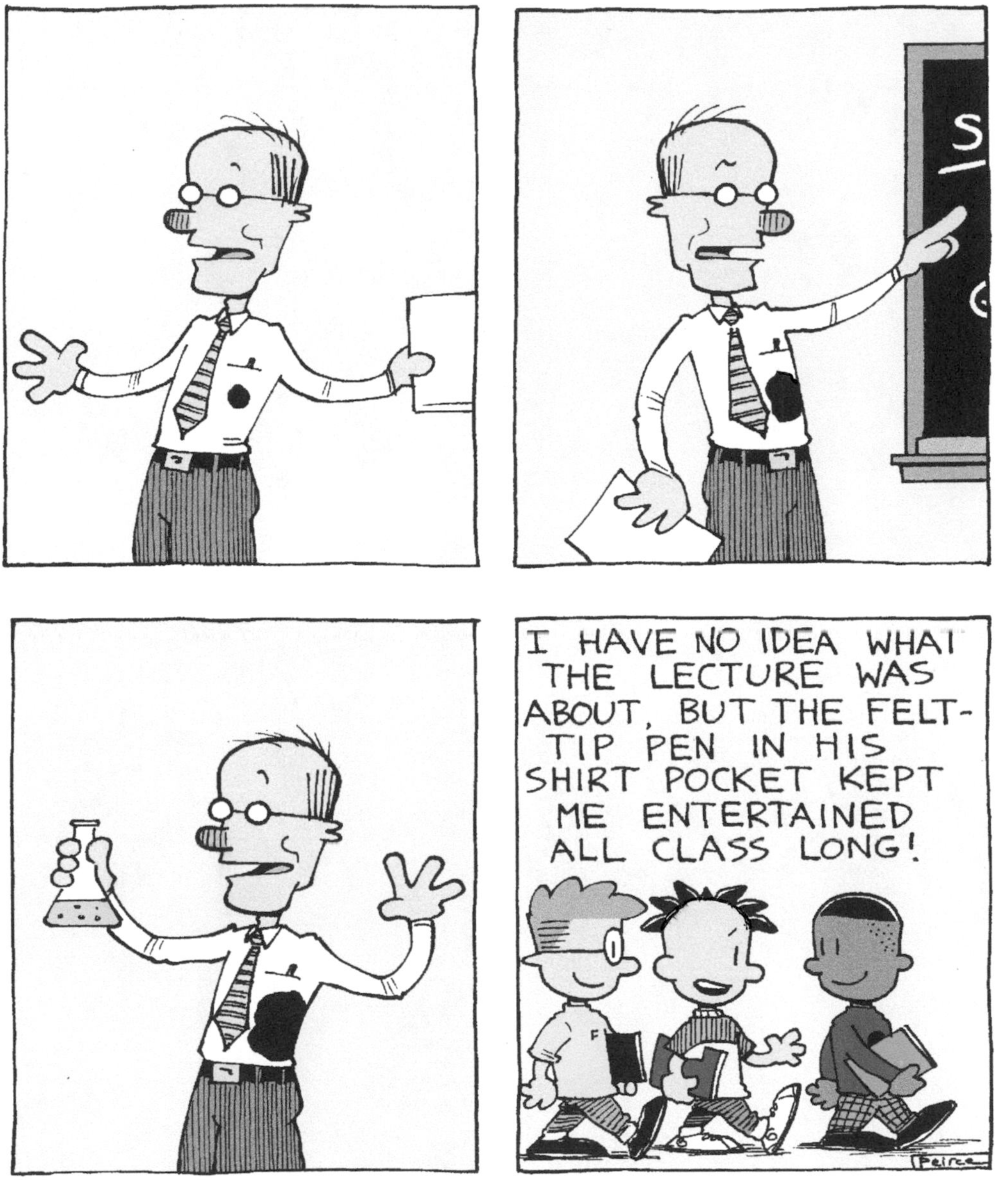

I HAVE NO IDEA WHAT THE LECTURE WAS ABOUT, BUT THE FELT-TIP PEN IN HIS SHIRT POCKET KEPT ME ENTERTAINED ALL CLASS LONG!
Peirce

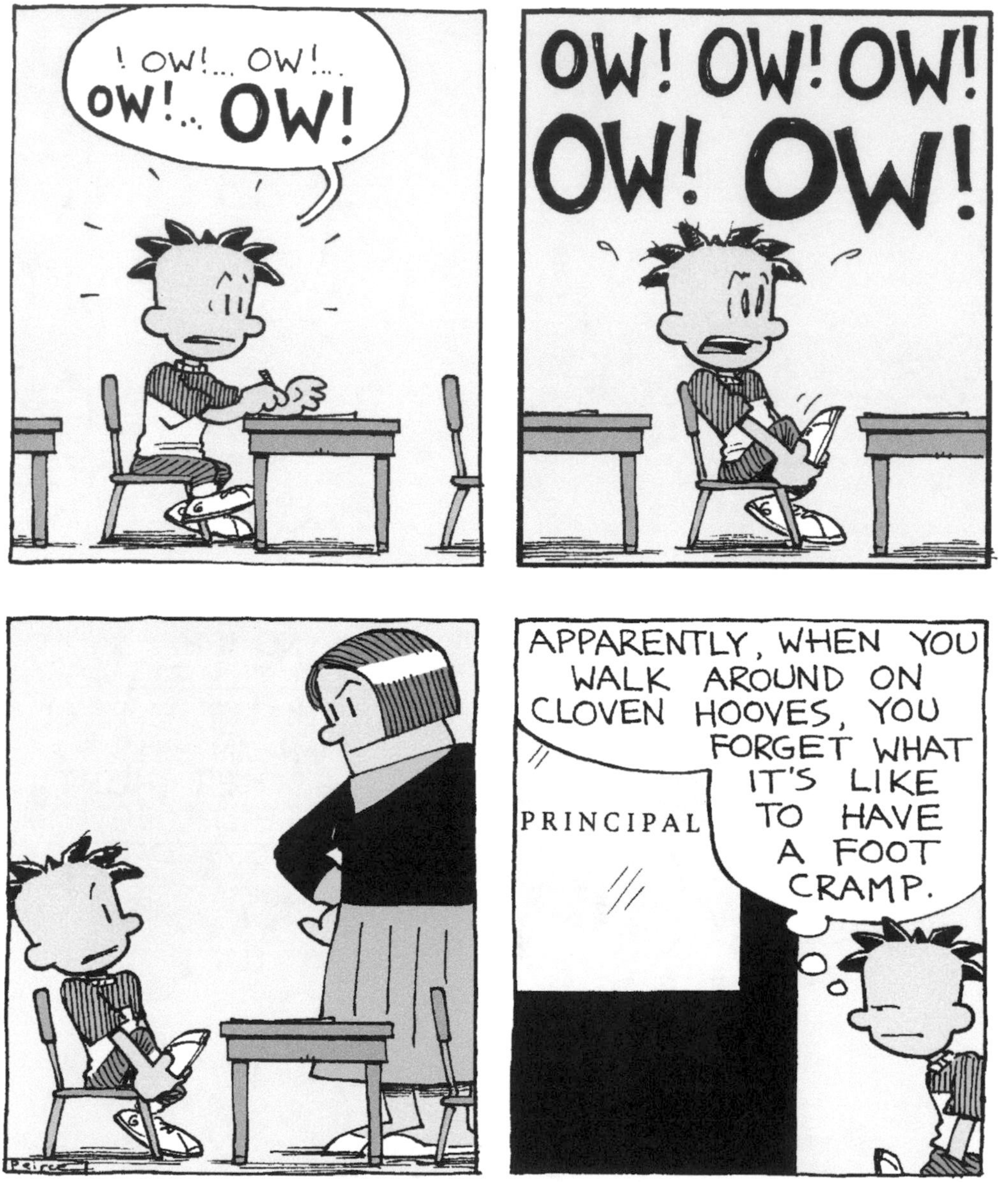

! OW!... OW!... OW!.. OW!
OW! OW! OW! OW! OW!
APPARENTLY, WHEN YOU WALK AROUND ON CLOVEN HOOVES, YOU FORGET WHAT IT'S LIKE TO HAVE A FOOT CRAMP.
PRINCIPAL

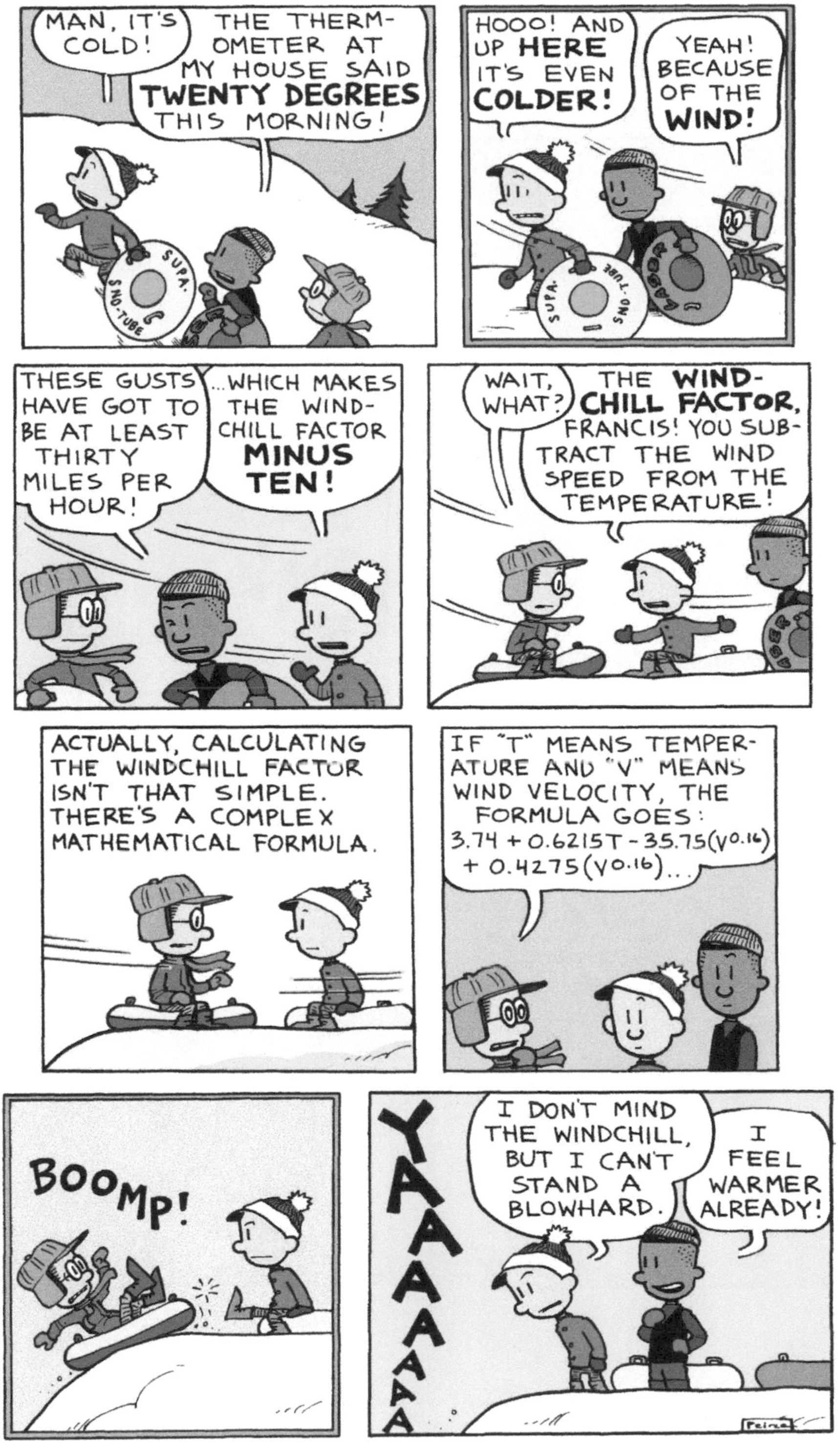
MAN, IT'S COLD!
THE THERMOMETER AT MY HOUSE SAID TWENTY DEGREES THIS MORNING!
SUPA. SNO-TUBE
HOOO! AND UP HERE IT'S EVEN COLDER!
YEAH! BECAUSE OF THE WIND!
THESE GUSTS HAVE GOT TO BE AT LEAST THIRTY MILES PER HOUR!
...WHICH MAKES THE WIND-CHILL FACTOR MINUS TEN!
WAIT, WHAT?
THE WIND-CHILL FACTOR, FRANCIS! YOU SUBTRACT THE WIND SPEED FROM THE TEMPERATURE!
ACTUALLY, CALCULATING THE WINDCHILL FACTOR ISN'T THAT SIMPLE. THERE'S A COMPLEX MATHEMATICAL FORMULA.
IF "T" MEANS TEMPERATURE AND "V" MEANS WIND VELOCITY, THE FORMULA GOES: $3.74 + 0.6215T - 35.75(V^{0.16}) + 0.4275(V^{0.16})$...
BOOMP!
YAAAAAAA
I DON'T MIND THE WINDCHILL, BUT I CAN'T STAND A BLOWHARD.
I FEEL WARMER ALREADY!

THREE PAGES ON THE BOSTON TEA PARTY! HOW AM I GONNA WRITE THREE WHOLE PAGES ON THE BOSTON TEA PARTY?
PERSON-ALLY, I'M NOT **GOING** TO WRITE THREE PAGES!
WHAT DO YOU MEAN?
I'M GOING TO WRITE **ONE** PAGE, THEN **TURN IT INTO** THREE!
HOW ARE YOU GONNA MANAGE THAT?
ONE WORD, TEDDY: **FONT SIZE!**
THAT'S TWO WORDS, NIM-ROD.
I'LL GO WITH A TIMES ROMAN TWENTY-FOUR! NO, TWENTY-**EIGHT!**
TICKA TICKA TIK TIK TAK

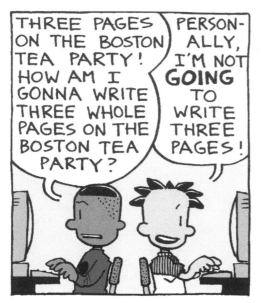

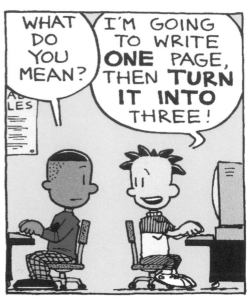

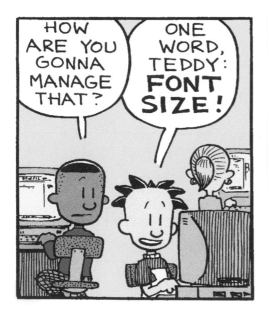

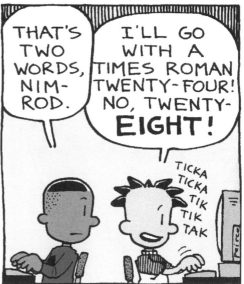

OBSERVE, TEDDY, AS I DEMONSTRATE THE TRANSFORMATIVE POWER OF FONTS!
GODFREY SAID WE HAD TO TYPE THESE USING A 14-POINT FONT, RIGHT? WELL, BOTH OF THESE ARE 14-POINT FONTS!
TIKKA TAKKA TIK TIKKITY TAK TIK
The Boston Tea Party, which took place on December 16, 1773, was a very significant event in United States history.
The Boston Tea Party, which took place on December 16, 1773, was a very significant event in United States history.
IT... IT'S A MIRACLE!
AMEN, BROTHER!
TIKKA TIKKA TIK TAK
Peirce

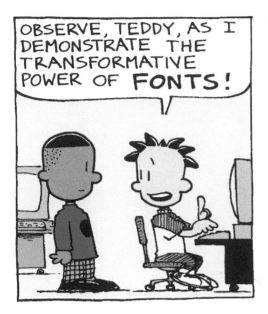

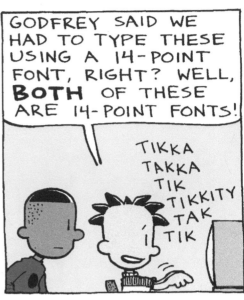

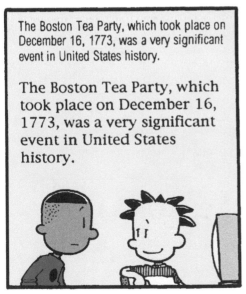

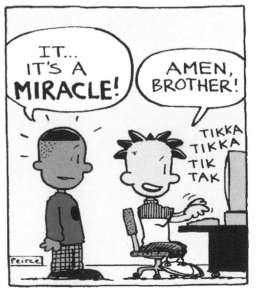

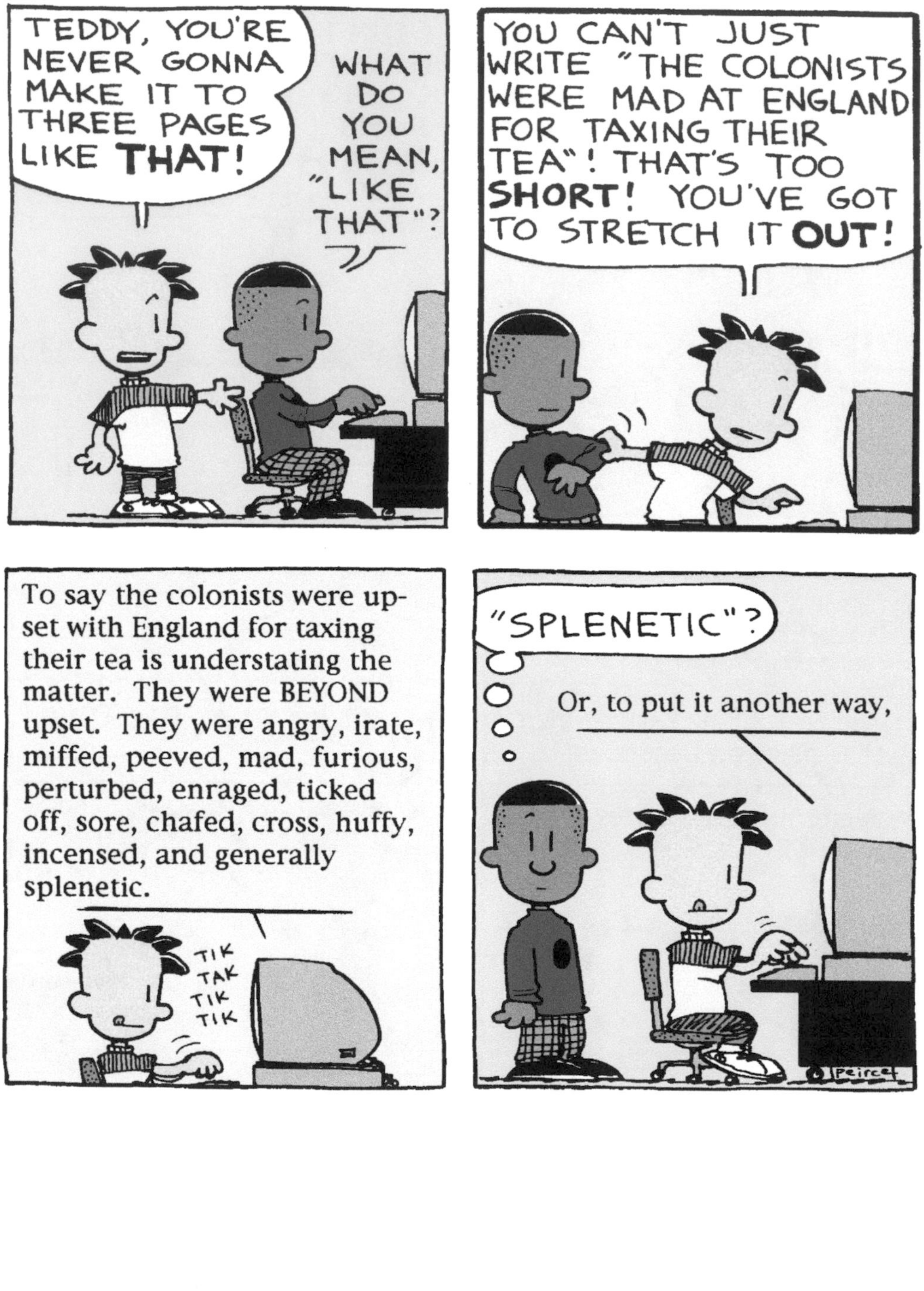
TEDDY, YOU'RE NEVER GONNA MAKE IT TO THREE PAGES LIKE **THAT**!
WHAT DO YOU MEAN, "LIKE THAT"?
YOU CAN'T JUST WRITE "THE COLONISTS WERE MAD AT ENGLAND FOR TAXING THEIR TEA"! THAT'S TOO **SHORT**! YOU'VE GOT TO STRETCH IT **OUT**!
To say the colonists were upset with England for taxing their tea is understating the matter. They were BEYOND upset. They were angry, irate, miffed, peeved, mad, furious, perturbed, enraged, ticked off, sore, chafed, cross, huffy, incensed, and generally splenetic.
TIK TAK TIK TIK
"SPLENETIC"?
Or, to put it another way,
Peirce

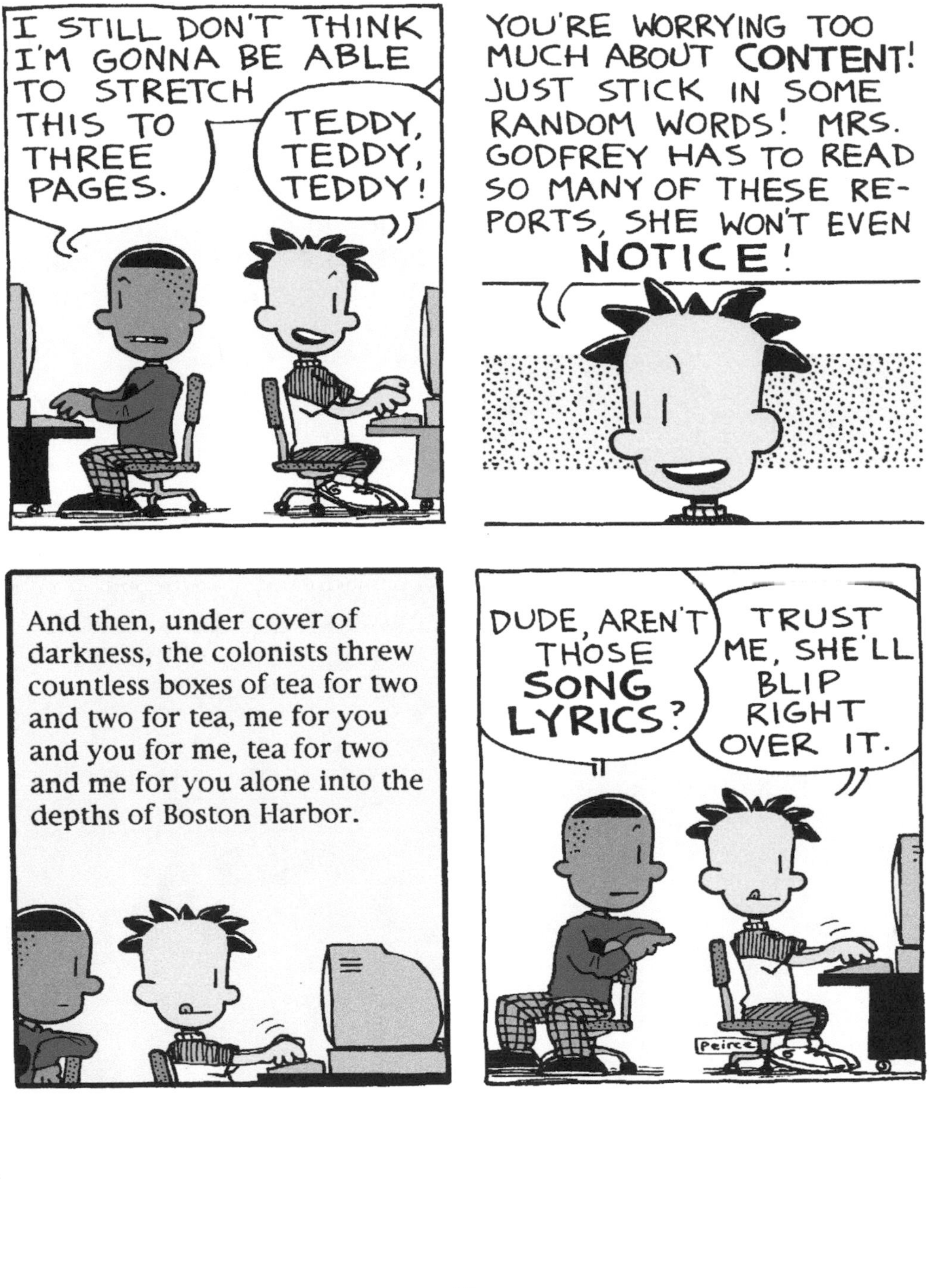
I STILL DON'T THINK I'M GONNA BE ABLE TO STRETCH THIS TO THREE PAGES.
TEDDY, TEDDY, TEDDY!
YOU'RE WORRYING TOO MUCH ABOUT CONTENT! JUST STICK IN SOME RANDOM WORDS! MRS. GODFREY HAS TO READ SO MANY OF THESE REPORTS, SHE WON'T EVEN NOTICE!
And then, under cover of darkness, the colonists threw countless boxes of tea for two and two for tea, me for you and you for me, tea for two and me for you alone into the depths of Boston Harbor.
DUDE, AREN'T THOSE SONG LYRICS?
TRUST ME, SHE'LL BLIP RIGHT OVER IT.
Peirce

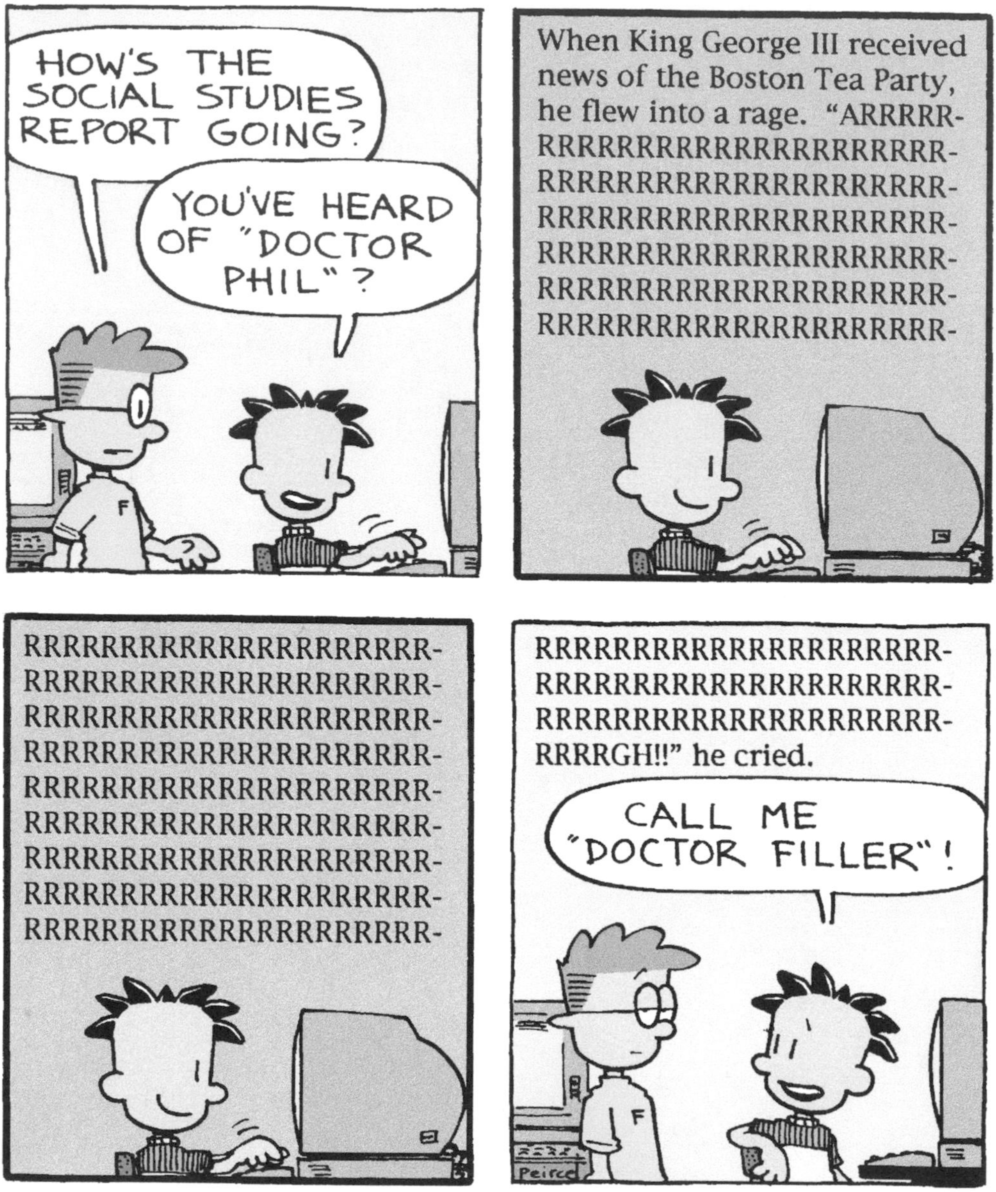
HOW'S THE SOCIAL STUDIES REPORT GOING?
YOU'VE HEARD OF "DOCTOR PHIL"?
When King George III received news of the Boston Tea Party, he flew into a rage. “ARRRRR-
RRRRRRRRRRRRRRRRRRRRR-
RRRRRRRRRRRRRRRRRRRRR-
RRRRRRRRRRRRRRRRRRRRR-
RRRRRRRRRRRRRRRRRRRRR-
RRRRRRRRRRRRRRRRRRRRR-
RRRRRRRRRRRRRRRRRRRRR-
RRRRRRRRRRRRRRRRRRRRR-
RRRRRRRRRRRRRRRRRRRRR-
RRRRRRRRRRRRRRRRRRRRR-
RRRRRRRRRRRRRRRRRRRRR-
RRRRRRRRRRRRRRRRRRRRR-
RRRRRRRRRRRRRRRRRRRRR-
RRRRRRRRRRRRRRRRRRRRR-
RRRRRRRRRRRRRRRRRRRRR-
RRRRRRRRRRRRRRRRRRRRR-
RRRRRRRRRRRRRRRRRRRRR-
RRRRRRRRRRRRRRRRRRRRR-
RRRRRRRRRRRRRRRRRRRRR-
RRRRGH!!” he cried.
CALL ME "DOCTOR FILLER"!
Peirce

THE BOSTON TEA PARTY
by Amanda Dreissen

The Boston Tea Party was one of the most important events in our nation's history. It happened on December 16, 1773 in the city of

THE BOSTON TEA PARTY
Teddy Ortiz

One of the major events leading up to the Revolutionary War was called the Boston

THE BOSTON TEA PARTY
by Caitlin Embry

The Boston Tea Party is one of the first examples of the thirteen colonies fighting back against some of England's most

BEDLAM IN BEANTOWN!
by Nate Wright

It was quiet that night on the cobblestoned streets of Boston.
Too quiet.
The inky black waters of Boston Harbor lay like a

SIGH

Peirce

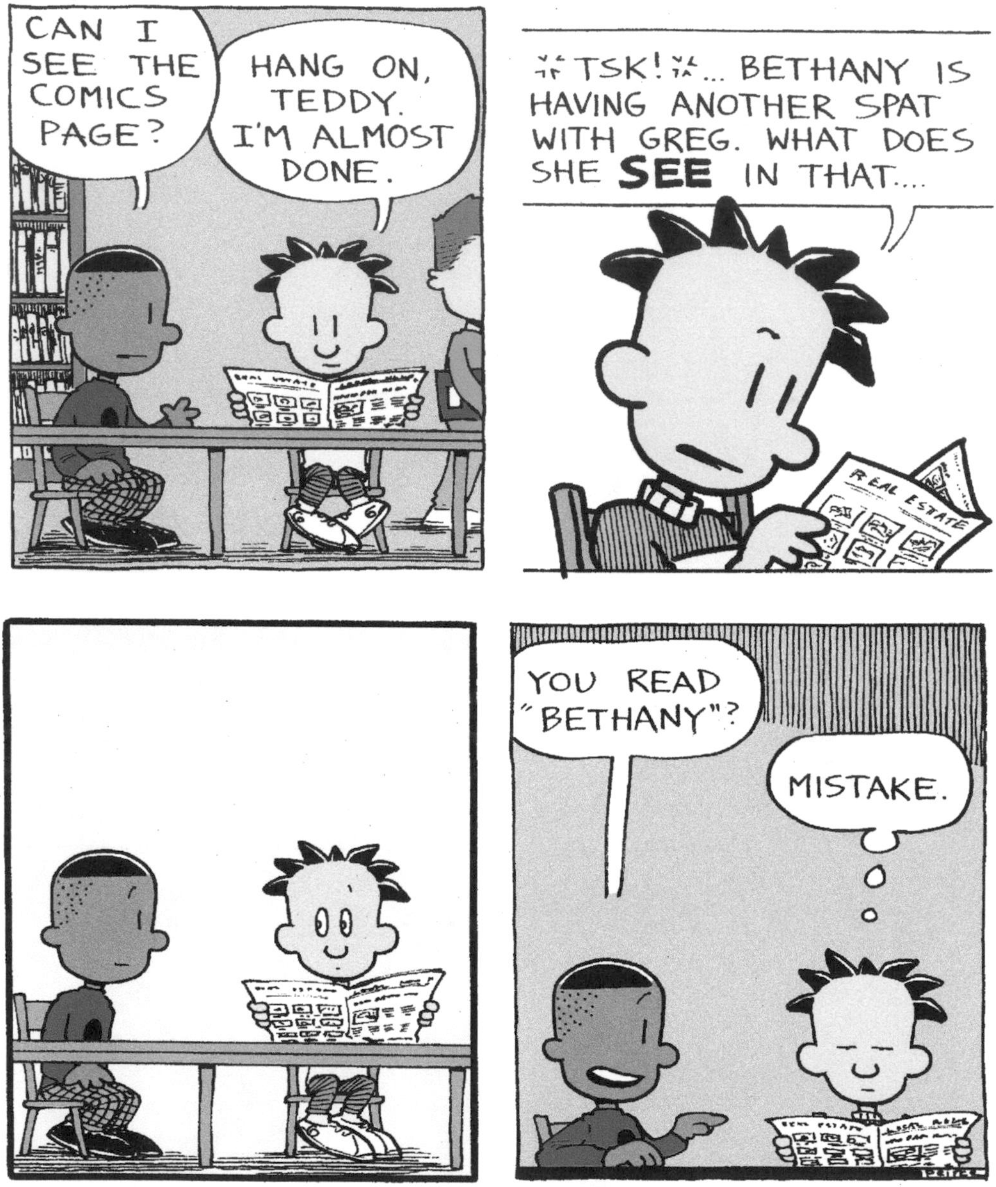
CAN I SEE THE COMICS PAGE?
HANG ON, TEDDY. I'M ALMOST DONE.
TSK!... BETHANY IS HAVING ANOTHER SPAT WITH GREG. WHAT DOES SHE SEE IN THAT...
REAL ESTATE
YOU READ "BETHANY"?
MISTAKE.

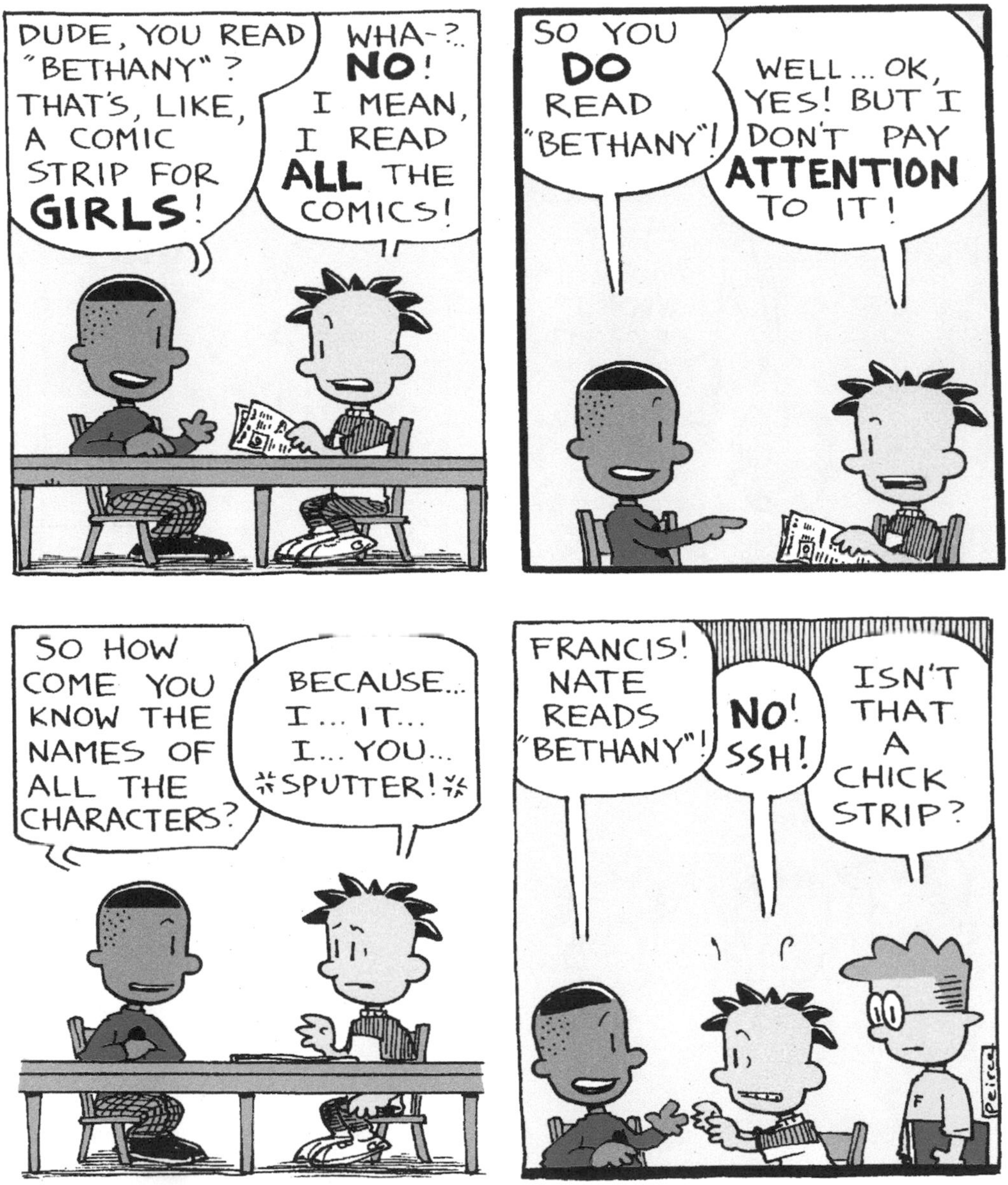
DUDE, YOU READ "BETHANY"? THAT'S, LIKE, A COMIC STRIP FOR **GIRLS**!
WHA-?.. **NO**! I MEAN, I READ **ALL** THE COMICS!
SO YOU **DO** READ "BETHANY"!
WELL... OK, YES! BUT I DON'T PAY **ATTENTION** TO IT!
SO HOW COME YOU KNOW THE NAMES OF ALL THE CHARACTERS?
BECAUSE... I... IT... I... YOU... *SPUTTER!*
FRANCIS! NATE READS "BETHANY"!
NO! SSH!
ISN'T THAT A CHICK STRIP?
Peirce

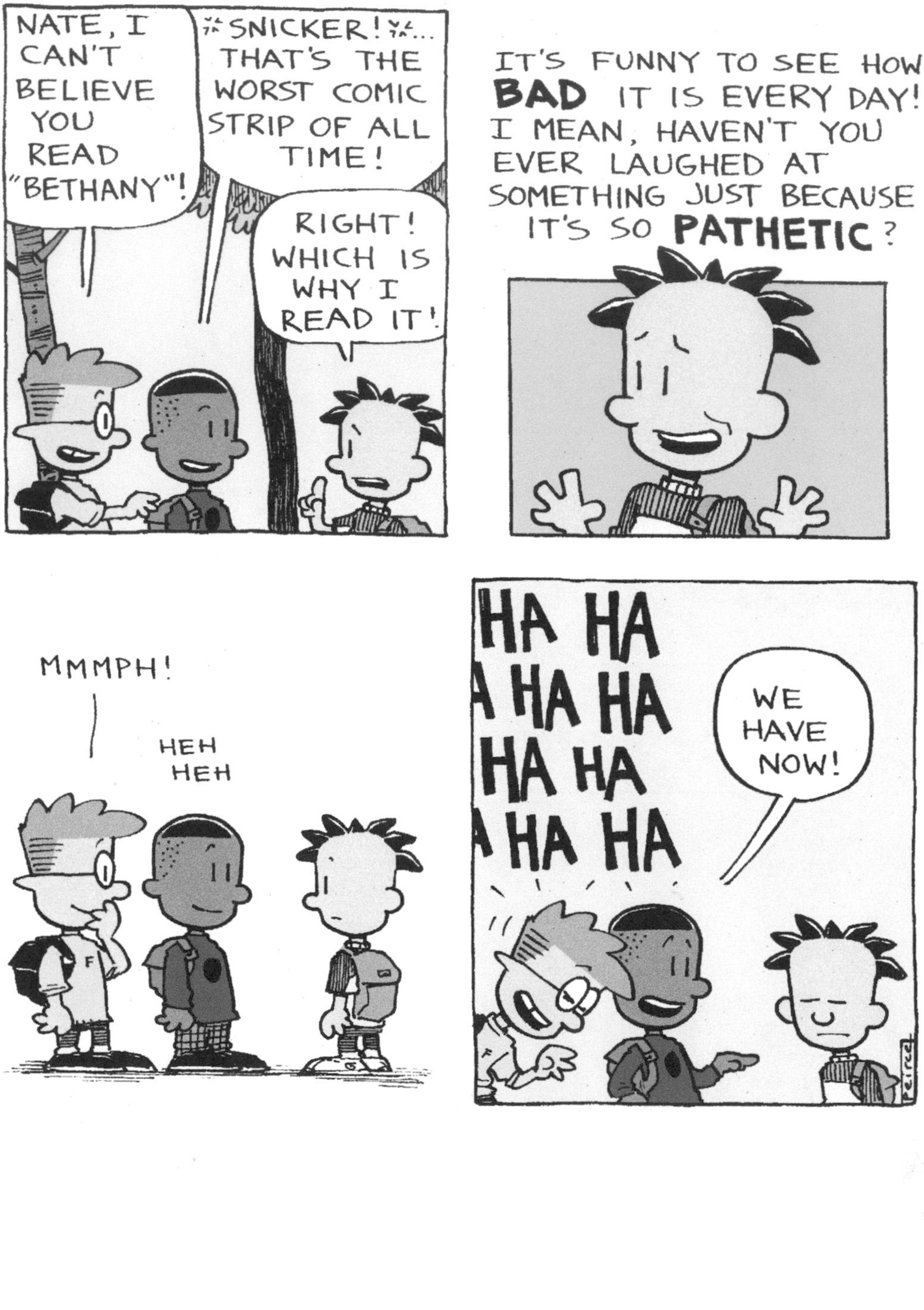
NATE, I CAN'T BELIEVE YOU READ "BETHANY"!
SNICKER!... THAT'S THE WORST COMIC STRIP OF ALL TIME!
RIGHT! WHICH IS WHY I READ IT!
IT'S FUNNY TO SEE HOW BAD IT IS EVERY DAY! I MEAN, HAVEN'T YOU EVER LAUGHED AT SOMETHING JUST BECAUSE IT'S SO PATHETIC?
MMMPH!
HEH HEH
HA HA A HA HA HA HA A HA HA
WE HAVE NOW!
PEIRCE

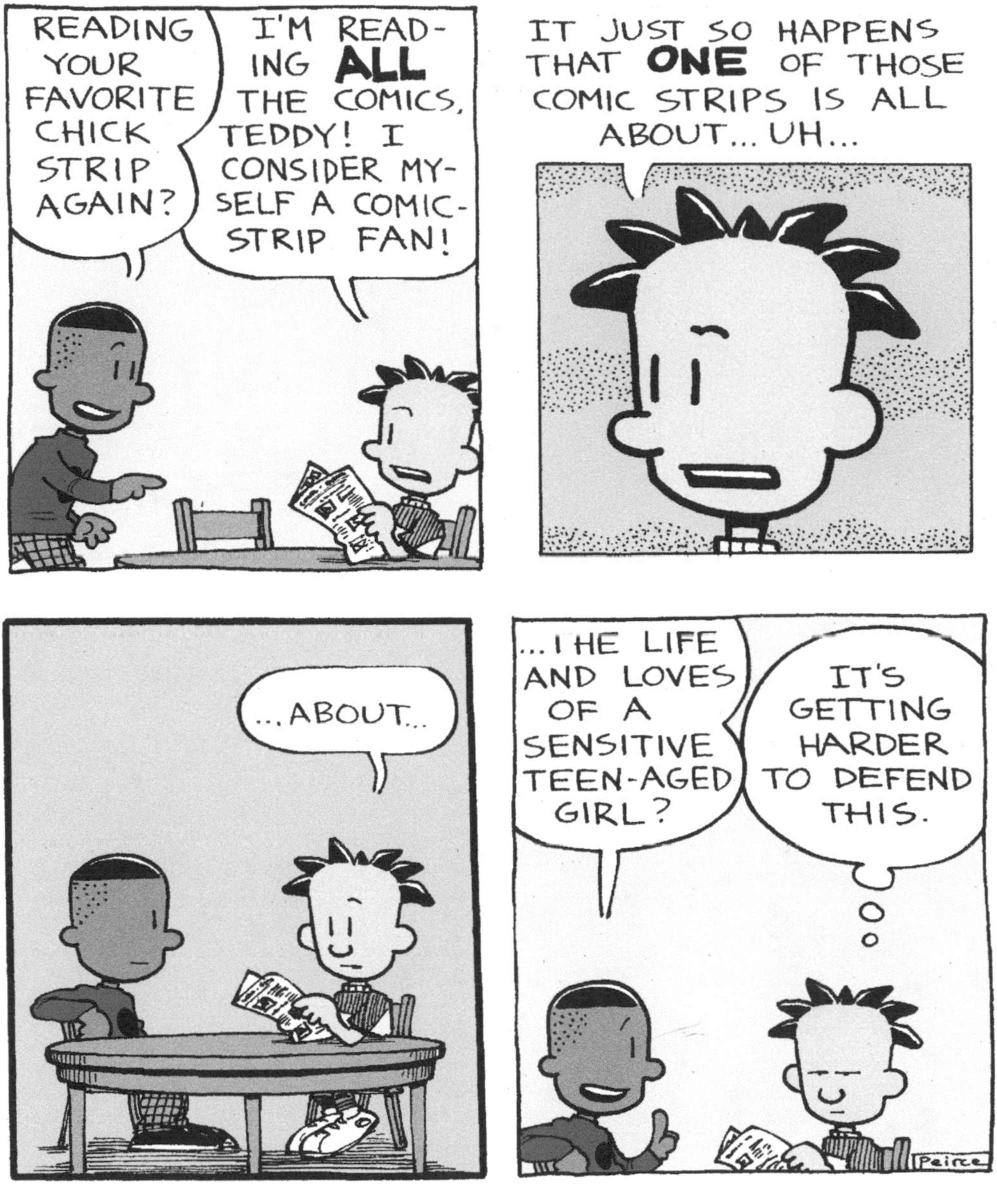
READING YOUR FAVORITE CHICK STRIP AGAIN?
I'M READING ALL THE COMICS, TEDDY! I CONSIDER MYSELF A COMIC-STRIP FAN!
IT JUST SO HAPPENS THAT ONE OF THOSE COMIC STRIPS IS ALL ABOUT... UH...
...ABOUT...
...THE LIFE AND LOVES OF A SENSITIVE TEEN-AGED GIRL?
IT'S GETTING HARDER TO DEFEND THIS.
Peirce

LISTEN, TEDDY, STOP HARSHING ON ME FOR READING "BETHANY"!

BUT IT'S HILARIOUS THAT YOU'RE A FAN OF SUCH A LAME COMIC STRIP!

I'M NOT A **FAN**, I JUST READ IT BECAUSE IT'S **THERE**! IT'S LIKE... IT'S LIKE...

REMEMBER THAT WEEK YOU WERE HOME WITH STREP THROAT AND YOU ENDED UP GETTING ADDICTED TO "THE VIEW"?

SAY **WHAT**?

DUDE, YOU PROMISED.

I HAD A POINT TO MAKE.

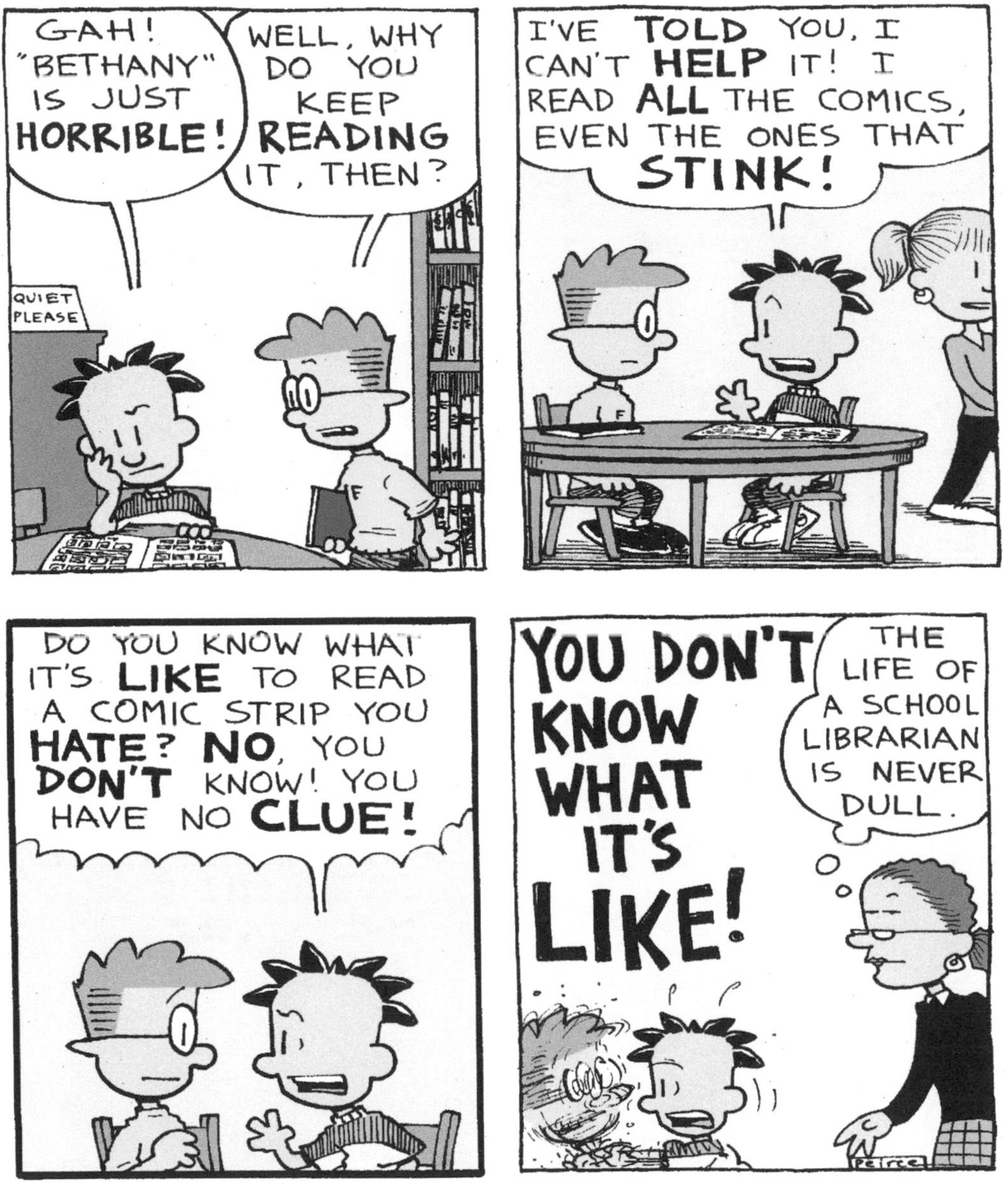
GAH! "BETHANY" IS JUST HORRIBLE!
WELL, WHY DO YOU KEEP READING IT, THEN?
QUIET PLEASE
I'VE TOLD YOU, I CAN'T HELP IT! I READ ALL THE COMICS, EVEN THE ONES THAT STINK!
DO YOU KNOW WHAT IT'S LIKE TO READ A COMIC STRIP YOU HATE? NO, YOU DON'T KNOW! YOU HAVE NO CLUE!
YOU DON'T KNOW WHAT IT'S LIKE!
THE LIFE OF A SCHOOL LIBRARIAN IS NEVER DULL.
Peirce

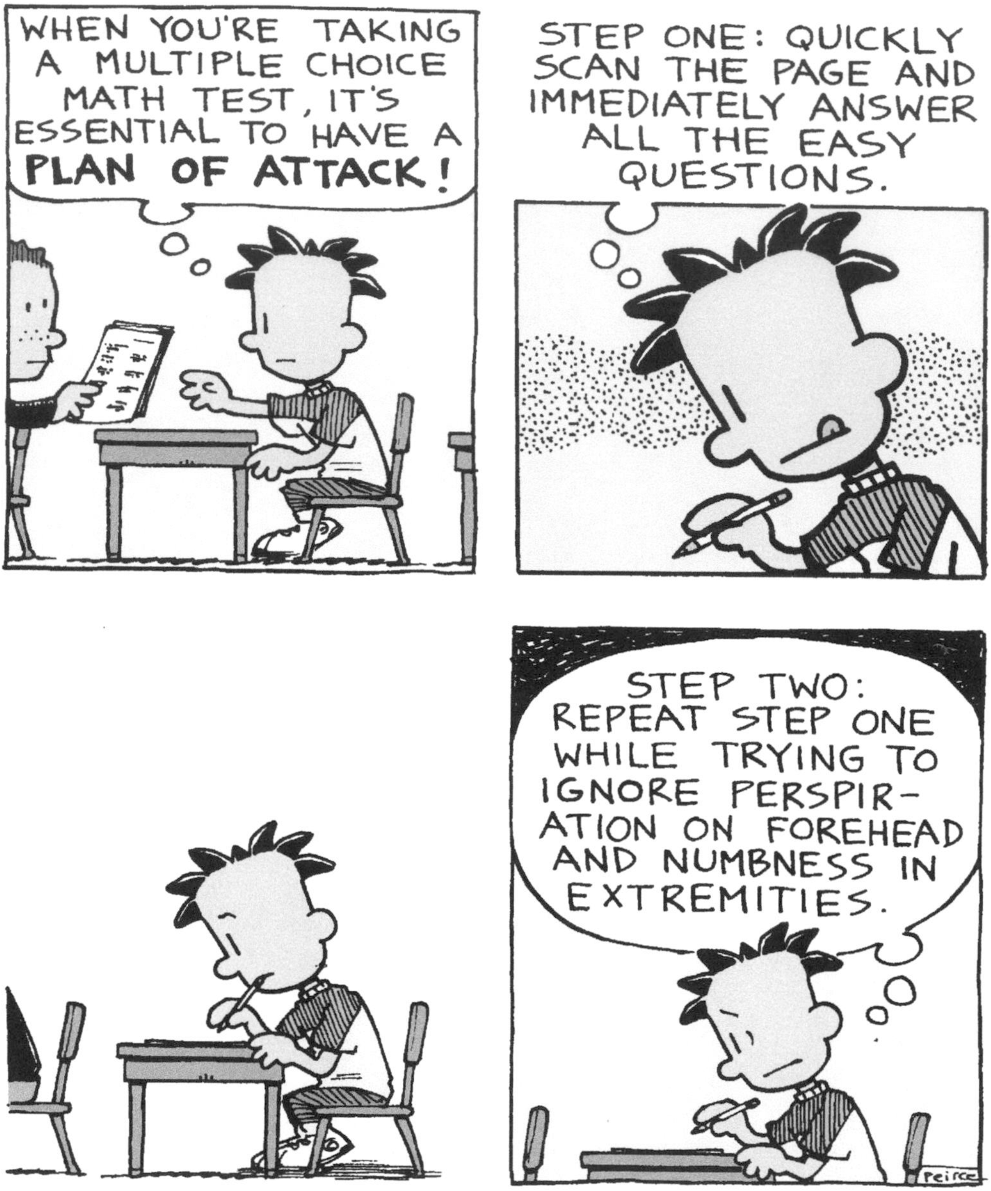
WHEN YOU'RE TAKING A MULTIPLE CHOICE MATH TEST, IT'S ESSENTIAL TO HAVE A **PLAN OF ATTACK!**
STEP ONE: QUICKLY SCAN THE PAGE AND IMMEDIATELY ANSWER ALL THE EASY QUESTIONS.
STEP TWO: REPEAT STEP ONE WHILE TRYING TO IGNORE PERSPIR- ATION ON FOREHEAD AND NUMBNESS IN EXTREMITIES.
PEIRCE

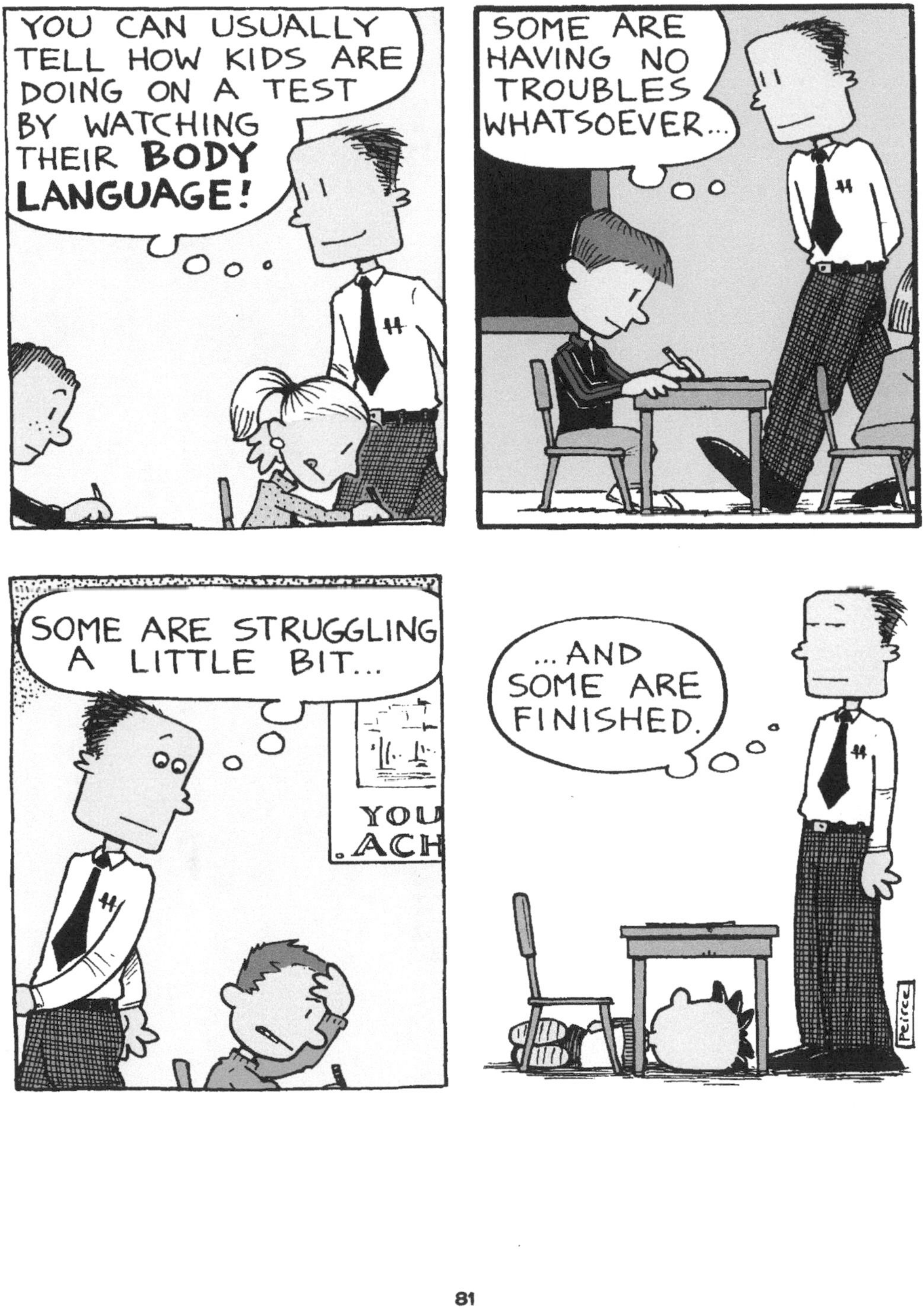
YOU CAN USUALLY TELL HOW KIDS ARE DOING ON A TEST BY WATCHING THEIR **BODY LANGUAGE!**
SOME ARE HAVING NO TROUBLES WHATSOEVER...
SOME ARE STRUGGLING A LITTLE BIT...
YOU
ACH
...AND SOME ARE FINISHED.
Peirce

NATE, YOU SEEM TO BE STRUGGLING A BIT WITH MATH.
WELL... YEAH, I GUESS.
MR. STAPLES
I THINK YOU MIGHT BENEFIT FROM WORKING WITH A TUTOR.
A TUTOR? YOU MEAN LIKE A HIGH SCHOOL STUDENT?
NO, I ACTUALLY HAD SOMEONE ELSE IN MIND.
MR. STAPLES
HALLO! I AM REPORTED FOR TUTOR DUTIES!
ARTUR!!
Peirce

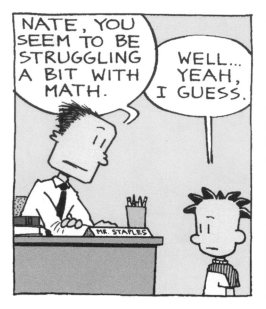

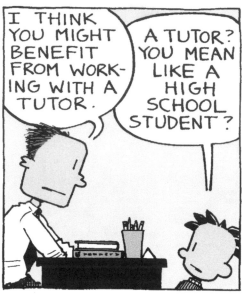

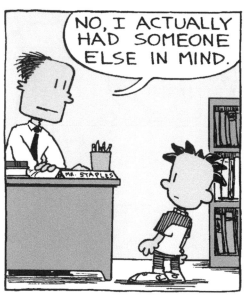

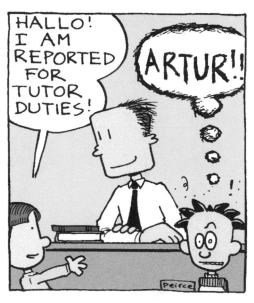

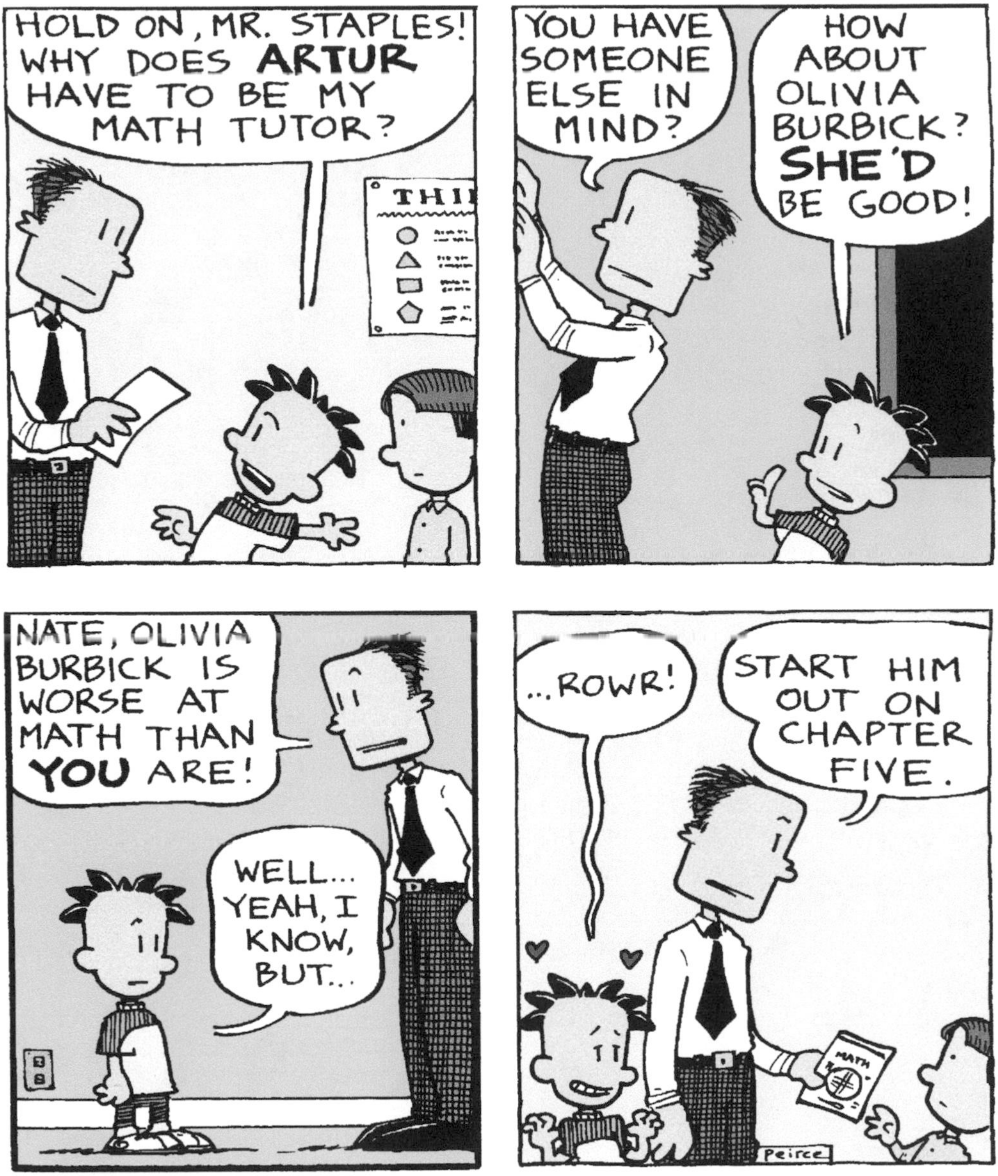
HOLD ON, MR. STAPLES! WHY DOES **ARTUR** HAVE TO BE MY MATH TUTOR?
YOU HAVE SOMEONE ELSE IN MIND?
HOW ABOUT OLIVIA BURBICK? **SHE'D** BE GOOD!
NATE, OLIVIA BURBICK IS WORSE AT MATH THAN **YOU** ARE!
WELL... YEAH, I KNOW, BUT...
...ROWR!
START HIM OUT ON CHAPTER FIVE.
MATH
Peirce

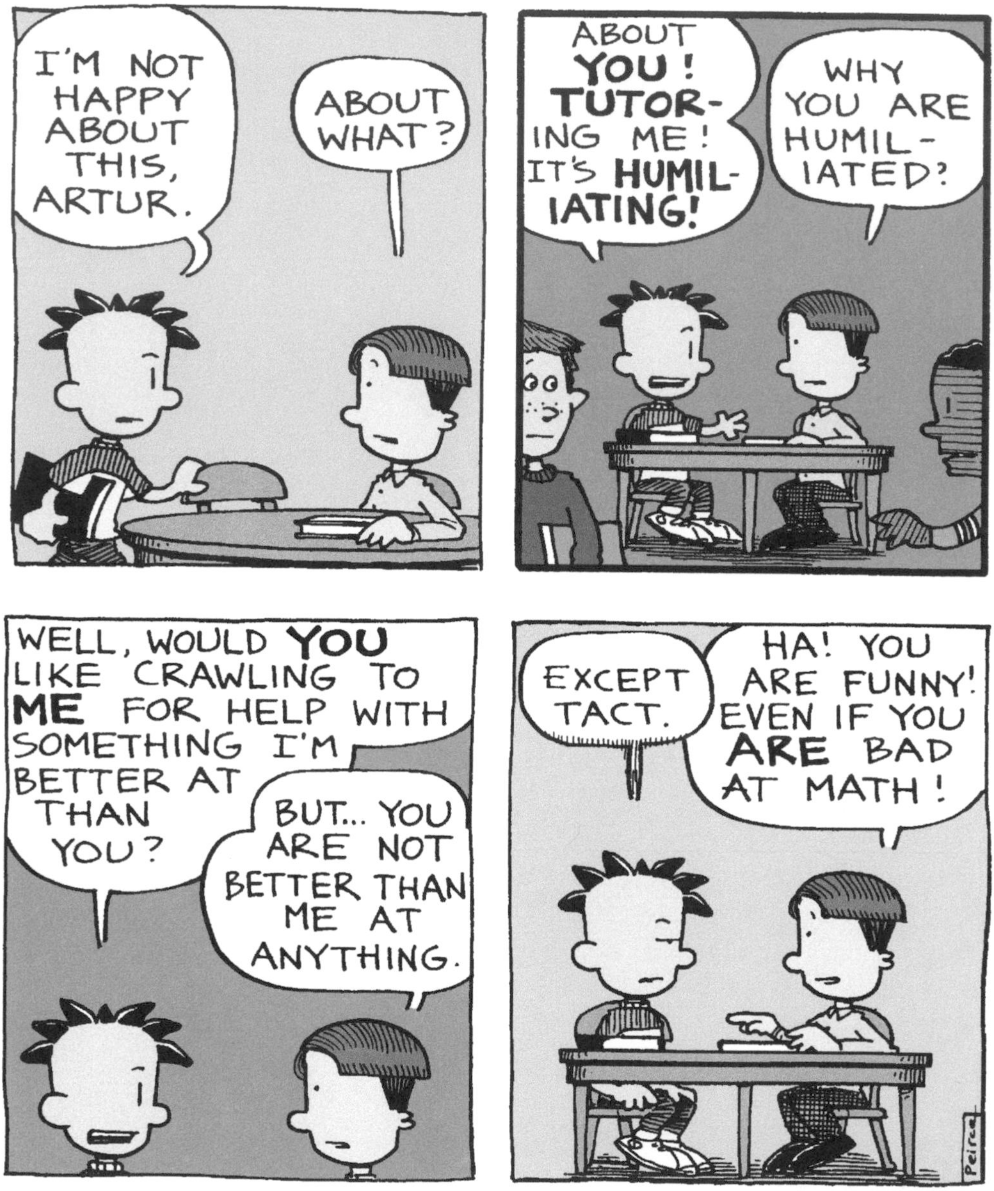
I'M NOT HAPPY ABOUT THIS, ARTUR.
ABOUT WHAT?
ABOUT **YOU**! **TUTOR**-ING ME! IT'S **HUMIL**-**IATING**!
WHY YOU ARE HUMIL-IATED?
WELL, WOULD **YOU** LIKE CRAWLING TO **ME** FOR HELP WITH SOMETHING I'M BETTER AT THAN YOU?
BUT... YOU ARE NOT BETTER THAN ME AT ANYTHING.
EXCEPT TACT.
HA! YOU ARE FUNNY! EVEN IF YOU **ARE** BAD AT MATH!
Peirce

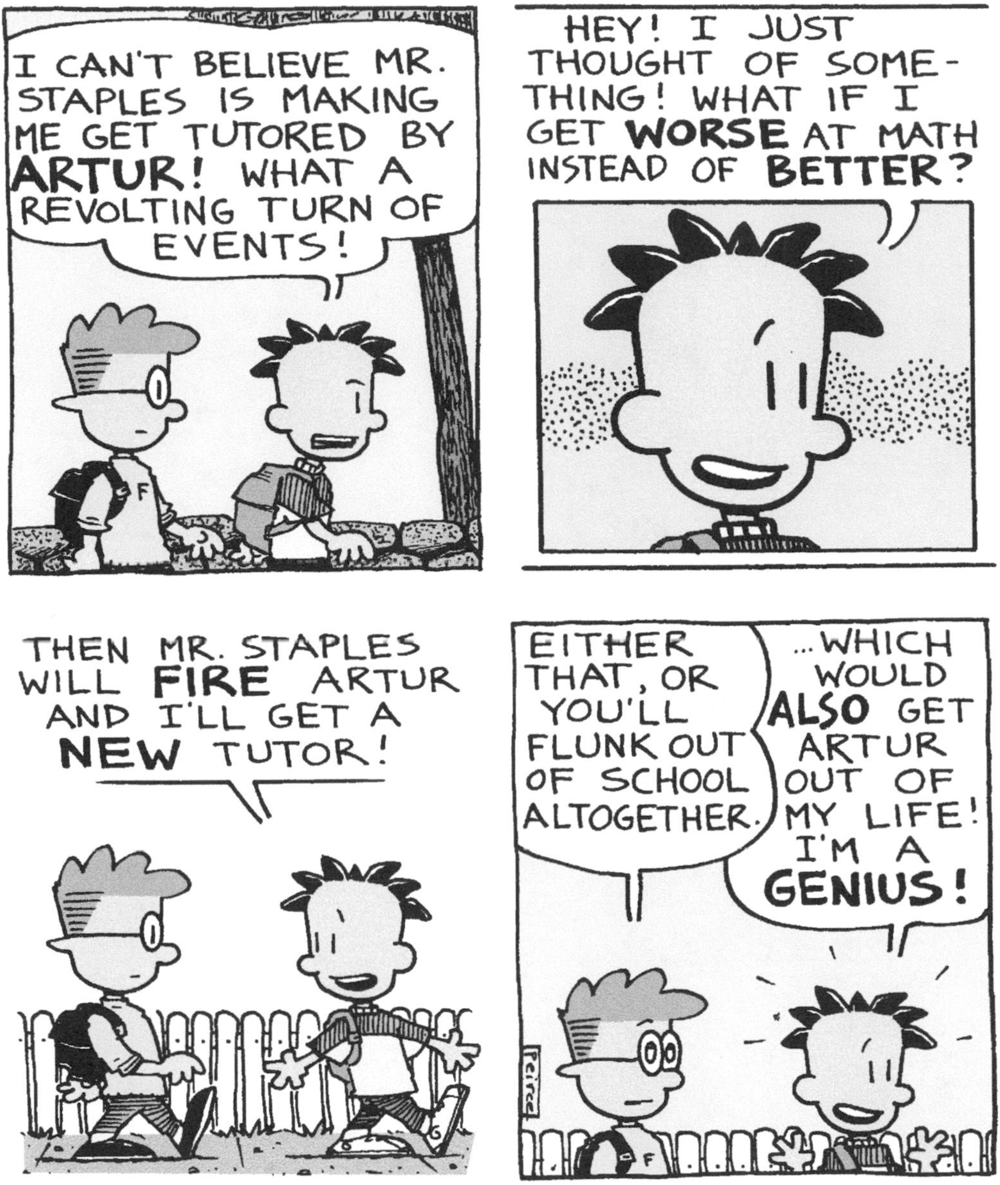
I CAN'T BELIEVE MR. STAPLES IS MAKING ME GET TUTORED BY ARTUR! WHAT A REVOLTING TURN OF EVENTS!
HEY! I JUST THOUGHT OF SOMETHING! WHAT IF I GET WORSE AT MATH INSTEAD OF BETTER?
THEN MR. STAPLES WILL FIRE ARTUR AND I'LL GET A NEW TUTOR!
EITHER THAT, OR YOU'LL FLUNK OUT OF SCHOOL ALTOGETHER.
...WHICH WOULD ALSO GET ARTUR OUT OF MY LIFE! I'M A GENIUS!
Peirce

WHAT'S THAT THING?
IT'S A "DIABOLO".
IT'S PART YO-YO, PART JUGGLING... OOP!
KONK!
... PART MARTIAL ARTS.
HI.
Peirce

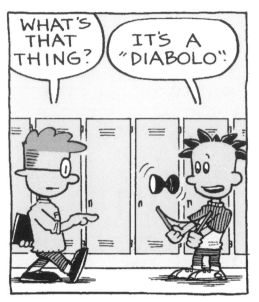

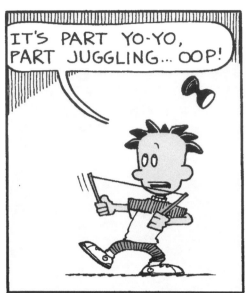

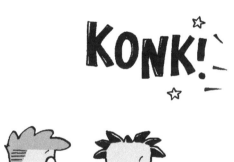

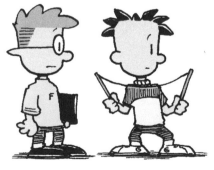

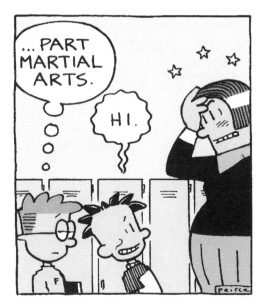

HERE FOR DETENTION, NATE?
YUP.
WHAT DID YOU DO THIS TIME?
I HIT MRS. GODFREY IN THE HEAD WITH A "DIABOLO."
CLAP! CLAP! CLAP!
CLAP! CLAP!
CLAP! CLAP!
CLAP! CLAP!
YOU'RE LIVIN' THE DREAM, MAN.
THANK YOU, BOYS! THANK YOU!
SIGH...
CLAP!
CLAP!
CLAP!
PEIRCE

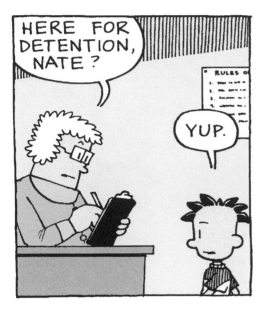

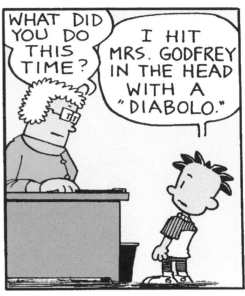

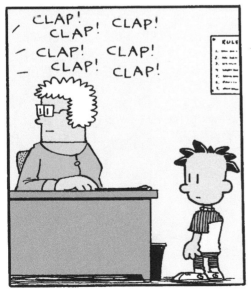

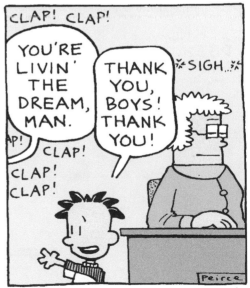

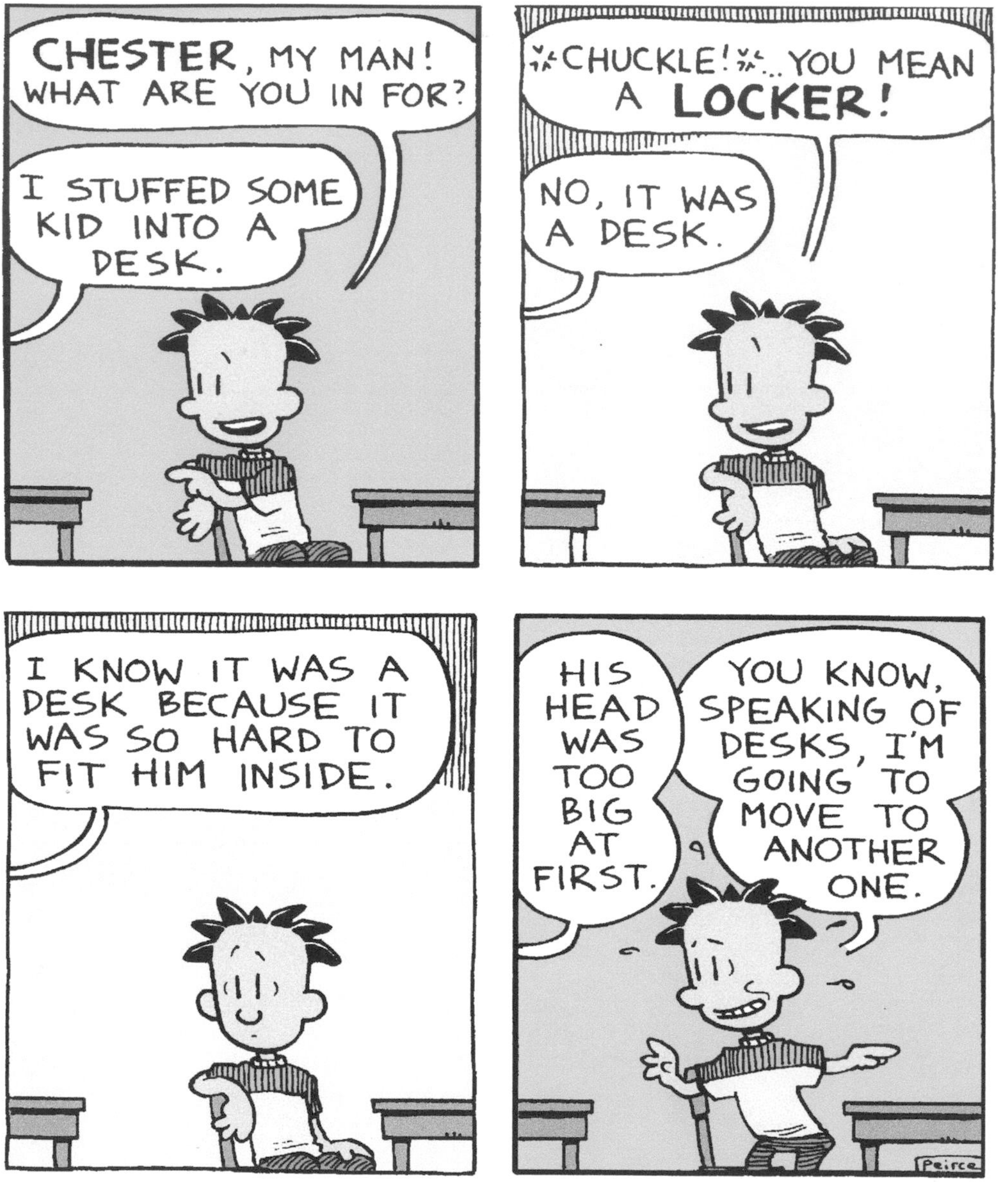
CHESTER, MY MAN! WHAT ARE YOU IN FOR?
I STUFFED SOME KID INTO A DESK.
CHUCKLE! ... YOU MEAN A LOCKER!
NO, IT WAS A DESK.
I KNOW IT WAS A DESK BECAUSE IT WAS SO HARD TO FIT HIM INSIDE.
HIS HEAD WAS TOO BIG AT FIRST.
YOU KNOW, SPEAKING OF DESKS, I'M GOING TO MOVE TO ANOTHER ONE.
Peirce

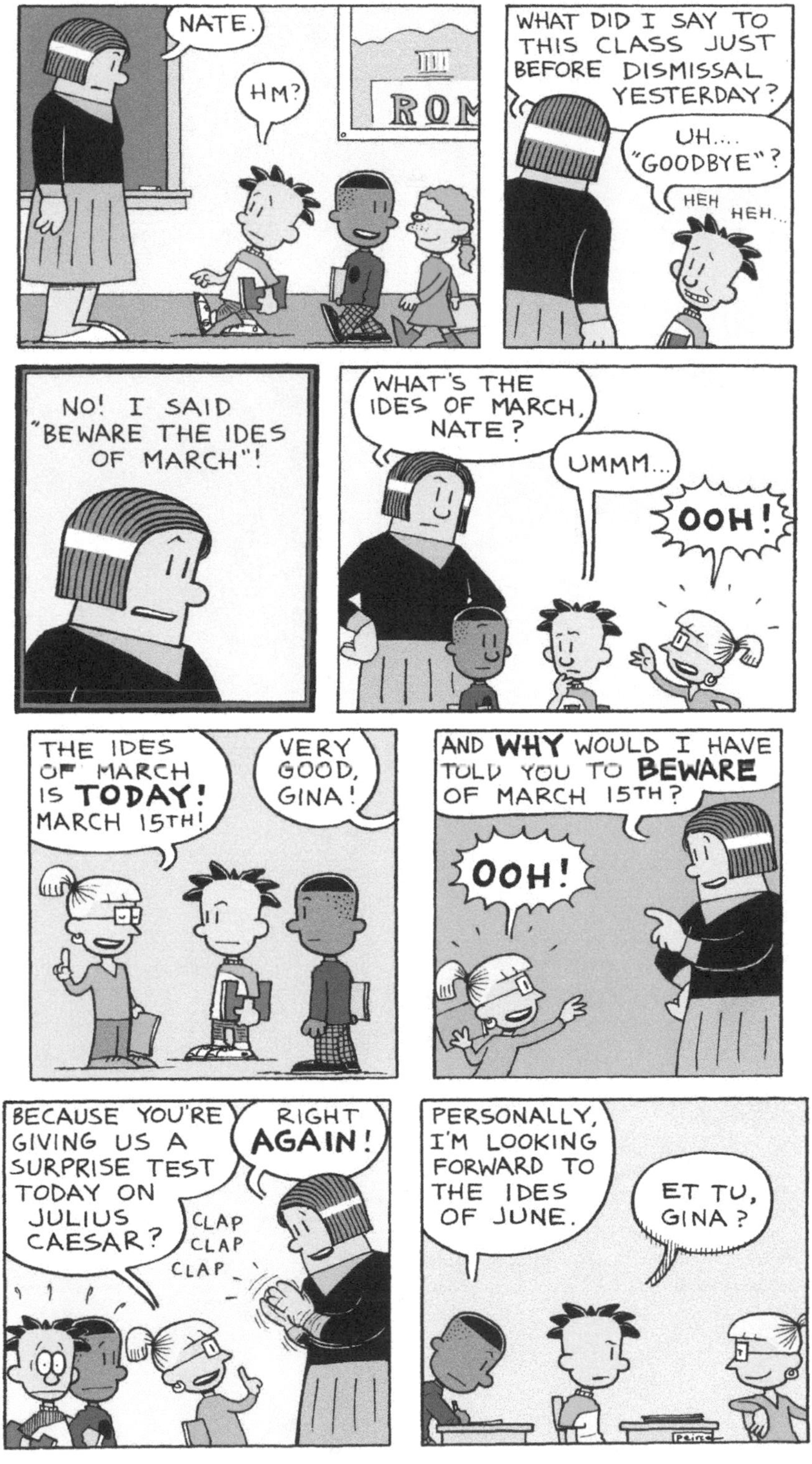
NATE.
HM?
ROM
WHAT DID I SAY TO THIS CLASS JUST BEFORE DISMISSAL YESTERDAY?
UH.... "GOODBYE"?
HEH HEH...
NO! I SAID "BEWARE THE IDES OF MARCH"!
WHAT'S THE IDES OF MARCH, NATE?
UMMM...
OOH!
THE IDES OF MARCH IS TODAY! MARCH 15TH!
VERY GOOD, GINA!
AND WHY WOULD I HAVE TOLD YOU TO BEWARE OF MARCH 15TH?
OOH!
BECAUSE YOU'RE GIVING US A SURPRISE TEST TODAY ON JULIUS CAESAR?
RIGHT AGAIN!
CLAP CLAP CLAP
PERSONALLY, I'M LOOKING FORWARD TO THE IDES OF JUNE.
ET TU, GINA?

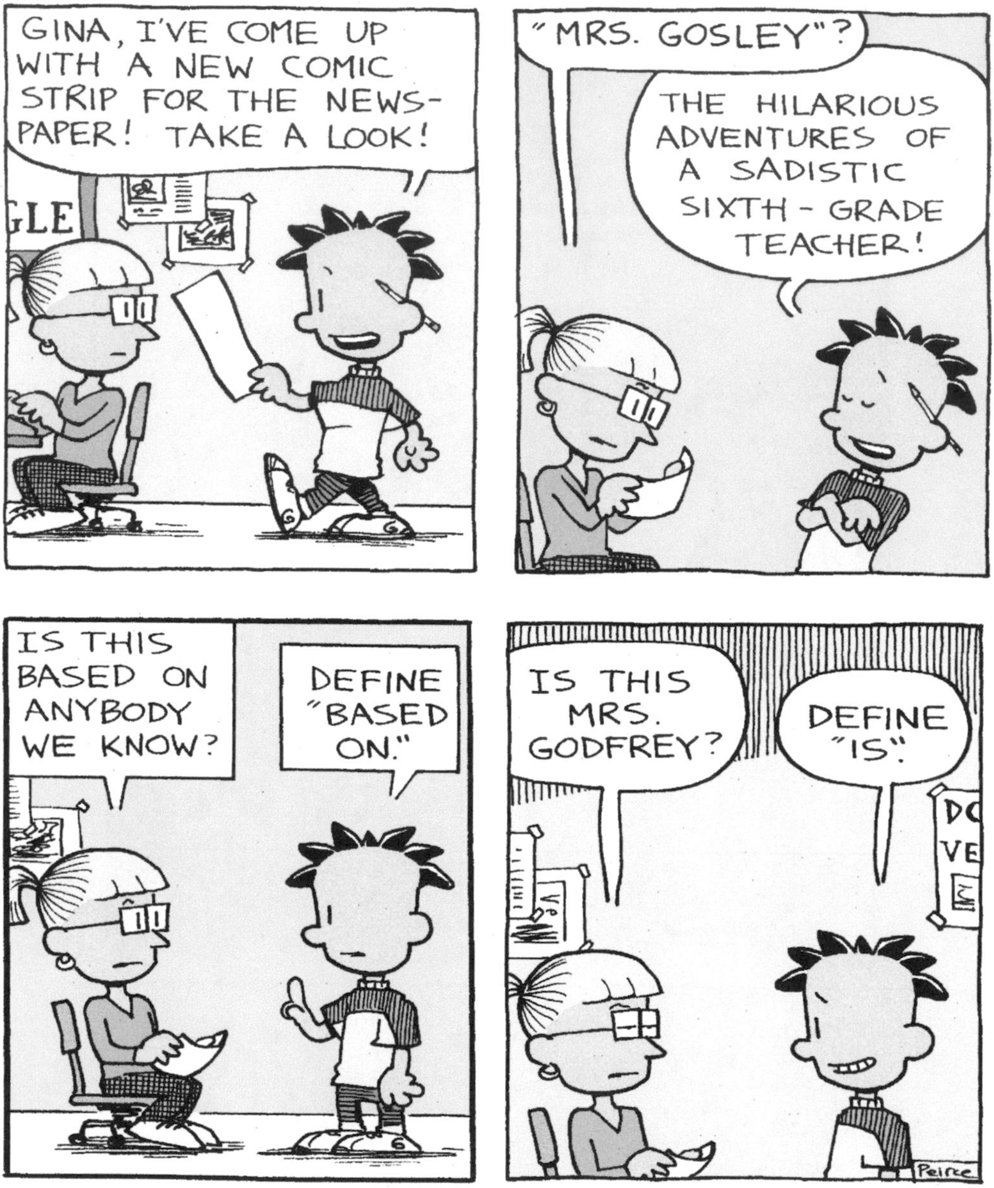
GINA, I'VE COME UP WITH A NEW COMIC STRIP FOR THE NEWS-PAPER! TAKE A LOOK!
GLE
"MRS. GOSLEY"?
THE HILARIOUS ADVENTURES OF A SADISTIC SIXTH-GRADE TEACHER!
IS THIS BASED ON ANYBODY WE KNOW?
DEFINE "BASED ON."
IS THIS MRS. GODFREY?
DEFINE "IS."
Peirce

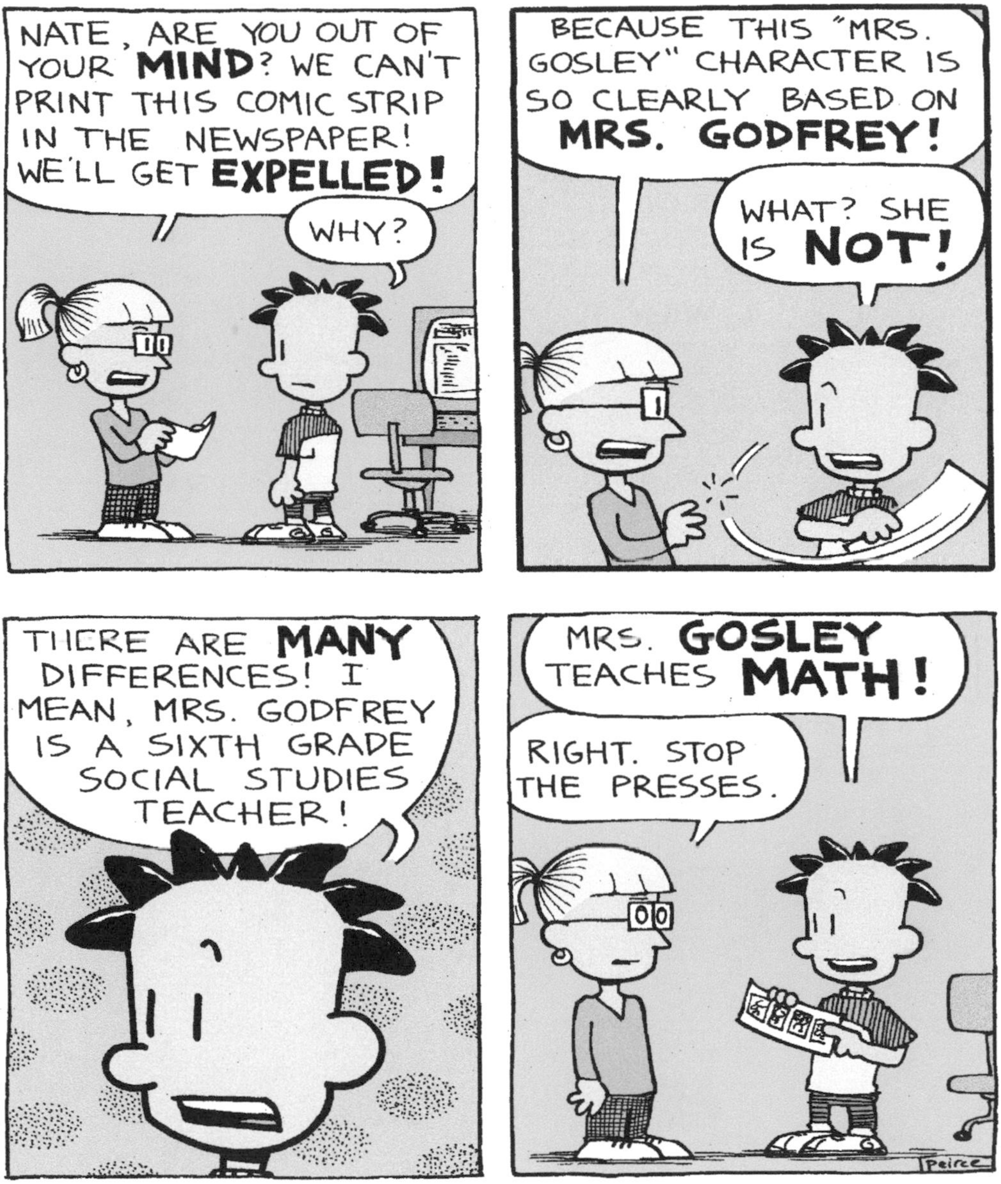
NATE, ARE YOU OUT OF YOUR MIND? WE CAN'T PRINT THIS COMIC STRIP IN THE NEWSPAPER! WE'LL GET EXPELLED!
WHY?
BECAUSE THIS "MRS. GOSLEY" CHARACTER IS SO CLEARLY BASED ON MRS. GODFREY!
WHAT? SHE IS NOT!
THERE ARE MANY DIFFERENCES! I MEAN, MRS. GODFREY IS A SIXTH GRADE SOCIAL STUDIES TEACHER!
MRS. GOSLEY TEACHES MATH!
RIGHT. STOP THE PRESSES.
Peirce

LET ME GET THIS STRAIGHT, GINA: YOU WON'T PRINT MY COMIC STRIP?

YOUR COMIC STRIP ATTACKING MRS. GODFREY? NO, I **WON'T**!

THIS IS **CENSOR-SHIP**! "MRS. GOSLEY" DESERVES TO BE **SEEN**!

YOU THINK SO?

WELL, HERE COMES MRS. GODFREY. LET **HER** SEE IT.

RIP
RIP
RIP
RIP
RIP
RIP
RIP
RIP
RIP
RIP

ASH

Peirce

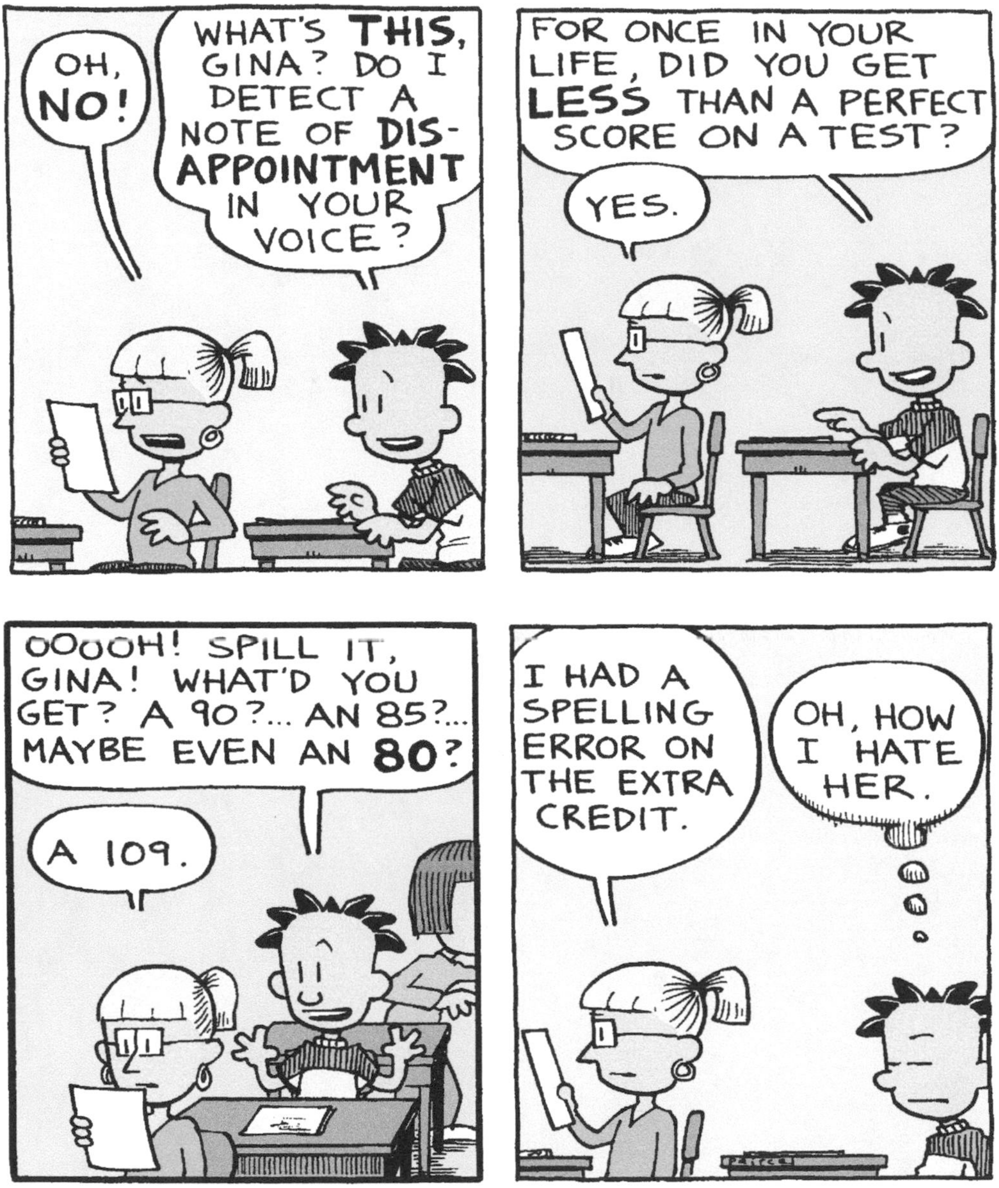
OH, NO!
WHAT'S THIS, GINA? DO I DETECT A NOTE OF DIS-APPOINTMENT IN YOUR VOICE?
FOR ONCE IN YOUR LIFE, DID YOU GET LESS THAN A PERFECT SCORE ON A TEST?
YES.
OOOOH! SPILL IT, GINA! WHAT'D YOU GET? A 90?... AN 85?... MAYBE EVEN AN 80?
A 109.
I HAD A SPELLING ERROR ON THE EXTRA CREDIT.
OH, HOW I HATE HER.

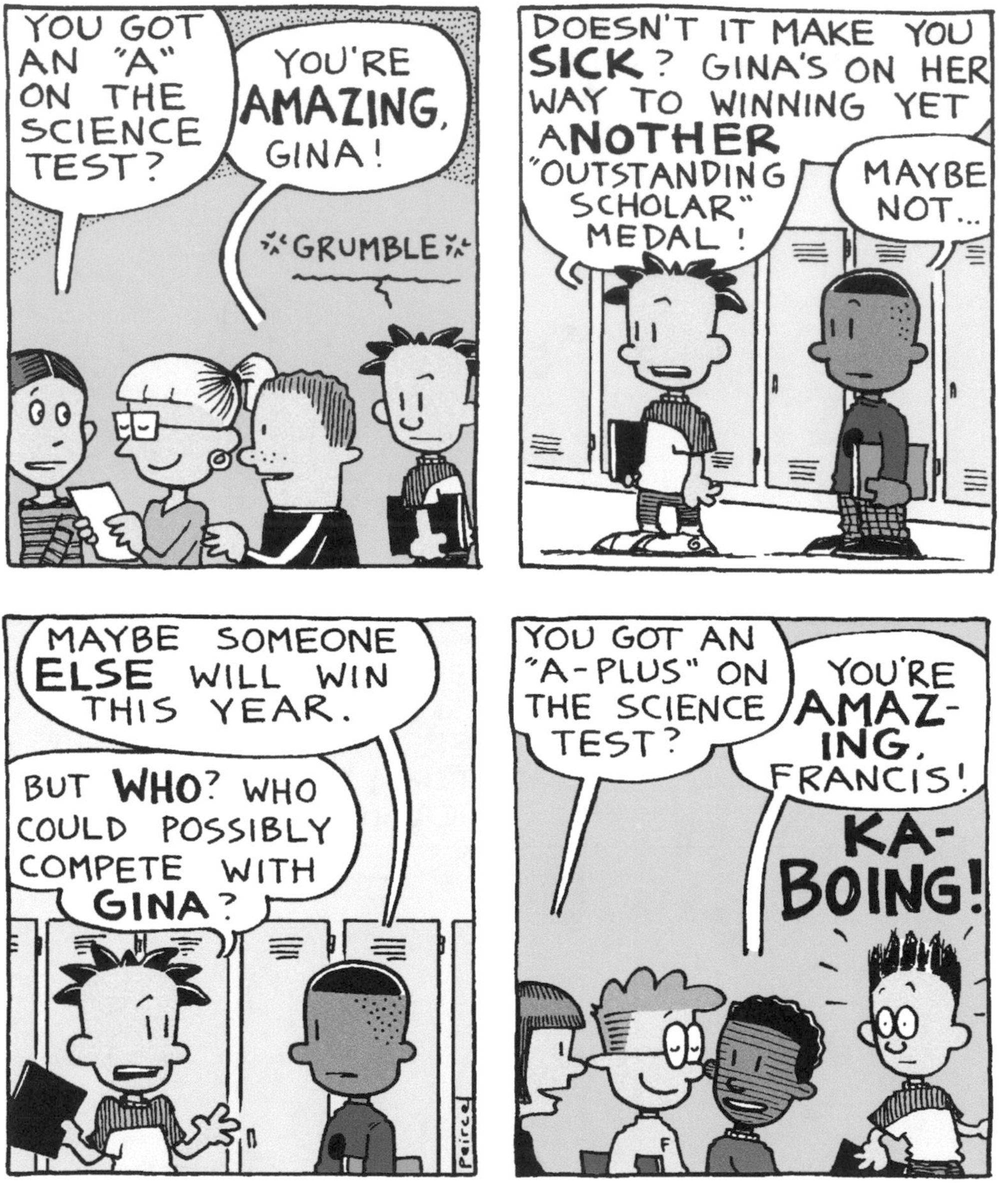
YOU GOT AN "A" ON THE SCIENCE TEST?
YOU'RE AMAZING, GINA!
GRUMBLE
DOESN'T IT MAKE YOU SICK? GINA'S ON HER WAY TO WINNING YET ANOTHER "OUTSTANDING SCHOLAR" MEDAL!
MAYBE NOT...
MAYBE SOMEONE ELSE WILL WIN THIS YEAR.
BUT WHO? WHO COULD POSSIBLY COMPETE WITH GINA?
Peirce
YOU GOT AN "A-PLUS" ON THE SCIENCE TEST?
YOU'RE AMAZ-ING, FRANCIS!
KA-BOING!

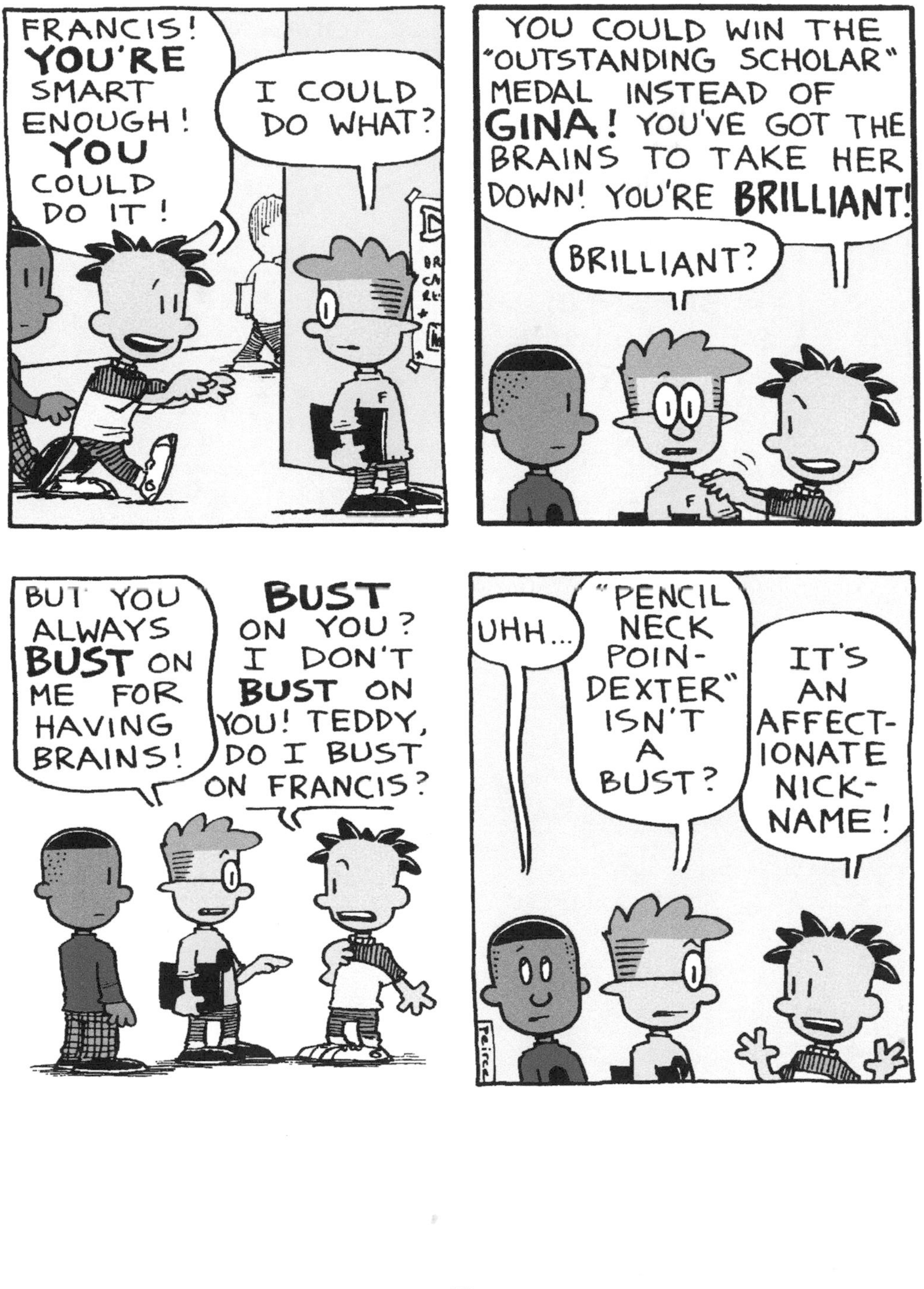
FRANCIS! YOU'RE SMART ENOUGH! YOU COULD DO IT!
I COULD DO WHAT?
YOU COULD WIN THE "OUTSTANDING SCHOLAR" MEDAL INSTEAD OF GINA! YOU'VE GOT THE BRAINS TO TAKE HER DOWN! YOU'RE BRILLIANT!
BRILLIANT?
BUT YOU ALWAYS BUST ON ME FOR HAVING BRAINS!
BUST ON YOU? I DON'T BUST ON YOU! TEDDY, DO I BUST ON FRANCIS?
UHH...
"PENCIL NECK POIN-DEXTER" ISN'T A BUST?
IT'S AN AFFECT-IONATE NICK-NAME!

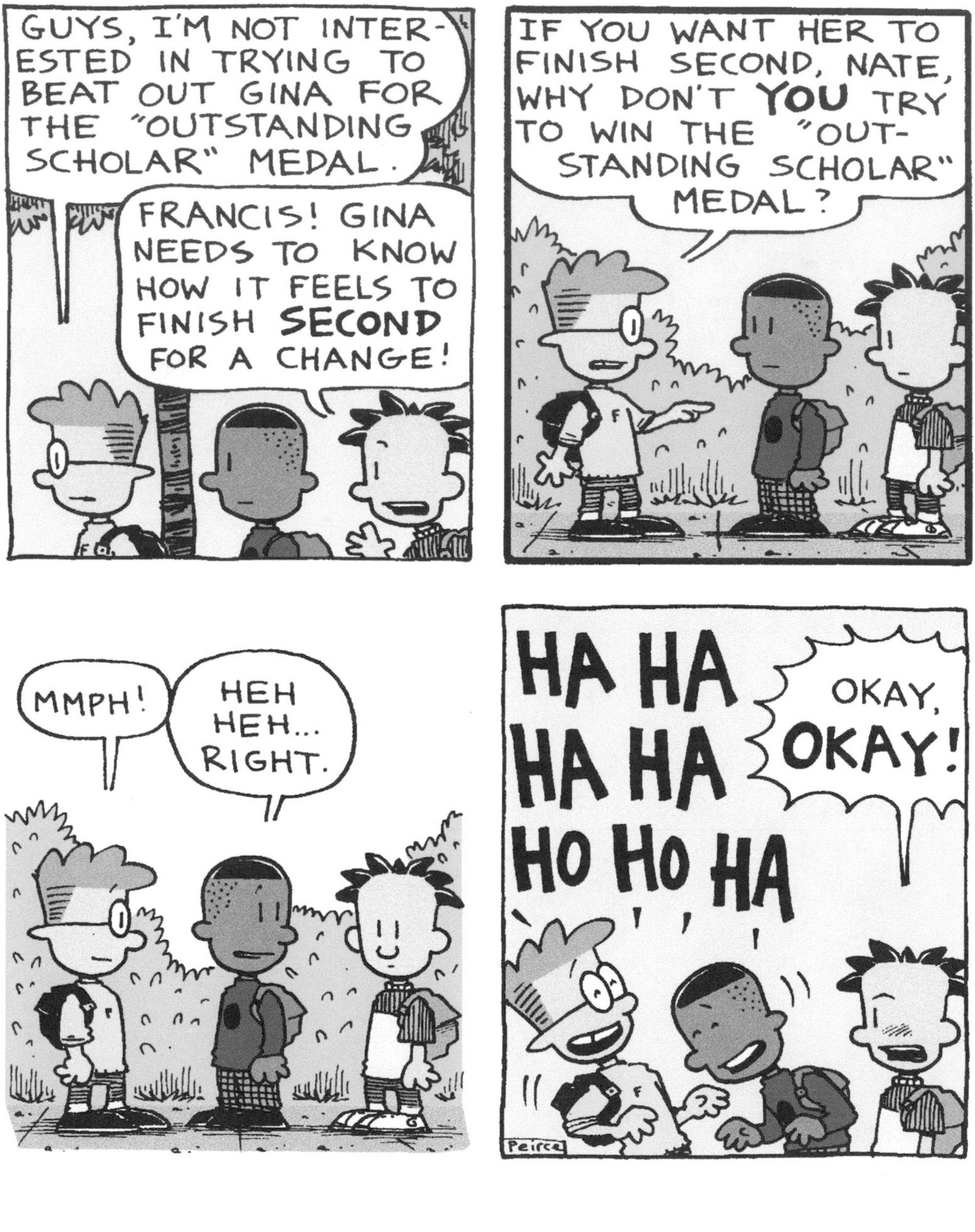
GUYS, I'M NOT INTERESTED IN TRYING TO BEAT OUT GINA FOR THE "OUTSTANDING SCHOLAR" MEDAL.
FRANCIS! GINA NEEDS TO KNOW HOW IT FEELS TO FINISH **SECOND** FOR A CHANGE!
IF YOU WANT HER TO FINISH SECOND, NATE, WHY DON'T **YOU** TRY TO WIN THE "OUTSTANDING SCHOLAR" MEDAL?
MMPH!
HEH HEH... RIGHT.
HA HA HA HA HO HO HA
OKAY, **OKAY!**
Peirce

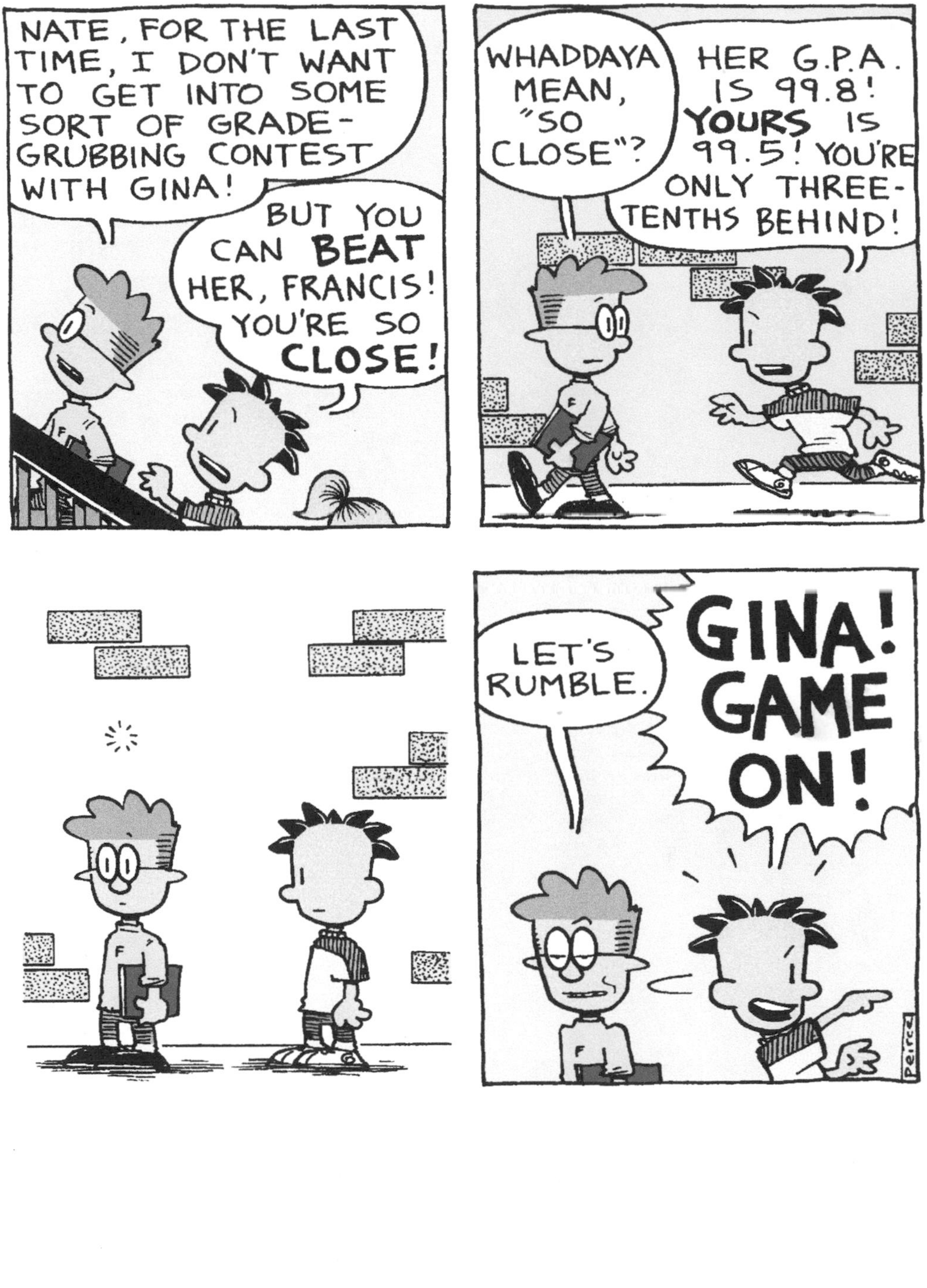
NATE, FOR THE LAST TIME, I DON'T WANT TO GET INTO SOME SORT OF GRADE-GRUBBING CONTEST WITH GINA!
BUT YOU CAN BEAT HER, FRANCIS! YOU'RE SO CLOSE!
WHADDAYA MEAN, "SO CLOSE"?
HER G.P.A. IS 99.8! YOURS IS 99.5! YOU'RE ONLY THREE-TENTHS BEHIND!
LET'S RUMBLE.
GINA! GAME ON!
PEIRCE

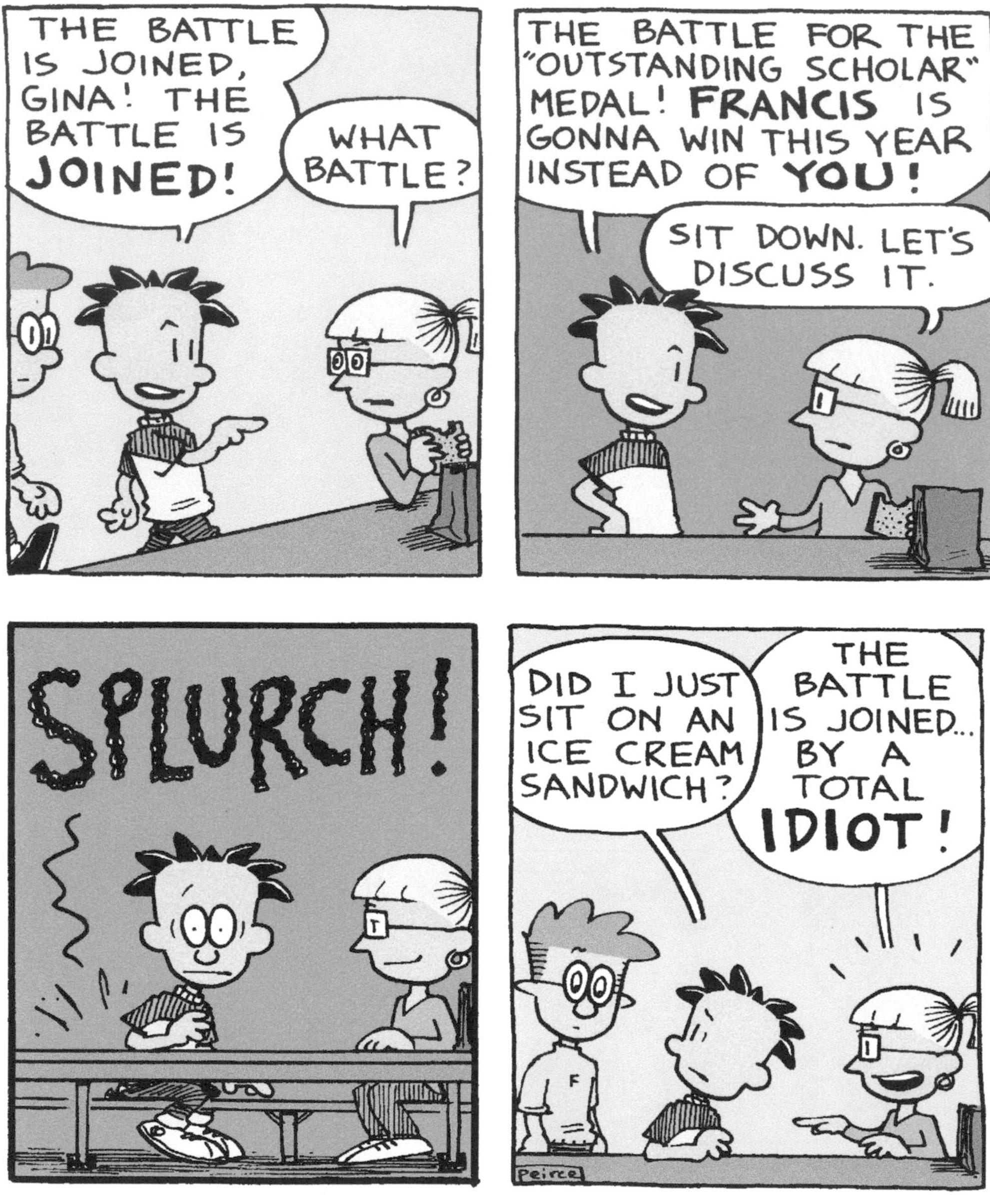
THE BATTLE IS JOINED, GINA! THE BATTLE IS JOINED!
WHAT BATTLE?
THE BATTLE FOR THE "OUTSTANDING SCHOLAR" MEDAL! FRANCIS IS GONNA WIN THIS YEAR INSTEAD OF YOU!
SIT DOWN. LET'S DISCUSS IT.
SPLURCH!
DID I JUST SIT ON AN ICE CREAM SANDWICH?
THE BATTLE IS JOINED... BY A TOTAL IDIOT!
Peirce

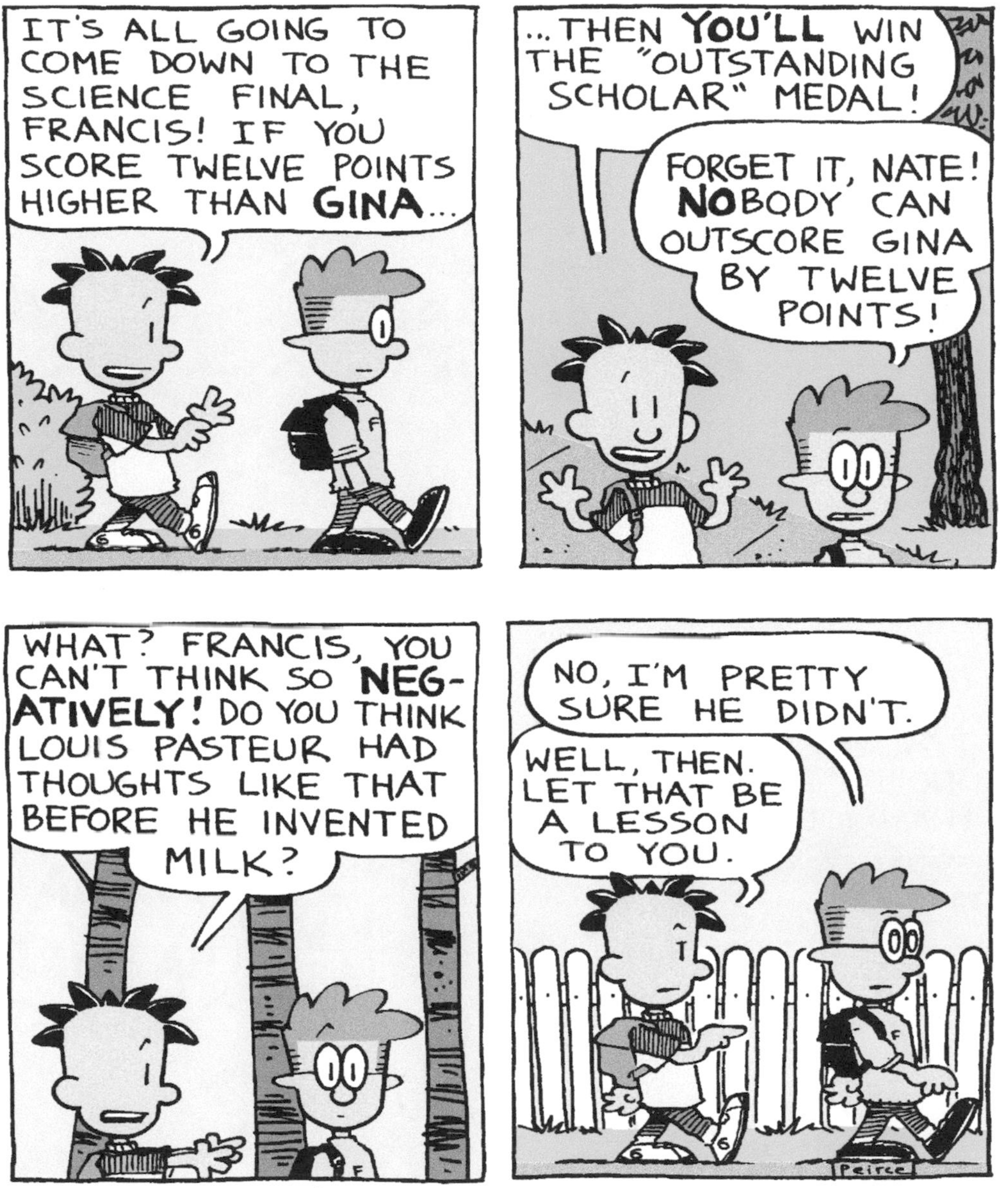
IT'S ALL GOING TO COME DOWN TO THE SCIENCE FINAL, FRANCIS! IF YOU SCORE TWELVE POINTS HIGHER THAN GINA...
...THEN YOU'LL WIN THE "OUTSTANDING SCHOLAR" MEDAL!
FORGET IT, NATE! NOBODY CAN OUTSCORE GINA BY TWELVE POINTS!
WHAT? FRANCIS, YOU CAN'T THINK SO NEG-ATIVELY! DO YOU THINK LOUIS PASTEUR HAD THOUGHTS LIKE THAT BEFORE HE INVENTED MILK?
NO, I'M PRETTY SURE HE DIDN'T.
WELL, THEN. LET THAT BE A LESSON TO YOU.
Peirce

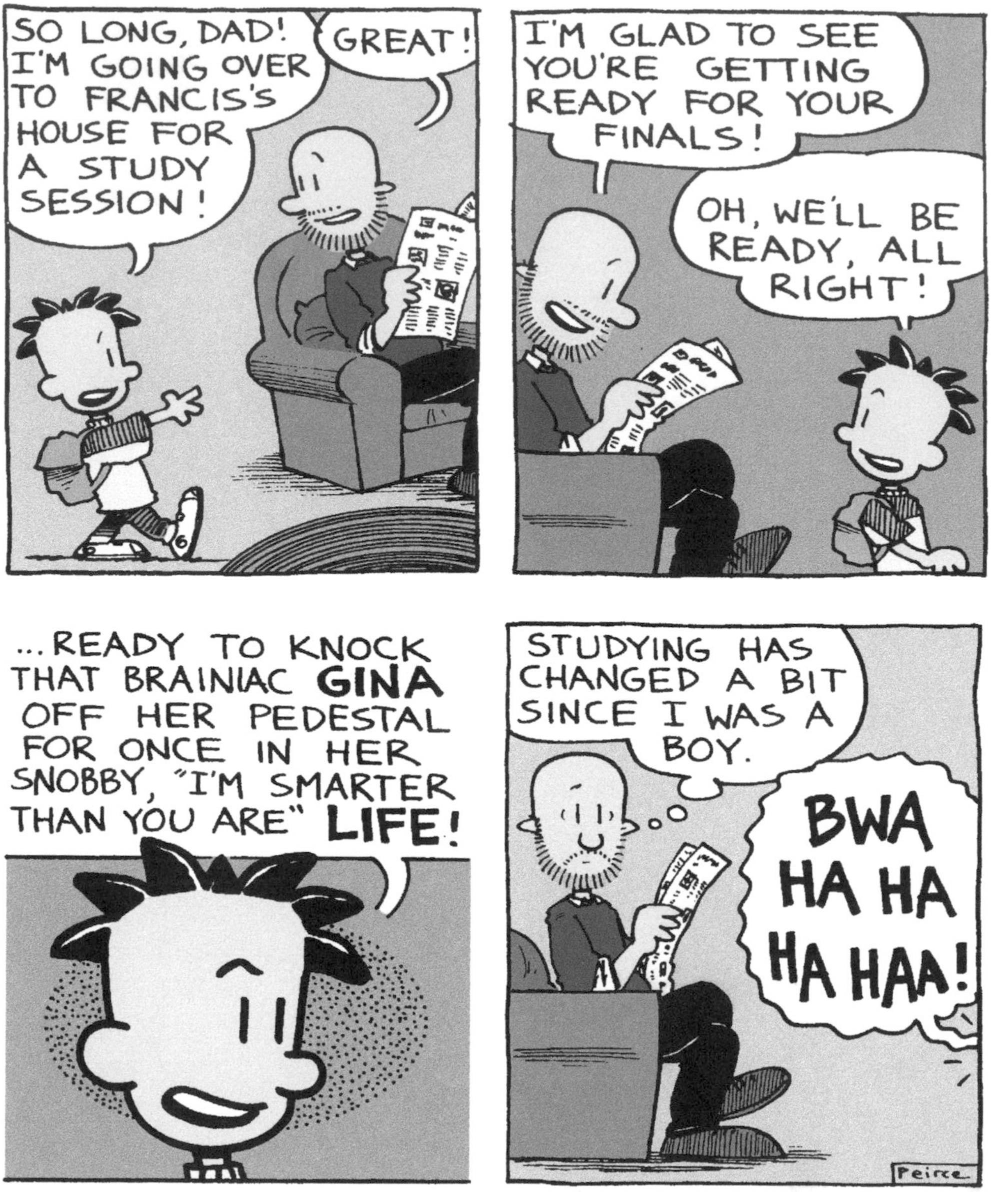
SO LONG, DAD! I'M GOING OVER TO FRANCIS'S HOUSE FOR A STUDY SESSION!
GREAT!
I'M GLAD TO SEE YOU'RE GETTING READY FOR YOUR FINALS!
OH, WE'LL BE READY, ALL RIGHT!
...READY TO KNOCK THAT BRAINIAC GINA OFF HER PEDESTAL FOR ONCE IN HER SNOBBY, "I'M SMARTER THAN YOU ARE" LIFE!
STUDYING HAS CHANGED A BIT SINCE I WAS A BOY.
BWA HA HA HA HAA!
Peirce

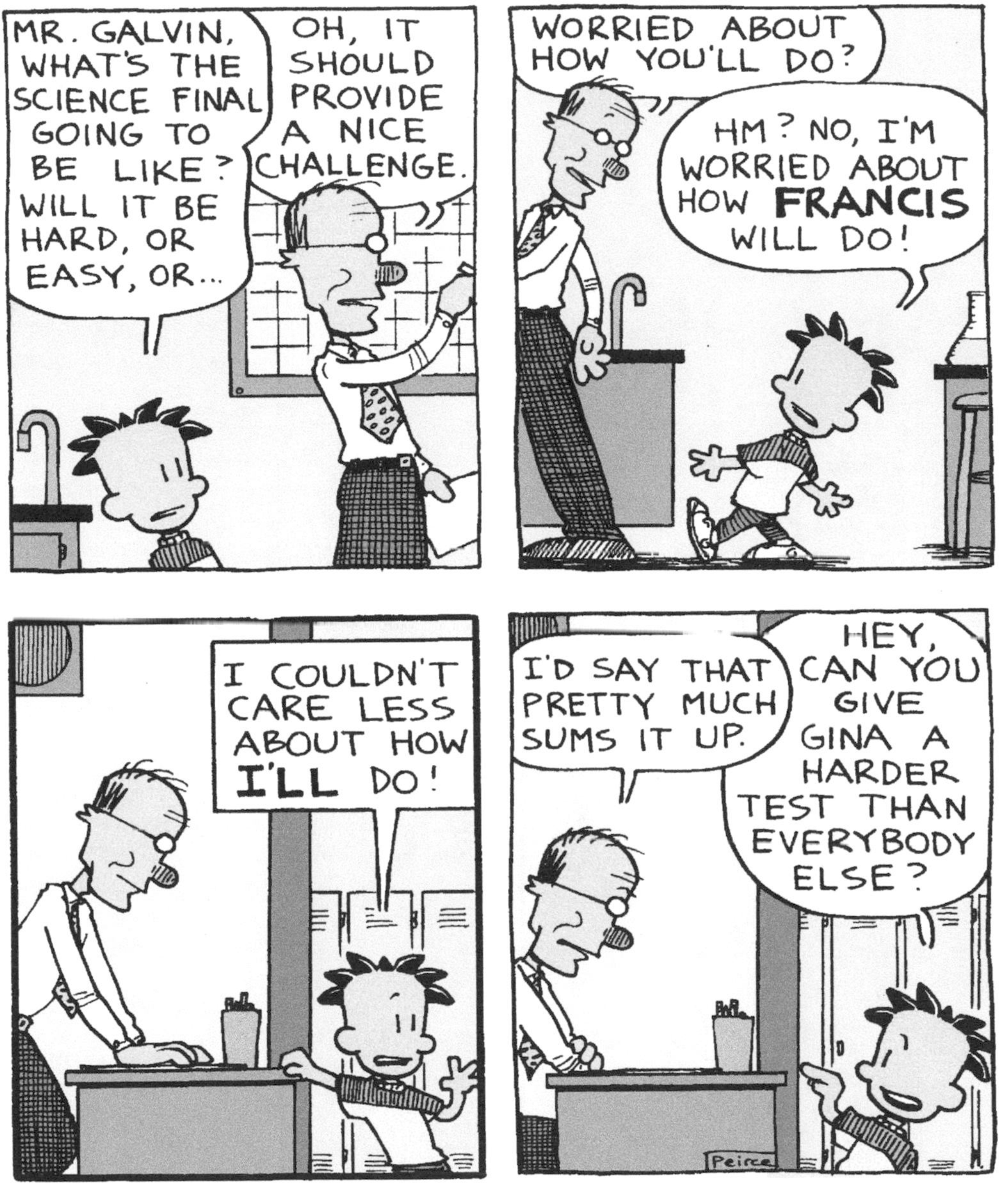
MR. GALVIN, WHAT'S THE SCIENCE FINAL GOING TO BE LIKE? WILL IT BE HARD, OR EASY, OR...
OH, IT SHOULD PROVIDE A NICE CHALLENGE.
WORRIED ABOUT HOW YOU'LL DO?
HM? NO, I'M WORRIED ABOUT HOW **FRANCIS** WILL DO!
I COULDN'T CARE LESS ABOUT HOW **I'LL** DO!
I'D SAY THAT PRETTY MUCH SUMS IT UP.
HEY, CAN YOU GIVE GINA A HARDER TEST THAN EVERYBODY ELSE?
Peirce

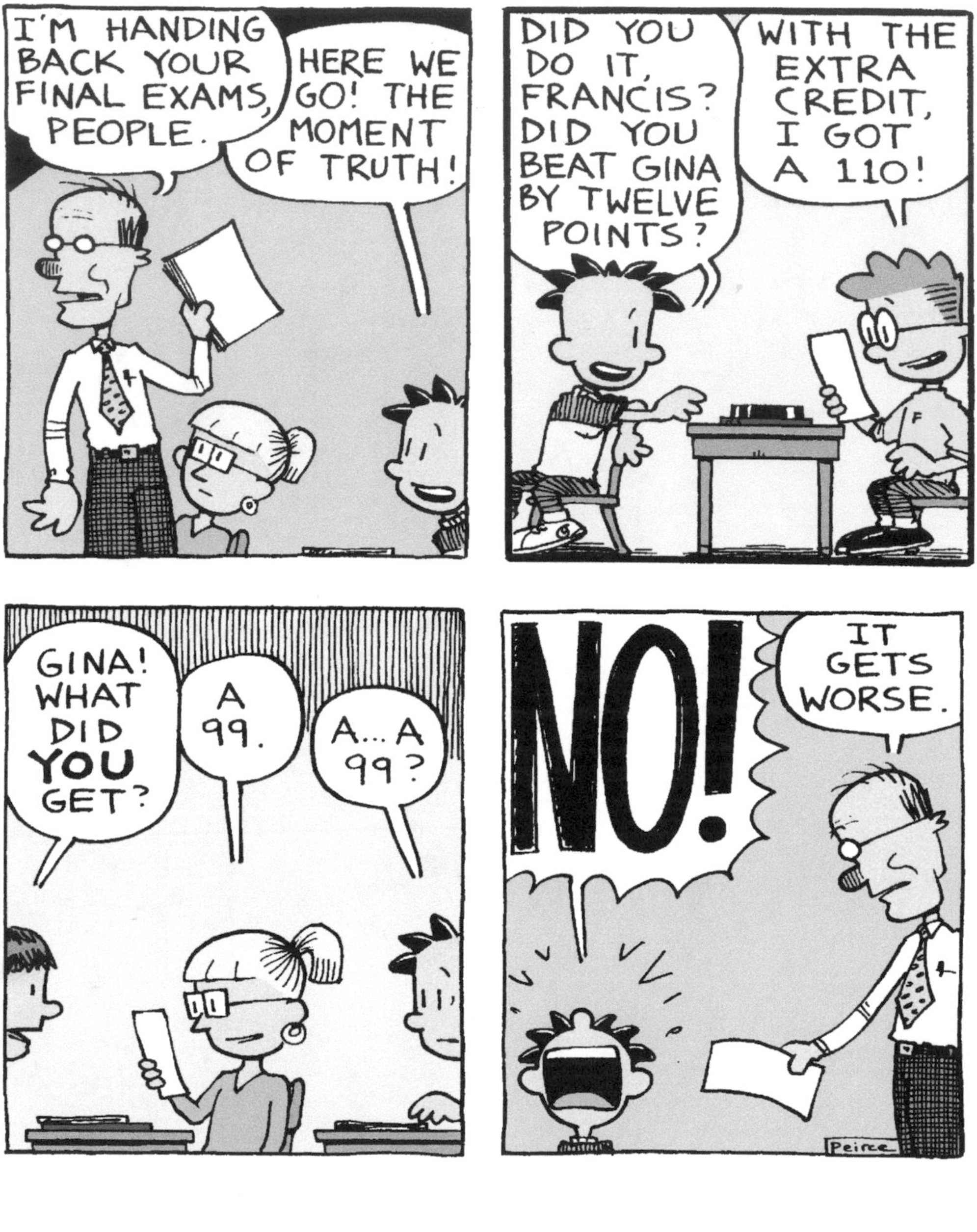
I'M HANDING BACK YOUR FINAL EXAMS, PEOPLE.
HERE WE GO! THE MOMENT OF TRUTH!
DID YOU DO IT, FRANCIS? DID YOU BEAT GINA BY TWELVE POINTS?
WITH THE EXTRA CREDIT, I GOT A 110!
GINA! WHAT DID **YOU** GET?
A 99.
A... A 99?
NO!
IT GETS WORSE.
Peirce

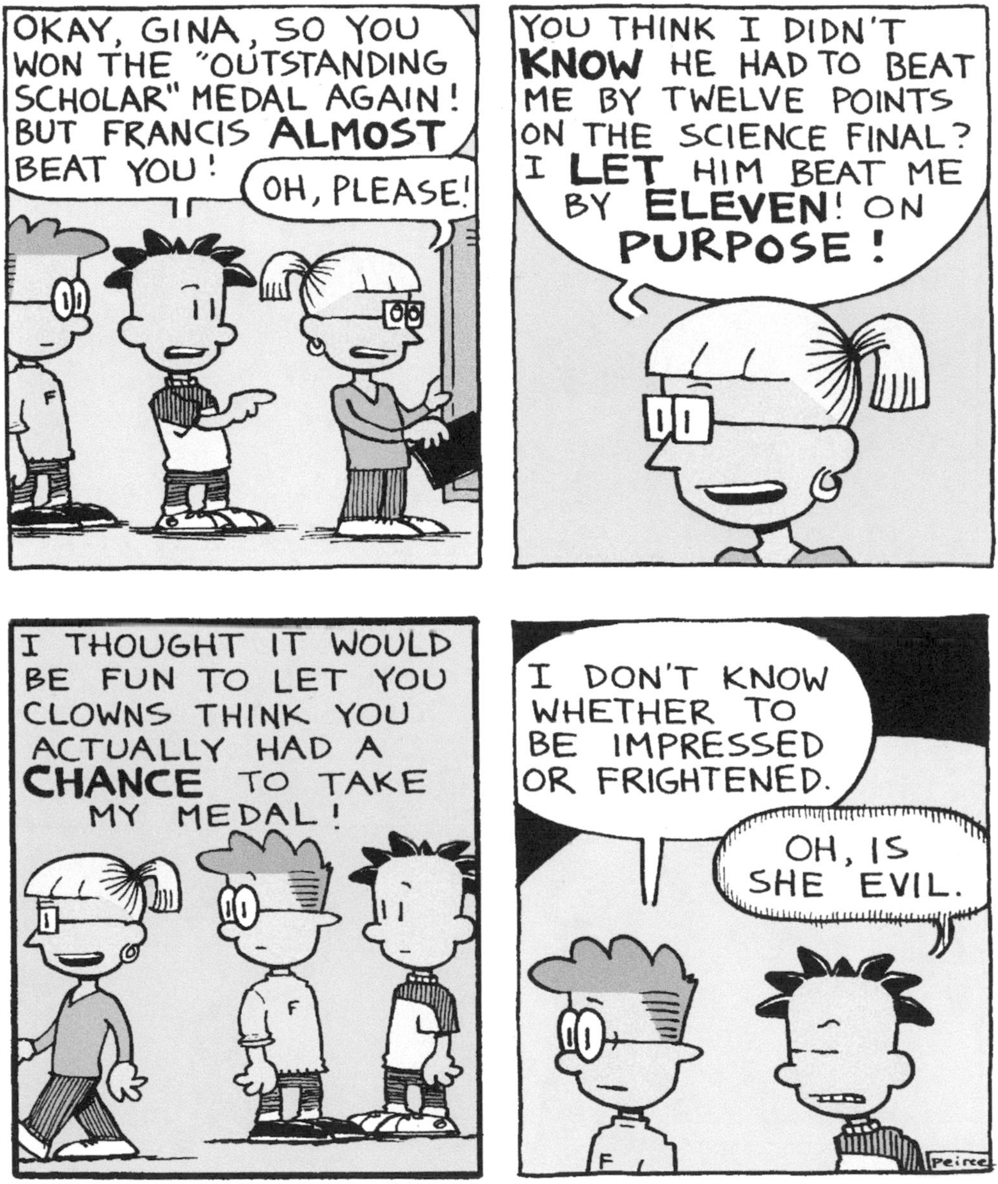
OKAY, GINA, SO YOU WON THE "OUTSTANDING SCHOLAR" MEDAL AGAIN! BUT FRANCIS ALMOST BEAT YOU!
OH, PLEASE!
YOU THINK I DIDN'T KNOW HE HAD TO BEAT ME BY TWELVE POINTS ON THE SCIENCE FINAL? I LET HIM BEAT ME BY ELEVEN! ON PURPOSE!
I THOUGHT IT WOULD BE FUN TO LET YOU CLOWNS THINK YOU ACTUALLY HAD A CHANCE TO TAKE MY MEDAL!
I DON'T KNOW WHETHER TO BE IMPRESSED OR FRIGHTENED.
OH, IS SHE EVIL.
Peirce

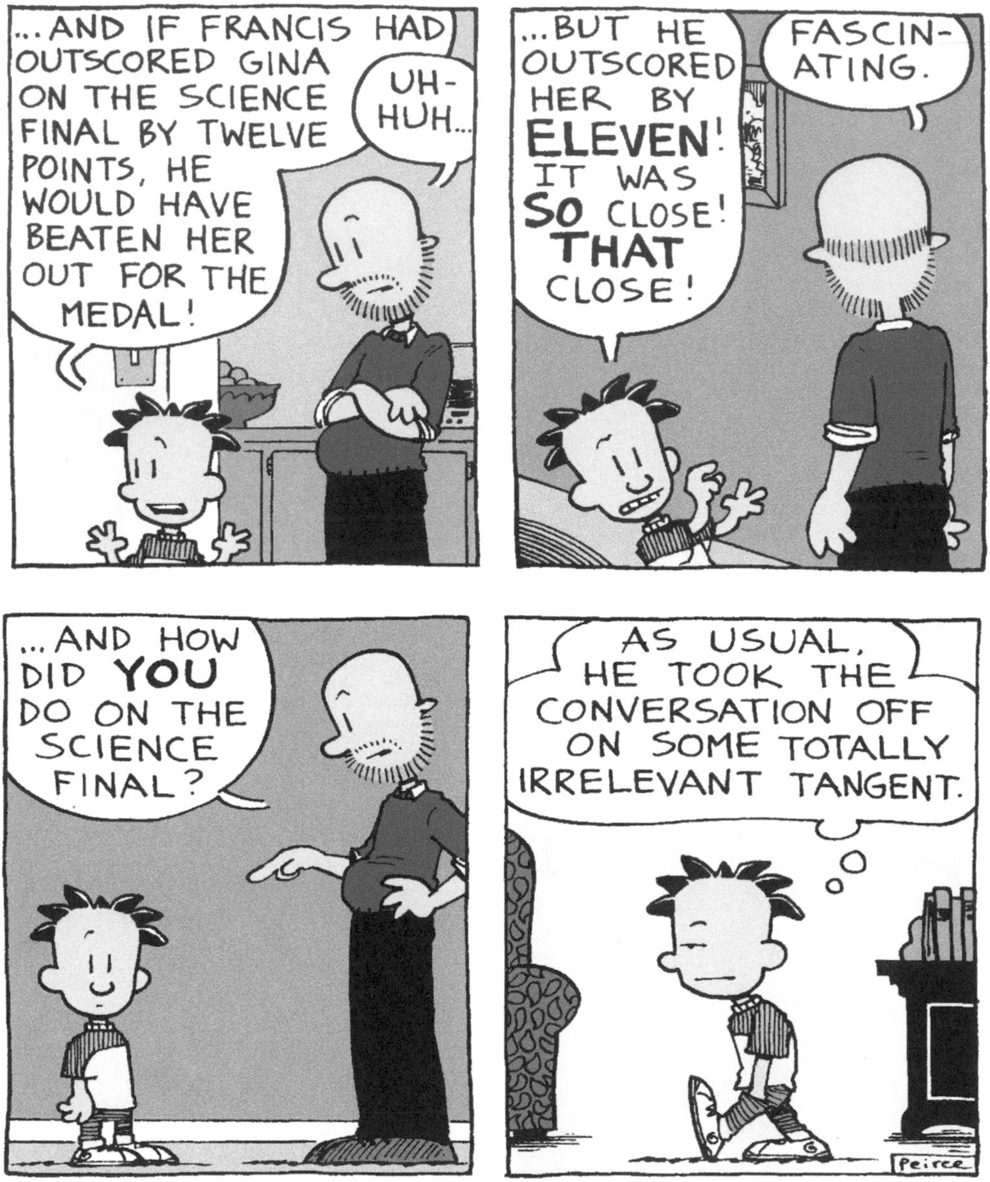
...AND IF FRANCIS HAD OUTSCORED GINA ON THE SCIENCE FINAL BY TWELVE POINTS, HE WOULD HAVE BEATEN HER OUT FOR THE MEDAL!
UH-HUH...
...BUT HE OUTSCORED HER BY ELEVEN! IT WAS SO CLOSE! THAT CLOSE!
FASCIN-ATING.
...AND HOW DID YOU DO ON THE SCIENCE FINAL?
AS USUAL, HE TOOK THE CONVERSATION OFF ON SOME TOTALLY IRRELEVANT TANGENT.
Peirce

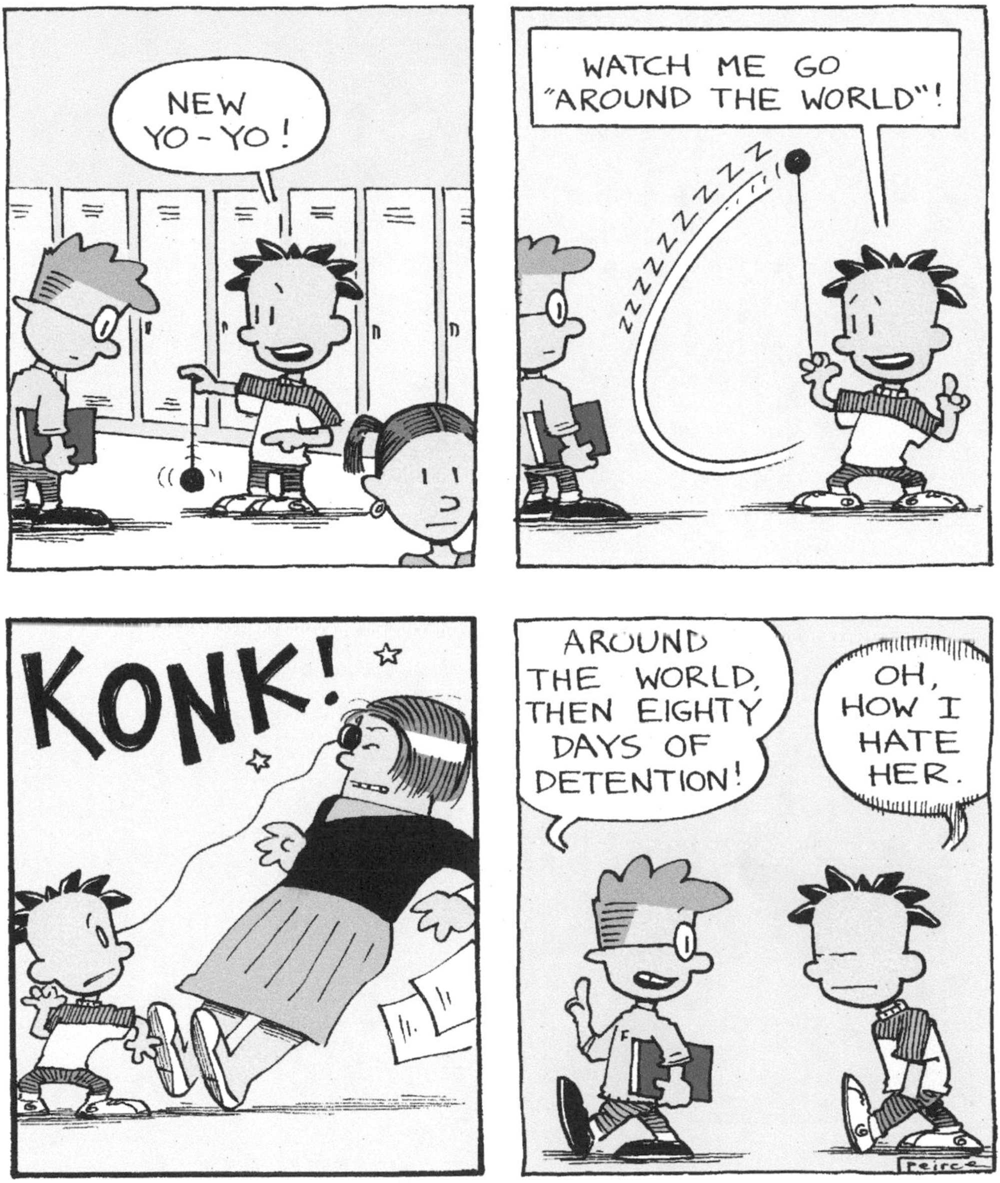
NEW YO-YO!
WATCH ME GO "AROUND THE WORLD"!
ZZZZZZZZZZ
KONK!
AROUND THE WORLD, THEN EIGHTY DAYS OF DETENTION!
OH, HOW I HATE HER.
peirce

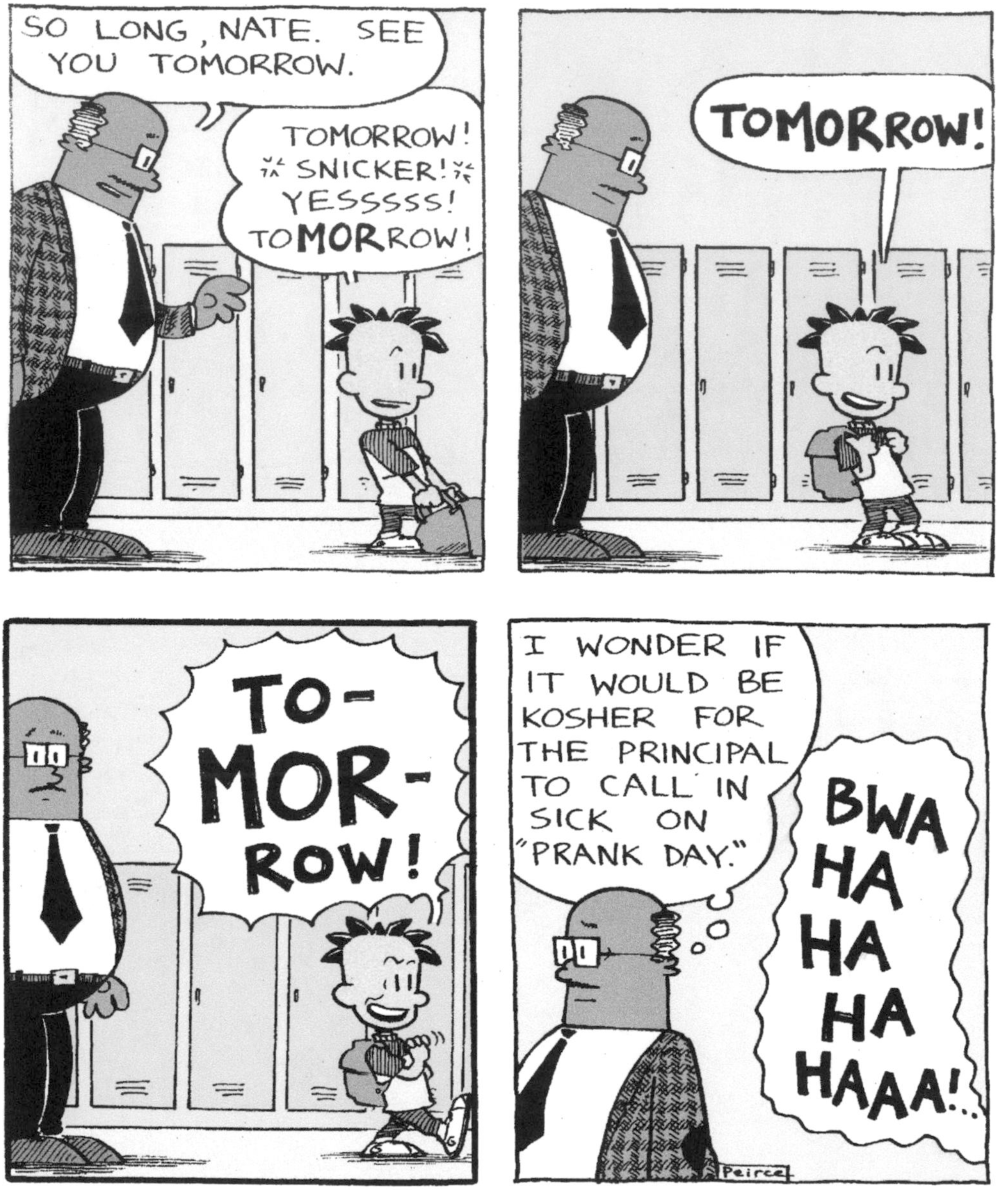
SO LONG, NATE. SEE YOU TOMORROW.
TOMORROW! SNICKER! YESSSSS! TOMORROW!
TOMORROW!
TO-MOR-ROW!
I WONDER IF IT WOULD BE KOSHER FOR THE PRINCIPAL TO CALL IN SICK ON "PRANK DAY."
BWA HA HA HA HA HAAA!
Peirce

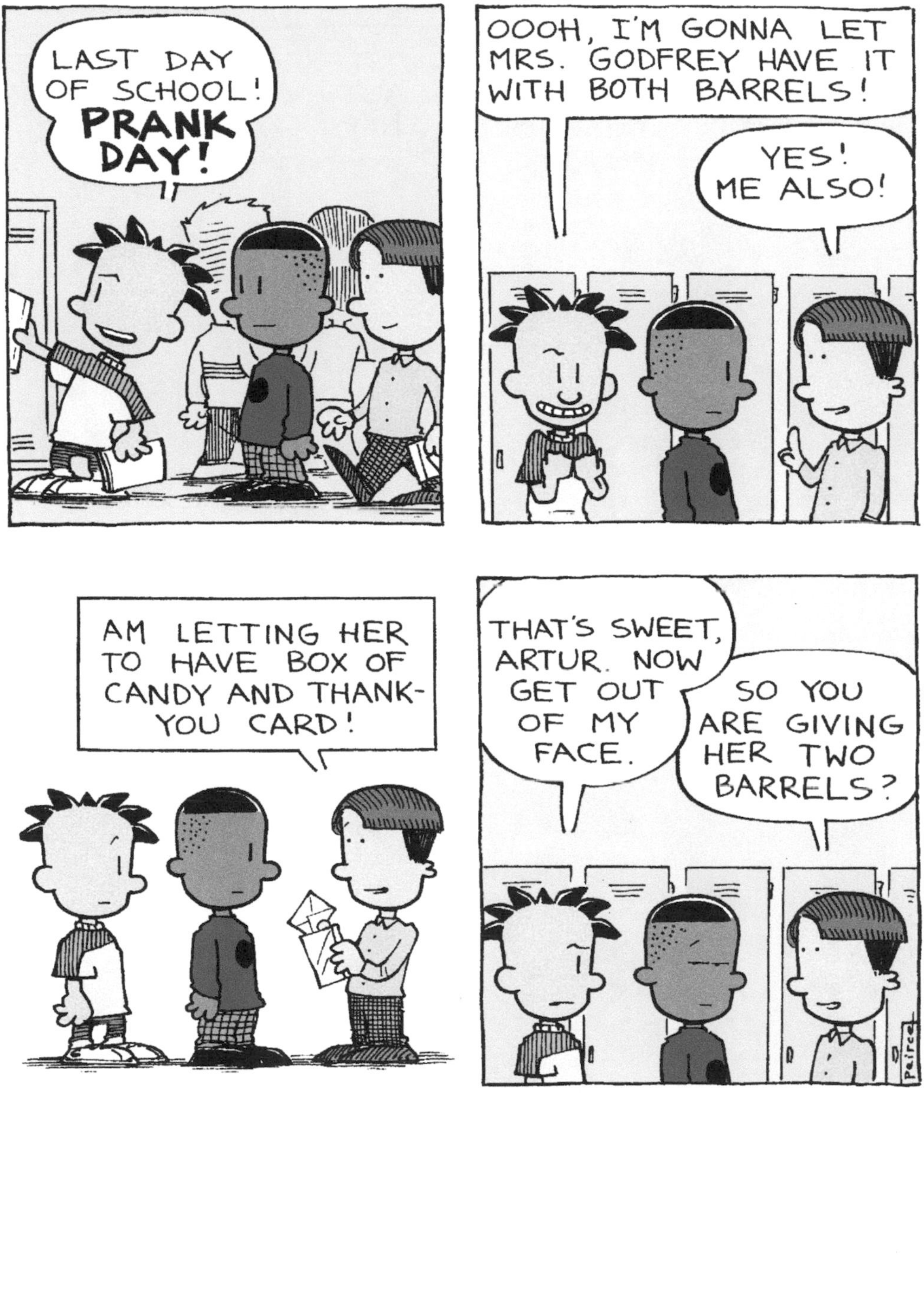
LAST DAY OF SCHOOL! PRANK DAY!
OOOH, I'M GONNA LET MRS. GODFREY HAVE IT WITH BOTH BARRELS!
YES! ME ALSO!
AM LETTING HER TO HAVE BOX OF CANDY AND THANK-YOU CARD!
THAT'S SWEET, ARTUR. NOW GET OUT OF MY FACE.
SO YOU ARE GIVING HER TWO BARRELS?
Peirce

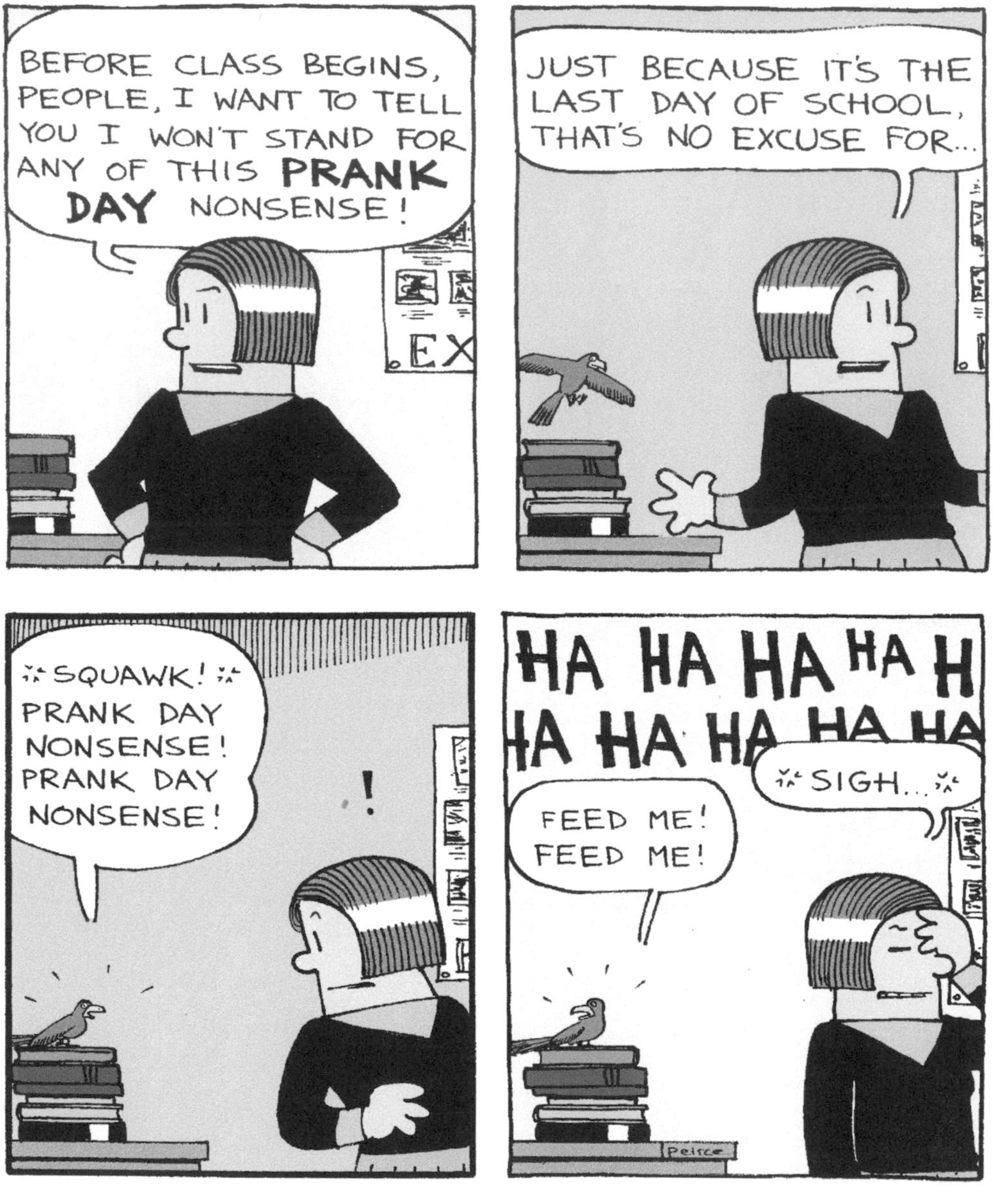
BEFORE CLASS BEGINS, PEOPLE, I WANT TO TELL YOU I WON'T STAND FOR ANY OF THIS PRANK DAY NONSENSE!
EX
JUST BECAUSE IT'S THE LAST DAY OF SCHOOL, THAT'S NO EXCUSE FOR...
SQUAWK! PRANK DAY NONSENSE! PRANK DAY NONSENSE!
!
HA HA HA HA H
HA HA HA HA HA
SIGH...
FEED ME! FEED ME!
Peirce

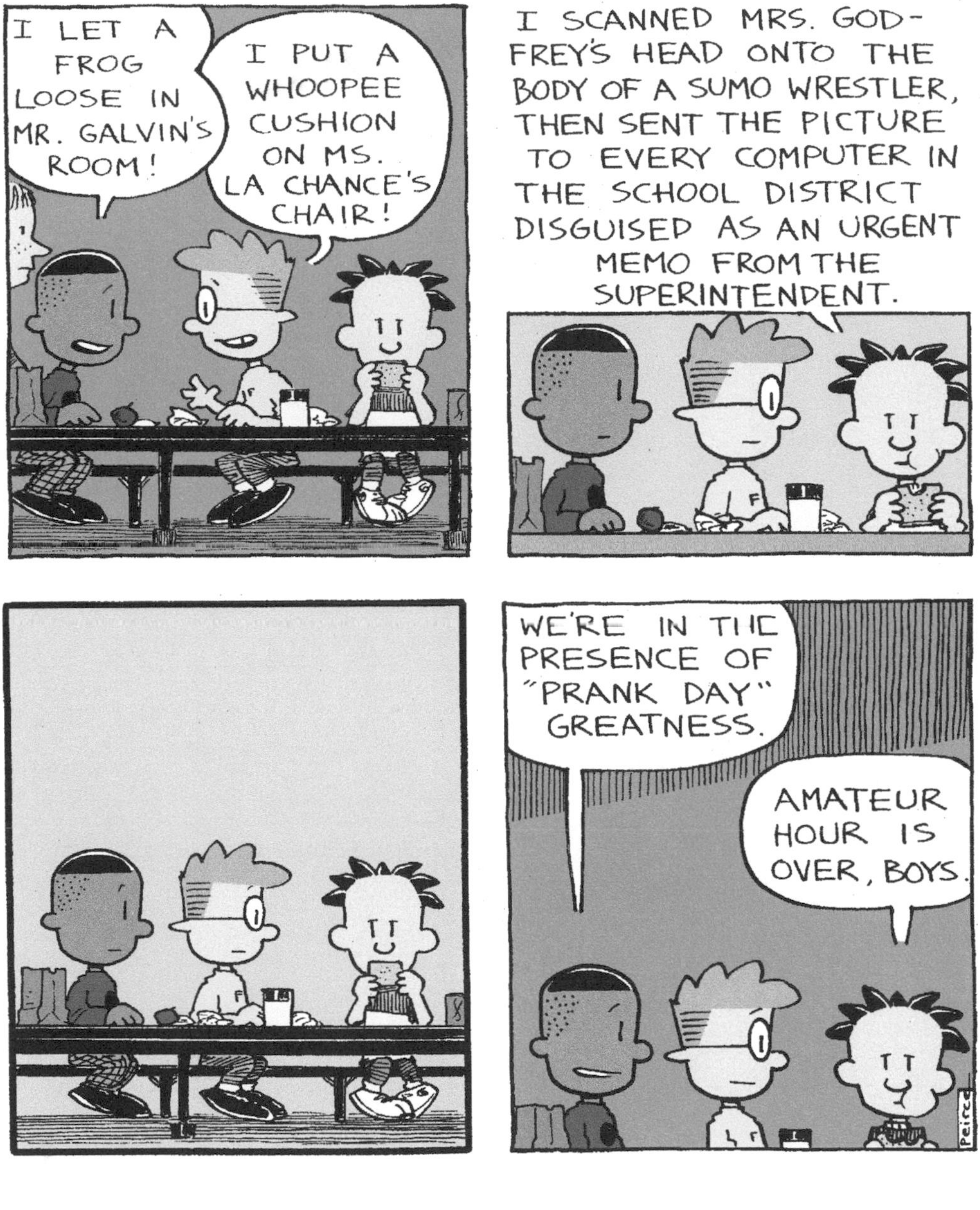
I LET A FROG LOOSE IN MR. GALVIN'S ROOM!
I PUT A WHOOPEE CUSHION ON MS. LA CHANCE'S CHAIR!
I SCANNED MRS. GODFREY'S HEAD ONTO THE BODY OF A SUMO WRESTLER, THEN SENT THE PICTURE TO EVERY COMPUTER IN THE SCHOOL DISTRICT DISGUISED AS AN URGENT MEMO FROM THE SUPERINTENDENT.
WE'RE IN THE PRESENCE OF "PRANK DAY" GREATNESS.
AMATEUR HOUR IS OVER, BOYS.
Peirce

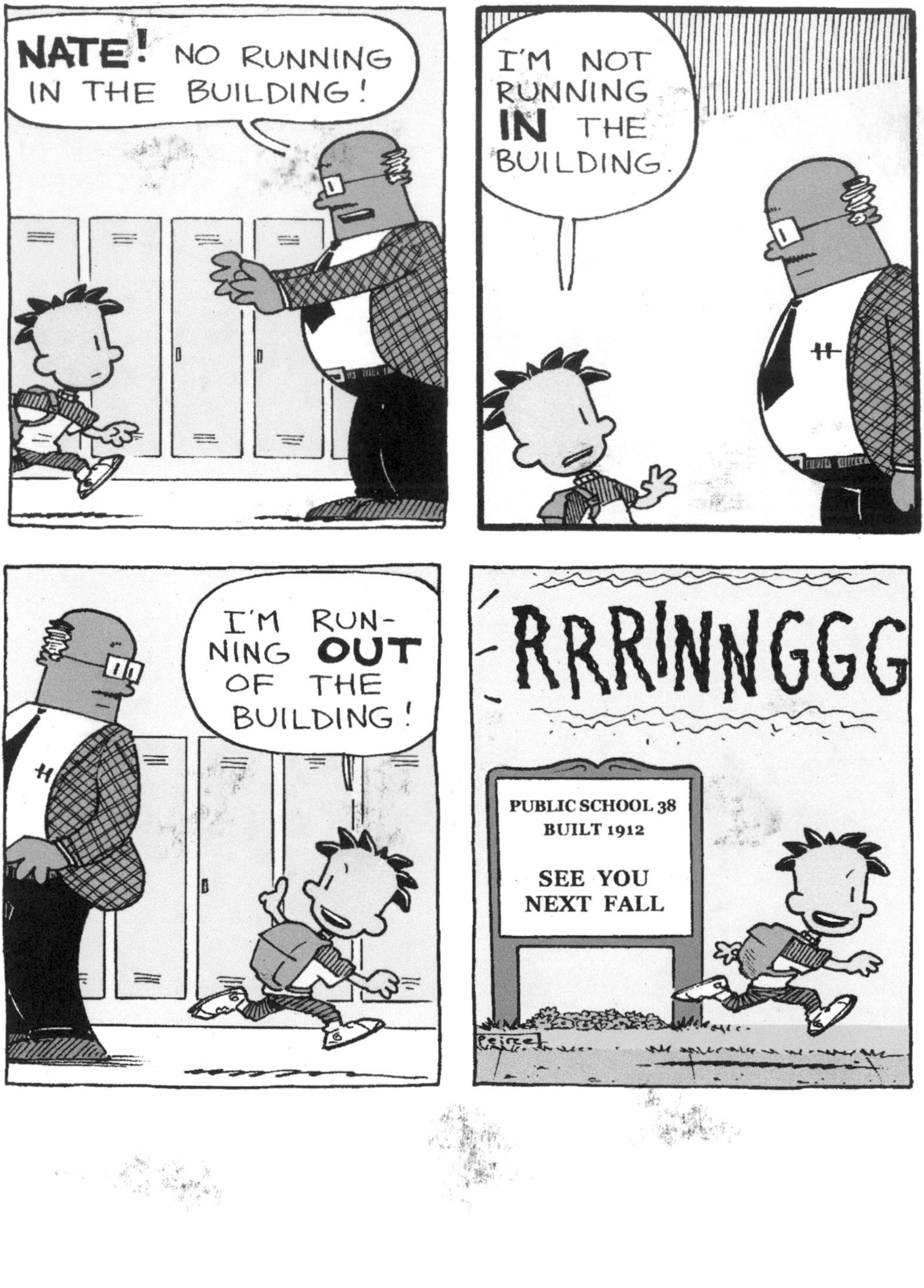
NATE! NO RUNNING IN THE BUILDING!
I'M NOT RUNNING IN THE BUILDING.
I'M RUN-NING OUT OF THE BUILDING!
RRRINNGGG
PUBLIC SCHOOL 38
BUILT 1912
SEE YOU NEXT FALL

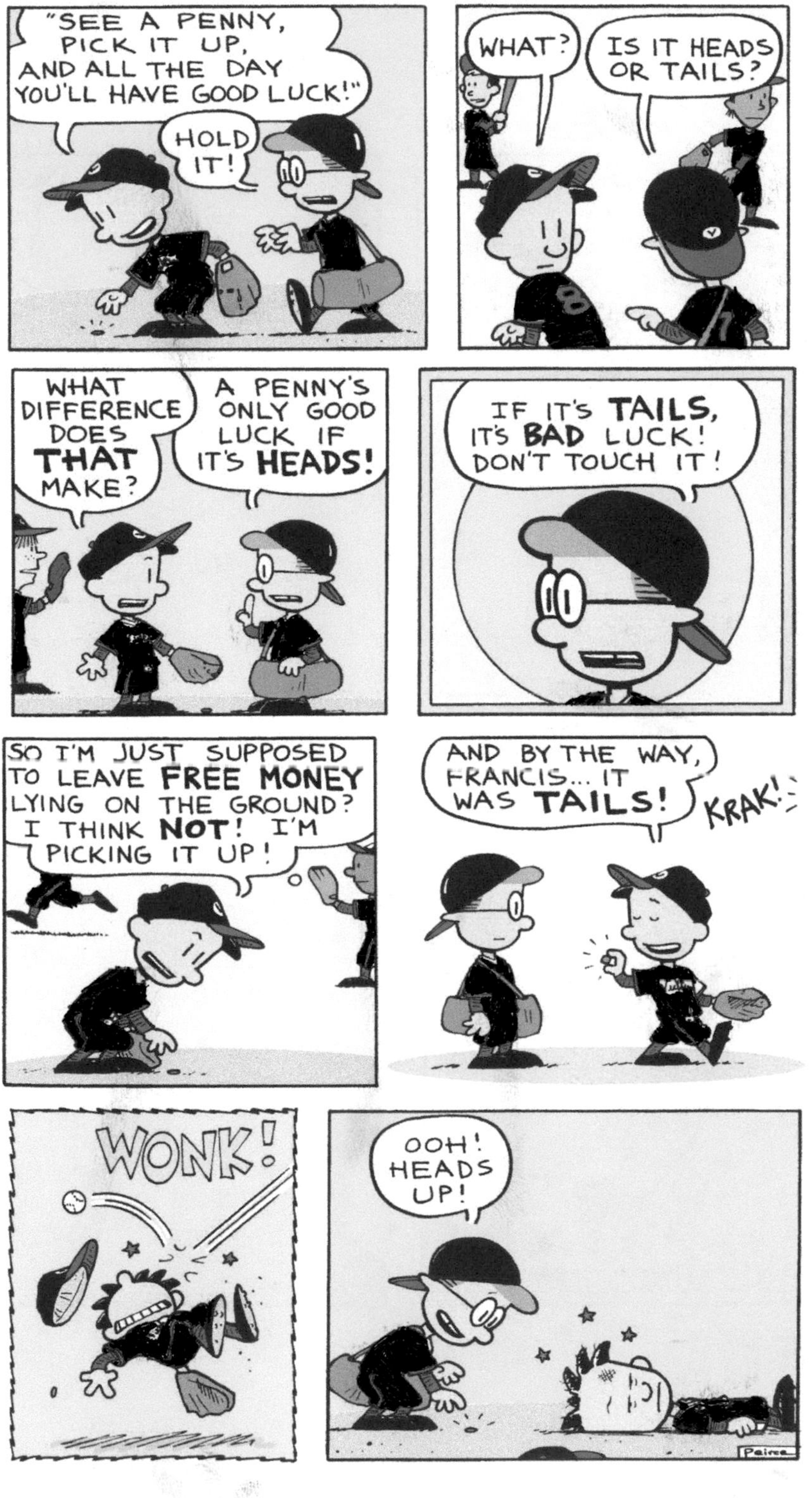
"SEE A PENNY, PICK IT UP, AND ALL THE DAY YOU'LL HAVE GOOD LUCK!"
HOLD IT!
WHAT?
IS IT HEADS OR TAILS?
WHAT DIFFERENCE DOES THAT MAKE?
A PENNY'S ONLY GOOD LUCK IF IT'S HEADS!
IF IT'S TAILS, IT'S BAD LUCK! DON'T TOUCH IT!
SO I'M JUST SUPPOSED TO LEAVE FREE MONEY LYING ON THE GROUND? I THINK NOT! I'M PICKING IT UP!
AND BY THE WAY, FRANCIS... IT WAS TAILS!
KRAK!
WONK!
OOH! HEADS UP!
Peirce

AH, FRISBEE GOLF!
OKAY, THIS IS A PAR THREE! THE TRASH CAN IS THE HOLE!...
THIS BLANKET IS THE TEE... THE DUNE GRASS IS THE ROUGH... THE PARKING LOT IS OUT-OF-BOUNDS...
ZING!
...AND THIS IS WHAT IS KNOWN AS A "HAZARD."

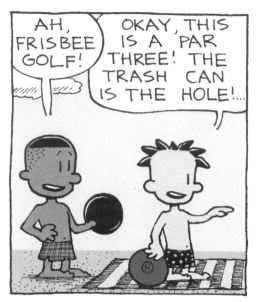

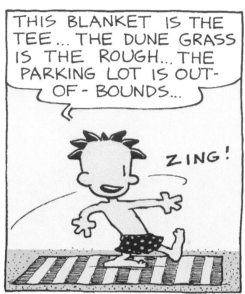

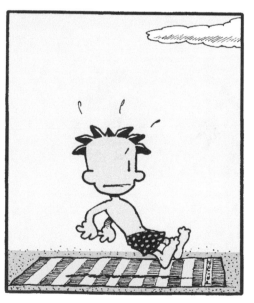

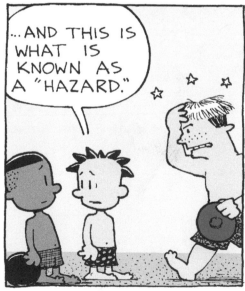

NATE! YOU ALMOST HIT ME WITH THAT FRISBEE!
SORRY, GINA, BUT THAT'S ONE OF THE HAZARDS OF BEING A SPECTATOR.
SPECTATOR? A SPEC-TATOR OF WHAT?
OUR FRISBEE GOLF TOURNAMENT!
YOUR WHAT? LOOK, I'M JUST TRYING TO READ!
THEN WHY ARE YOU SITTING IN THE MIDDLE OF THE TWELFTH FAIRWAY?
I HATE PEOPLE WHO DON'T LIKE SPORTS.
Peirce

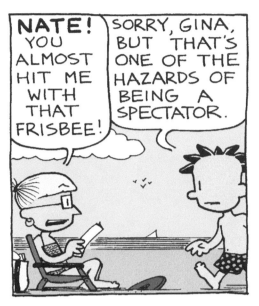

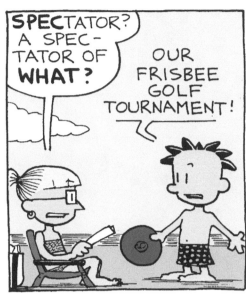

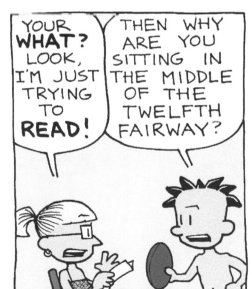

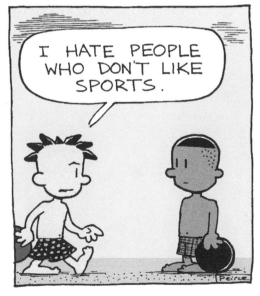

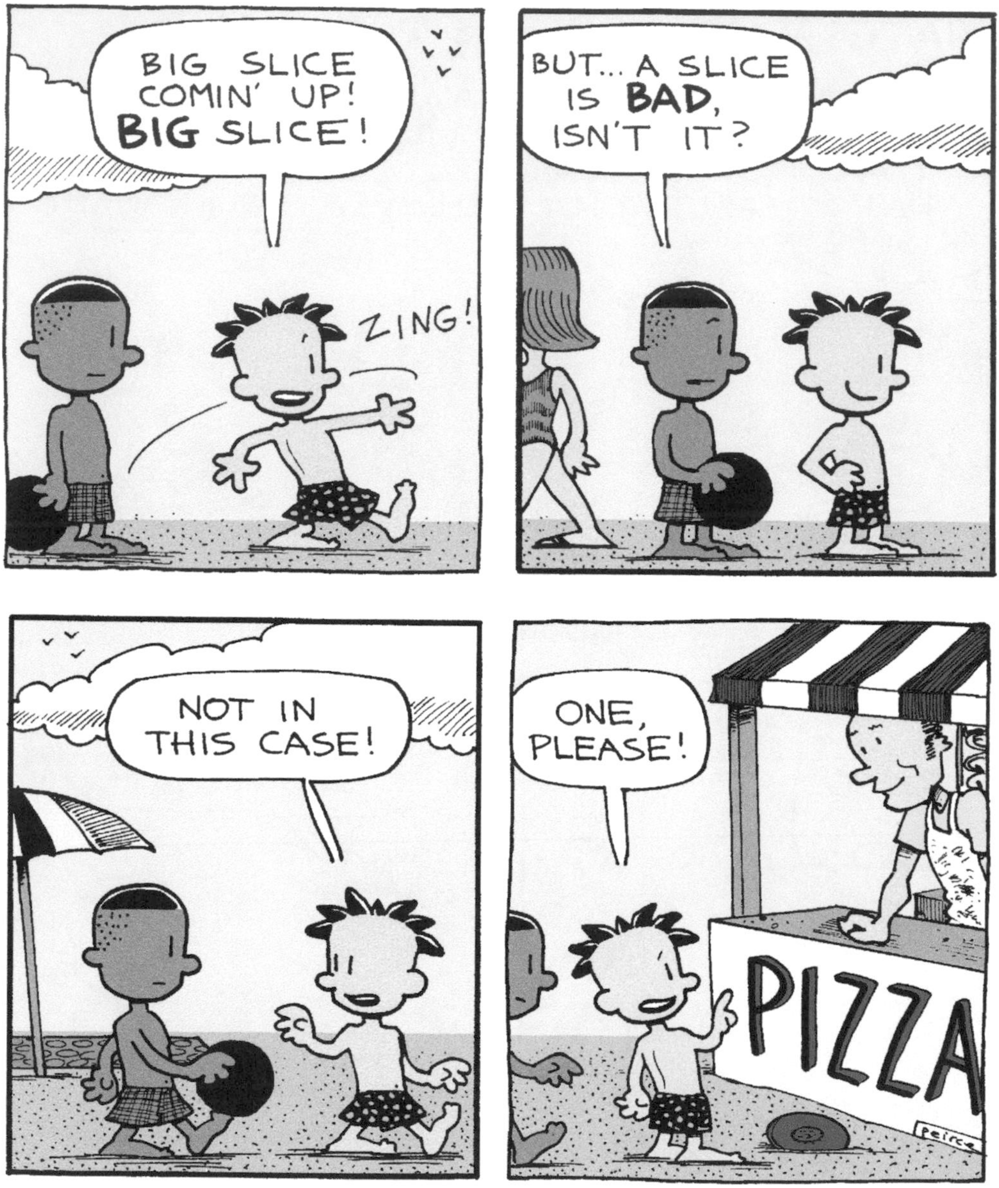
BIG SLICE COMIN' UP! BIG SLICE!
ZING!
BUT... A SLICE IS BAD, ISN'T IT?
NOT IN THIS CASE!
ONE, PLEASE!
PIZZA
peirce

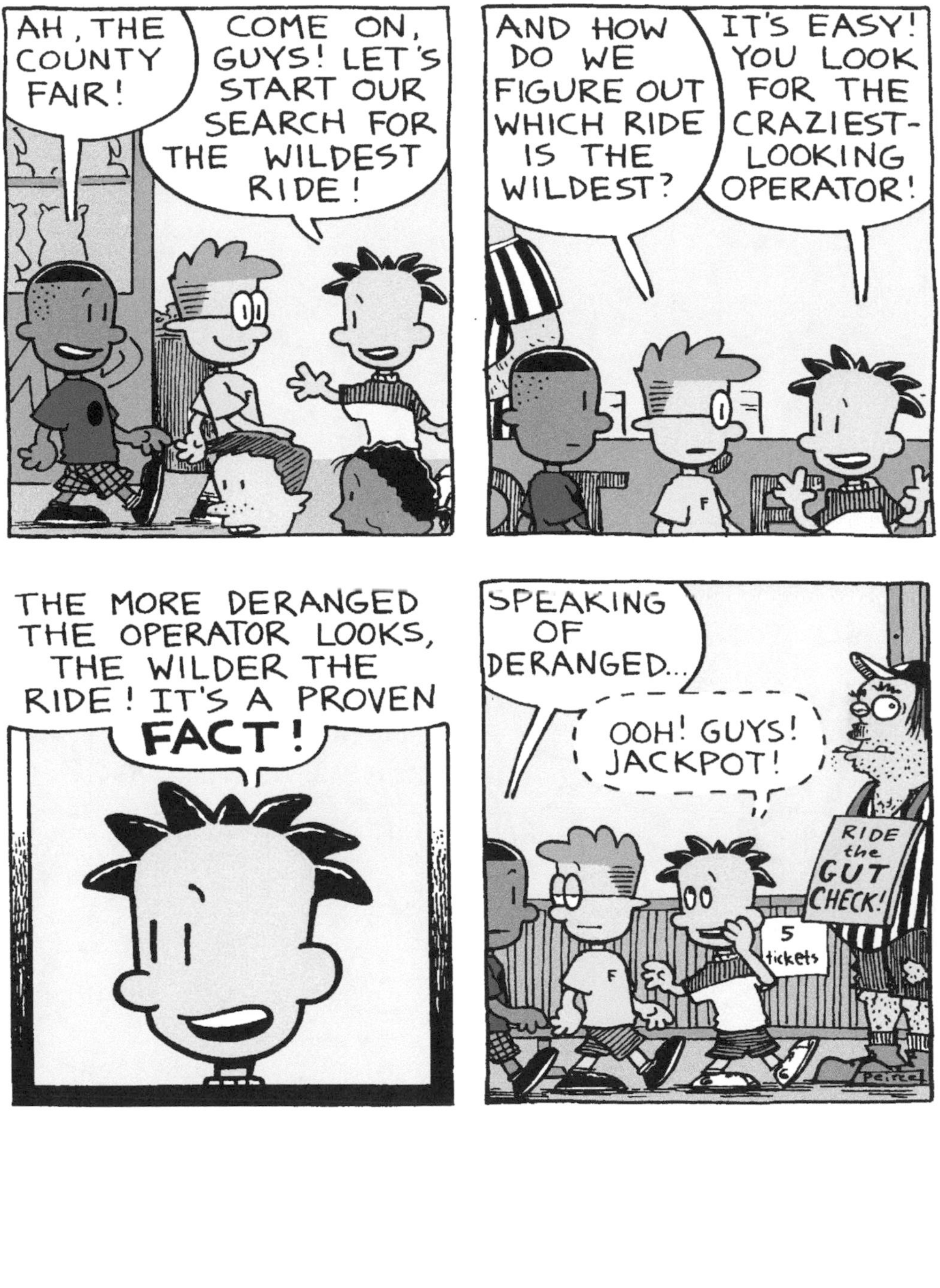
AH, THE COUNTY FAIR!
COME ON, GUYS! LET'S START OUR SEARCH FOR THE WILDEST RIDE!
AND HOW DO WE FIGURE OUT WHICH RIDE IS THE WILDEST?
IT'S EASY! YOU LOOK FOR THE CRAZIEST-LOOKING OPERATOR!
THE MORE DERANGED THE OPERATOR LOOKS, THE WILDER THE RIDE! IT'S A PROVEN **FACT**!
SPEAKING OF DERANGED...
OOH! GUYS! JACKPOT!
RIDE the GUT CHECK!
5 tickets
Peirce

AH! JENNY, M'LADY!
EWWW! NATE, THAT'S GROSS!
WHAT'S GROSS?
YOUR SHIRT! YOU GOT MOTION SICK ON ONE OF THE RIDES!
NO, I DIDN'T! I HAVEN'T EVEN GONE ON ANY RIDES YET!
HE'S JUST A SLOB!
LOOK, IS IT MY FAULT THEY OVER-STUFFED MY CHILI DOG?

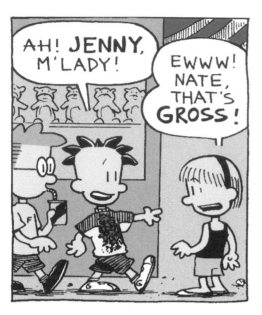

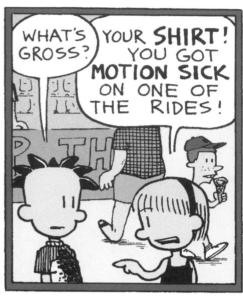

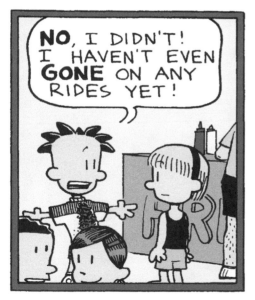

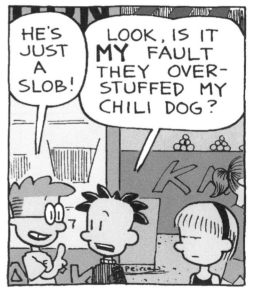

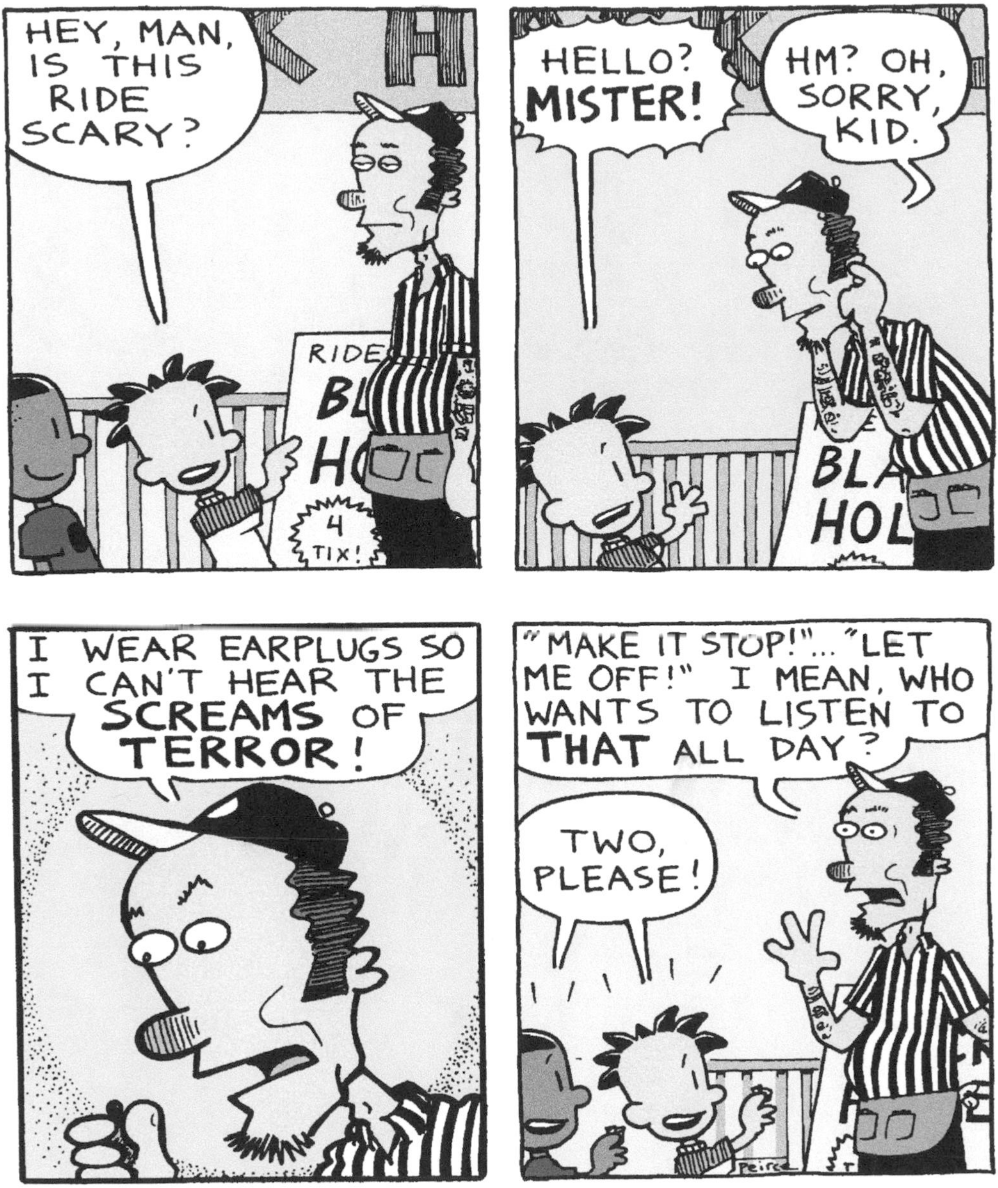
HEY, MAN, IS THIS RIDE SCARY?
RIDE
BL
HO
4 TIX!
HELLO? MISTER!
HM? OH, SORRY, KID.
BLA
HOL
I WEAR EARPLUGS SO I CAN'T HEAR THE SCREAMS OF TERROR!
"MAKE IT STOP!"... "LET ME OFF!" I MEAN, WHO WANTS TO LISTEN TO THAT ALL DAY?
TWO, PLEASE!
PEIRCE

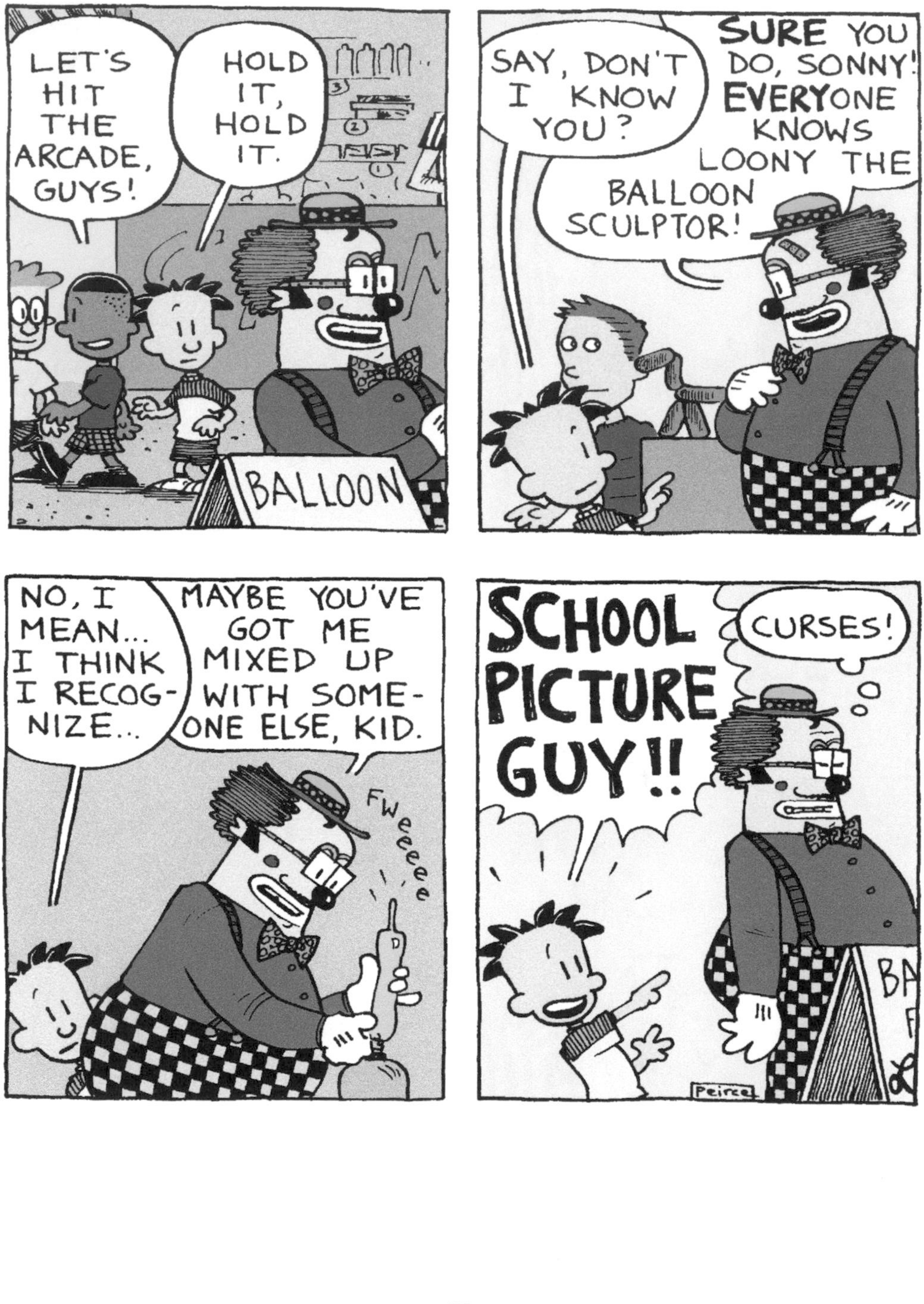
LET'S HIT THE ARCADE, GUYS!
HOLD IT, HOLD IT.
BALLOON
SAY, DON'T I KNOW YOU?
SURE YOU DO, SONNY! EVERYONE KNOWS LOONY THE BALLOON SCULPTOR!
NO, I MEAN... I THINK I RECOG-NIZE...
MAYBE YOU'VE GOT ME MIXED UP WITH SOME-ONE ELSE, KID.
FWeeeee
SCHOOL PICTURE GUY!!
CURSES!
Peirce

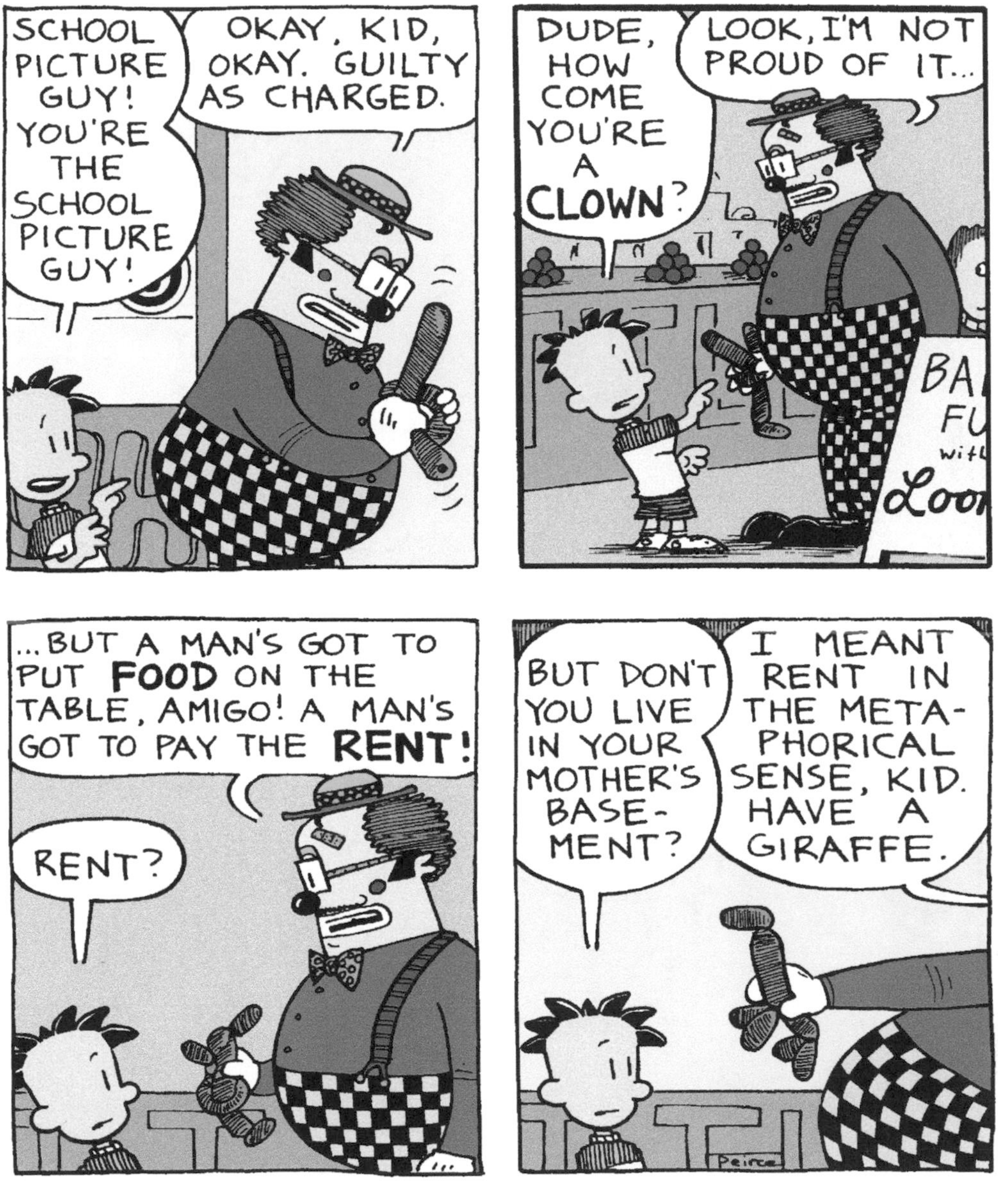
SCHOOL PICTURE GUY! YOU'RE THE SCHOOL PICTURE GUY!
OKAY, KID, OKAY. GUILTY AS CHARGED.
DUDE, HOW COME YOU'RE A **CLOWN**?
LOOK, I'M NOT PROUD OF IT...
...BUT A MAN'S GOT TO PUT **FOOD** ON THE TABLE, AMIGO! A MAN'S GOT TO PAY THE **RENT**!
RENT?
BUT DON'T YOU LIVE IN YOUR MOTHER'S BASE-MENT?
I MEANT RENT IN THE META-PHORICAL SENSE, KID. HAVE A GIRAFFE.
Peirce

GAD, THIS INFERNAL COSTUME IS HOT!
COULDN'T YOU HAVE TAKEN A JOB WHERE YOU DIDN'T HAVE TO WEAR A COSTUME?
BALLOON FUN with Loons
COULDN'T YOU HAVE WORKED AT A FOOD BOOTH OR SOMETHING?
KID, KID! WORKING AT A FOOD BOOTH IS DRUDGERY!
I AM AN ARTISTE! I REQUIRE A JOB WHICH ALLOWS MY CREATIVE TALENTS TO BURST FORTH IN FULL FLOWER!
HEY, CLOWN. THIS FLAMINGO YOU SOLD MY KID IS LAME.
THAT, MY GOOD MAN, IS A DOUBLE-CRESTED CORMORANT.

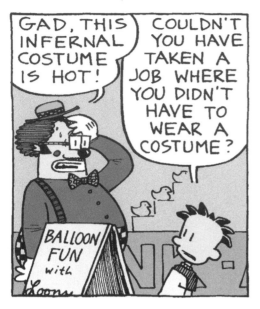

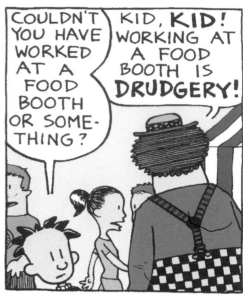

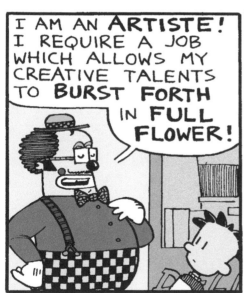

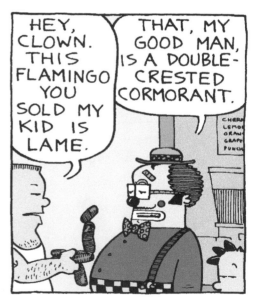

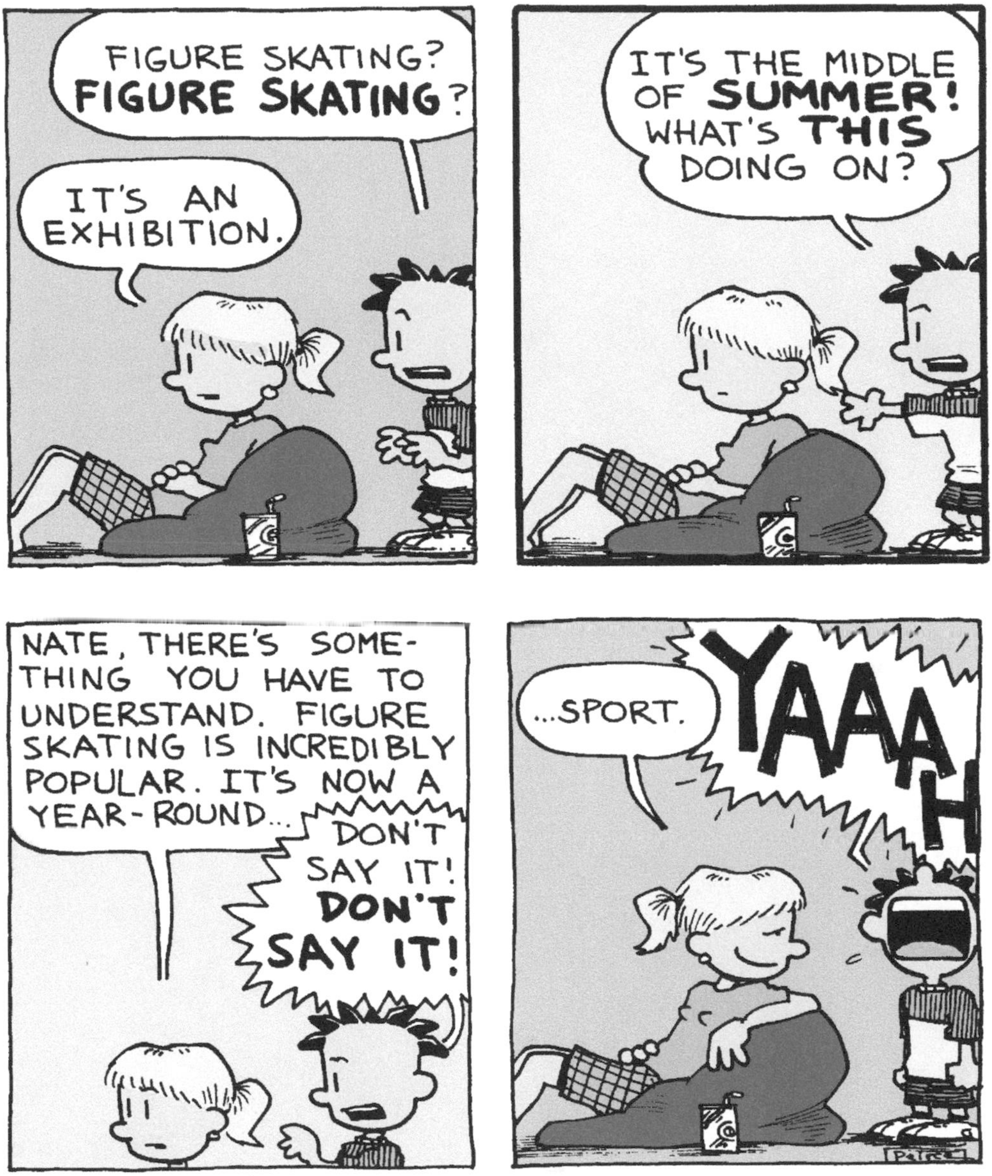
FIGURE SKATING? **FIGURE SKATING**?
IT'S AN EXHIBITION.
IT'S THE MIDDLE OF **SUMMER!** WHAT'S **THIS** DOING ON?
NATE, THERE'S SOME-THING YOU HAVE TO UNDERSTAND. FIGURE SKATING IS INCREDIBLY POPULAR. IT'S NOW A YEAR-ROUND...
DON'T SAY IT! **DON'T SAY IT!**
...SPORT.
YAAAH

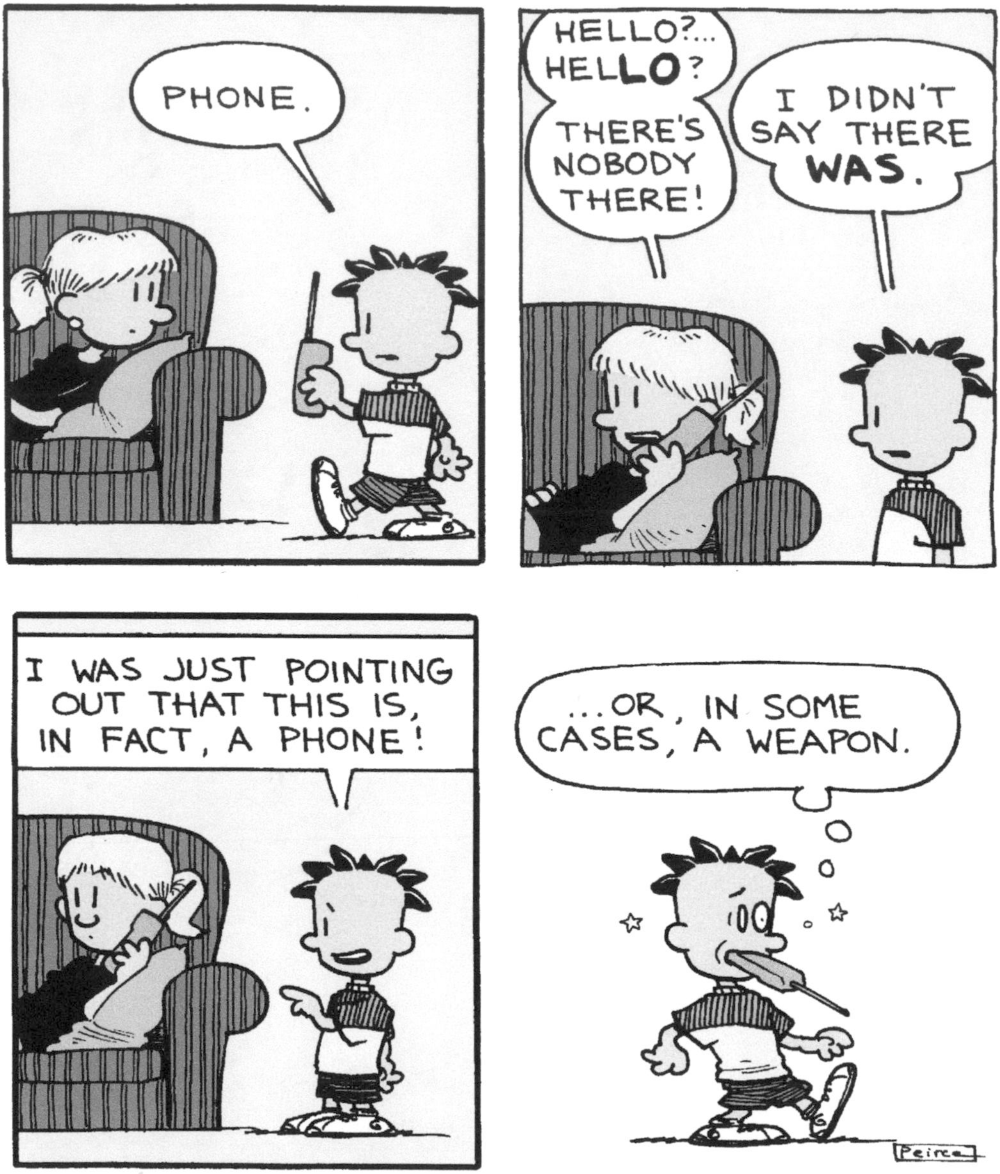
PHONE.
HELLO?... HELLO?
THERE'S NOBODY THERE!
I DIDN'T SAY THERE WAS.
I WAS JUST POINTING OUT THAT THIS IS, IN FACT, A PHONE!
...OR, IN SOME CASES, A WEAPON.
Peirce

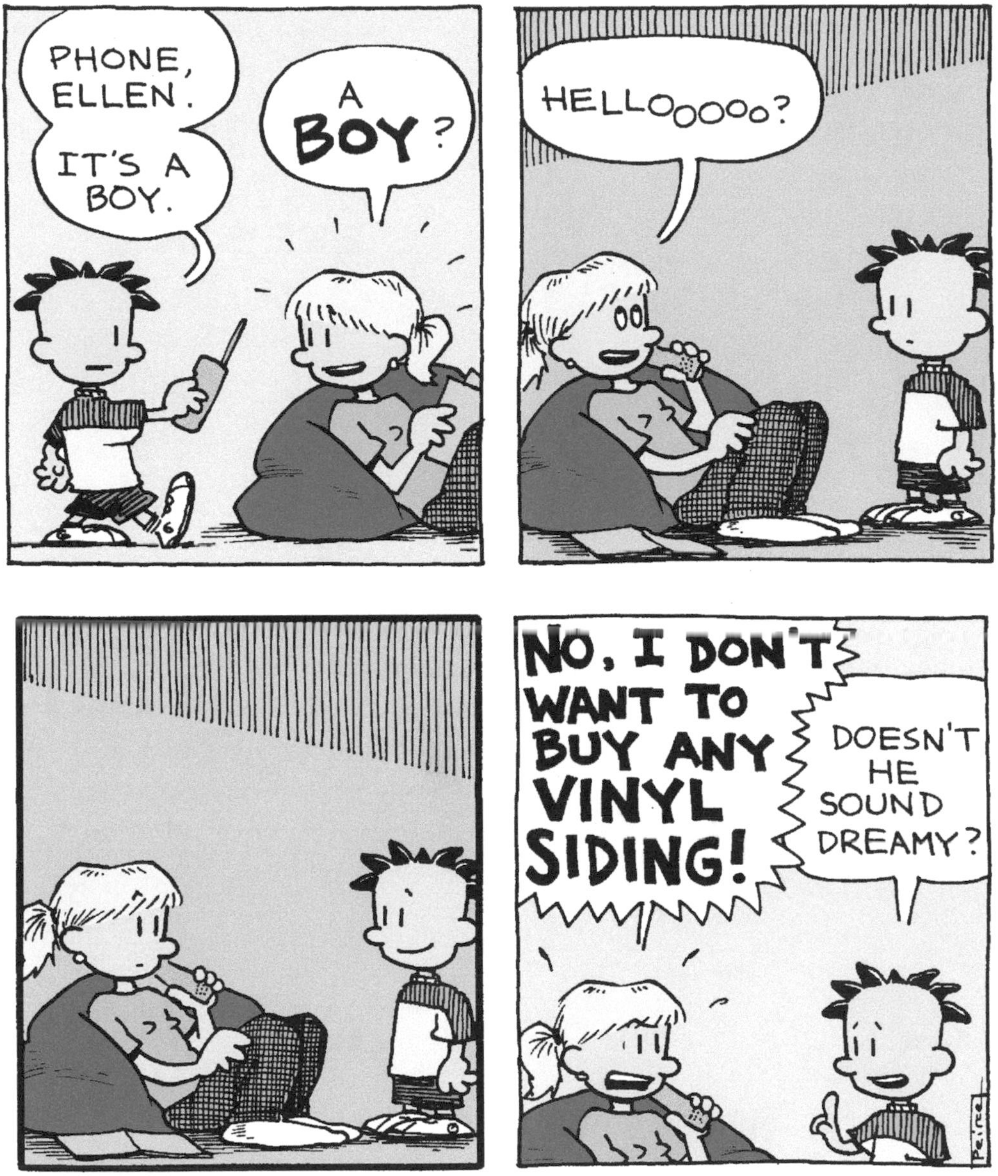
PHONE, ELLEN.
IT'S A BOY.
A BOY?
HELLOOOOO?
NO, I DON'T WANT TO BUY ANY VINYL SIDING!
DOESN'T HE SOUND DREAMY?
Peirce

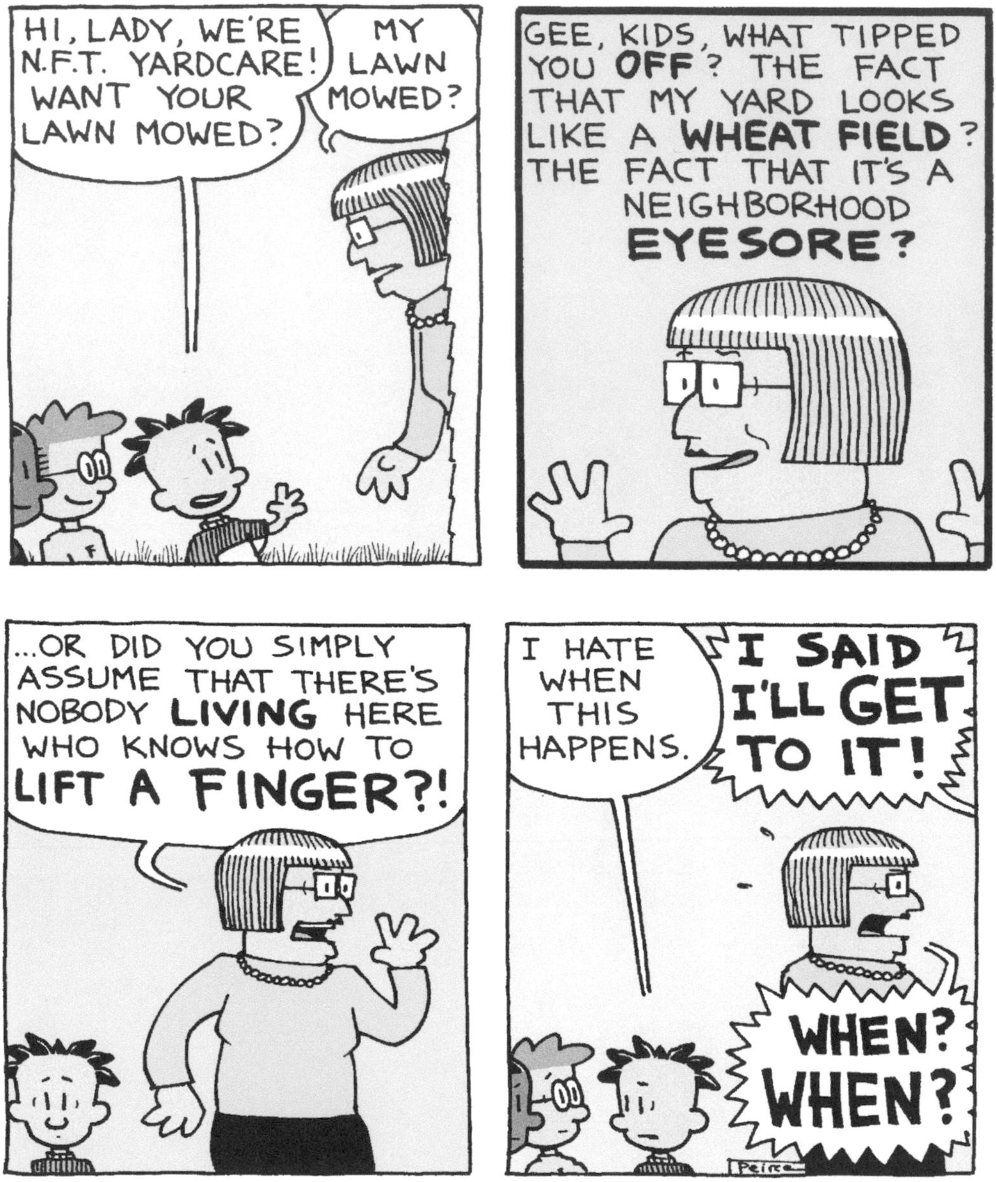
HI, LADY, WE'RE N.F.T. YARDCARE! WANT YOUR LAWN MOWED?
MY LAWN MOWED?
GEE, KIDS, WHAT TIPPED YOU **OFF**? THE FACT THAT MY YARD LOOKS LIKE A **WHEAT FIELD**? THE FACT THAT IT'S A NEIGHBORHOOD **EYESORE**?
...OR DID YOU SIMPLY ASSUME THAT THERE'S NOBODY **LIVING** HERE WHO KNOWS HOW TO **LIFT A FINGER?!**
I HATE WHEN THIS HAPPENS.
I SAID I'LL GET TO IT!
WHEN? WHEN?
Peirce

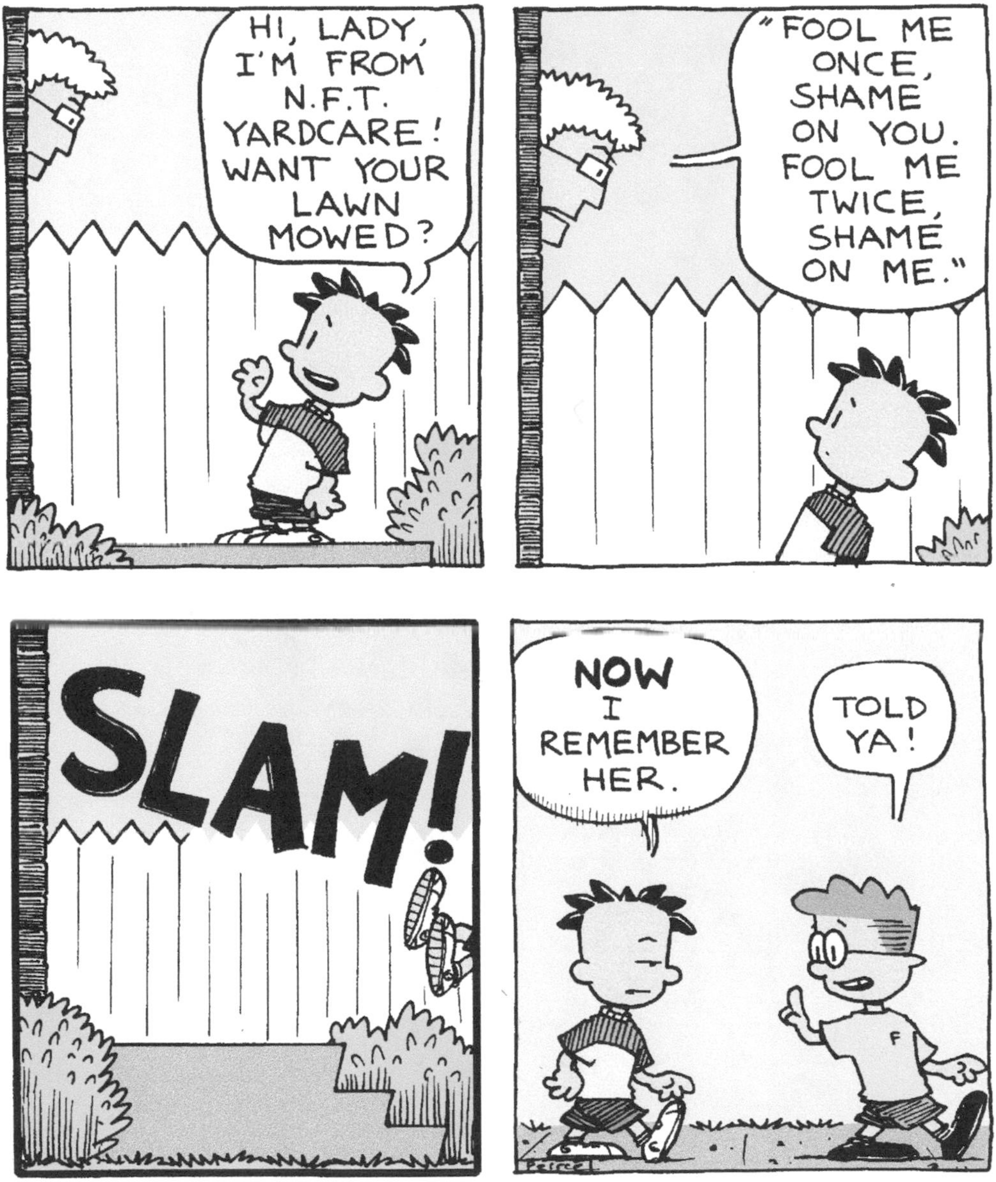
HI, LADY, I'M FROM N.F.T. YARDCARE! WANT YOUR LAWN MOWED?
"FOOL ME ONCE, SHAME ON YOU. FOOL ME TWICE, SHAME ON ME."
SLAM!
NOW I REMEMBER HER.
TOLD YA!

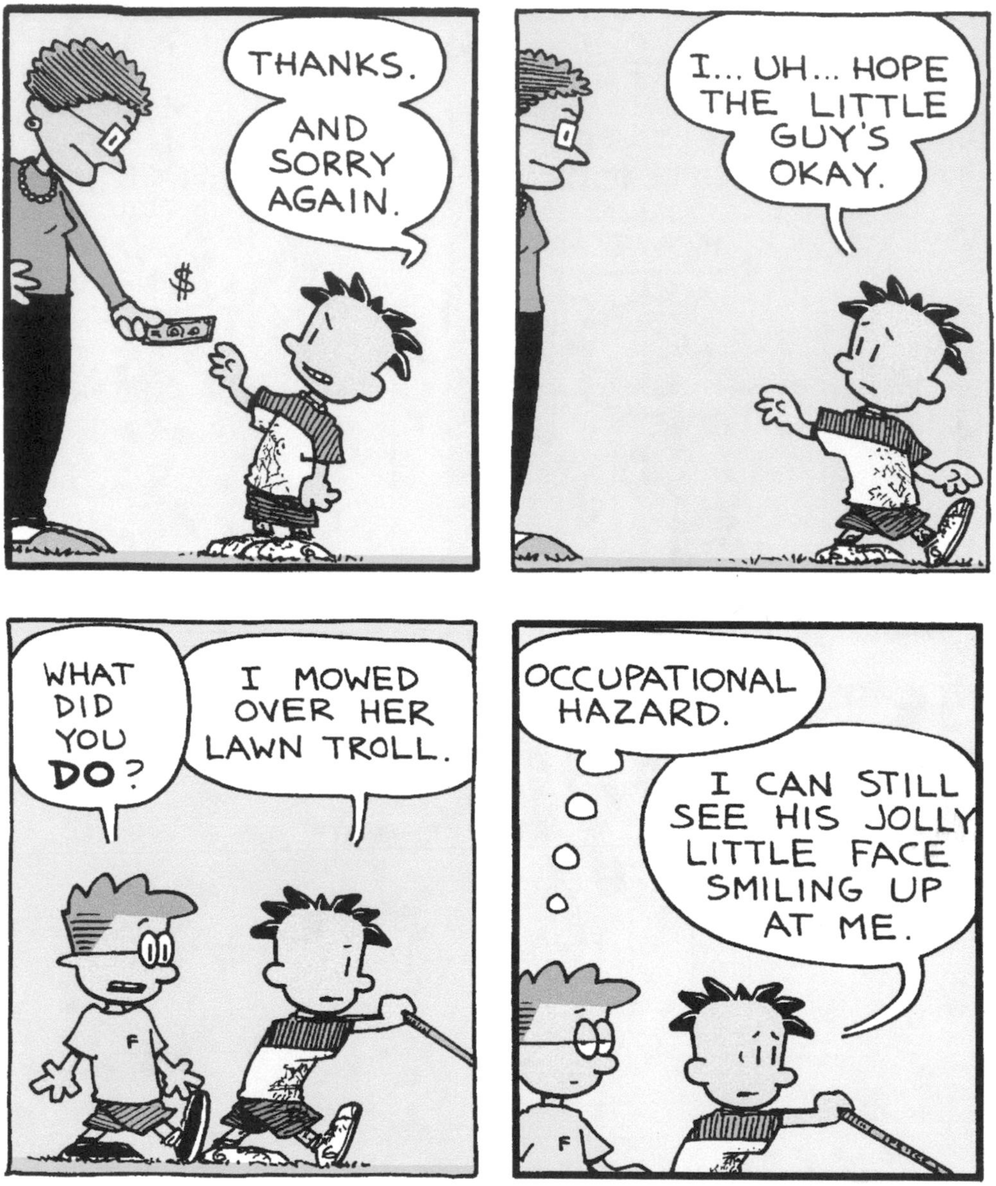
THANKS.
AND SORRY AGAIN.
$
I... UH... HOPE THE LITTLE GUY'S OKAY.
WHAT DID YOU **DO**?
I MOWED OVER HER LAWN TROLL.
OCCUPATIONAL HAZARD.
I CAN STILL SEE HIS JOLLY LITTLE FACE SMILING UP AT ME.

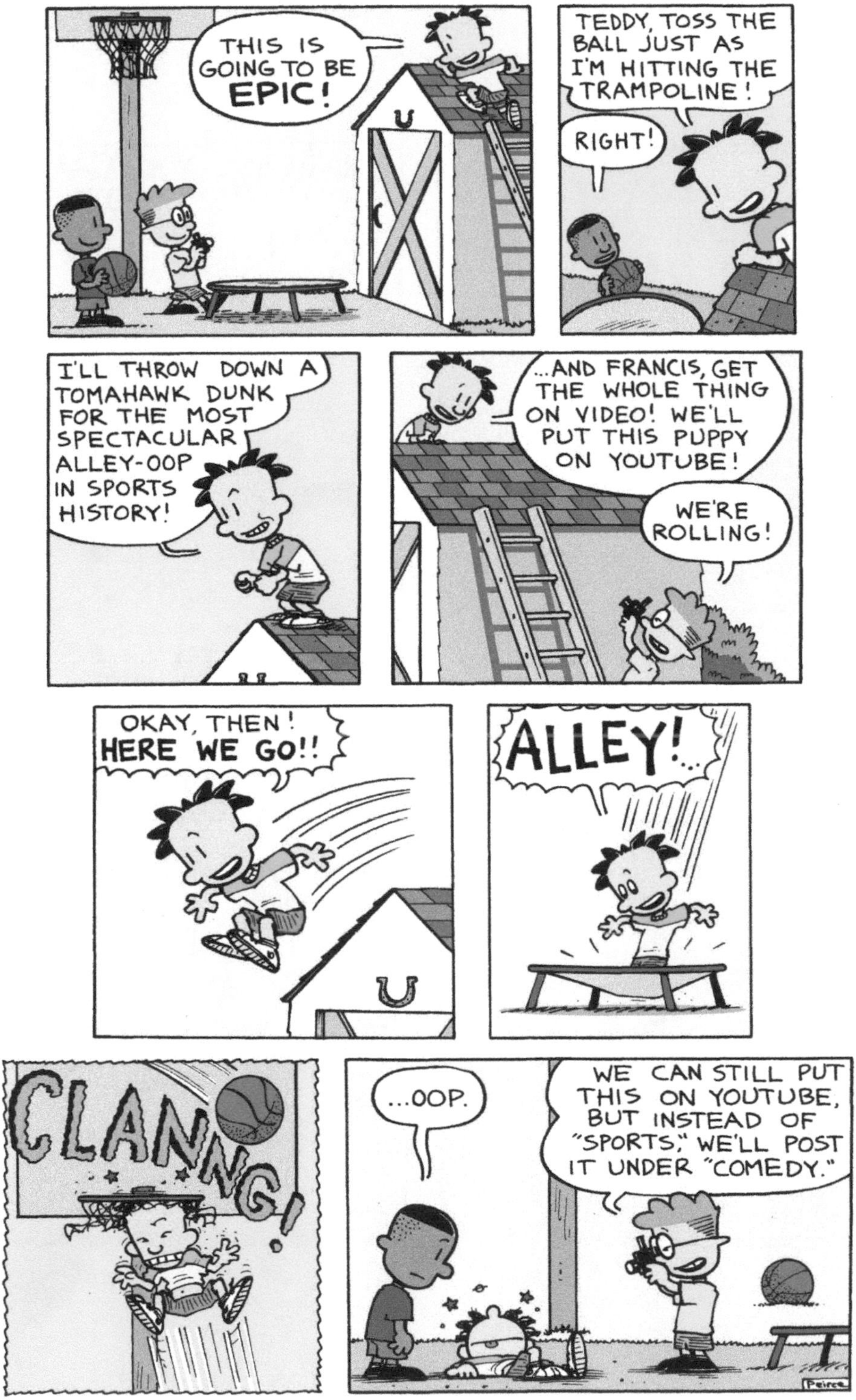
THIS IS GOING TO BE EPIC!
TEDDY, TOSS THE BALL JUST AS I'M HITTING THE TRAMPOLINE!
RIGHT!
I'LL THROW DOWN A TOMAHAWK DUNK FOR THE MOST SPECTACULAR ALLEY-OOP IN SPORTS HISTORY!
...AND FRANCIS, GET THE WHOLE THING ON VIDEO! WE'LL PUT THIS PUPPY ON YOUTUBE!
WE'RE ROLLING!
OKAY, THEN! HERE WE GO!!
ALLEY!...
CLANNG!
...OOP.
WE CAN STILL PUT THIS ON YOUTUBE, BUT INSTEAD OF "SPORTS," WE'LL POST IT UNDER "COMEDY."
Peirce

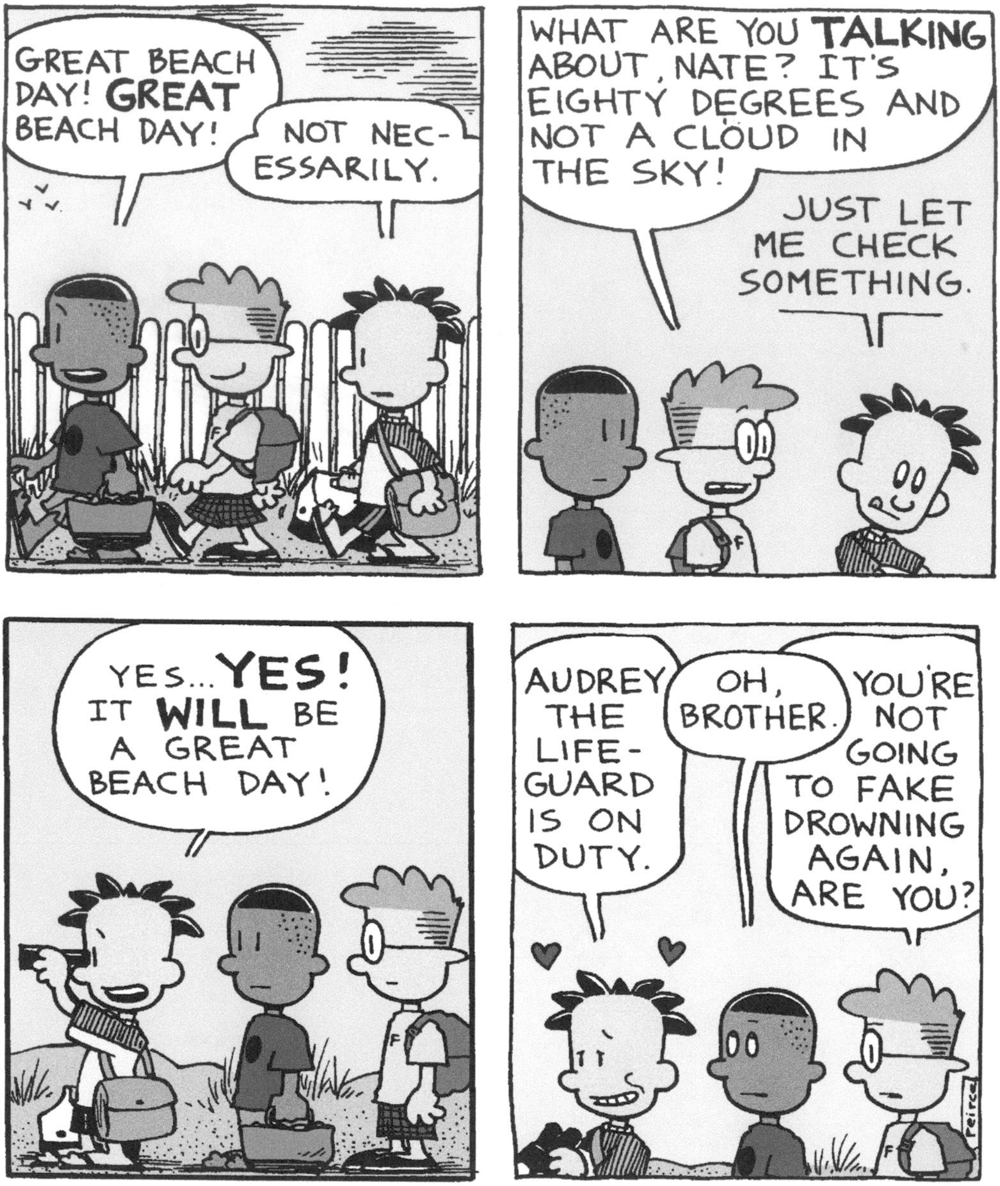
GREAT BEACH DAY! **GREAT** BEACH DAY!
NOT NEC- ESSARILY.
WHAT ARE YOU **TALKING** ABOUT, NATE? IT'S EIGHTY DEGREES AND NOT A CLOUD IN THE SKY!
JUST LET ME CHECK SOMETHING.
YES... **YES!** IT **WILL** BE A GREAT BEACH DAY!
AUDREY THE LIFE- GUARD IS ON DUTY.
OH, BROTHER.
YOU'RE NOT GOING TO FAKE DROWNING AGAIN, ARE YOU?
Peirce

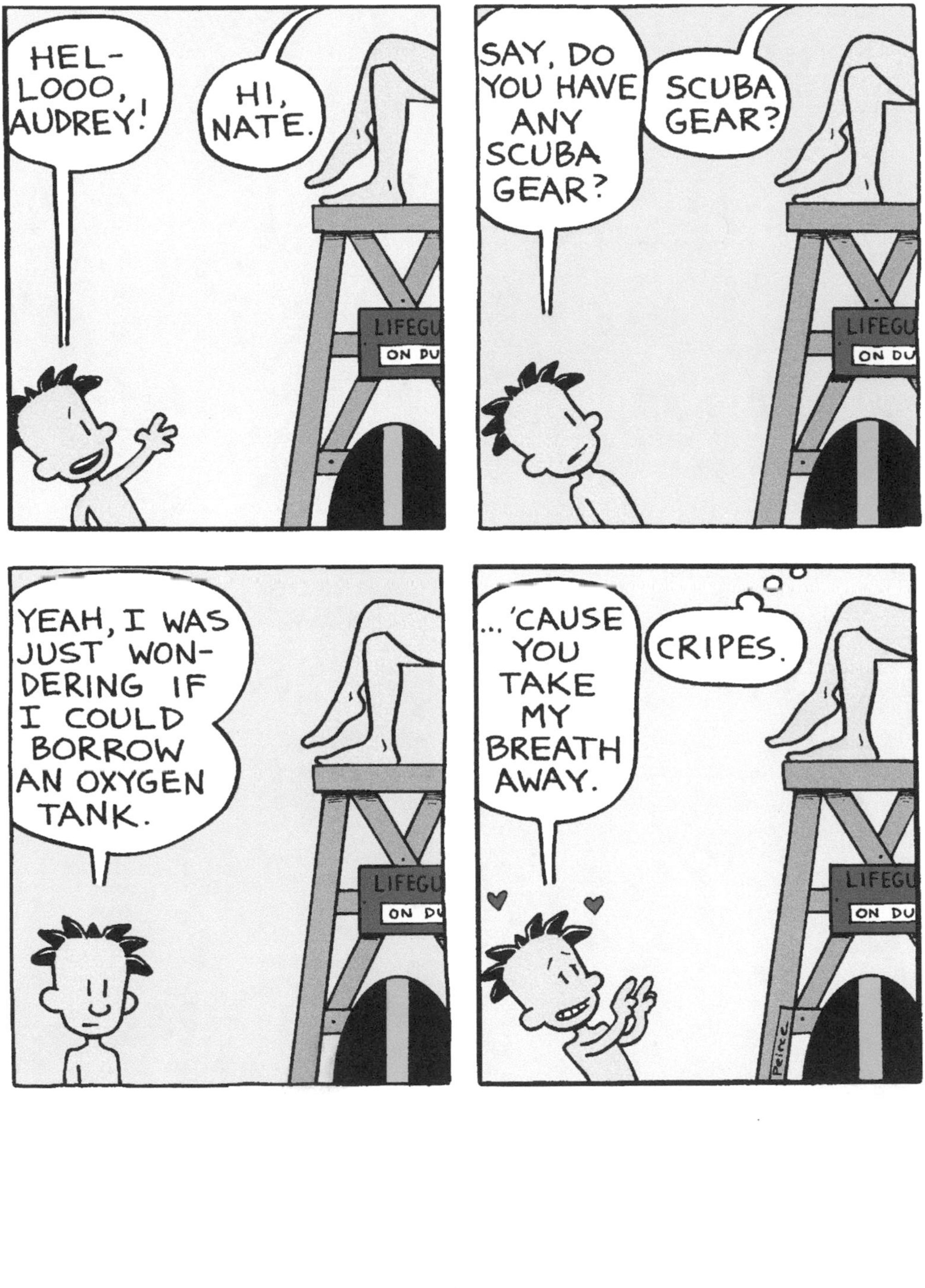
HEL-LOOO, AUDREY!
HI, NATE.
SAY, DO YOU HAVE ANY SCUBA GEAR?
SCUBA GEAR?
YEAH, I WAS JUST WON-DERING IF I COULD BORROW AN OXYGEN TANK.
...'CAUSE YOU TAKE MY BREATH AWAY.
CRIPES.

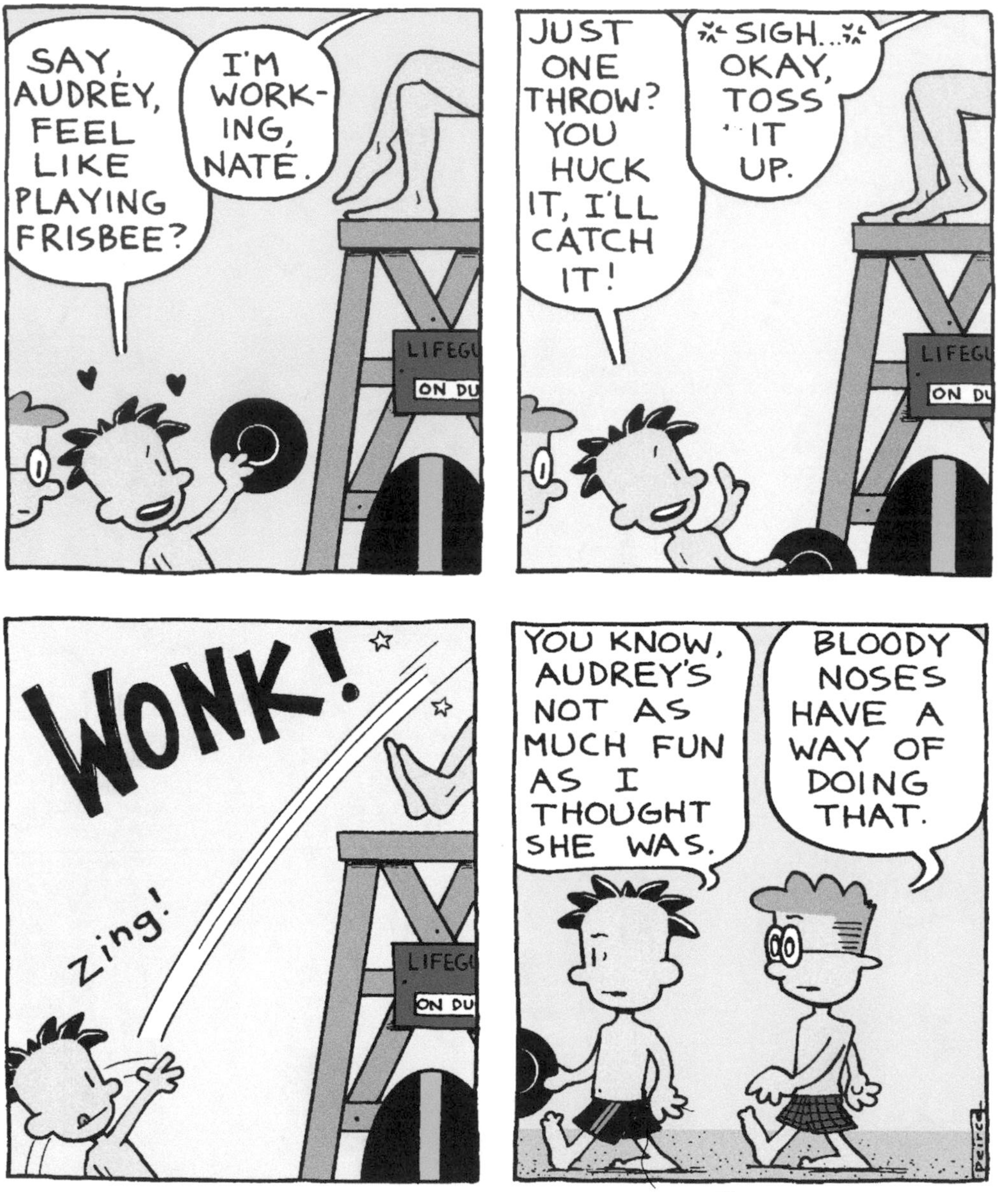

SAY, AUDREY, FEEL LIKE PLAYING FRISBEE?
I'M WORKING, NATE.
LIFEGU
ON DU
JUST ONE THROW? YOU HUCK IT, I'LL CATCH IT!
SIGH... OKAY, TOSS IT UP.
WONK!
zing!
YOU KNOW, AUDREY'S NOT AS MUCH FUN AS I THOUGHT SHE WAS.
BLOODY NOSES HAVE A WAY OF DOING THAT.

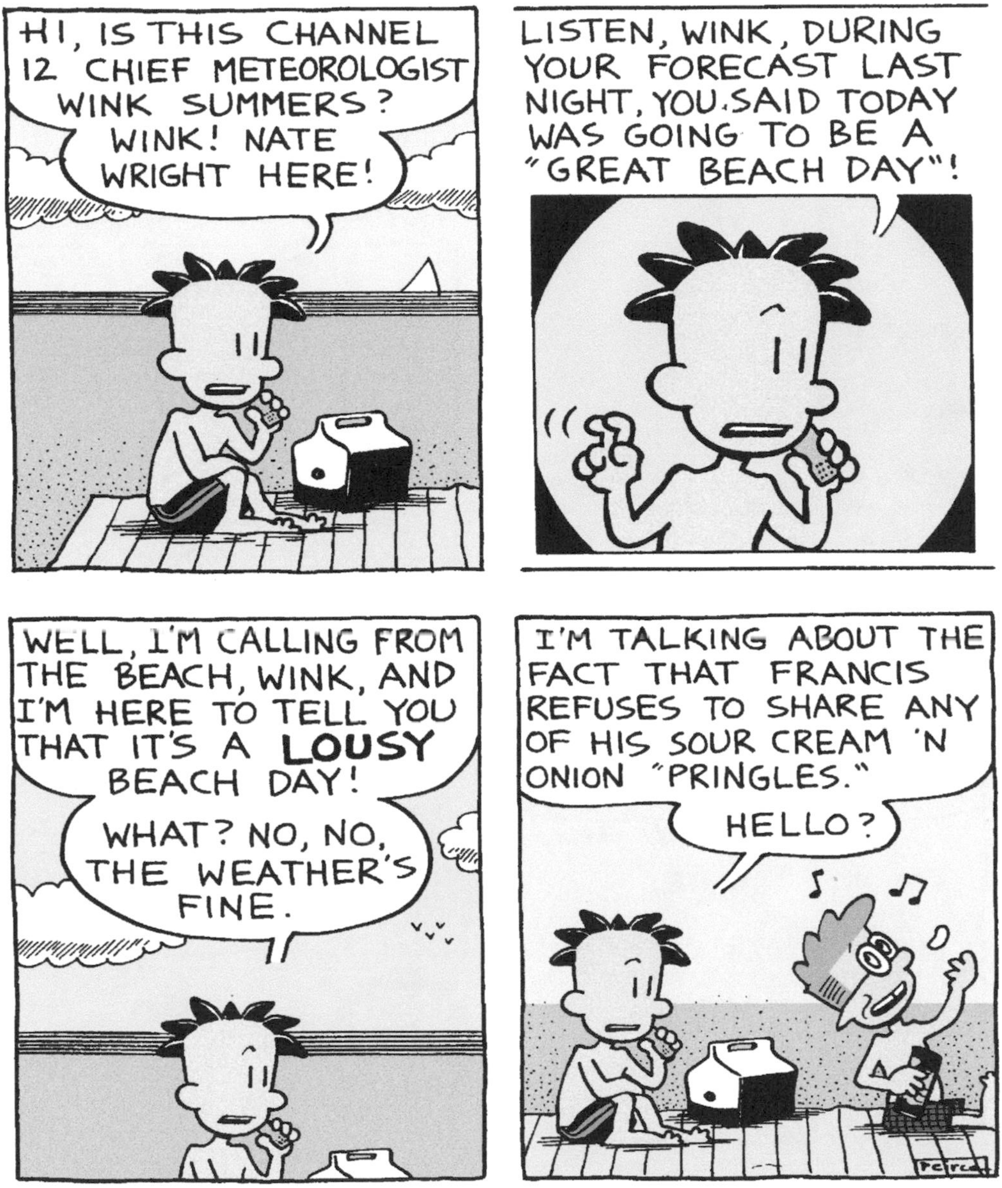
HI, IS THIS CHANNEL 12 CHIEF METEOROLOGIST WINK SUMMERS?
WINK! NATE WRIGHT HERE!
LISTEN, WINK, DURING YOUR FORECAST LAST NIGHT, YOU SAID TODAY WAS GOING TO BE A "GREAT BEACH DAY"!
WELL, I'M CALLING FROM THE BEACH, WINK, AND I'M HERE TO TELL YOU THAT IT'S A **LOUSY** BEACH DAY!
WHAT? NO, NO, THE WEATHER'S FINE.
I'M TALKING ABOUT THE FACT THAT FRANCIS REFUSES TO SHARE ANY OF HIS SOUR CREAM 'N ONION "PRINGLES."
HELLO?

LISTEN, WINK, AS LONG AS I'VE GOT YOU ON THE PHONE, LET ME LAY THIS SUGGESTION ON YOU:

DURING YOUR WEATHER FORECASTS, HOW ABOUT THROWING IN A **JOKE** NOW AND THEN? YOU KNOW, DROP A LITTLE **HUMOR** IN THERE!

I MEAN, RIGHT NOW THE ONLY THING FUNNY ABOUT THE NEWS IS THAT LAME **TOUPEE** OF YOURS!

"THAT'S MY REAL HAIR!" **GOOD** ONE, WINK!

THEY PROBABLY DON'T TELL YOU ABOUT STUFF LIKE THIS IN METEOROLOGY SCHOOL.

Peirce

TA-DAAH!
WHAT IS THAT?
IT'S A SELF-PORTRAIT, OBVIOUSLY!
IT'S A SAND SCULPTURE OF YOURS TRULY! SO NOW THERE ARE TWO OF ME!
peirce
ISN'T ONE OF YOU ENOUGH?
AMEN, BROTHER.
HEY, GUYS, I'M BESIDE MYSELF!
CHUCKLE

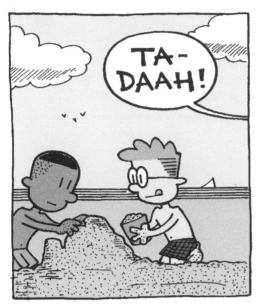

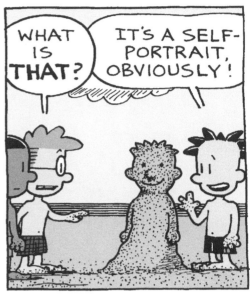

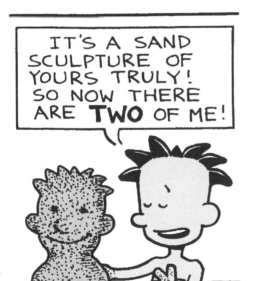

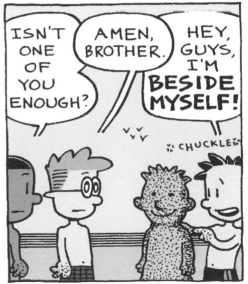

GOOD GRAVY! ARE YOU EATING **AGAIN?** THAT'S YOUR THIRD SNACK THIS AFTERNOON!
EASE **UP**, NATE! IT'S NOT HEALTHY TO STUFF FOOD INTO YOUR MOUTH WHENEVER YOU'VE GOT NOTHING ELSE TO DO!
FATHERLY CONCERN, DAD? OR... **JEALOUSY?**
PAT PAT
PARRA
JEALOUSY.
peirce

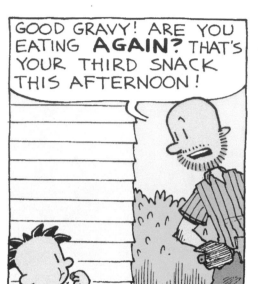

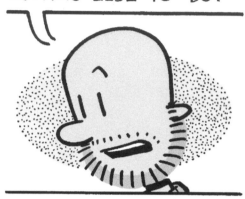

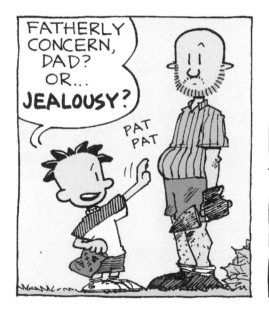

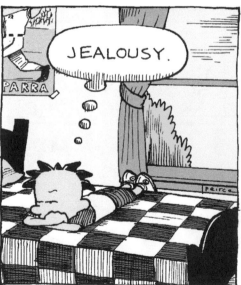

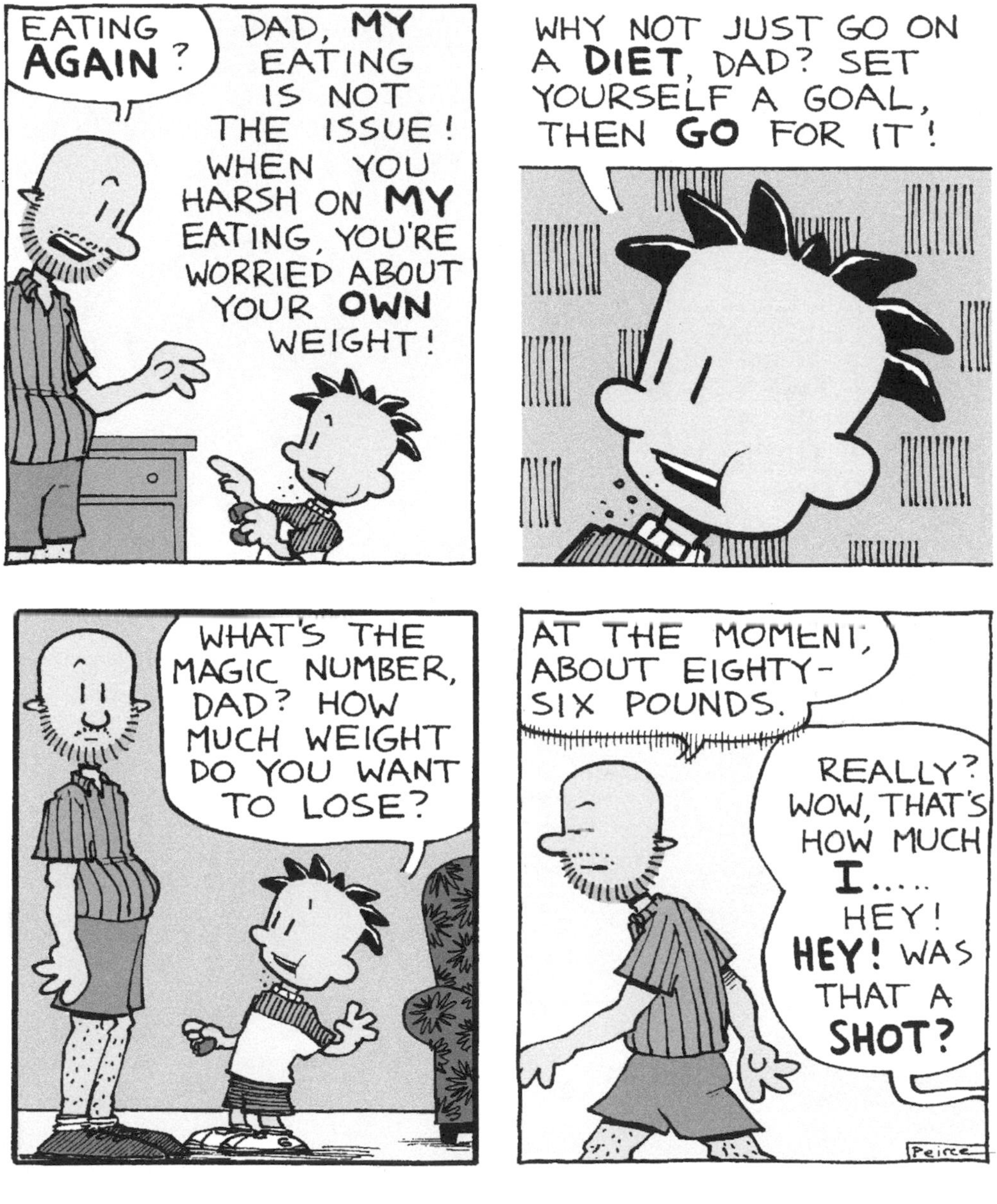
EATING AGAIN?
DAD, MY EATING IS NOT THE ISSUE! WHEN YOU HARSH ON MY EATING, YOU'RE WORRIED ABOUT YOUR OWN WEIGHT!
WHY NOT JUST GO ON A DIET, DAD? SET YOURSELF A GOAL, THEN GO FOR IT!
WHAT'S THE MAGIC NUMBER, DAD? HOW MUCH WEIGHT DO YOU WANT TO LOSE?
AT THE MOMENT, ABOUT EIGHTY-SIX POUNDS.
REALLY? WOW, THAT'S HOW MUCH I..... HEY! HEY! WAS THAT A SHOT?
Peirce

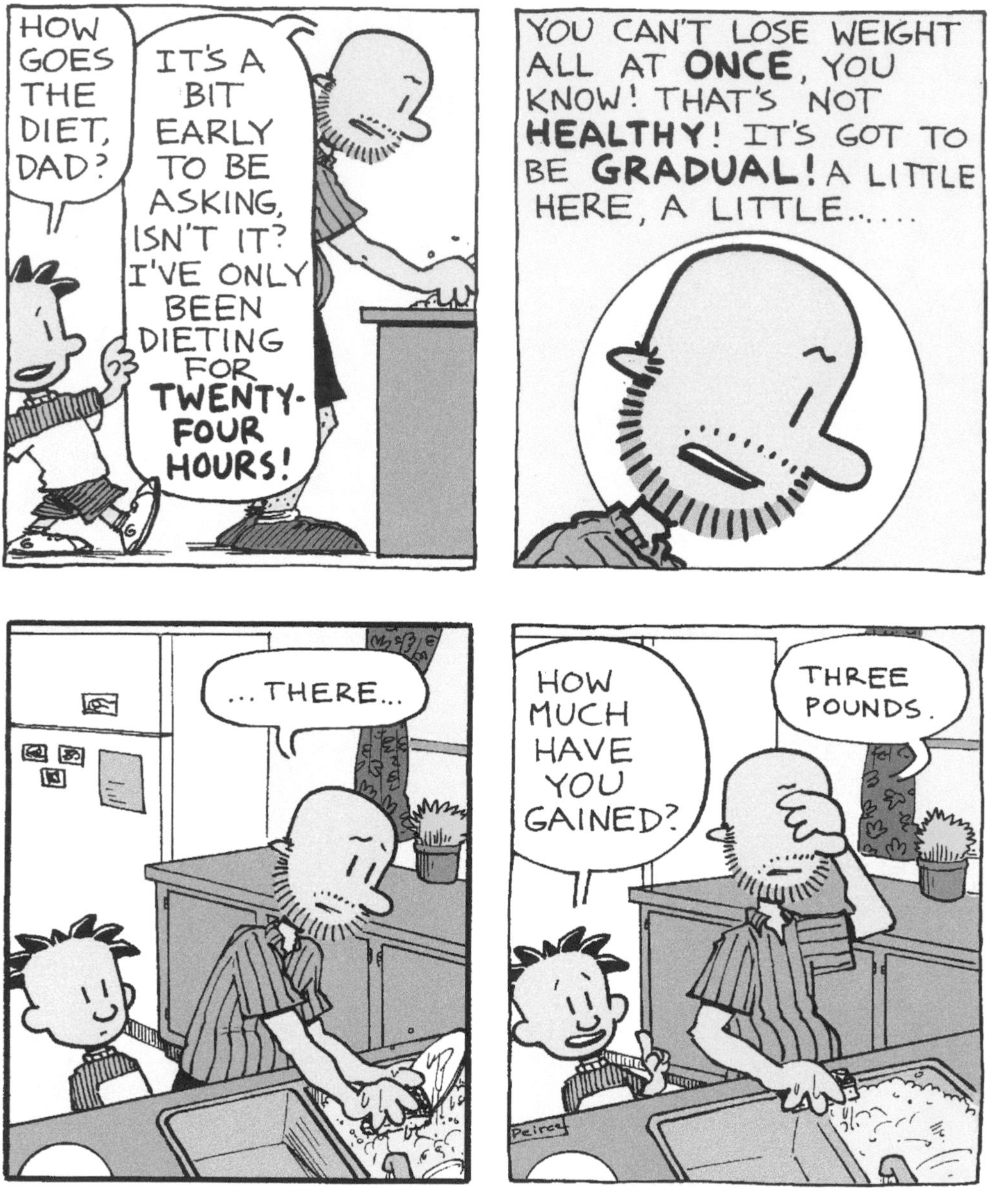
HOW GOES THE DIET, DAD?
IT'S A BIT EARLY TO BE ASKING, ISN'T IT? I'VE ONLY BEEN DIETING FOR **TWENTY-FOUR HOURS**!
YOU CAN'T LOSE WEIGHT ALL AT **ONCE**, YOU KNOW! THAT'S NOT **HEALTHY**! IT'S GOT TO BE **GRADUAL!** A LITTLE HERE, A LITTLE......
...THERE...
HOW MUCH HAVE YOU GAINED?
THREE POUNDS.
Peirce

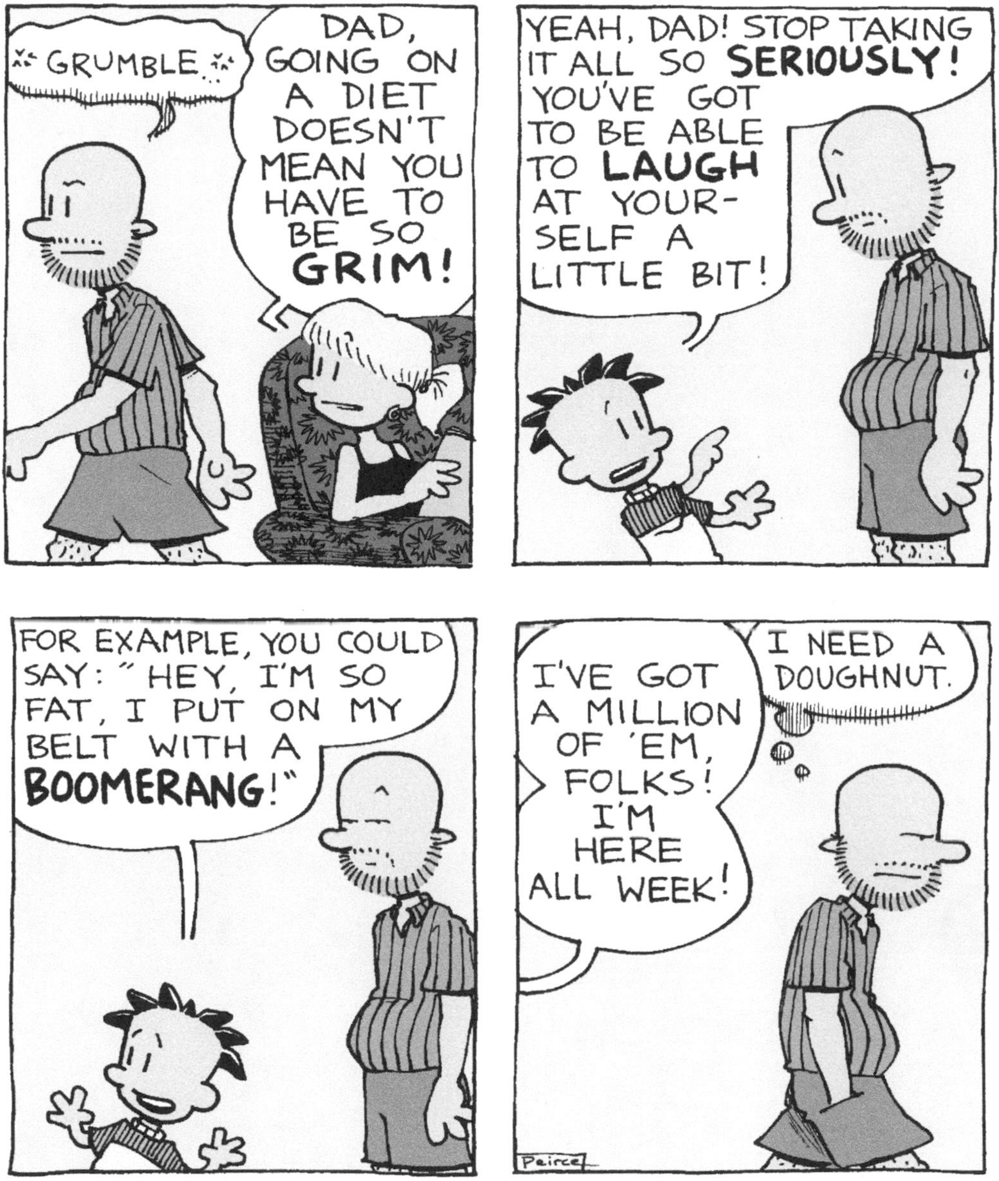
GRUMBLE
DAD, GOING ON A DIET DOESN'T MEAN YOU HAVE TO BE SO **GRIM**!
YEAH, DAD! STOP TAKING IT ALL SO **SERIOUSLY**! YOU'VE GOT TO BE ABLE TO **LAUGH** AT YOURSELF A LITTLE BIT!
FOR EXAMPLE, YOU COULD SAY: "HEY, I'M SO FAT, I PUT ON MY BELT WITH A **BOOMERANG**!"
I'VE GOT A MILLION OF 'EM, FOLKS! I'M HERE ALL WEEK!
I NEED A DOUGHNUT.
Peirce

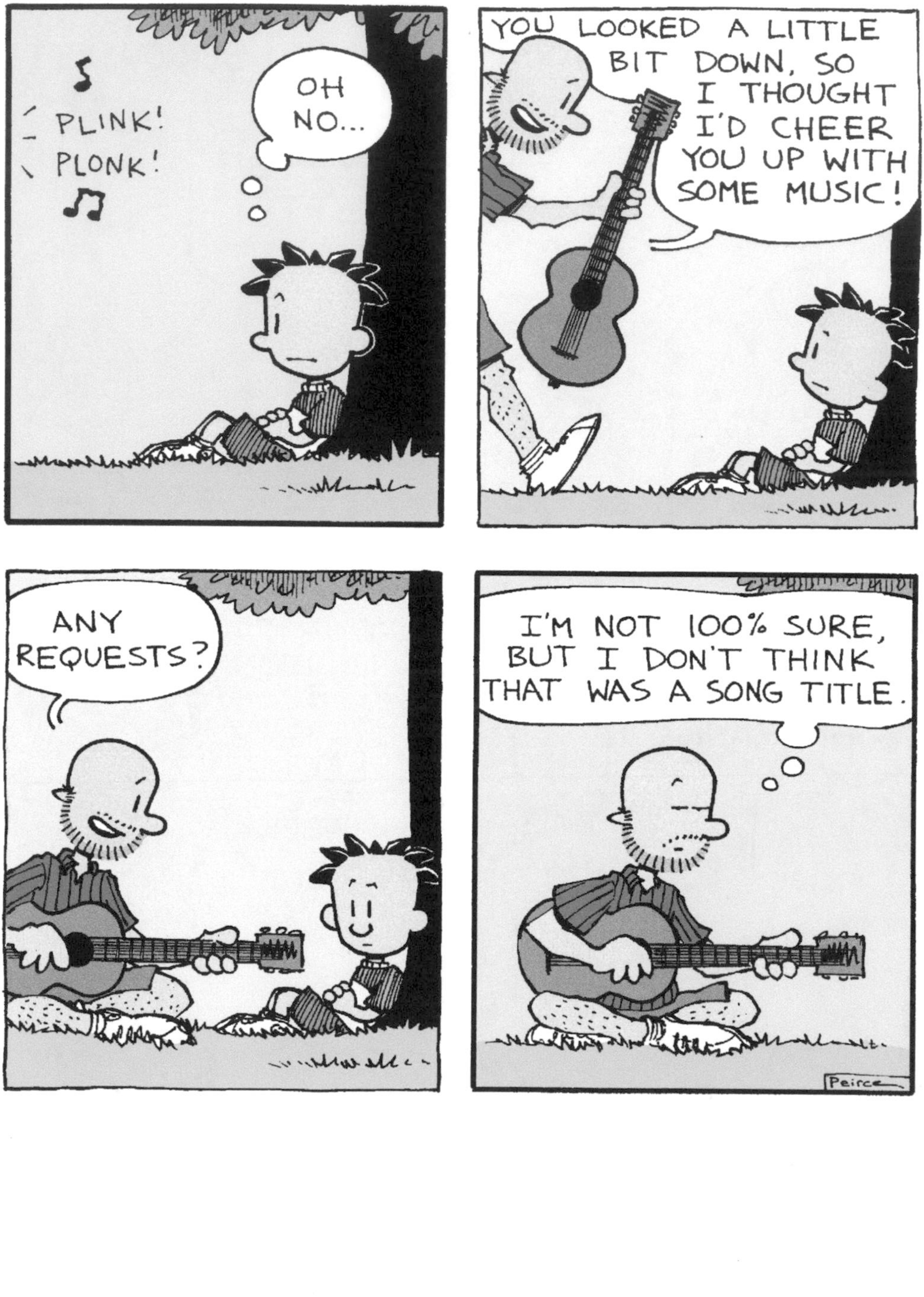
PLINK!
PLONK!
OH NO...
YOU LOOKED A LITTLE BIT DOWN, SO I THOUGHT I'D CHEER YOU UP WITH SOME MUSIC!
ANY REQUESTS?
I'M NOT 100% SURE, BUT I DON'T THINK THAT WAS A SONG TITLE.
Peirce

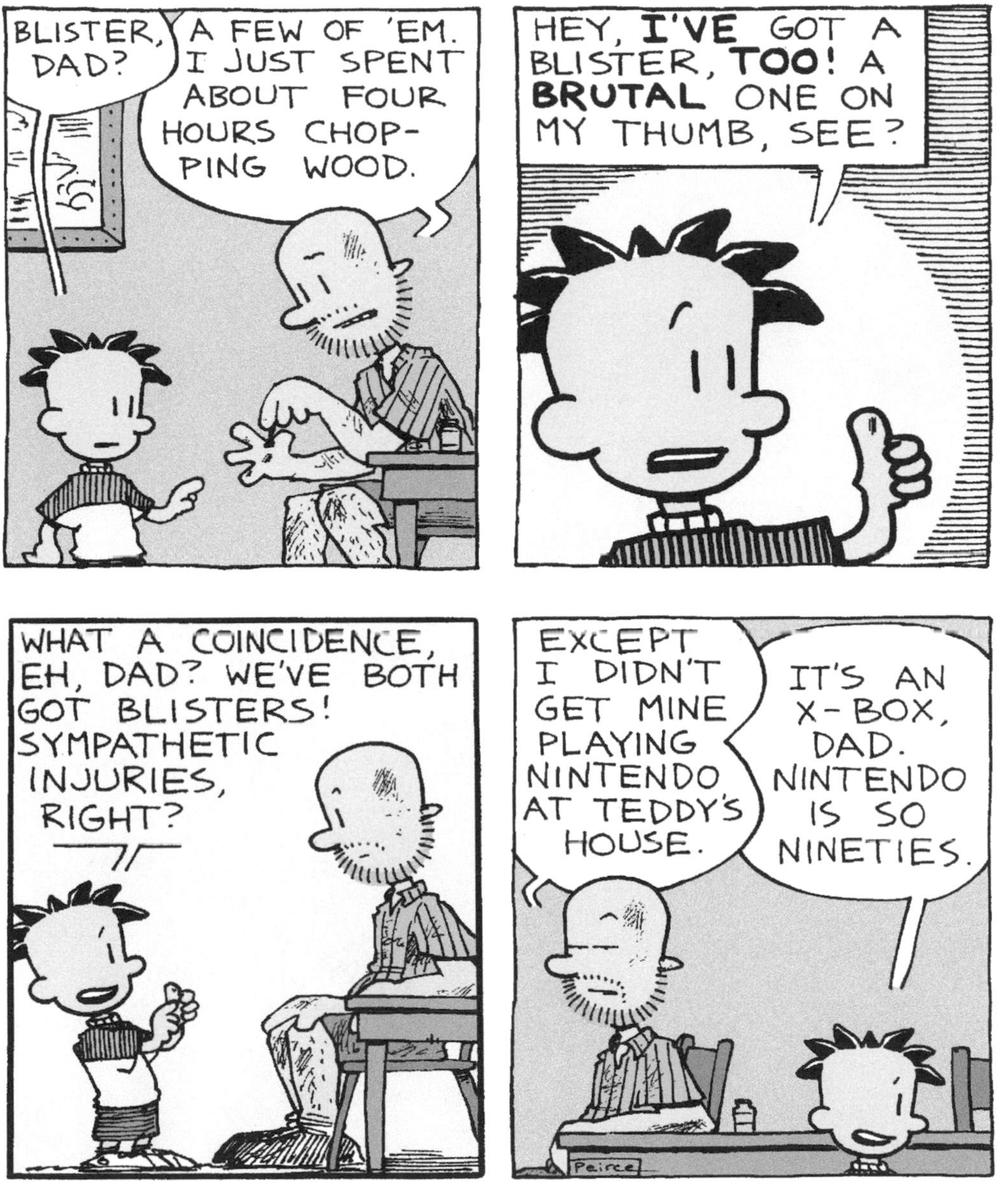
BLISTER, DAD?
A FEW OF 'EM. I JUST SPENT ABOUT FOUR HOURS CHOP-PING WOOD.
HEY, **I'VE** GOT A BLISTER, **TOO!** A **BRUTAL** ONE ON MY THUMB, SEE?
WHAT A COINCIDENCE, EH, DAD? WE'VE BOTH GOT BLISTERS! SYMPATHETIC INJURIES, RIGHT?
EXCEPT I DIDN'T GET MINE PLAYING NINTENDO AT TEDDY'S HOUSE.
IT'S AN X-BOX, DAD. NINTENDO IS SO NINETIES.
Peirce

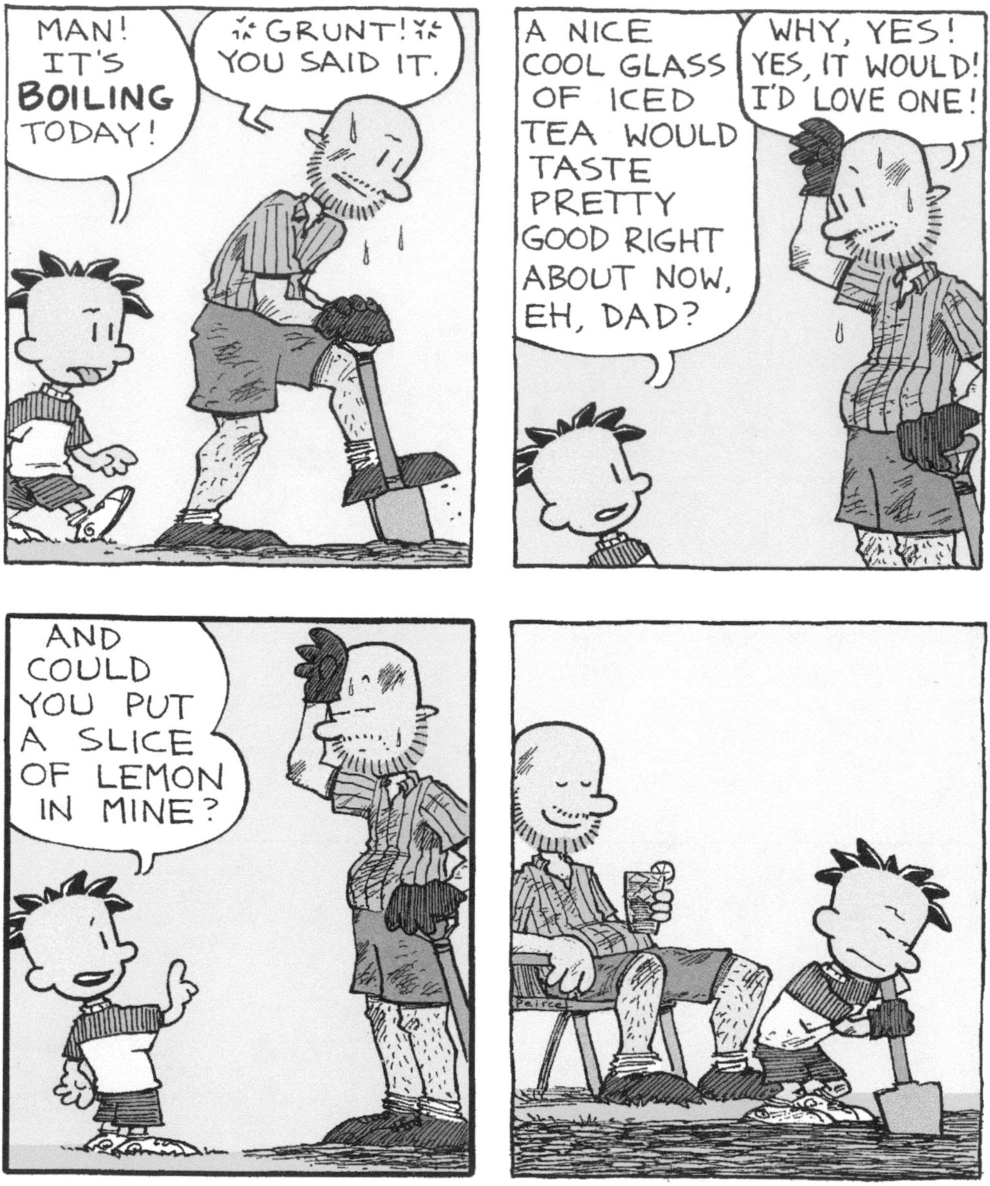
MAN! IT'S **BOILING** TODAY!
GRUNT! YOU SAID IT.
A NICE COOL GLASS OF ICED TEA WOULD TASTE PRETTY GOOD RIGHT ABOUT NOW, EH, DAD?
WHY, YES! YES, IT WOULD! I'D LOVE ONE!
AND COULD YOU PUT A SLICE OF LEMON IN MINE?
Peirce

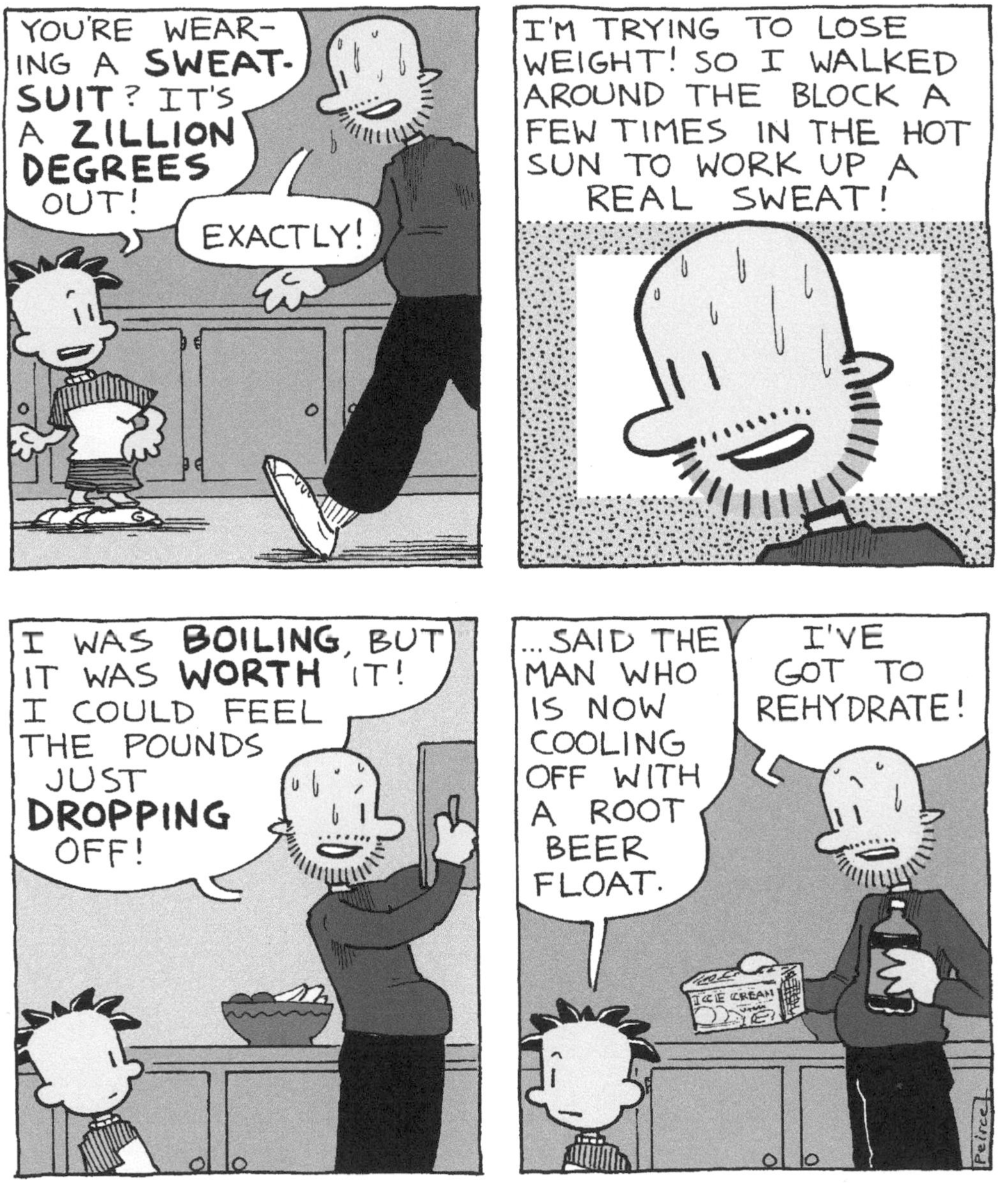
YOU'RE WEARING A **SWEAT-SUIT**? IT'S A **ZILLION DEGREES** OUT!
EXACTLY!
I'M TRYING TO LOSE WEIGHT! SO I WALKED AROUND THE BLOCK A FEW TIMES IN THE HOT SUN TO WORK UP A REAL SWEAT!
I WAS **BOILING**, BUT IT WAS **WORTH** IT! I COULD FEEL THE POUNDS JUST **DROPPING** OFF!
...SAID THE MAN WHO IS NOW COOLING OFF WITH A ROOT BEER FLOAT.
I'VE GOT TO REHYDRATE!
ICE CREAM
Peirce

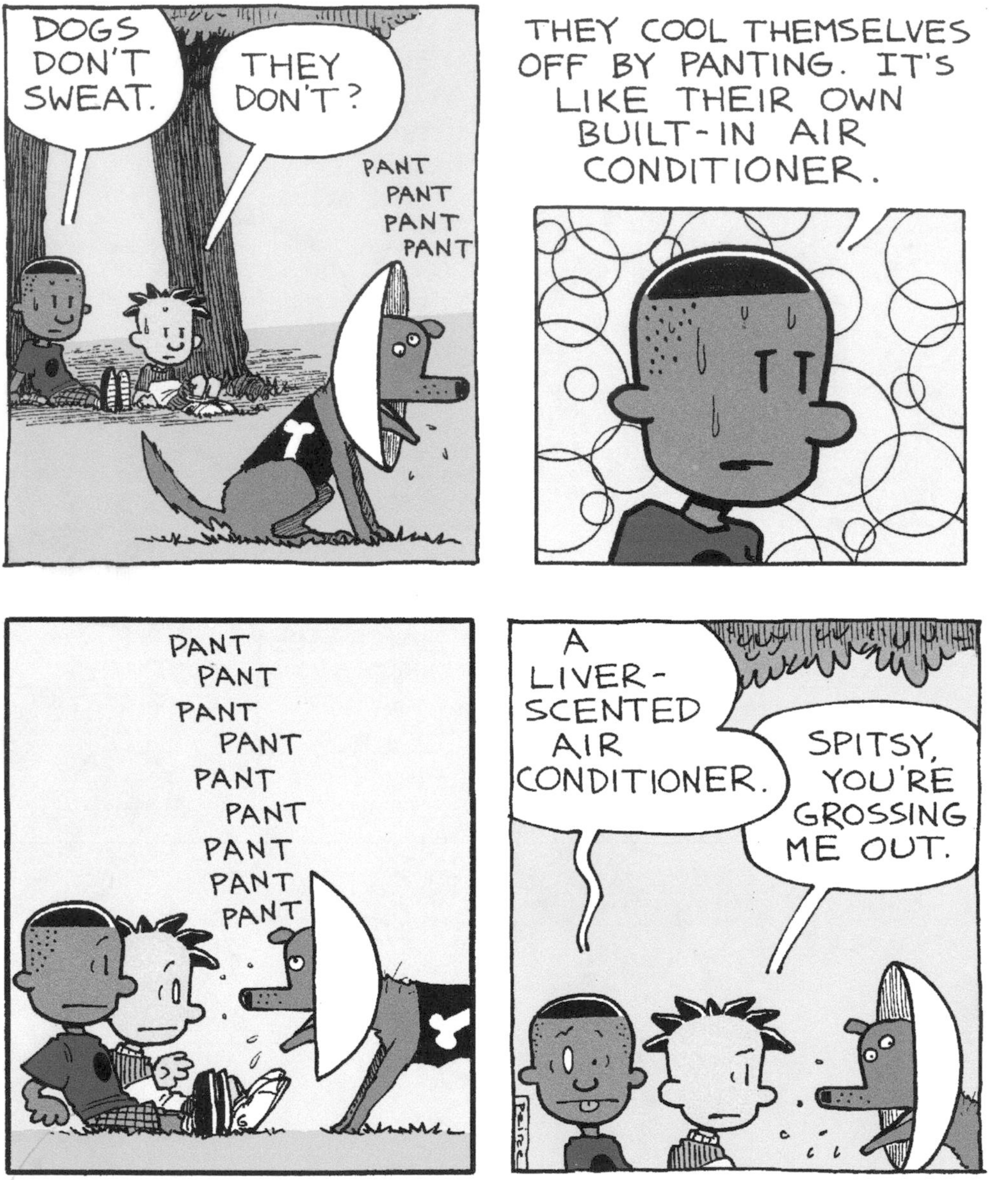
DOGS DON'T SWEAT.
THEY DON'T?
PANT PANT PANT PANT
THEY COOL THEMSELVES OFF BY PANTING. IT'S LIKE THEIR OWN BUILT-IN AIR CONDITIONER.
PANT PANT PANT PANT PANT PANT PANT PANT PANT
A LIVER-SCENTED AIR CONDITIONER.
SPITSY, YOU'RE GROSSING ME OUT.
PEIRCE

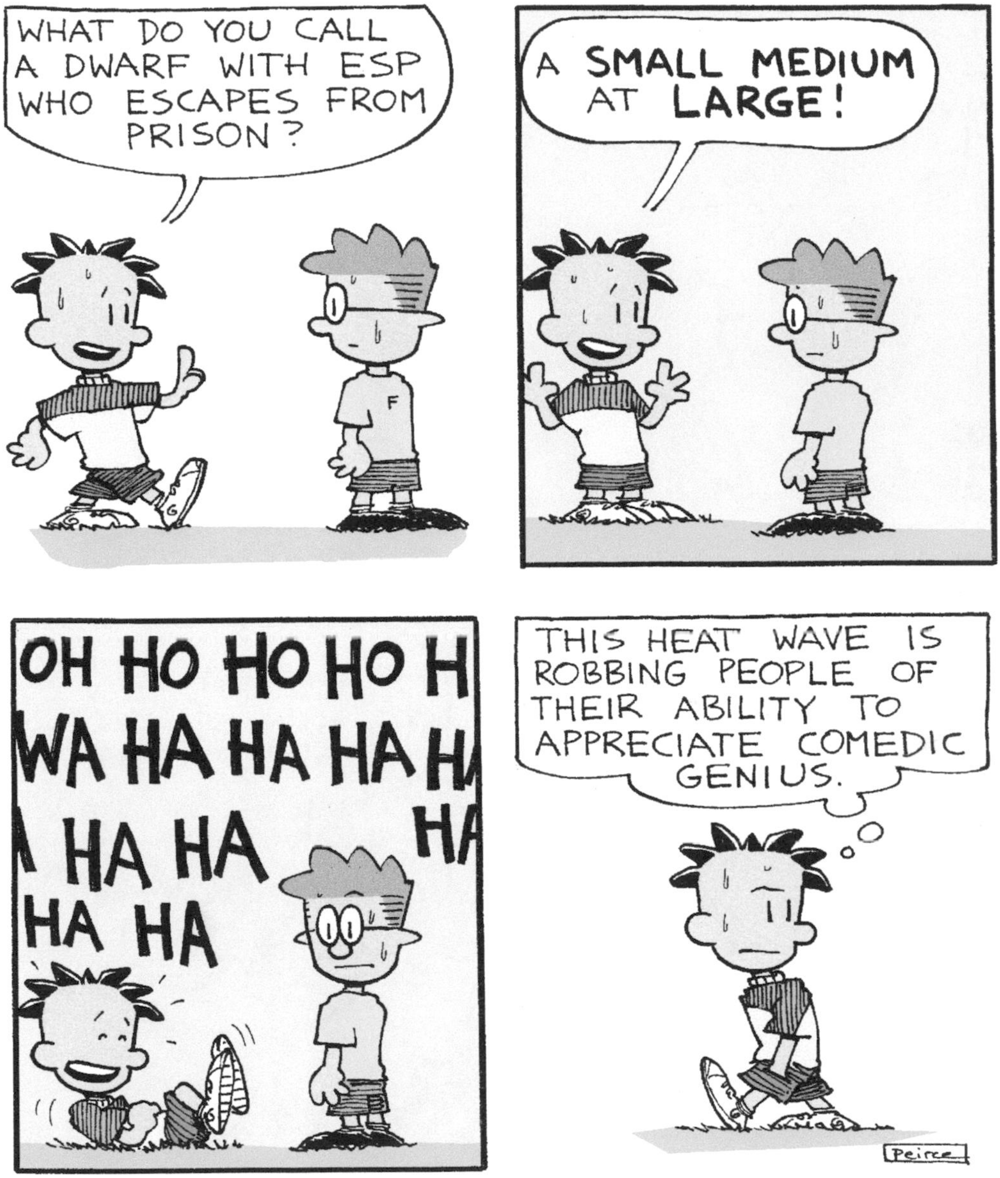
WHAT DO YOU CALL A DWARF WITH ESP WHO ESCAPES FROM PRISON?
A SMALL MEDIUM AT LARGE!
OH HO HO HO H
WA HA HA HA H
HA HA HA
HA HA
HA
THIS HEAT WAVE IS ROBBING PEOPLE OF THEIR ABILITY TO APPRECIATE COMEDIC GENIUS.
Peirce

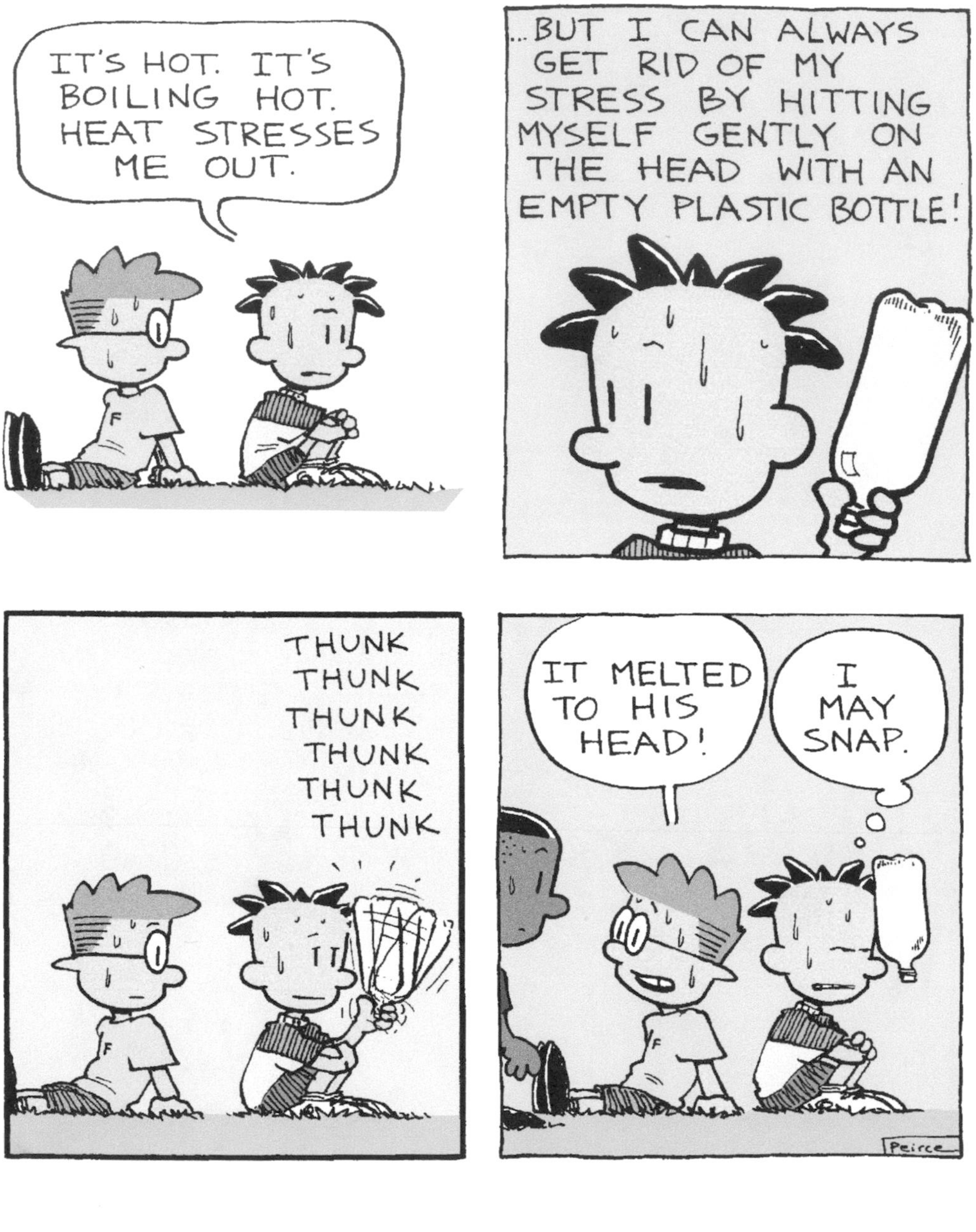
IT'S HOT. IT'S BOILING HOT. HEAT STRESSES ME OUT.
...BUT I CAN ALWAYS GET RID OF MY STRESS BY HITTING MYSELF GENTLY ON THE HEAD WITH AN EMPTY PLASTIC BOTTLE!
THUNK THUNK THUNK THUNK THUNK THUNK
IT MELTED TO HIS HEAD!
I MAY SNAP.
Peirce

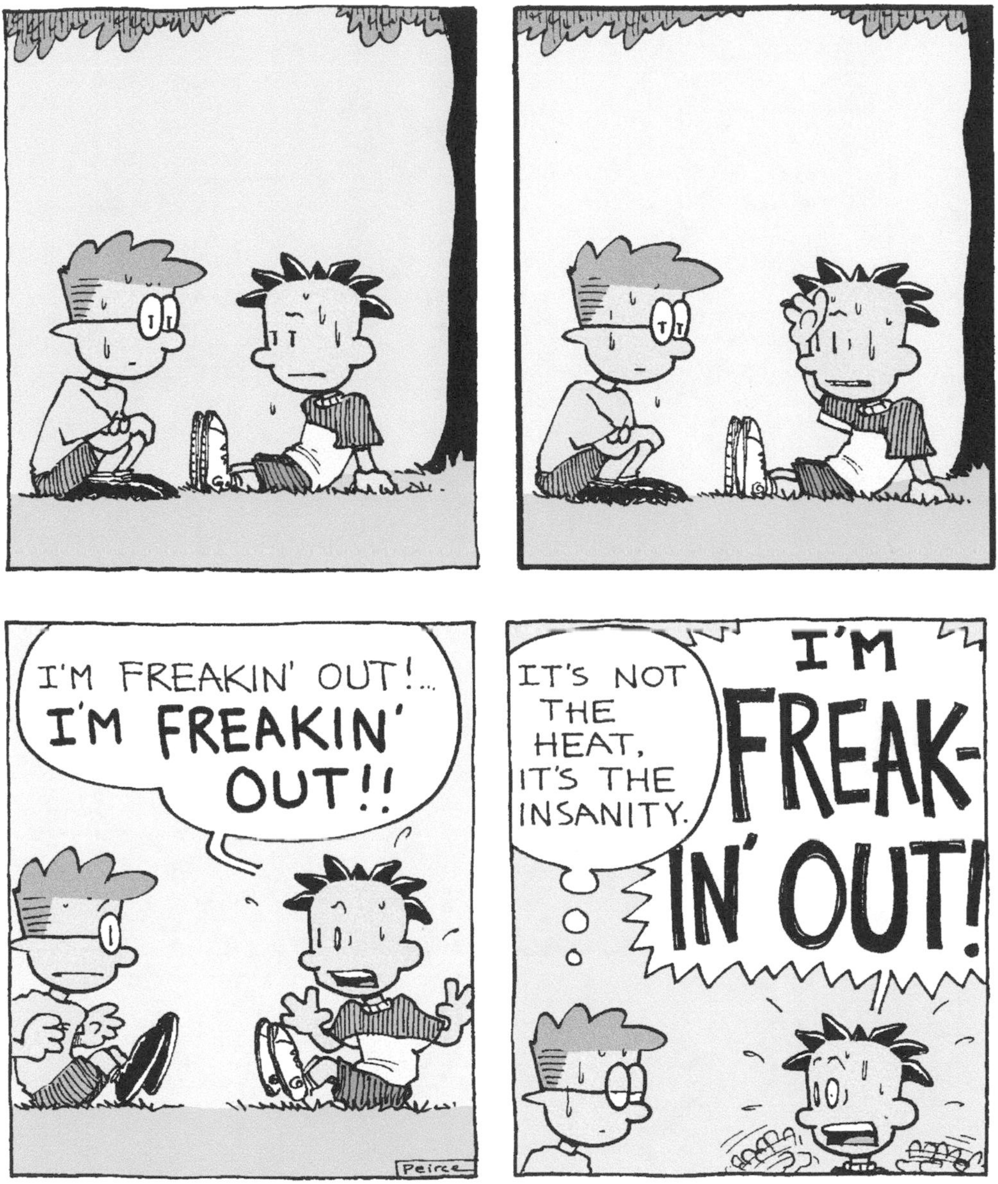
I'M FREAKIN' OUT!... I'M FREAKIN' OUT!!
IT'S NOT THE HEAT, IT'S THE INSANITY.
I'M FREAK-IN' OUT!
Peirce

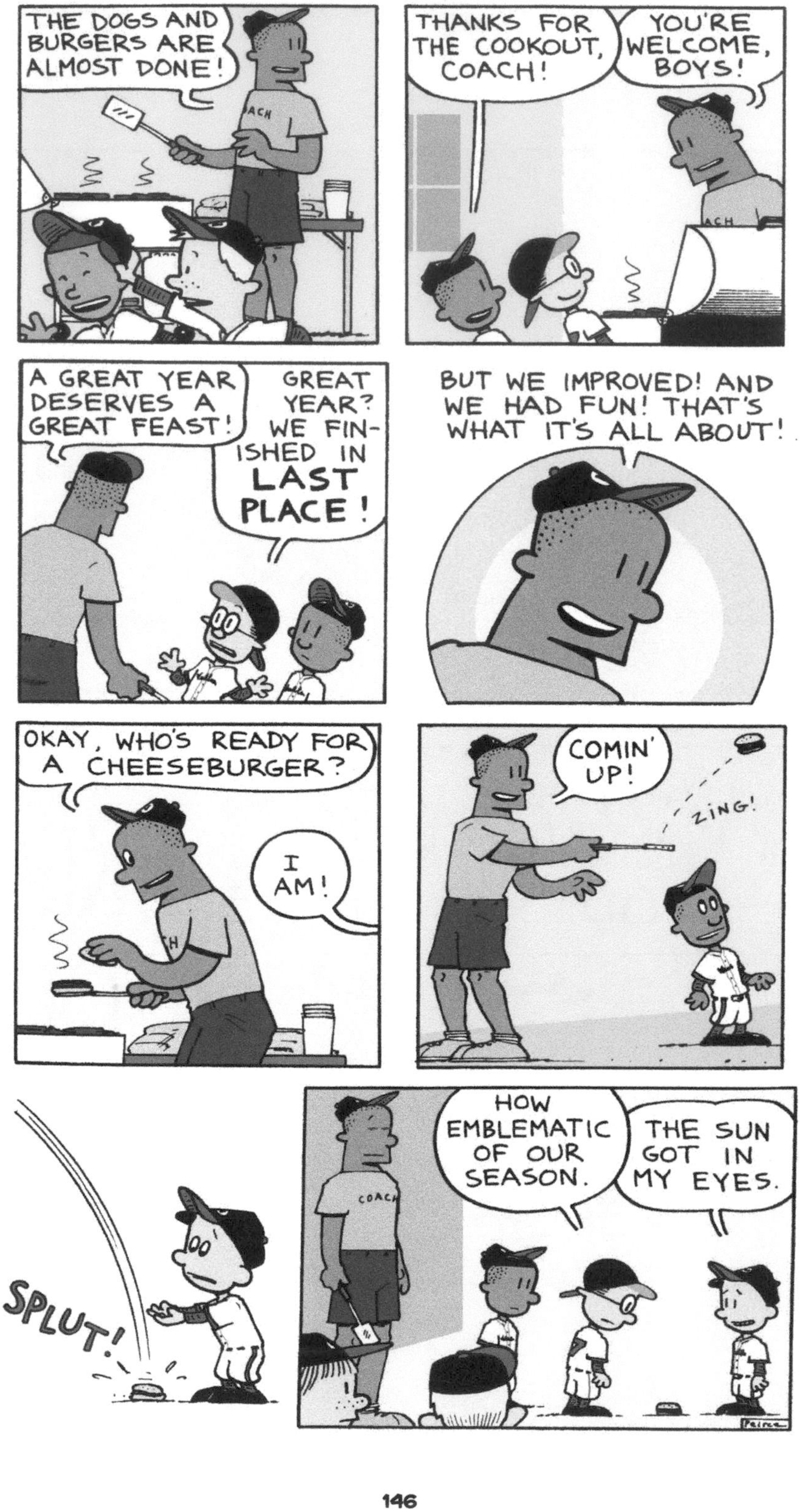
THE DOGS AND BURGERS ARE ALMOST DONE!
THANKS FOR THE COOKOUT, COACH!
YOU'RE WELCOME, BOYS!
A GREAT YEAR DESERVES A GREAT FEAST!
GREAT YEAR? WE FIN-ISHED IN **LAST PLACE**!
BUT WE IMPROVED! AND WE HAD FUN! THAT'S WHAT IT'S ALL ABOUT!
OKAY, WHO'S READY FOR A CHEESEBURGER?
I AM!
COMIN' UP!
ZING!
SPLUT!
HOW EMBLEMATIC OF OUR SEASON.
THE SUN GOT IN MY EYES.
Peirce

MR. EUSTIS, I'M HERE TO TELL YOU I'M GETTING OUT OF THE LAWN-MOWING BUSINESS.
I'M BURNED OUT, YOU KNOW WHAT I MEAN? THE GRIND IS JUST WEARING ME DOWN!
ANYWAY, SINCE YOU'RE ONE OF MY BEST CUSTOMERS, I JUST THOUGHT I'D LET YOU KNOW.
Peirce
BUT YOU'RE ONLY **HALFWAY THROUGH MY LAWN!!**
AS I SAID, I'M BURNED OUT.

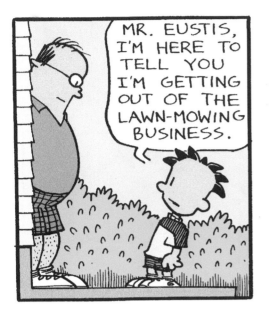

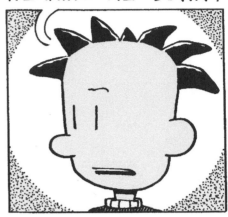

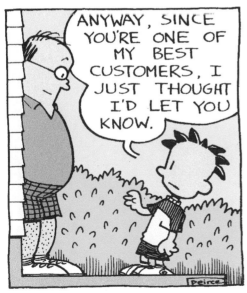

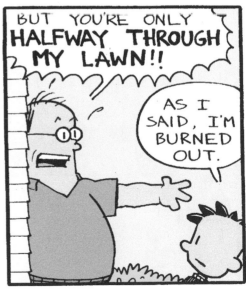

NATE, WAIT! YOU CAN'T JUST RETIRE FROM LAWN MOWING IN THE MIDDLE OF A JOB!!
IT'S NOT A MATTER OF CHOICE, MR. EUSTIS! IT'S JUST THE WAY IT IS! THE SPARK JUST ISN'T THERE ANYMORE!
MY MUSE HAS LEFT ME.
YOU HAVE A LAWN-MOWING MUSE?
PLUS, I WAS GETTING A REALLY BAD BLISTER.
PEIRCE

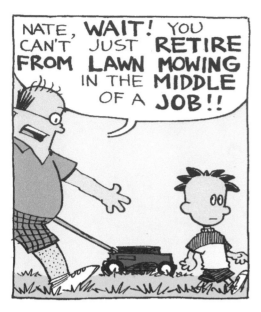

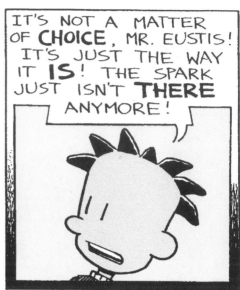

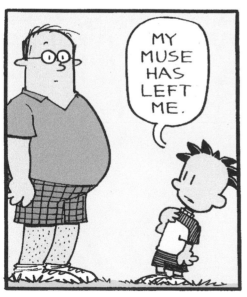

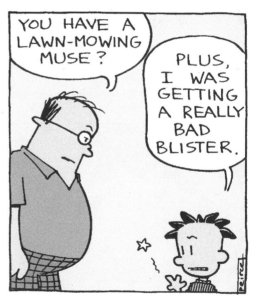

HERE'S THE REALITY, MR. EUSTIS: I CAN'T KEEP MOWING LAWNS IF MY **HEART'S** NOT IN IT!

THE GREAT ONES KNOW WHEN IT'S TIME TO SAY GOODBYE, AND **THIS** IS **MY** TIME!

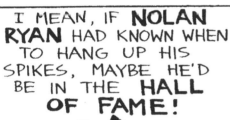

I MEAN, IF **NOLAN RYAN** HAD KNOWN WHEN TO HANG UP HIS SPIKES, MAYBE HE'D BE IN THE **HALL OF FAME!**

NOLAN RYAN **IS** IN THE HALL OF FAME.

OKAY, WHAT-EVER. THE POINT IS, I'M SICK OF MOWING LAWNS.

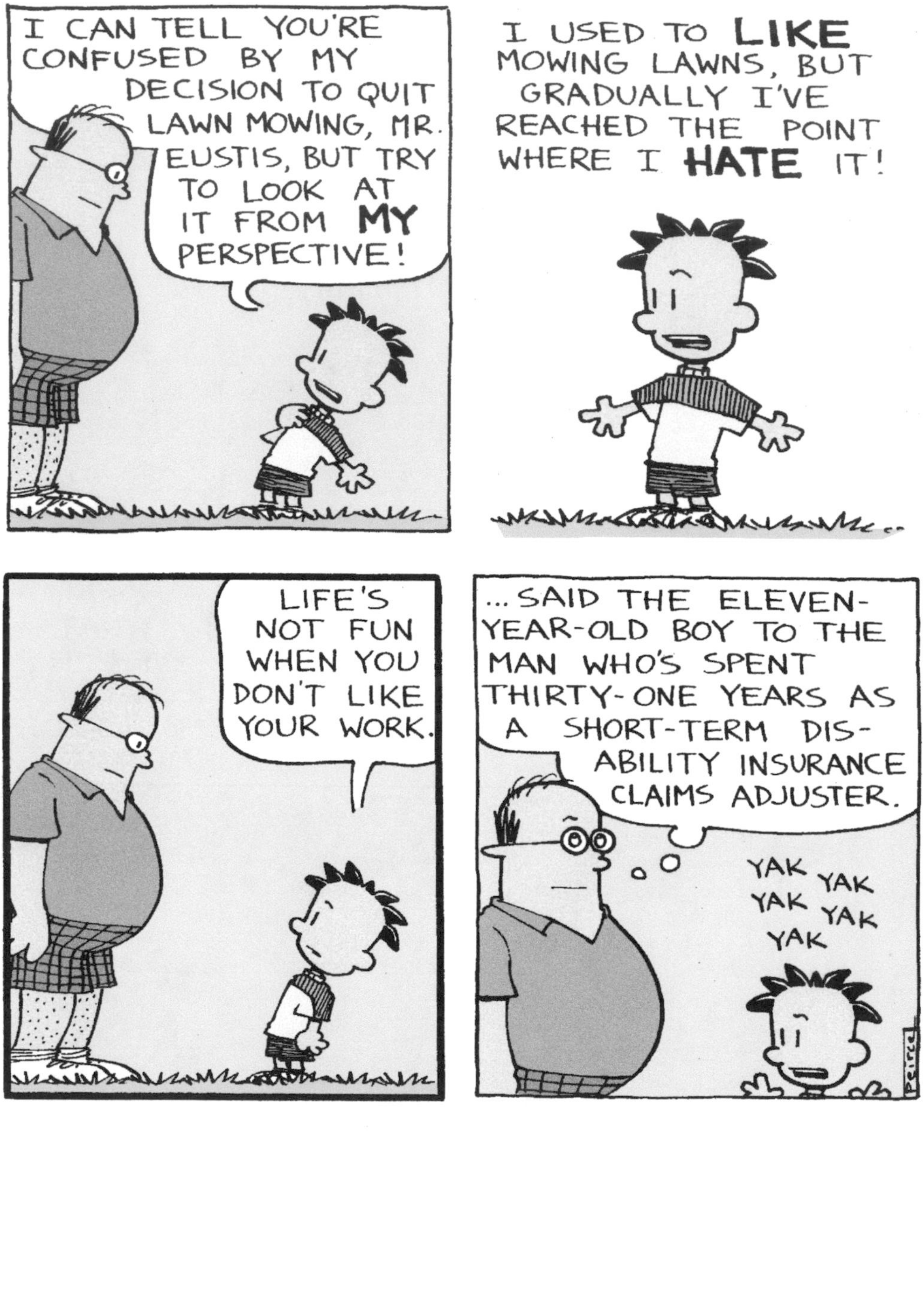
I CAN TELL YOU'RE CONFUSED BY MY DECISION TO QUIT LAWN MOWING, MR. EUSTIS, BUT TRY TO LOOK AT IT FROM MY PERSPECTIVE!
I USED TO LIKE MOWING LAWNS, BUT GRADUALLY I'VE REACHED THE POINT WHERE I HATE IT!
LIFE'S NOT FUN WHEN YOU DON'T LIKE YOUR WORK.
...SAID THE ELEVEN-YEAR-OLD BOY TO THE MAN WHO'S SPENT THIRTY-ONE YEARS AS A SHORT-TERM DIS-ABILITY INSURANCE CLAIMS ADJUSTER.
YAK YAK YAK YAK YAK
PEIRCE

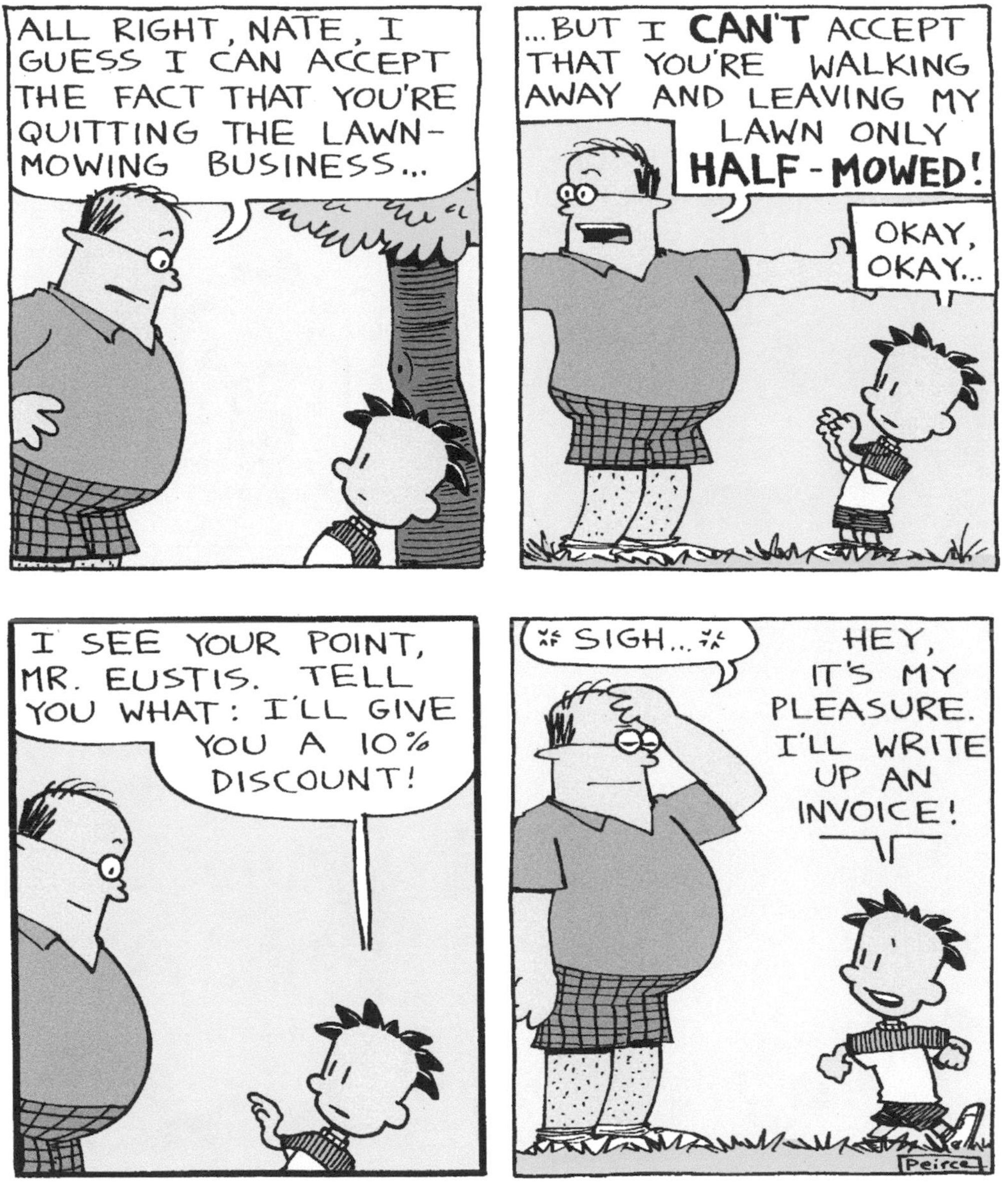
ALL RIGHT, NATE, I GUESS I CAN ACCEPT THE FACT THAT YOU'RE QUITTING THE LAWN-MOWING BUSINESS...
...BUT I **CAN'T** ACCEPT THAT YOU'RE WALKING AWAY AND LEAVING MY LAWN ONLY **HALF-MOWED!**
OKAY, OKAY...
I SEE YOUR POINT, MR. EUSTIS. TELL YOU WHAT: I'LL GIVE YOU A 10% DISCOUNT!
SIGH...
HEY, IT'S MY PLEASURE. I'LL WRITE UP AN INVOICE!
Peirce

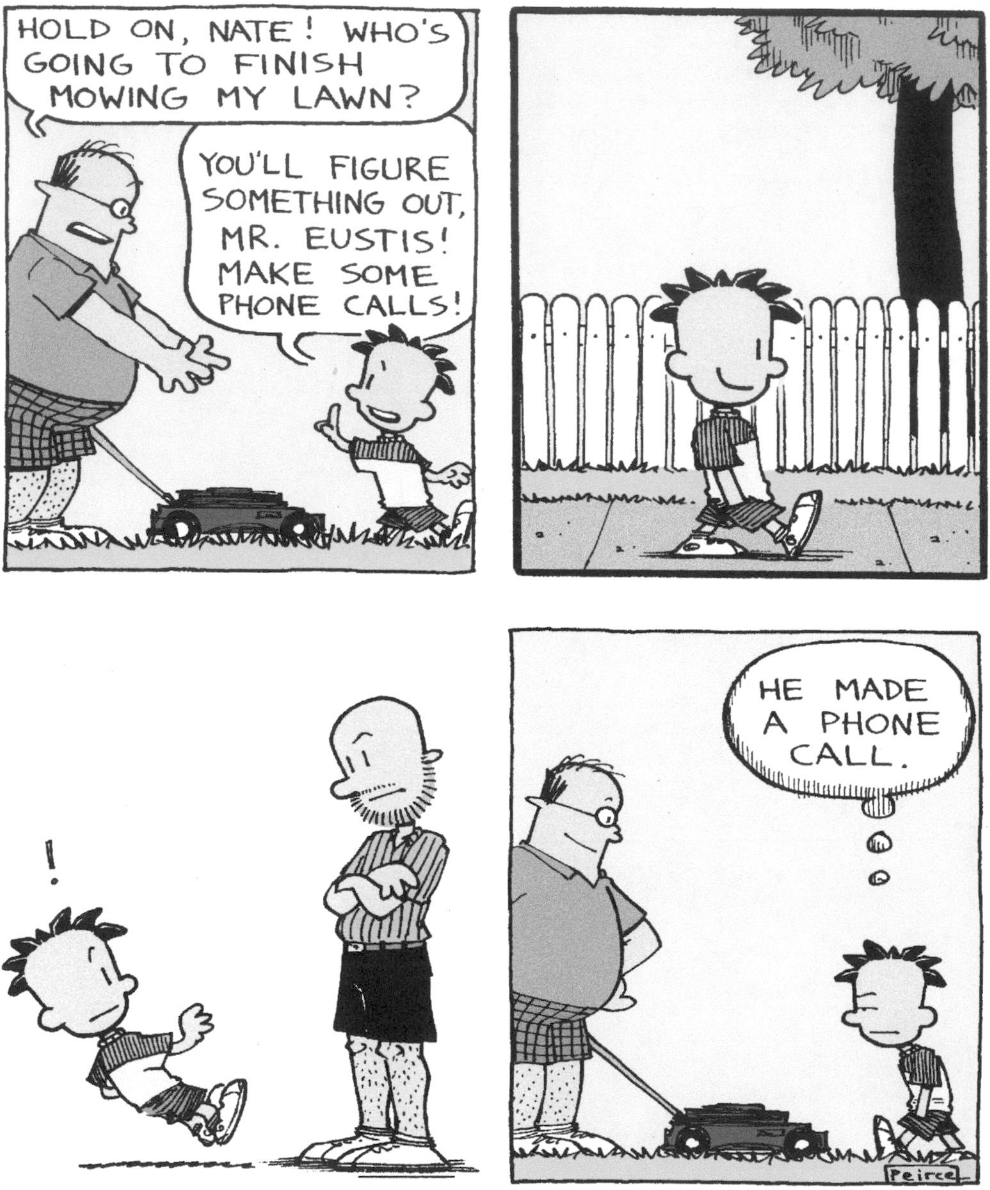
HOLD ON, NATE! WHO'S GOING TO FINISH MOWING MY LAWN?
YOU'LL FIGURE SOMETHING OUT, MR. EUSTIS! MAKE SOME PHONE CALLS!
!
HE MADE A PHONE CALL.
Peirce

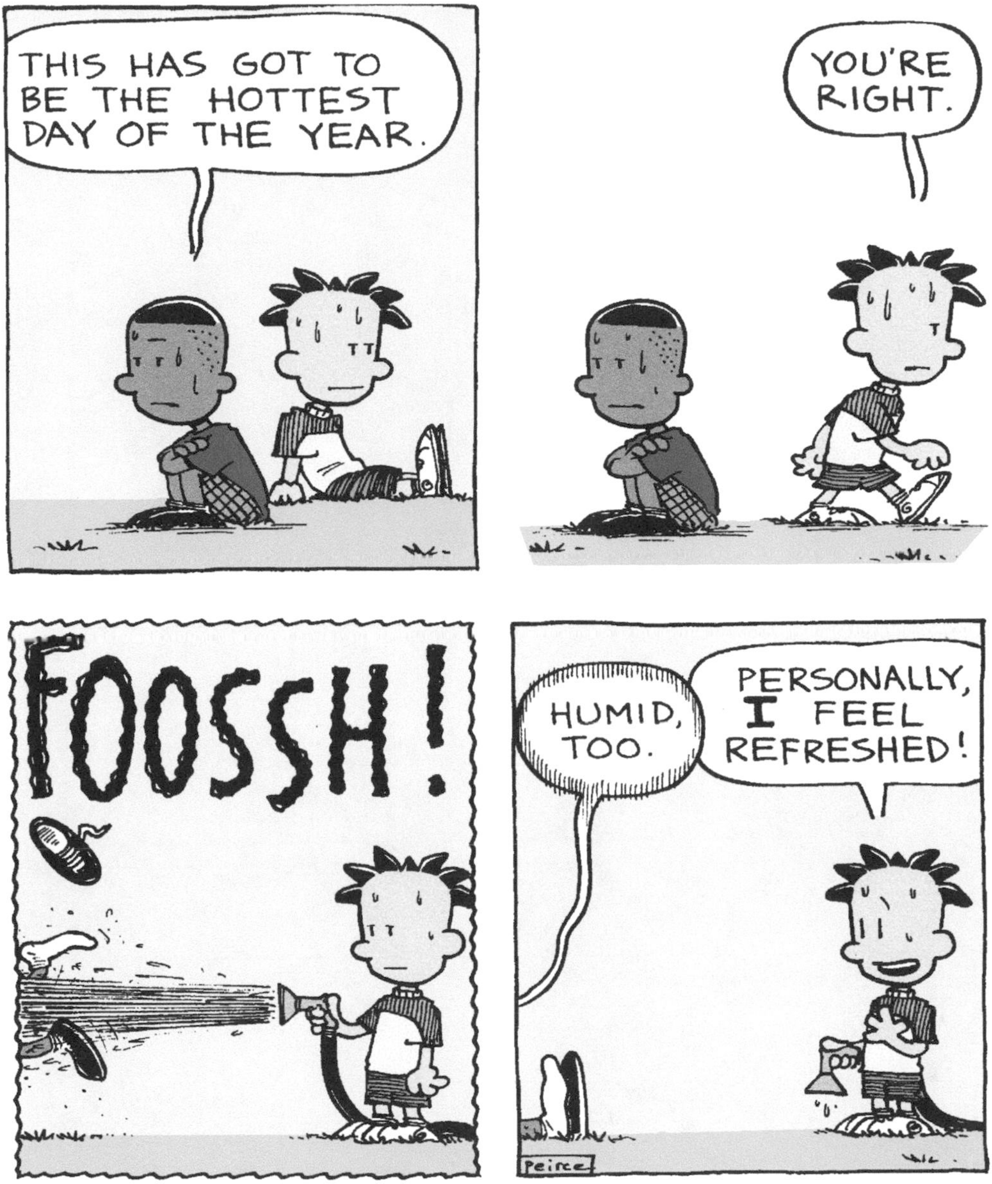
THIS HAS GOT TO BE THE HOTTEST DAY OF THE YEAR.
YOU'RE RIGHT.
FOOSSH!
HUMID, TOO.
PERSONALLY, I FEEL REFRESHED!
Peirce

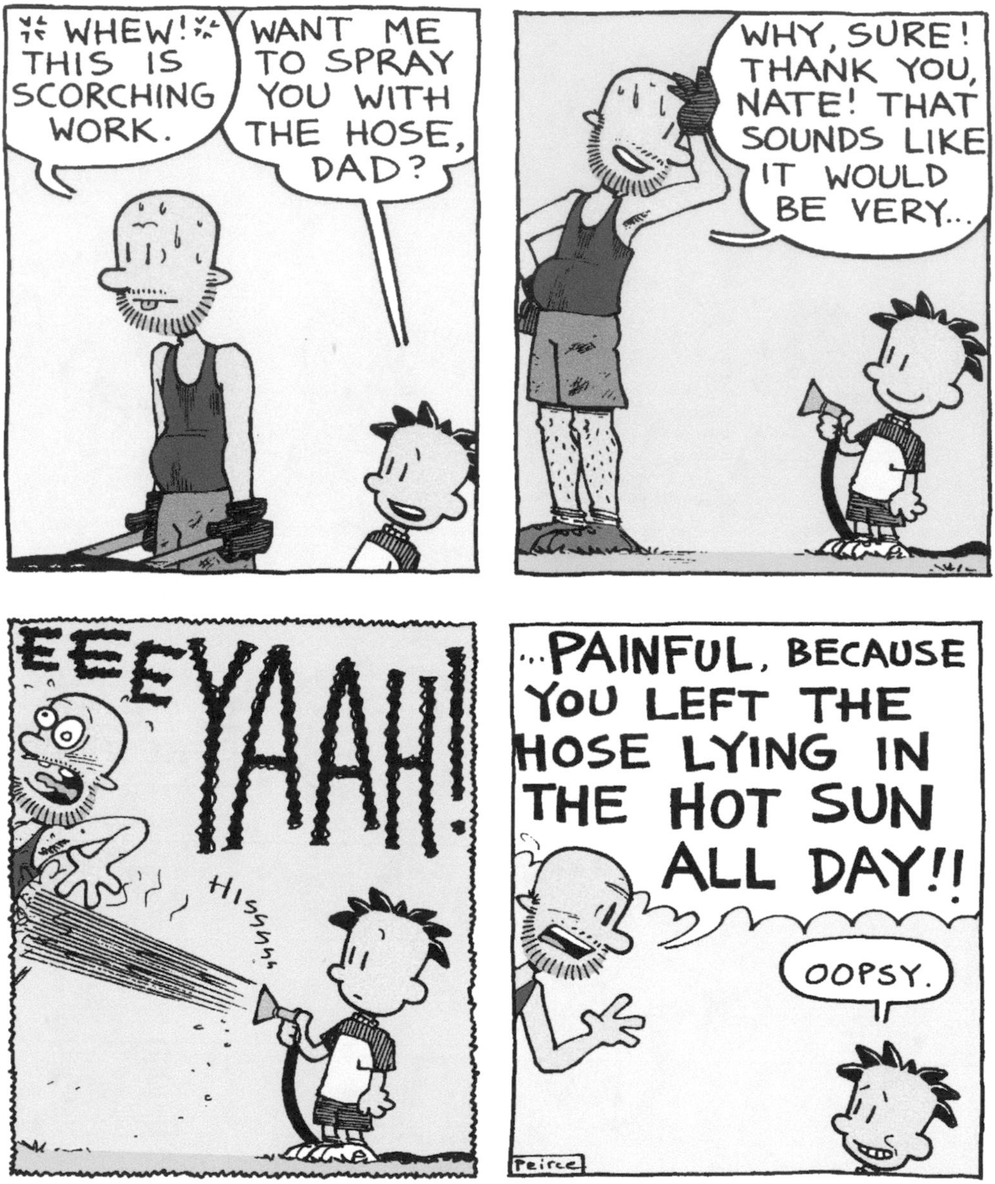
WHEW! THIS IS SCORCHING WORK.
WANT ME TO SPRAY YOU WITH THE HOSE, DAD?
WHY, SURE! THANK YOU, NATE! THAT SOUNDS LIKE IT WOULD BE VERY...
EEEYAAH!
HISSSSS
...PAINFUL, BECAUSE YOU LEFT THE HOSE LYING IN THE HOT SUN ALL DAY!!
OOPSY.
Peirce

UGH! WHAT A MISERABLY HOT DAY!
HEY, ELLEN! FOR A DOLLAR, I'LL COOL YOU OFF WITH THE HOSE!
A DOLLAR? FORGET IT!
FIFTY CENTS?
NO.
A QUARTER?
NO!
A DIME?
NO!
FOOSSH!
HOW 'BOUT I PAY YOU?
OH, YOU'RE GOING TO PAY, ALL RIGHT.
Peirce

JENNY, M'LADY! WANT TO THROW AROUND THE OL' PIGSKIN?
WITH YOU? I'D RATHER STICK A FORK IN MY EYE.
HOW 'BOUT TOSSING A BASEBALL?
WITH YOU? I THINK NOT.
WANNA SHOOT HOOPS?
WITH YOU? NO.
KICK A SOCCER BALL?
NOT WITH YOU.
PLAY PING PONG?
NO!
SOME PEOPLE JUST DON'T LIKE SPORTS.
Peirce

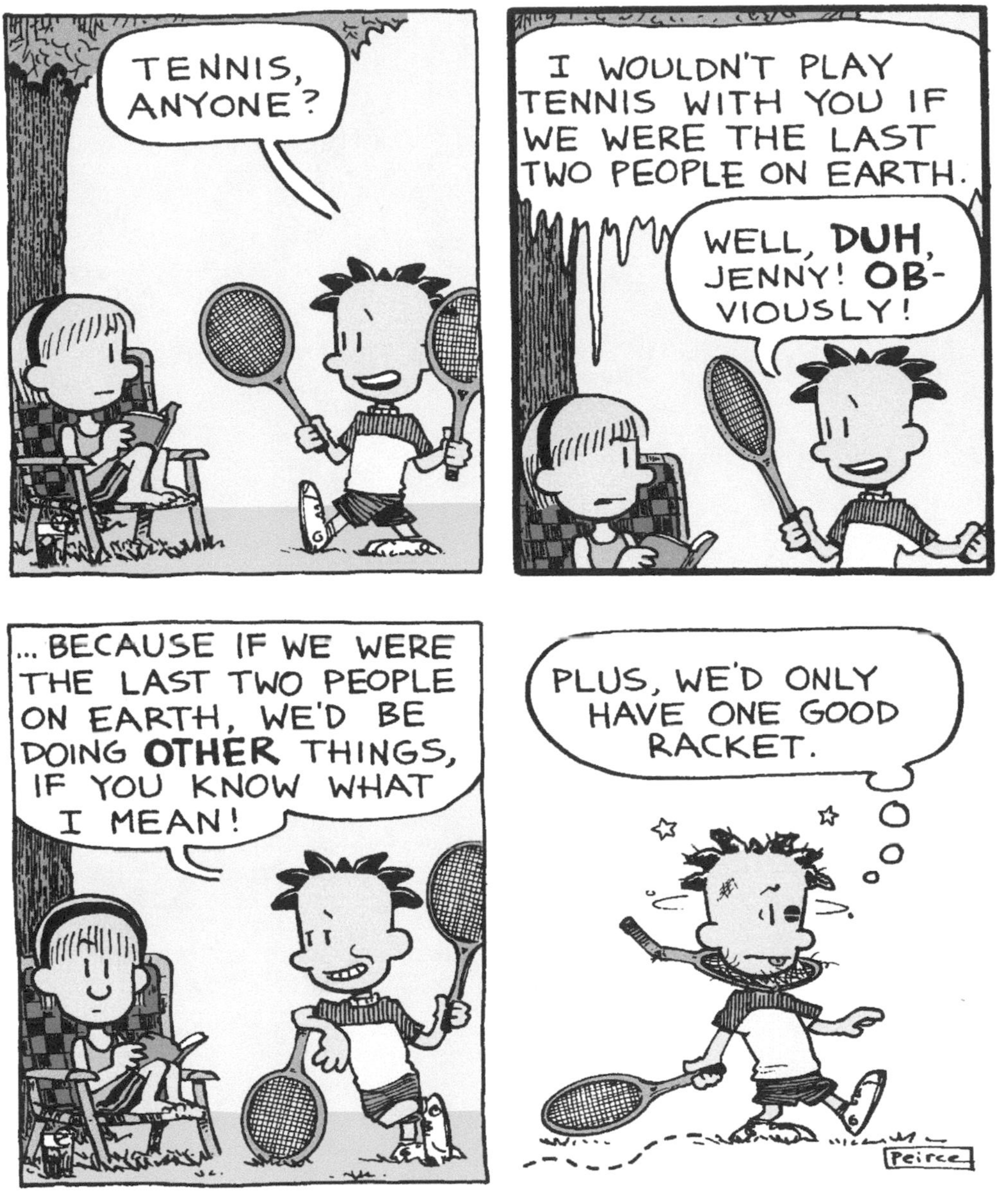
TENNIS, ANYONE?
I WOULDN'T PLAY TENNIS WITH YOU IF WE WERE THE LAST TWO PEOPLE ON EARTH.
WELL, DUH, JENNY! OB-VIOUSLY!
... BECAUSE IF WE WERE THE LAST TWO PEOPLE ON EARTH, WE'D BE DOING OTHER THINGS, IF YOU KNOW WHAT I MEAN!
PLUS, WE'D ONLY HAVE ONE GOOD RACKET.
Peirce

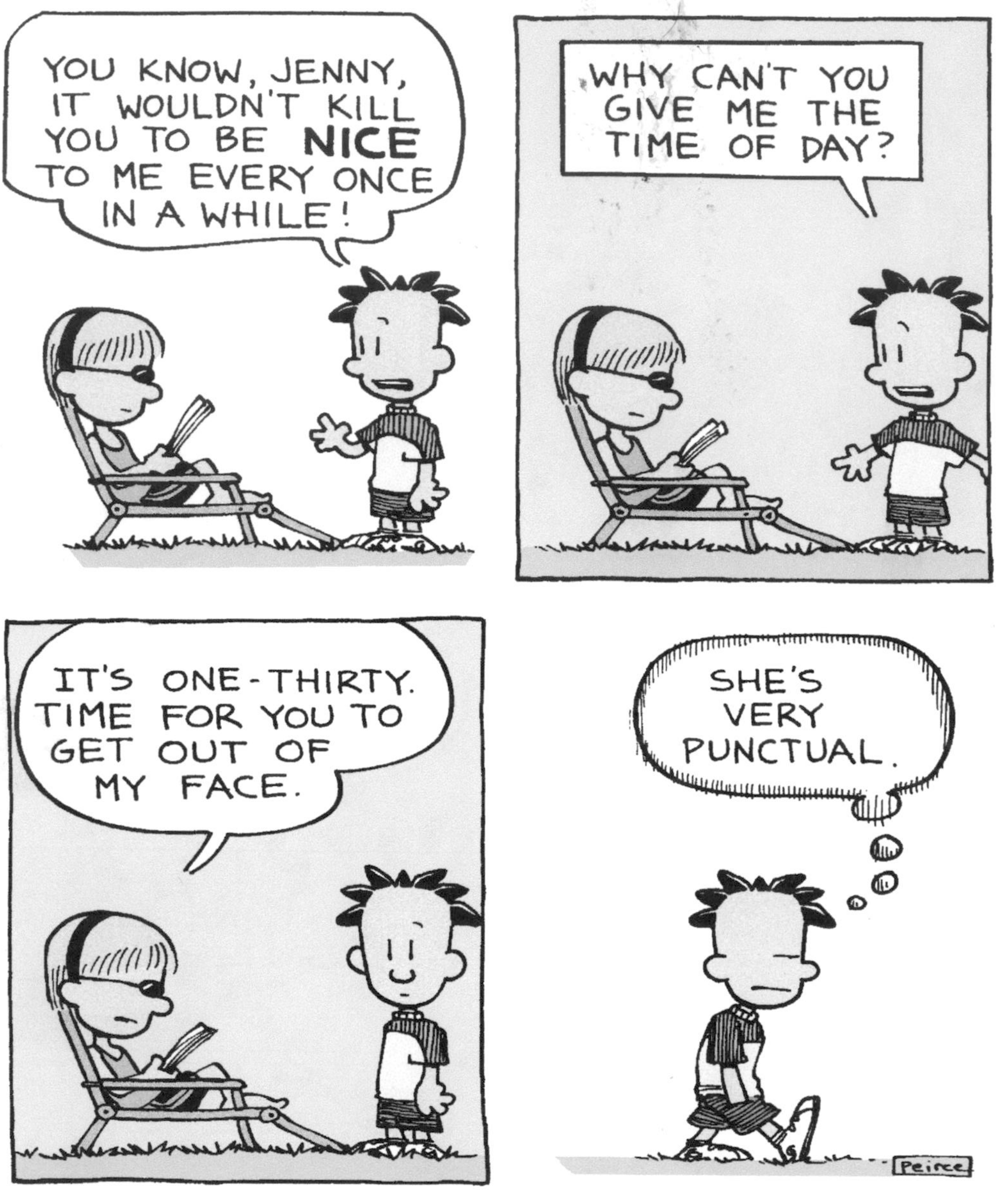
YOU KNOW, JENNY, IT WOULDN'T KILL YOU TO BE **NICE** TO ME EVERY ONCE IN A WHILE!
WHY CAN'T YOU GIVE ME THE TIME OF DAY?
IT'S ONE-THIRTY. TIME FOR YOU TO GET OUT OF MY FACE.
SHE'S VERY PUNCTUAL.
Peirce

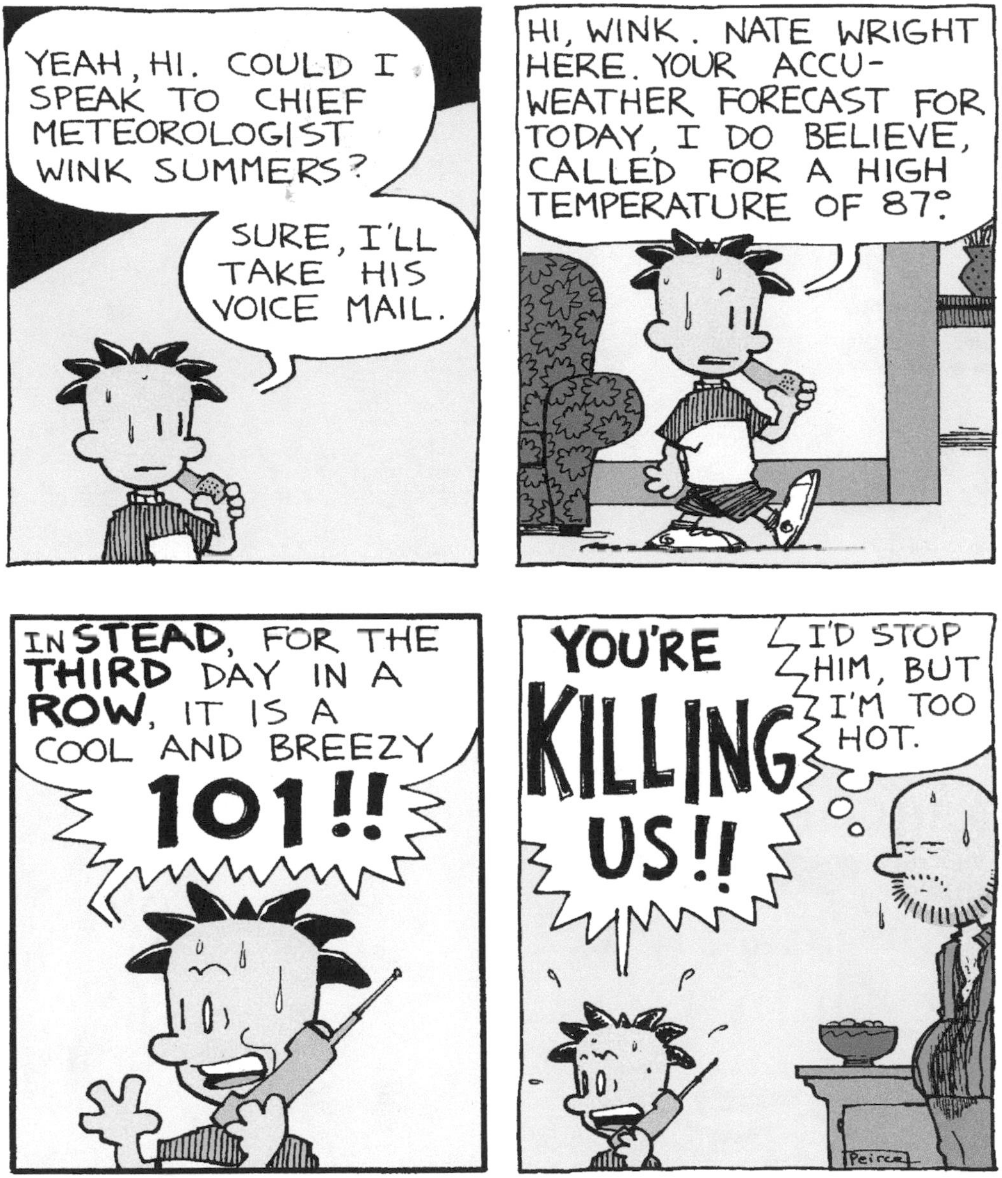
YEAH, HI. COULD I SPEAK TO CHIEF METEOROLOGIST WINK SUMMERS?
SURE, I'LL TAKE HIS VOICE MAIL.
HI, WINK. NATE WRIGHT HERE. YOUR ACCU-WEATHER FORECAST FOR TODAY, I DO BELIEVE, CALLED FOR A HIGH TEMPERATURE OF 87°.
INSTEAD, FOR THE THIRD DAY IN A ROW, IT IS A COOL AND BREEZY
101!!
YOU'RE KILLING US!!
I'D STOP HIM, BUT I'M TOO HOT.
Peirce

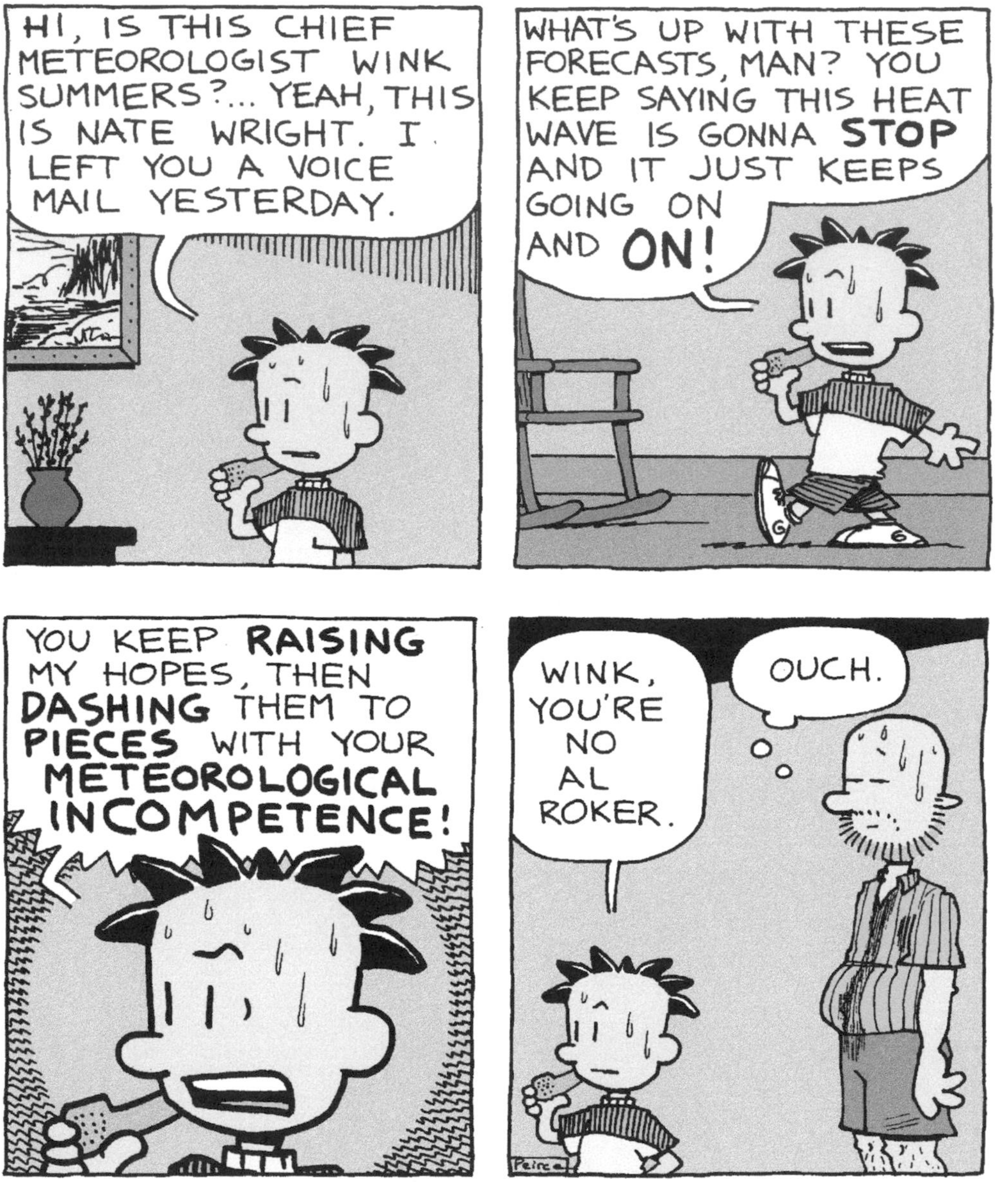
HI, IS THIS CHIEF METEOROLOGIST WINK SUMMERS?... YEAH, THIS IS NATE WRIGHT. I LEFT YOU A VOICE MAIL YESTERDAY.
WHAT'S UP WITH THESE FORECASTS, MAN? YOU KEEP SAYING THIS HEAT WAVE IS GONNA STOP AND IT JUST KEEPS GOING ON AND ON!
YOU KEEP RAISING MY HOPES, THEN DASHING THEM TO PIECES WITH YOUR METEOROLOGICAL INCOMPETENCE!
WINK, YOU'RE NO AL ROKER.
OUCH.
Peirce

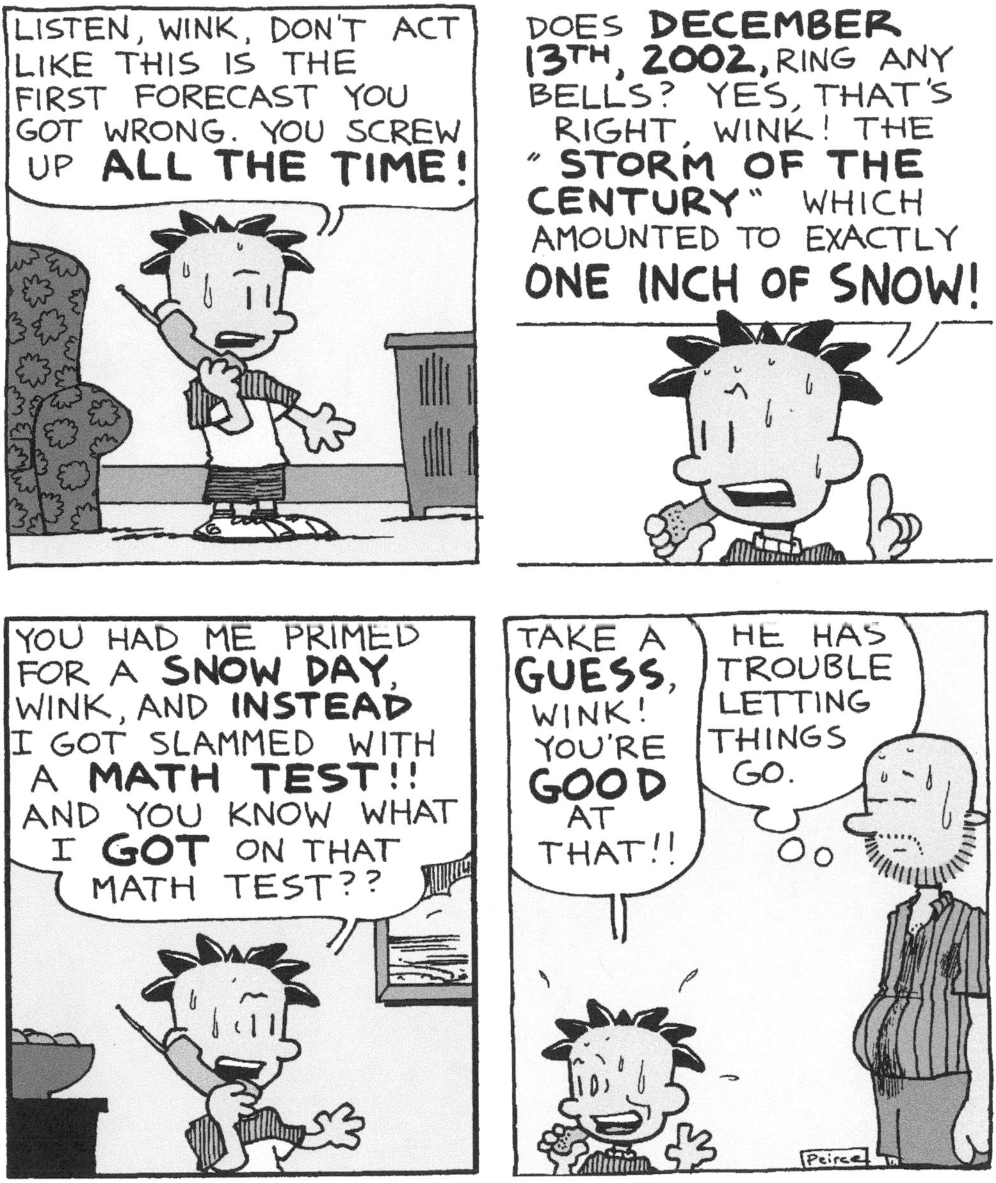
LISTEN, WINK, DON'T ACT LIKE THIS IS THE FIRST FORECAST YOU GOT WRONG. YOU SCREW UP **ALL THE TIME!**
DOES **DECEMBER 13TH, 2002,** RING ANY BELLS? YES, THAT'S RIGHT, WINK! THE "**STORM OF THE CENTURY**" WHICH AMOUNTED TO EXACTLY **ONE INCH OF SNOW!**
YOU HAD ME PRIMED FOR A **SNOW DAY**, WINK, AND **INSTEAD** I GOT SLAMMED WITH A **MATH TEST!!** AND YOU KNOW WHAT I **GOT** ON THAT MATH TEST??
TAKE A **GUESS**, WINK! YOU'RE **GOOD** AT THAT!!
HE HAS TROUBLE LETTING THINGS GO.
Peirce

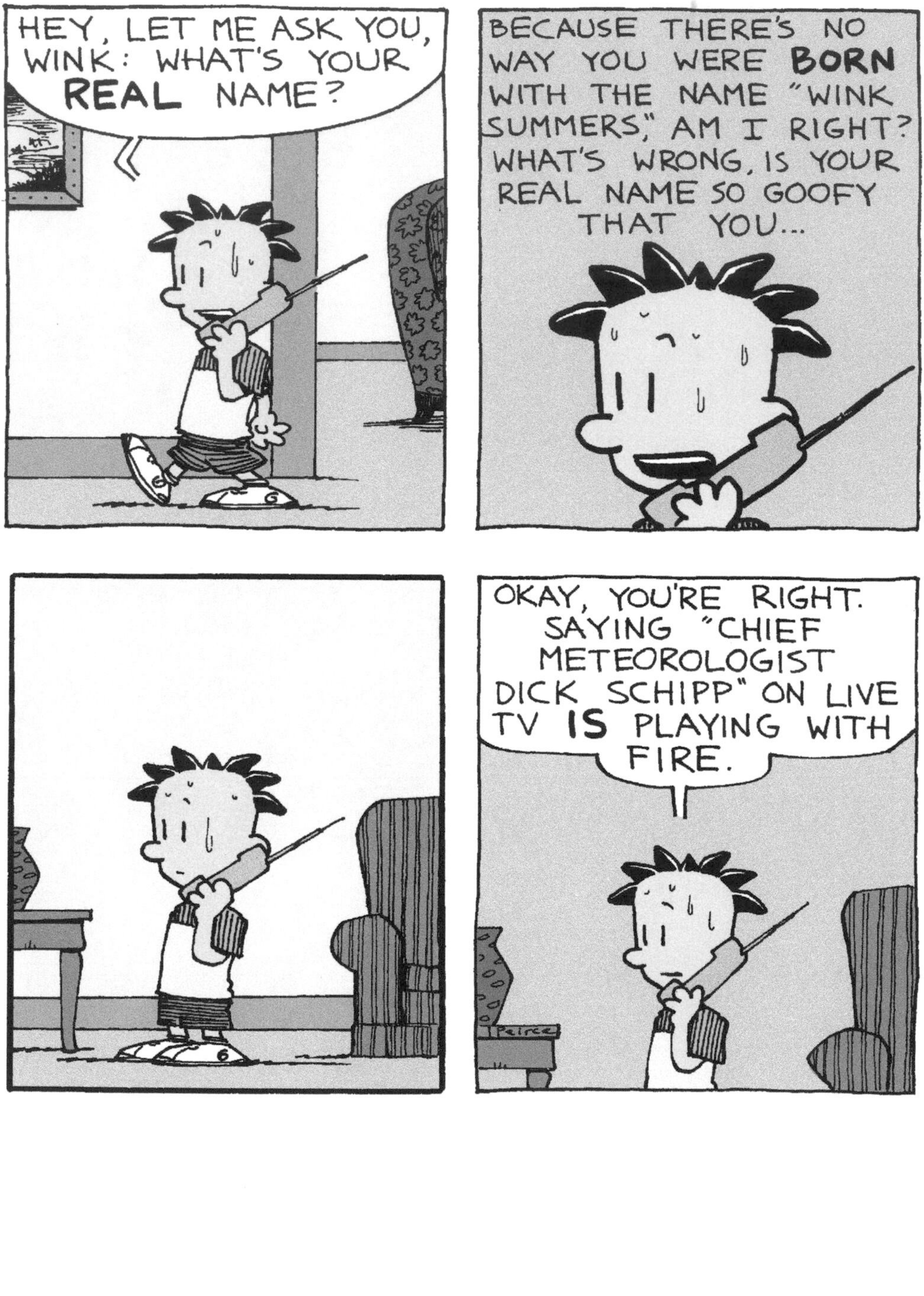
HEY, LET ME ASK YOU, WINK: WHAT'S YOUR **REAL** NAME?
BECAUSE THERE'S NO WAY YOU WERE **BORN** WITH THE NAME "WINK SUMMERS," AM I RIGHT? WHAT'S WRONG, IS YOUR REAL NAME SO GOOFY THAT YOU...
OKAY, YOU'RE RIGHT. SAYING "CHIEF METEOROLOGIST DICK SCHIPP" ON LIVE TV **IS** PLAYING WITH FIRE.
Peirce

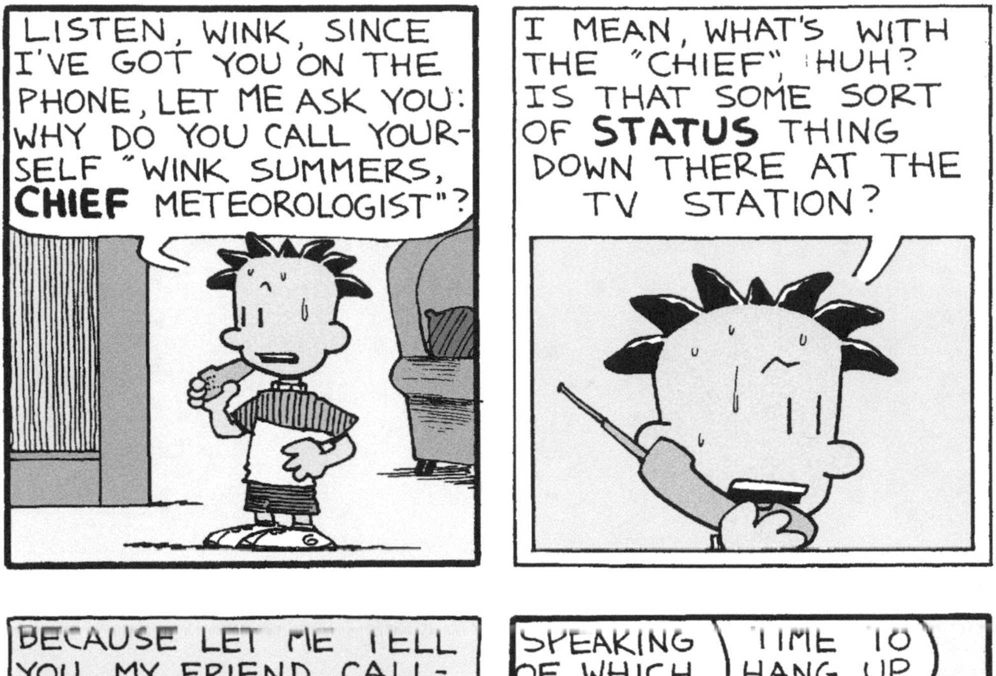

LISTEN, WINK, SINCE I'VE GOT YOU ON THE PHONE, LET ME ASK YOU: WHY DO YOU CALL YOURSELF "WINK SUMMERS, **CHIEF** METEOROLOGIST"?

 I MEAN, WHAT'S WITH THE "CHIEF", HUH? IS THAT SOME SORT OF **STATUS** THING DOWN THERE AT THE TV STATION?

BECAUSE LET ME TELL YOU, MY FRIEND, CALL-ING YOURSELF "**CHIEF**" DOESN'T MAKE YOU MORE IMPORTANT THAN THE NEWS GUY OR THE SPORTS GUY, OR **ESPECIALLY** THE LADY WHO REVIEWS MOVIES!

 SPEAKING OF WHICH... COULD I SPEAK TO HER, PLEASE?

TIME TO HANG UP, SON.

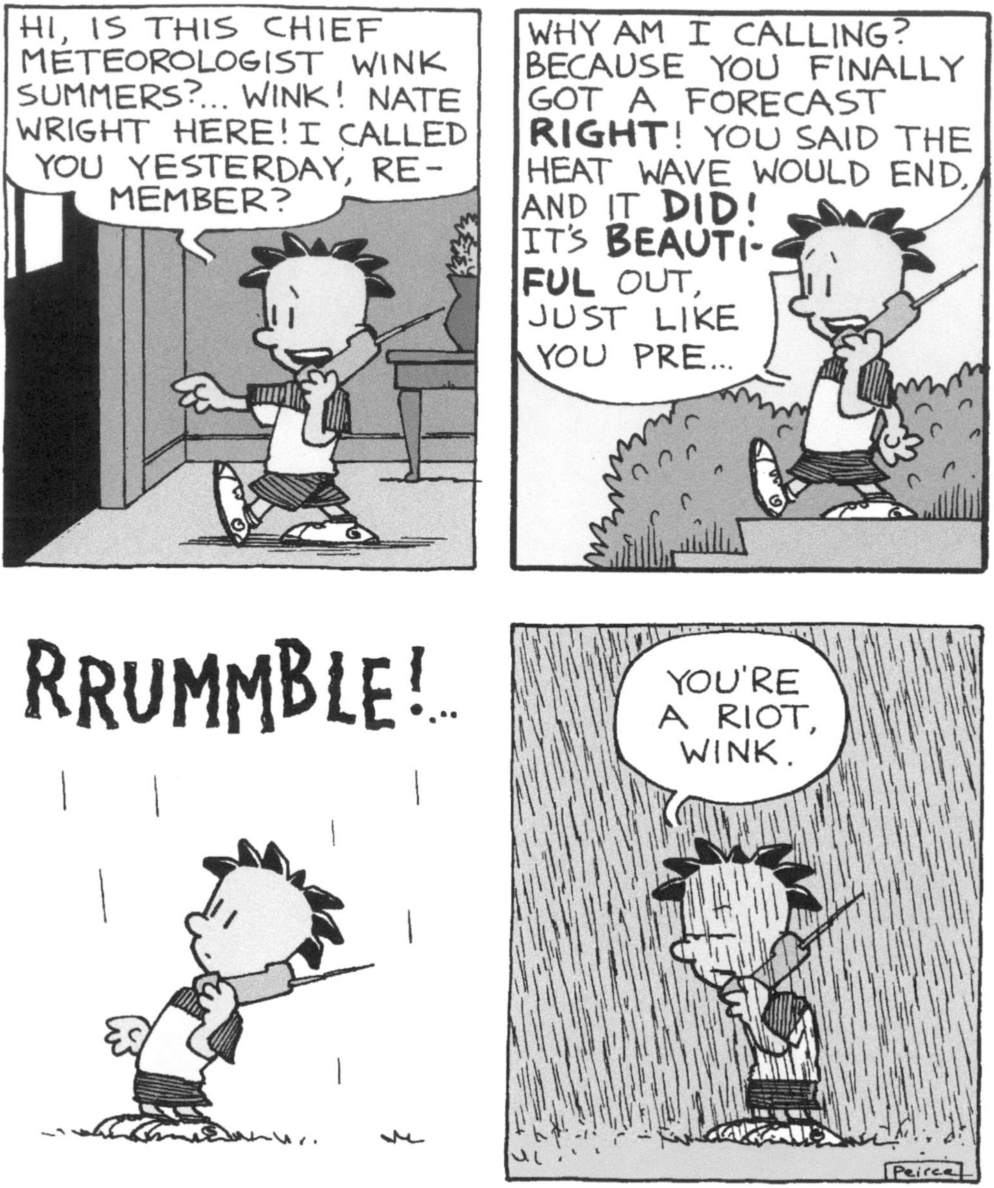
HI, IS THIS CHIEF METEOROLOGIST WINK SUMMERS?... WINK! NATE WRIGHT HERE! I CALLED YOU YESTERDAY, REMEMBER?
WHY AM I CALLING? BECAUSE YOU FINALLY GOT A FORECAST **RIGHT**! YOU SAID THE HEAT WAVE WOULD END, AND IT **DID**! IT'S **BEAUTIFUL** OUT, JUST LIKE YOU PRE...
RRUMMBLE!...
YOU'RE A RIOT, WINK.
Peirce

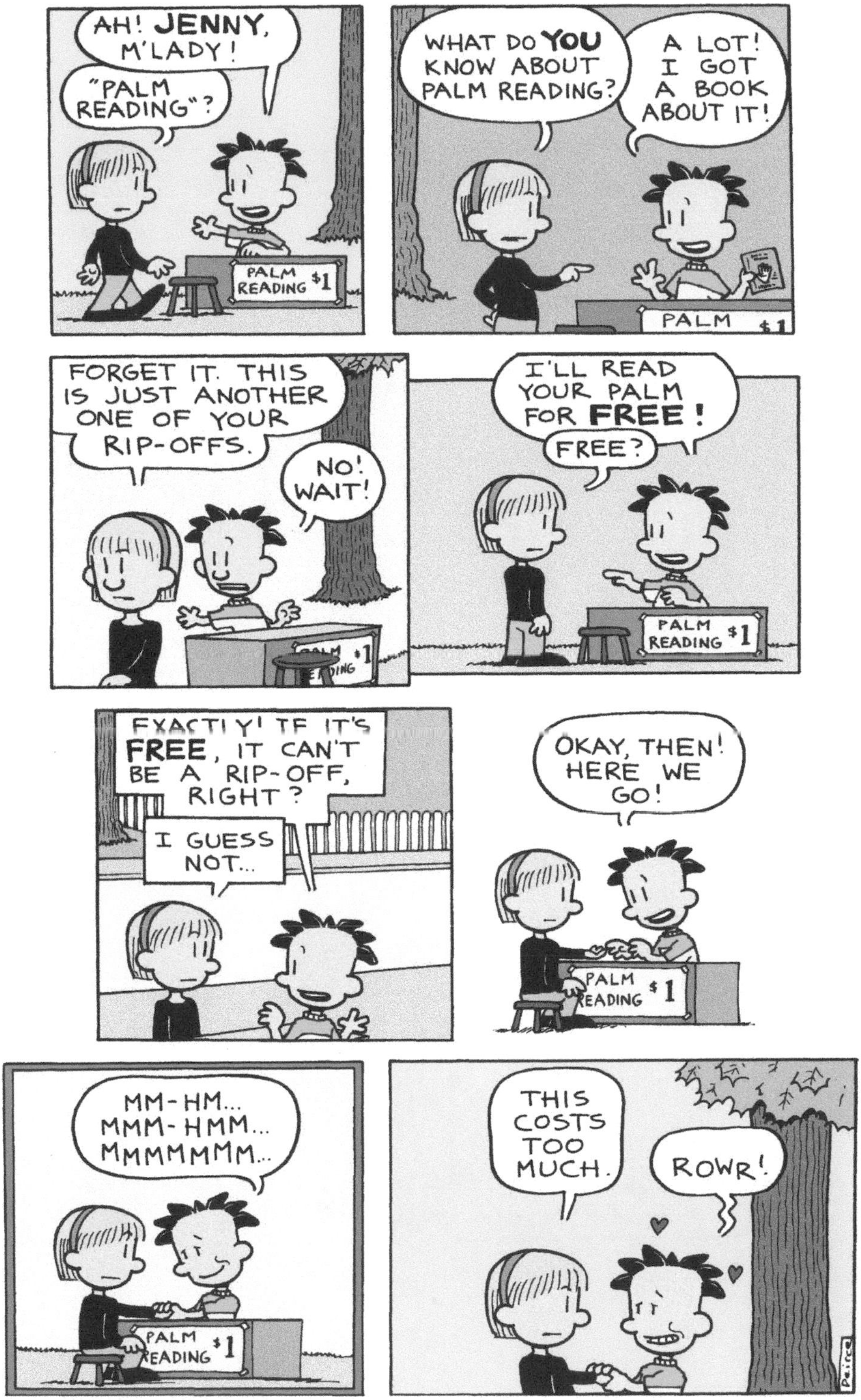
AH! JENNY, M'LADY!
"PALM READING"?
PALM READING $1
WHAT DO YOU KNOW ABOUT PALM READING?
A LOT! I GOT A BOOK ABOUT IT!
PALM $1
FORGET IT. THIS IS JUST ANOTHER ONE OF YOUR RIP-OFFS.
NO! WAIT!
I'LL READ YOUR PALM FOR FREE!
FREE?
PALM READING $1
EXACTLY! IF IT'S FREE, IT CAN'T BE A RIP-OFF, RIGHT?
I GUESS NOT...
OKAY, THEN! HERE WE GO!
PALM READING $1
MM-HM... MMM-HMM... MMMMMMM...
PALM READING $1
THIS COSTS TOO MUCH.
ROWR!
Peirce

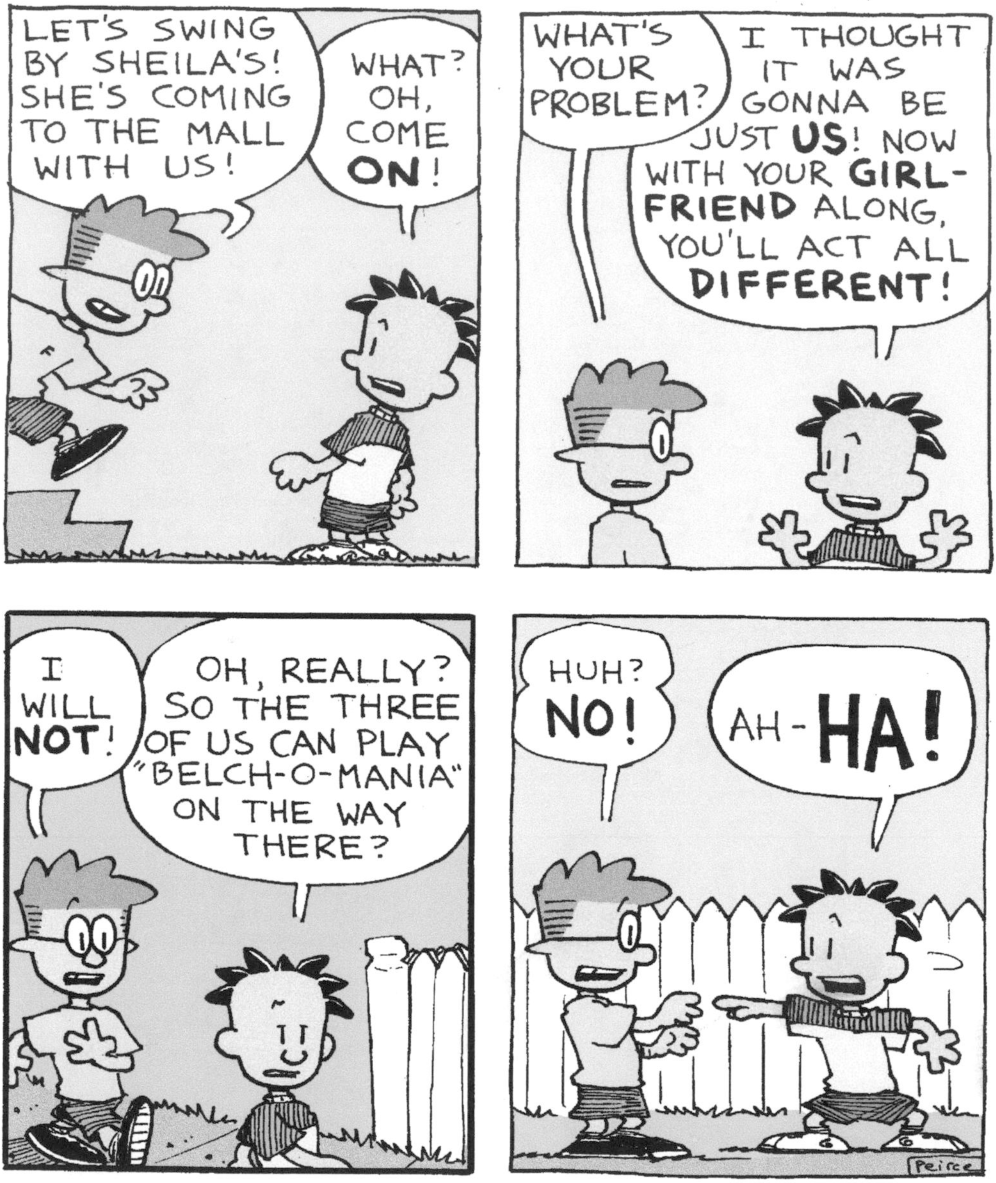
LET'S SWING BY SHEILA'S! SHE'S COMING TO THE MALL WITH US!
WHAT? OH, COME **ON**!
WHAT'S YOUR PROBLEM?
I THOUGHT IT WAS GONNA BE JUST **US**! NOW WITH YOUR **GIRL-FRIEND** ALONG, YOU'LL ACT ALL **DIFFERENT**!
I WILL **NOT**!
OH, REALLY? SO THE THREE OF US CAN PLAY "BELCH-O-MANIA" ON THE WAY THERE?
HUH? **NO**!
AH-**HA**!
Peirce

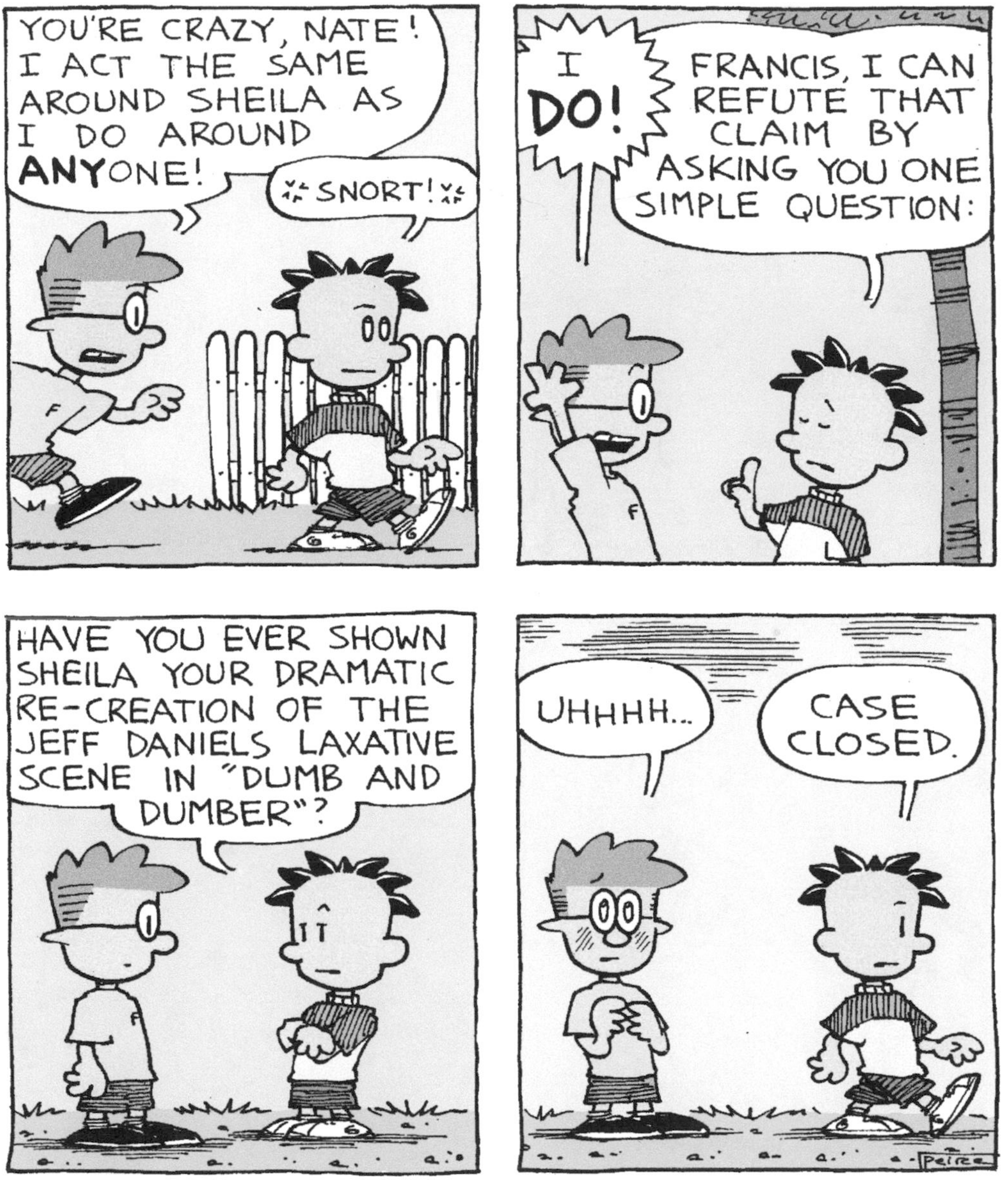
YOU'RE CRAZY, NATE! I ACT THE SAME AROUND SHEILA AS I DO AROUND ANYONE!
SNORT!
I DO!
FRANCIS, I CAN REFUTE THAT CLAIM BY ASKING YOU ONE SIMPLE QUESTION:
HAVE YOU EVER SHOWN SHEILA YOUR DRAMATIC RE-CREATION OF THE JEFF DANIELS LAXATIVE SCENE IN "DUMB AND DUMBER"?
UHHHH...
CASE CLOSED.
PEIRCE

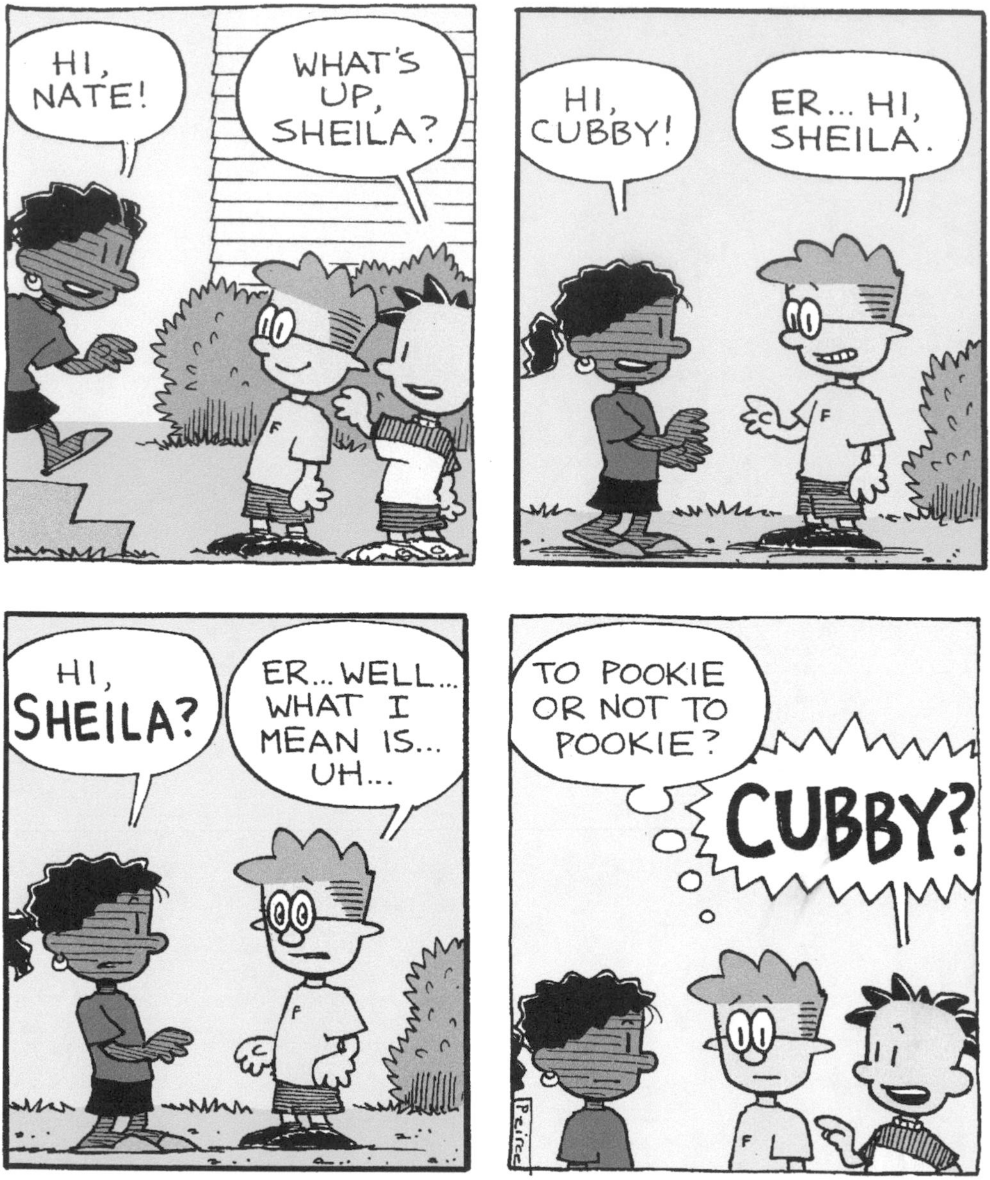
HI, NATE!
WHAT'S UP, SHEILA?
HI, CUBBY!
ER... HI, SHEILA.
HI, SHEILA?
ER... WELL... WHAT I MEAN IS... UH...
TO POOKIE OR NOT TO POOKIE?
CUBBY?
Peirce

SO! YOU GUYS HAVE PET NAMES FOR EACH OTHER! HOW **SWEET!**
OH, COME ON, NATE! IT'S SO OBVIOUS YOU'RE JEALOUS!
JEALOUS?
SURE! YOU'D **LOVE** TO HAVE A PET NAME! BECAUSE **THAT** WOULD MEAN YOU HAD A **GIRL-FRIEND!**
BUT DON'T FEEL LEFT OUT! UNTIL YOU MANAGE TO HOOK UP WITH SOME-BODY, **WE'LL** COME UP WITH A PET NAME FOR YOU!
THIS CONVERSATION ISN'T GOING QUITE AS I'D HOPED.
AFTER ALL, WHAT ARE FRIENDS FOR?
HOW ABOUT "URKEL"?
Peirce

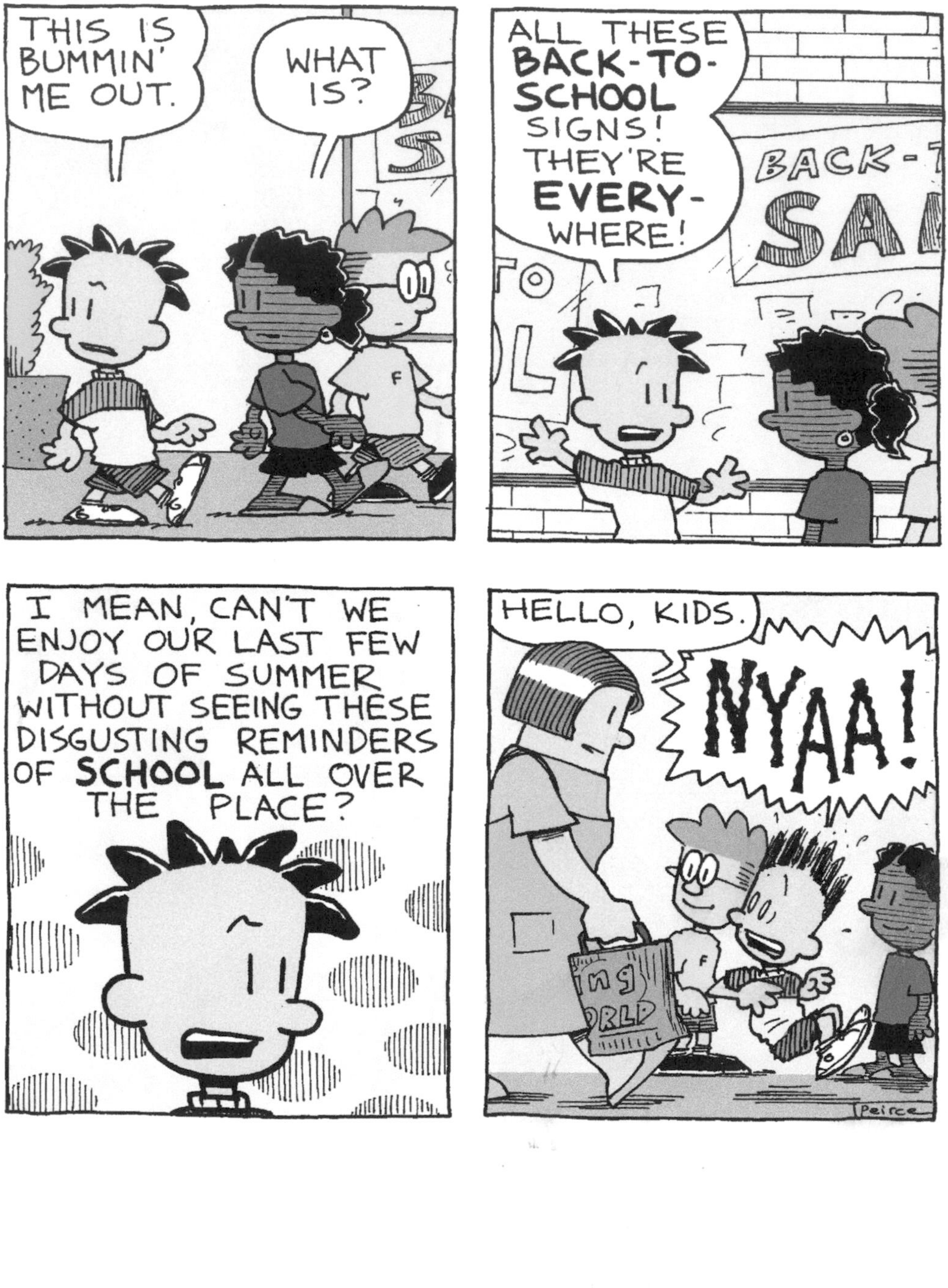
THIS IS BUMMIN' ME OUT.
WHAT IS?
ALL THESE **BACK-TO-SCHOOL** SIGNS! THEY'RE **EVERY-**WHERE!
BACK-T
SA
I MEAN, CAN'T WE ENJOY OUR LAST FEW DAYS OF SUMMER WITHOUT SEEING THESE DISGUSTING REMINDERS OF **SCHOOL** ALL OVER THE PLACE?
HELLO, KIDS.
NYAA!
Peirce

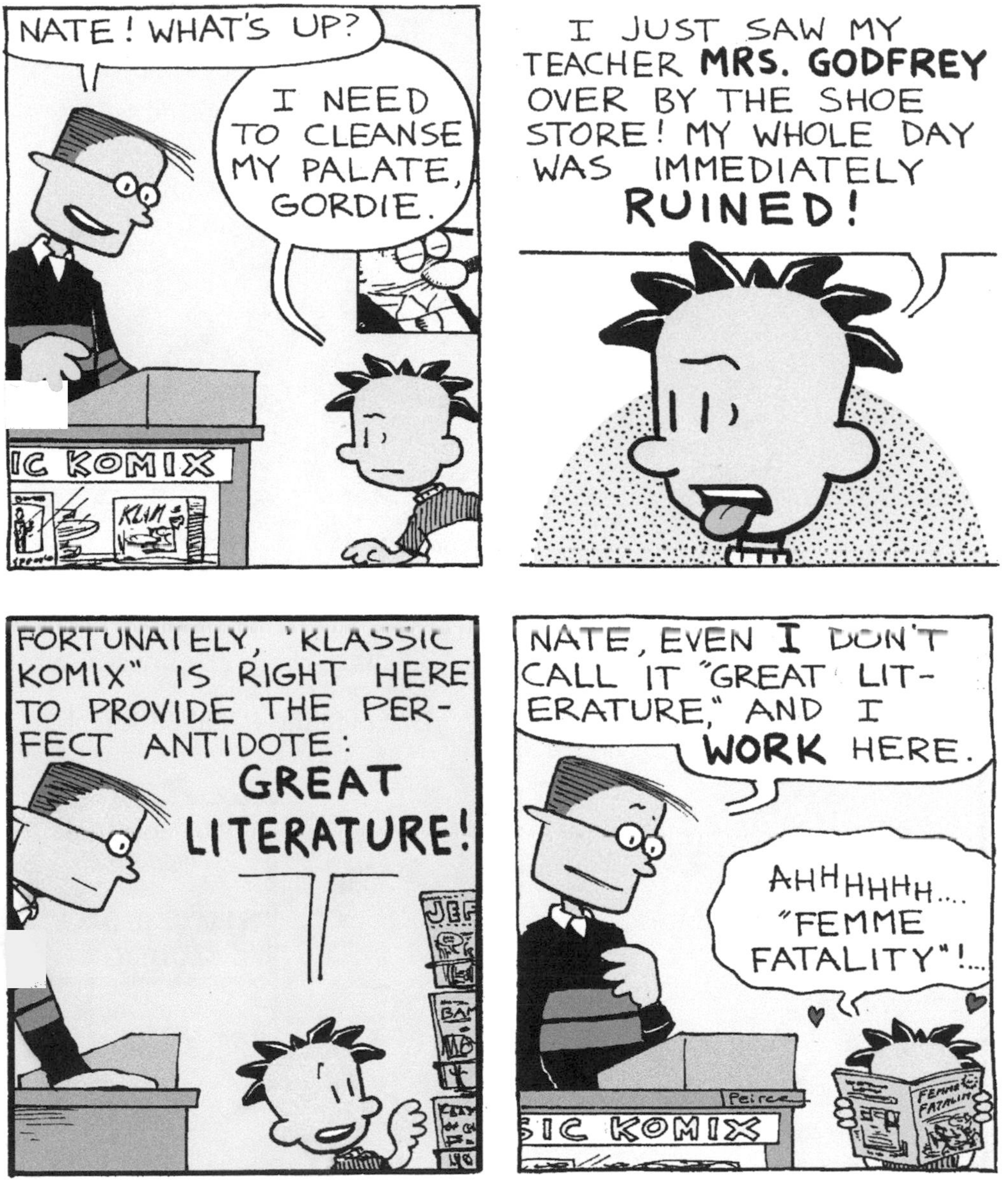
NATE! WHAT'S UP?
I NEED TO CLEANSE MY PALATE, GORDIE.
IC KOMIX
I JUST SAW MY TEACHER MRS. GODFREY OVER BY THE SHOE STORE! MY WHOLE DAY WAS IMMEDIATELY RUINED!
FORTUNATELY, "KLASSIC KOMIX" IS RIGHT HERE TO PROVIDE THE PERFECT ANTIDOTE: GREAT LITERATURE!
NATE, EVEN I DON'T CALL IT "GREAT LITERATURE," AND I WORK HERE.
AHHHHHH.... "FEMME FATALITY"!...
SIC KOMIX
Peirce

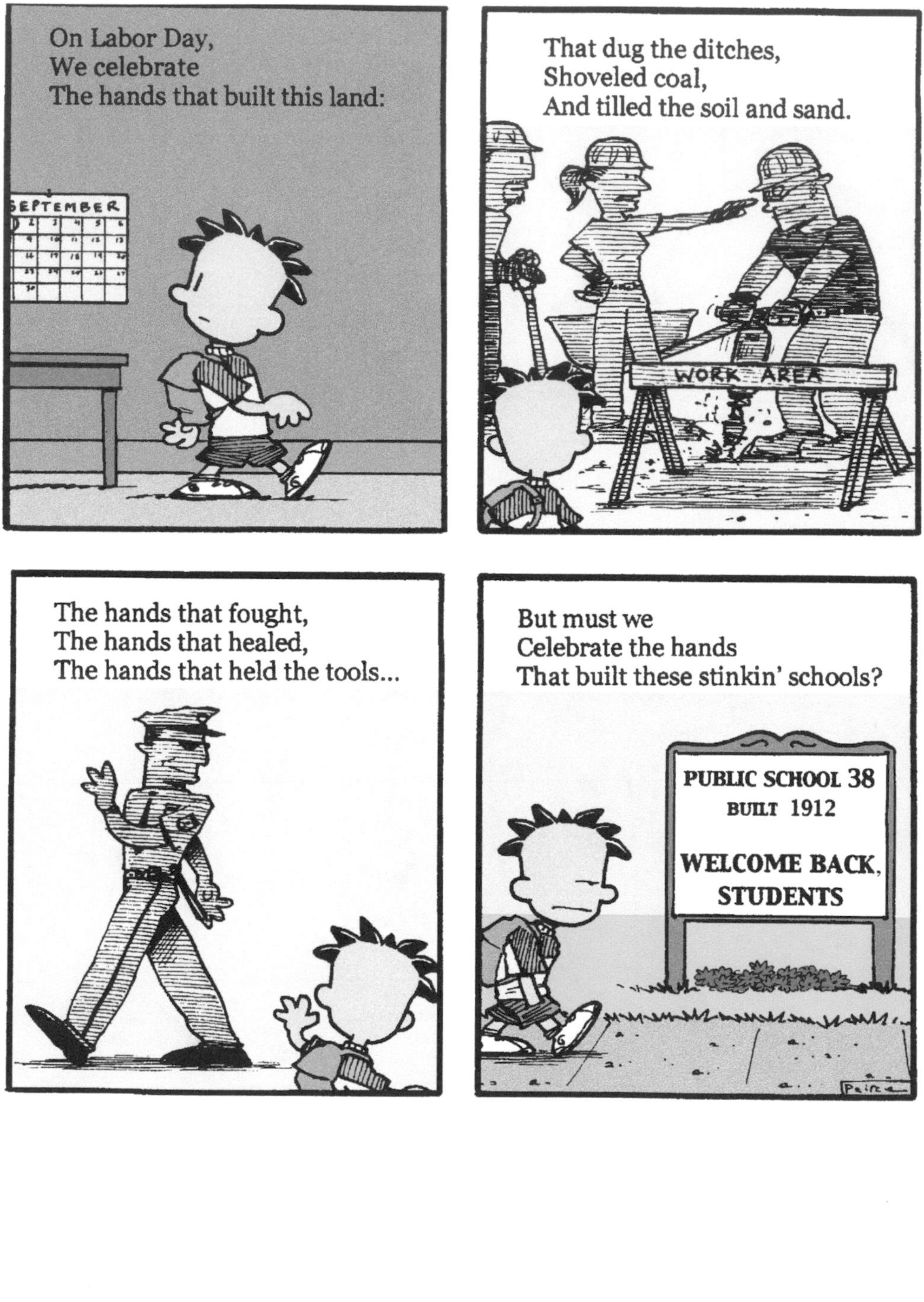
On Labor Day,
We celebrate
The hands that built this land:
SEPTEMBER
That dug the ditches,
Shoveled coal,
And tilled the soil and sand.
WORK AREA
The hands that fought,
The hands that healed,
The hands that held the tools...
But must we
Celebrate the hands
That built these stinkin' schools?
PUBLIC SCHOOL 38
BUILT 1912
WELCOME BACK,
STUDENTS

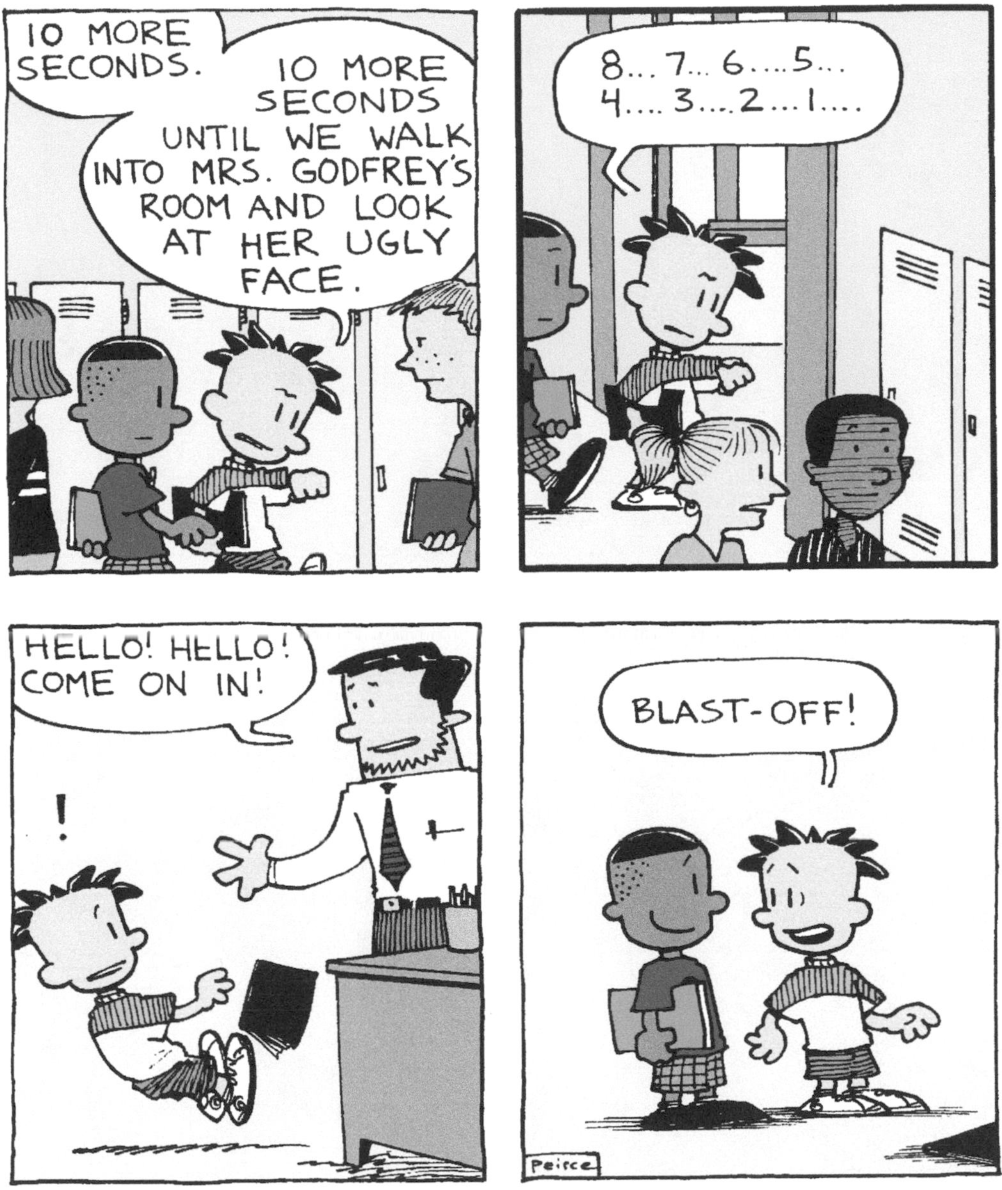
10 MORE SECONDS.
10 MORE SECONDS UNTIL WE WALK INTO MRS. GODFREY'S ROOM AND LOOK AT HER UGLY FACE.
8... 7... 6.... 5... 4.... 3.... 2... 1....
HELLO! HELLO! COME ON IN!
!
BLAST-OFF!
Peirce

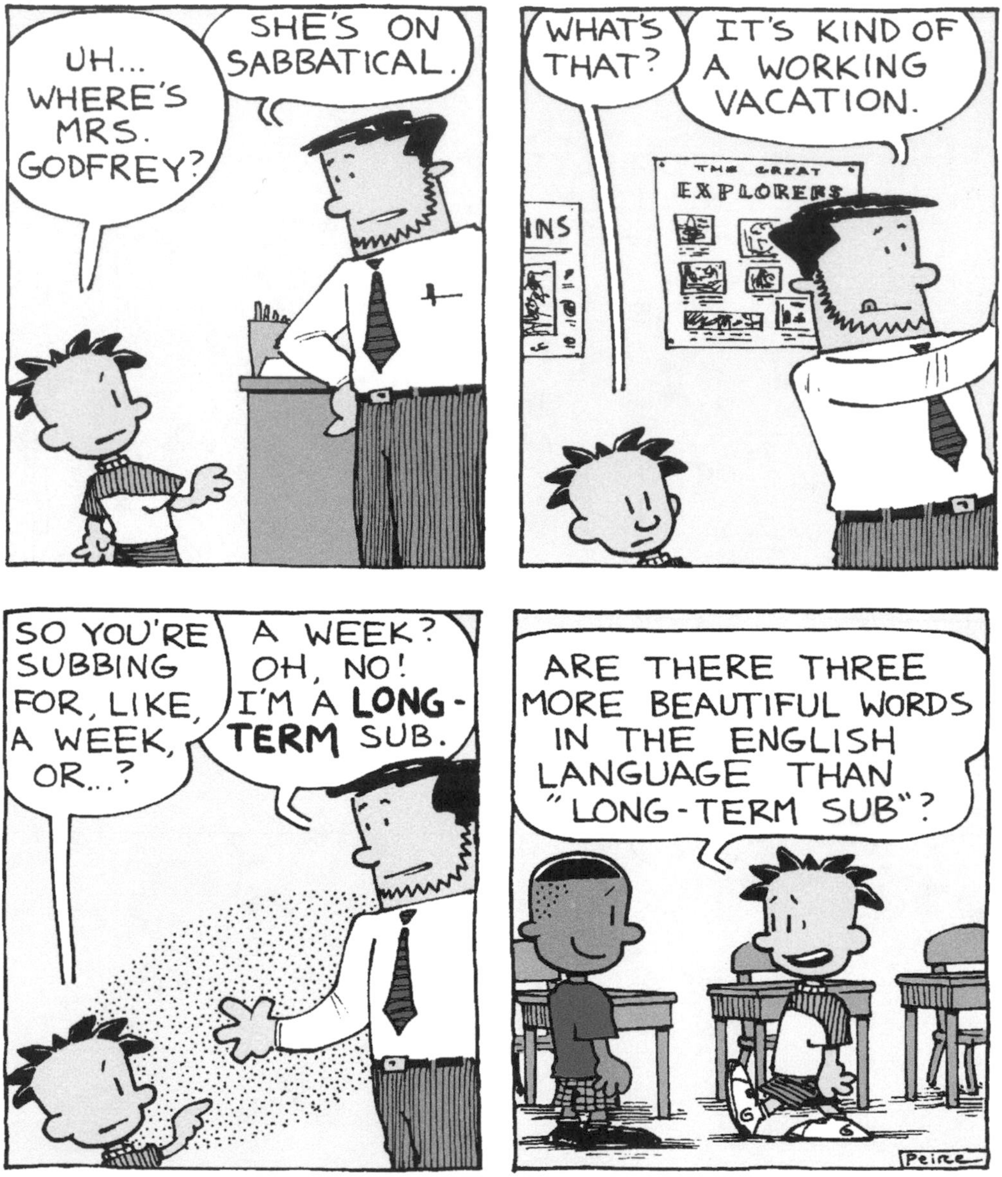
UH... WHERE'S MRS. GODFREY?
SHE'S ON SABBATICAL.
WHAT'S THAT?
IT'S KIND OF A WORKING VACATION.
THE GREAT EXPLORERS
SO YOU'RE SUBBING FOR, LIKE, A WEEK, OR...?
A WEEK? OH, NO! I'M A **LONG-TERM** SUB.
ARE THERE THREE MORE BEAUTIFUL WORDS IN THE ENGLISH LANGUAGE THAN "LONG-TERM SUB"?
Peirce

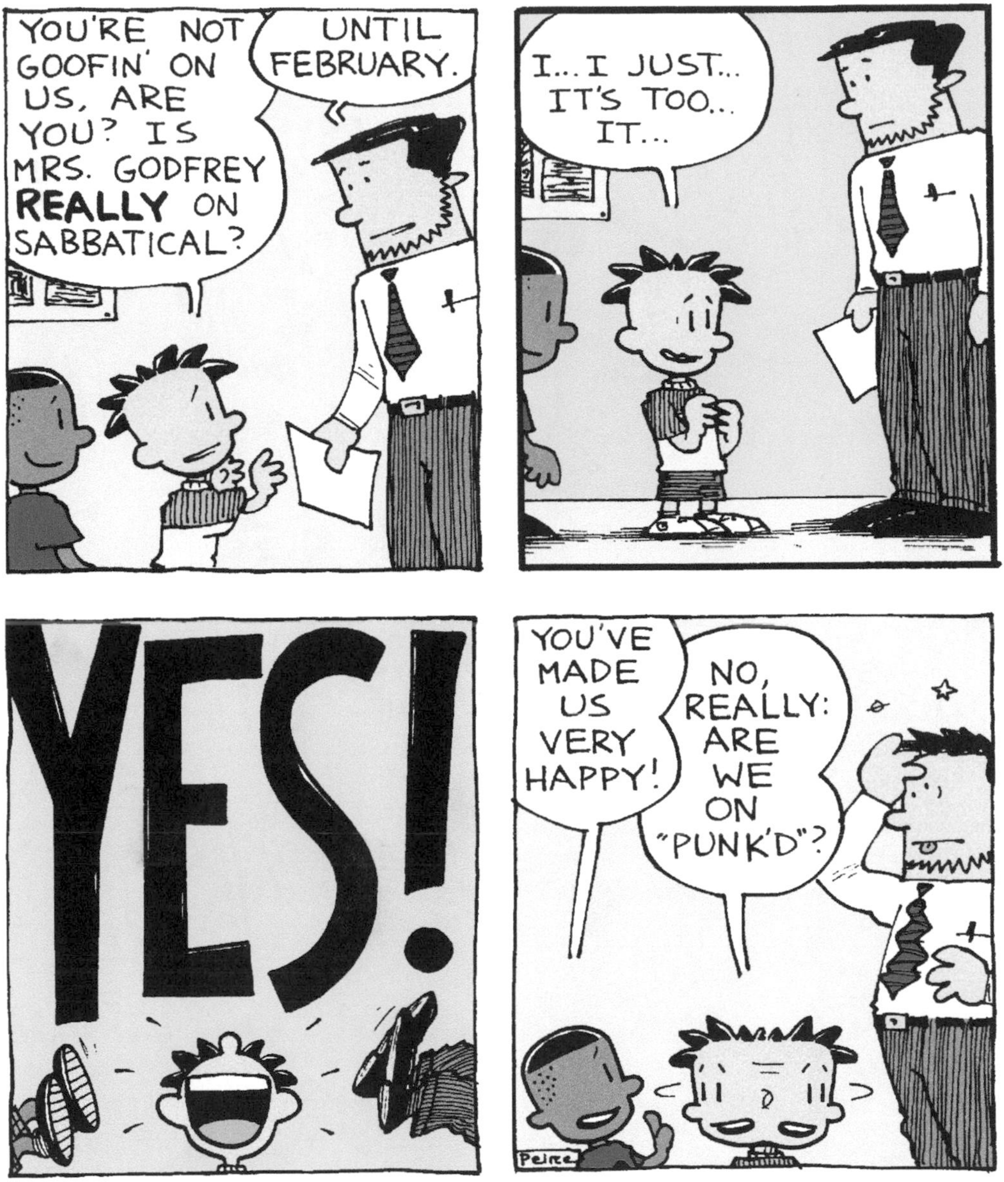
YOU'RE NOT GOOFIN' ON US, ARE YOU? IS MRS. GODFREY **REALLY** ON SABBATICAL?
UNTIL FEBRUARY.
I... I JUST... IT'S TOO... IT...
YES!
YOU'VE MADE US VERY HAPPY!
NO, REALLY: ARE WE ON "PUNK'D"?
Peirce

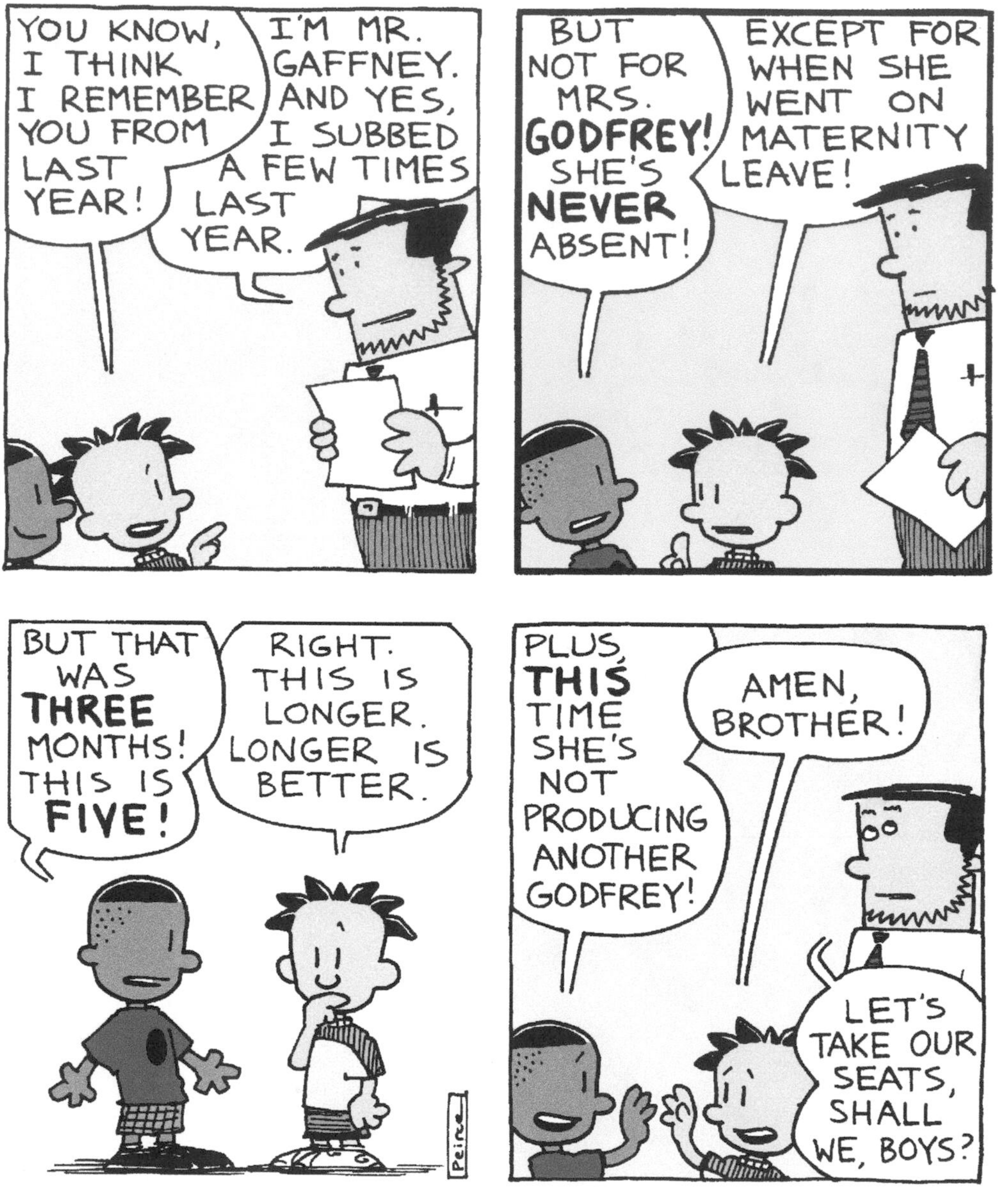
YOU KNOW, I THINK I REMEMBER YOU FROM LAST YEAR!
I'M MR. GAFFNEY. AND YES, I SUBBED A FEW TIMES LAST YEAR.
BUT NOT FOR MRS. GODFREY! SHE'S NEVER ABSENT!
EXCEPT FOR WHEN SHE WENT ON MATERNITY LEAVE!
BUT THAT WAS THREE MONTHS! THIS IS FIVE!
RIGHT. THIS IS LONGER. LONGER IS BETTER.
Peirce
PLUS, THIS TIME SHE'S NOT PRODUCING ANOTHER GODFREY!
AMEN, BROTHER!
LET'S TAKE OUR SEATS, SHALL WE, BOYS?

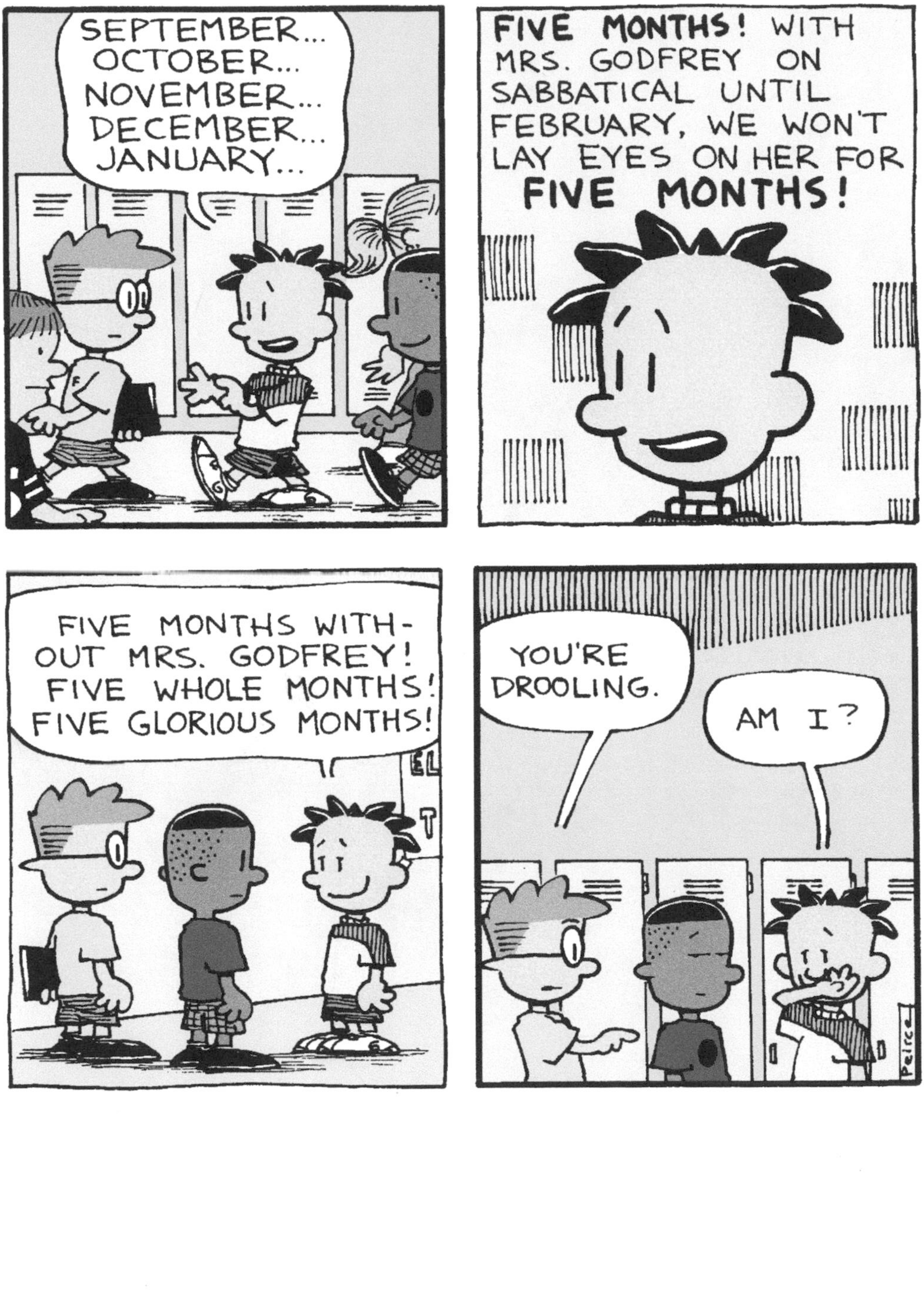
SEPTEMBER... OCTOBER... NOVEMBER... DECEMBER... JANUARY...
FIVE MONTHS! WITH MRS. GODFREY ON SABBATICAL UNTIL FEBRUARY, WE WON'T LAY EYES ON HER FOR FIVE MONTHS!
FIVE MONTHS WITH-OUT MRS. GODFREY! FIVE WHOLE MONTHS! FIVE GLORIOUS MONTHS!
YOU'RE DROOLING.
AM I?
Peirce

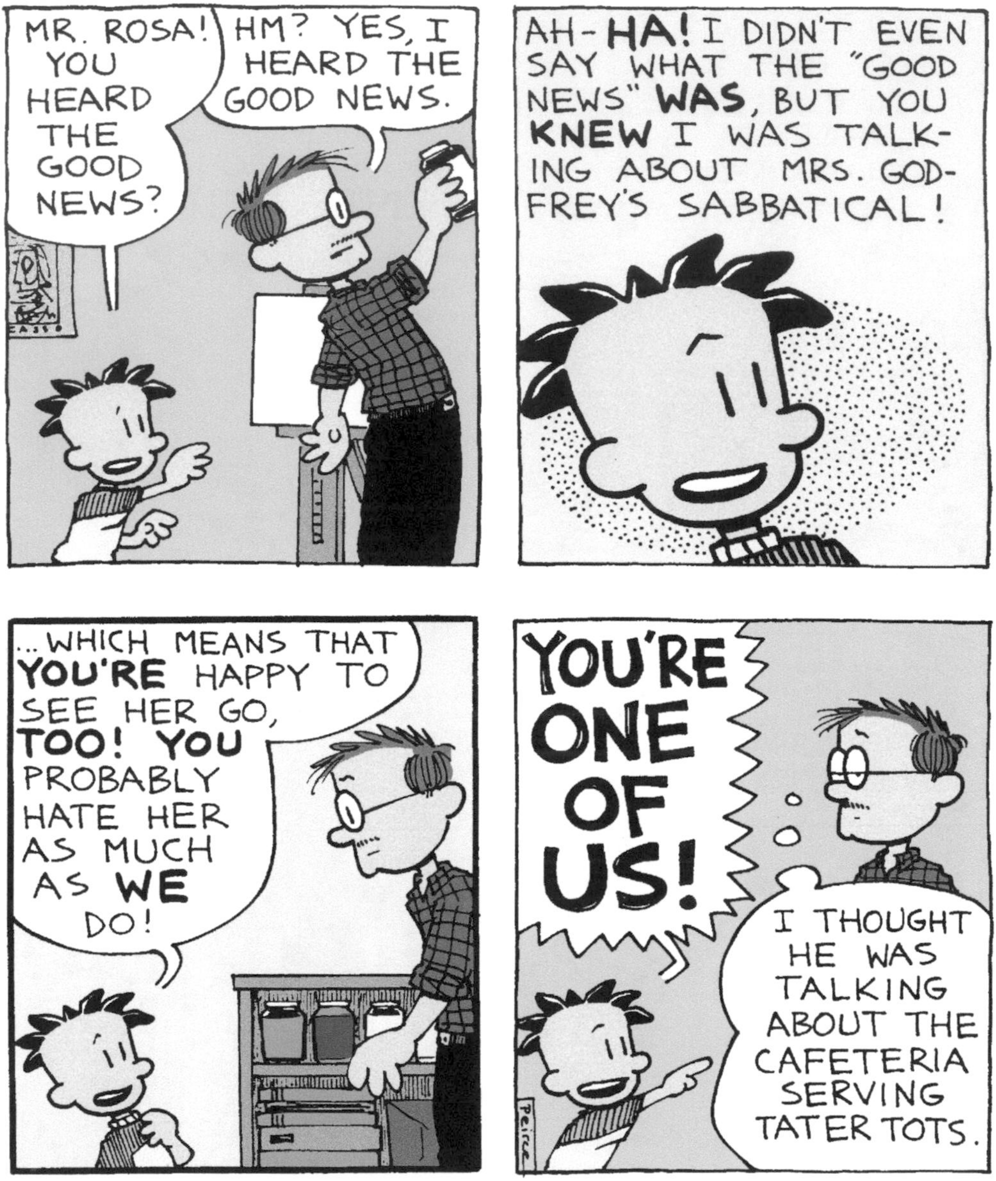
MR. ROSA! YOU HEARD THE GOOD NEWS?
HM? YES, I HEARD THE GOOD NEWS.
AH-HA! I DIDN'T EVEN SAY WHAT THE "GOOD NEWS" WAS, BUT YOU KNEW I WAS TALKING ABOUT MRS. GODFREY'S SABBATICAL!
...WHICH MEANS THAT YOU'RE HAPPY TO SEE HER GO, TOO! YOU PROBABLY HATE HER AS MUCH AS WE DO!
YOU'RE ONE OF US!
I THOUGHT HE WAS TALKING ABOUT THE CAFETERIA SERVING TATER TOTS.
PEIRCE

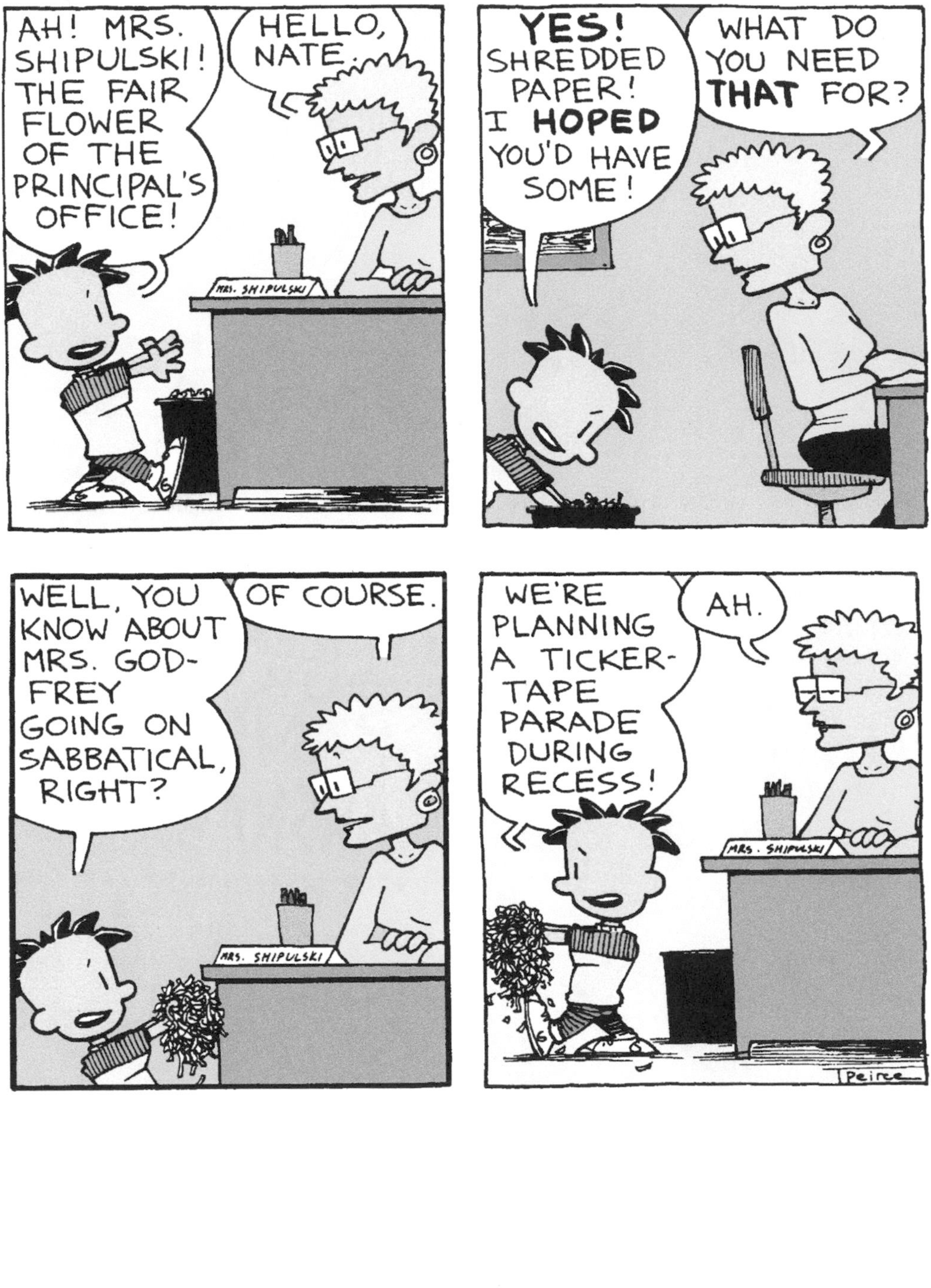
AH! MRS. SHIPULSKI! THE FAIR FLOWER OF THE PRINCIPAL'S OFFICE!
HELLO, NATE.
MRS. SHIPULSKI
YES! SHREDDED PAPER! I HOPED YOU'D HAVE SOME!
WHAT DO YOU NEED THAT FOR?
WELL, YOU KNOW ABOUT MRS. GOD-FREY GOING ON SABBATICAL, RIGHT?
OF COURSE.
MRS. SHIPULSKI
WE'RE PLANNING A TICKER-TAPE PARADE DURING RECESS!
AH.
MRS. SHIPULSKI
Peirce

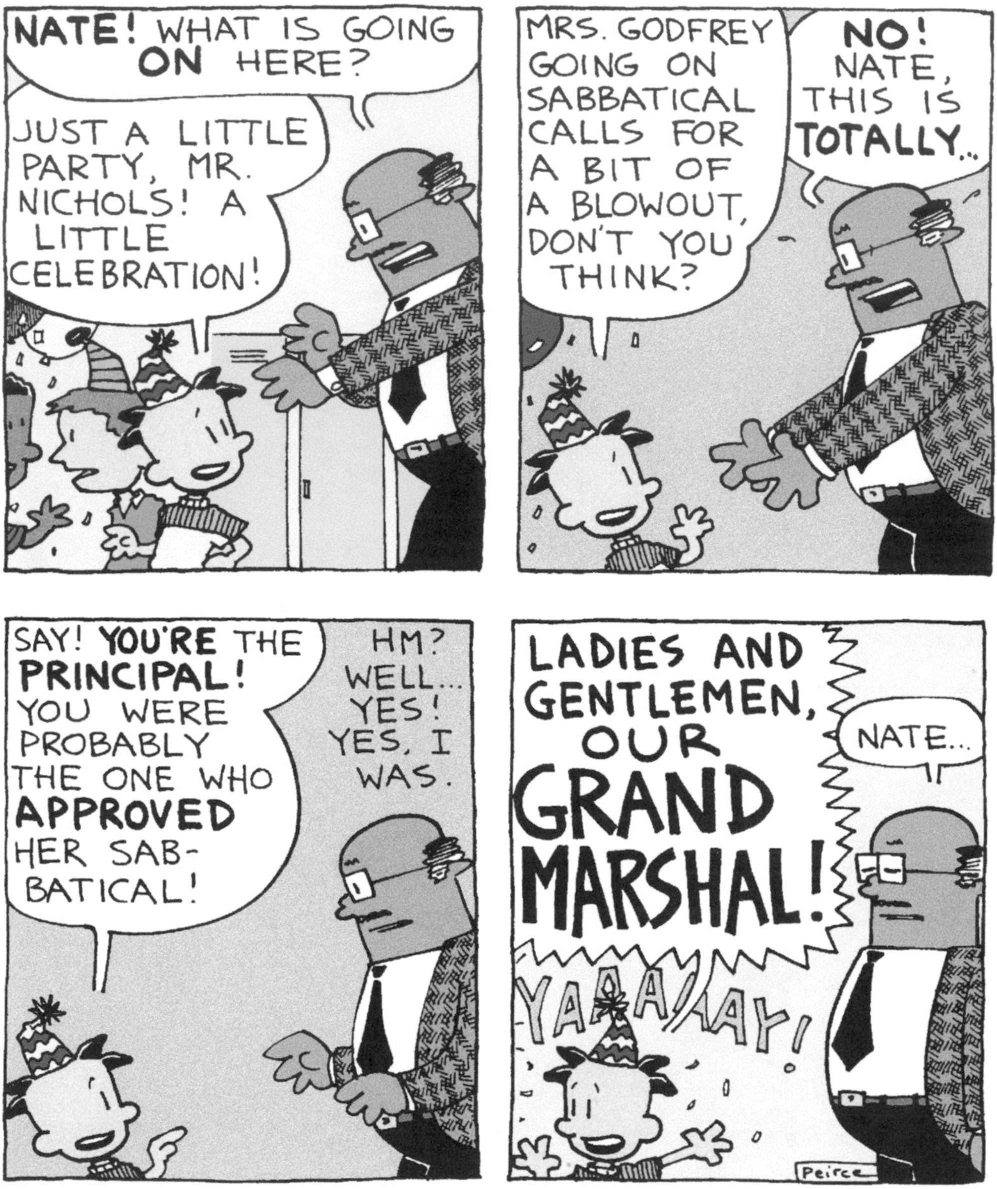
NATE! WHAT IS GOING ON HERE?
JUST A LITTLE PARTY, MR. NICHOLS! A LITTLE CELEBRATION!
MRS. GODFREY GOING ON SABBATICAL CALLS FOR A BIT OF A BLOWOUT, DON'T YOU THINK?
NO! NATE, THIS IS TOTALLY...
SAY! YOU'RE THE PRINCIPAL! YOU WERE PROBABLY THE ONE WHO APPROVED HER SAB-BATICAL!
HM? WELL... YES! YES, I WAS.
LADIES AND GENTLEMEN, OUR GRAND MARSHAL!
NATE...
YAAAAAY!
Peirce

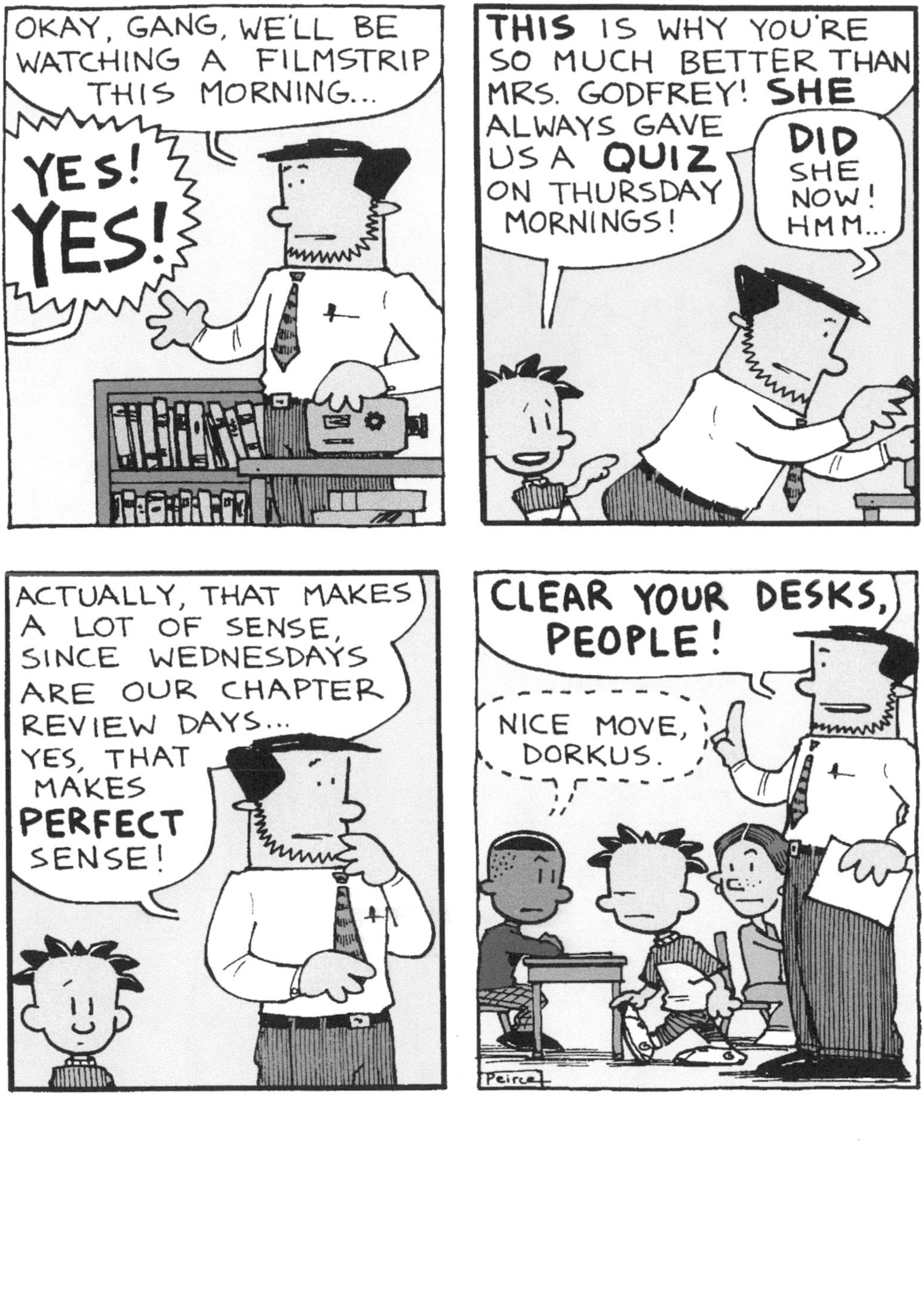
OKAY, GANG, WE'LL BE WATCHING A FILMSTRIP THIS MORNING...
YES! YES!
THIS IS WHY YOU'RE SO MUCH BETTER THAN MRS. GODFREY! SHE ALWAYS GAVE US A QUIZ ON THURSDAY MORNINGS!
DID SHE NOW! HMM...
ACTUALLY, THAT MAKES A LOT OF SENSE, SINCE WEDNESDAYS ARE OUR CHAPTER REVIEW DAYS... YES, THAT MAKES PERFECT SENSE!
CLEAR YOUR DESKS, PEOPLE!
NICE MOVE, DORKUS.
Peirce

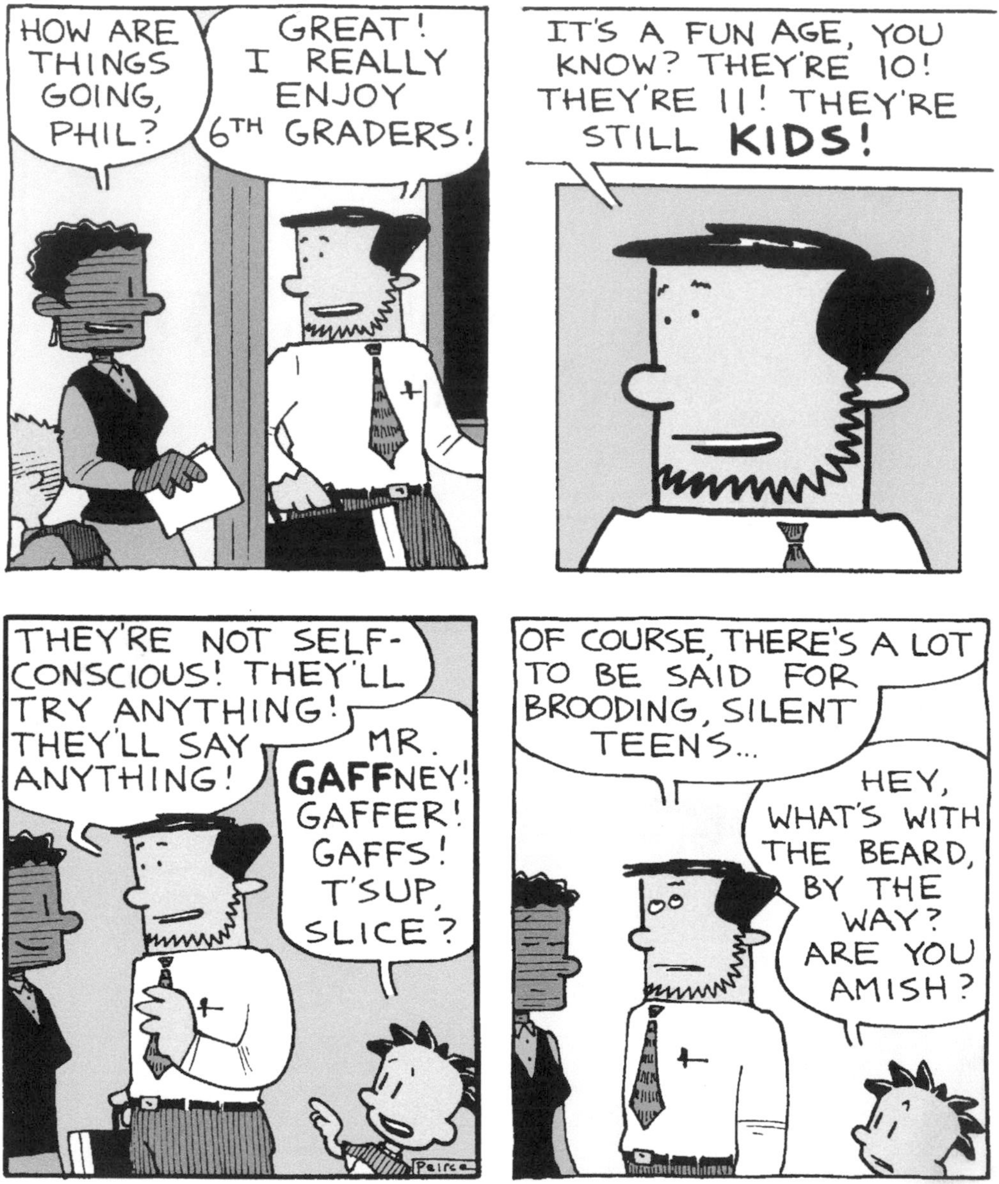
HOW ARE THINGS GOING, PHIL?
GREAT! I REALLY ENJOY 6TH GRADERS!
IT'S A FUN AGE, YOU KNOW? THEY'RE 10! THEY'RE 11! THEY'RE STILL **KIDS!**
THEY'RE NOT SELF-CONSCIOUS! THEY'LL TRY ANYTHING! THEY'LL SAY ANYTHING!
MR. **GAFF**NEY! GAFFER! GAFFS! T'SUP, SLICE?
Peirce
OF COURSE, THERE'S A LOT TO BE SAID FOR BROODING, SILENT TEENS...
HEY, WHAT'S WITH THE BEARD, BY THE WAY? ARE YOU AMISH?

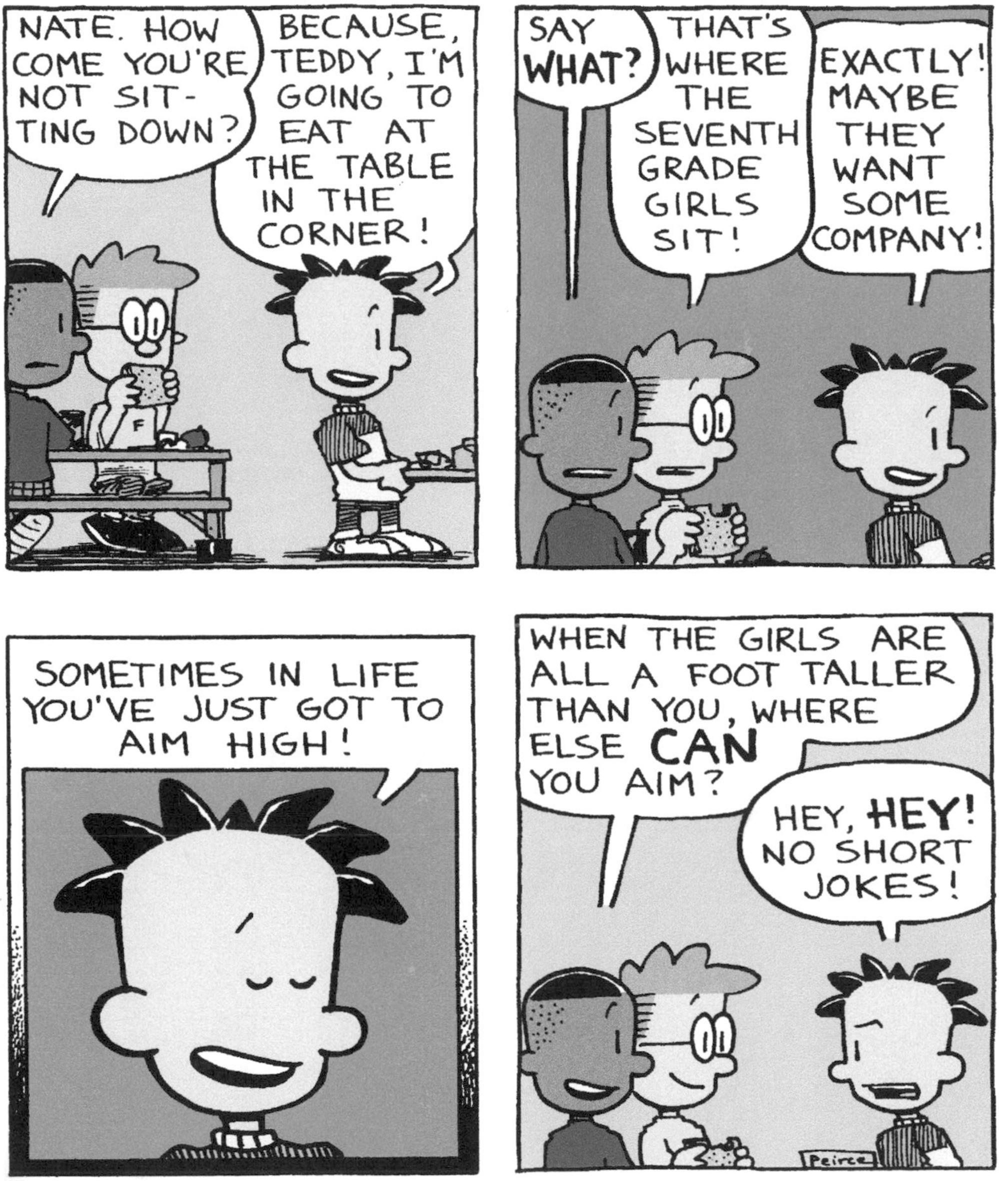
NATE. HOW COME YOU'RE NOT SITTING DOWN?
BECAUSE, TEDDY, I'M GOING TO EAT AT THE TABLE IN THE CORNER!
SAY WHAT?
THAT'S WHERE THE SEVENTH GRADE GIRLS SIT!
EXACTLY! MAYBE THEY WANT SOME COMPANY!
SOMETIMES IN LIFE YOU'VE JUST GOT TO AIM HIGH!
WHEN THE GIRLS ARE ALL A FOOT TALLER THAN YOU, WHERE ELSE CAN YOU AIM?
HEY, HEY! NO SHORT JOKES!
Peirce

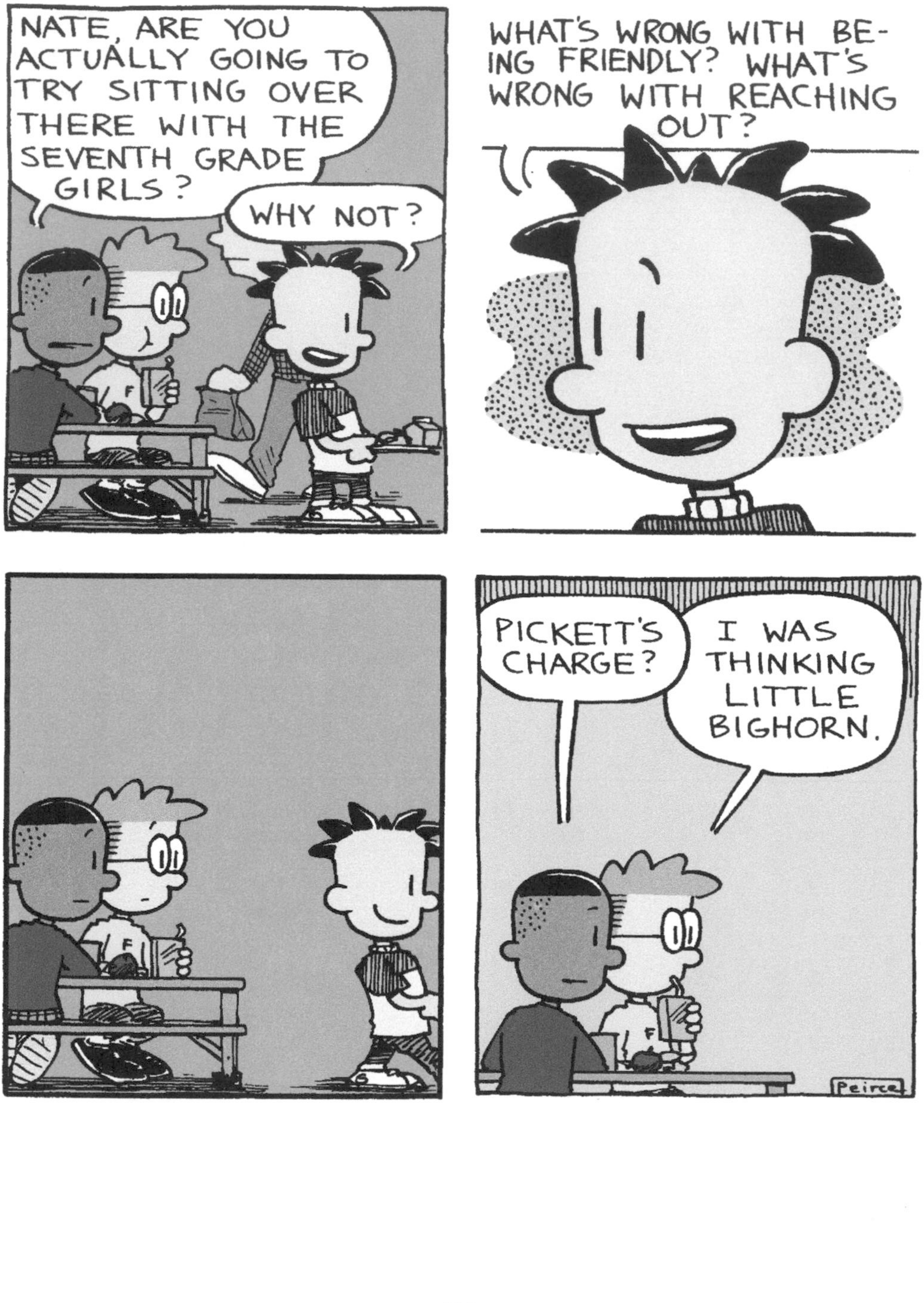

NATE, ARE YOU ACTUALLY GOING TO TRY SITTING OVER THERE WITH THE SEVENTH GRADE GIRLS?
WHY NOT?
WHAT'S WRONG WITH BEING FRIENDLY? WHAT'S WRONG WITH REACHING OUT?
PICKETT'S CHARGE?
I WAS THINKING LITTLE BIGHORN.
Peirce

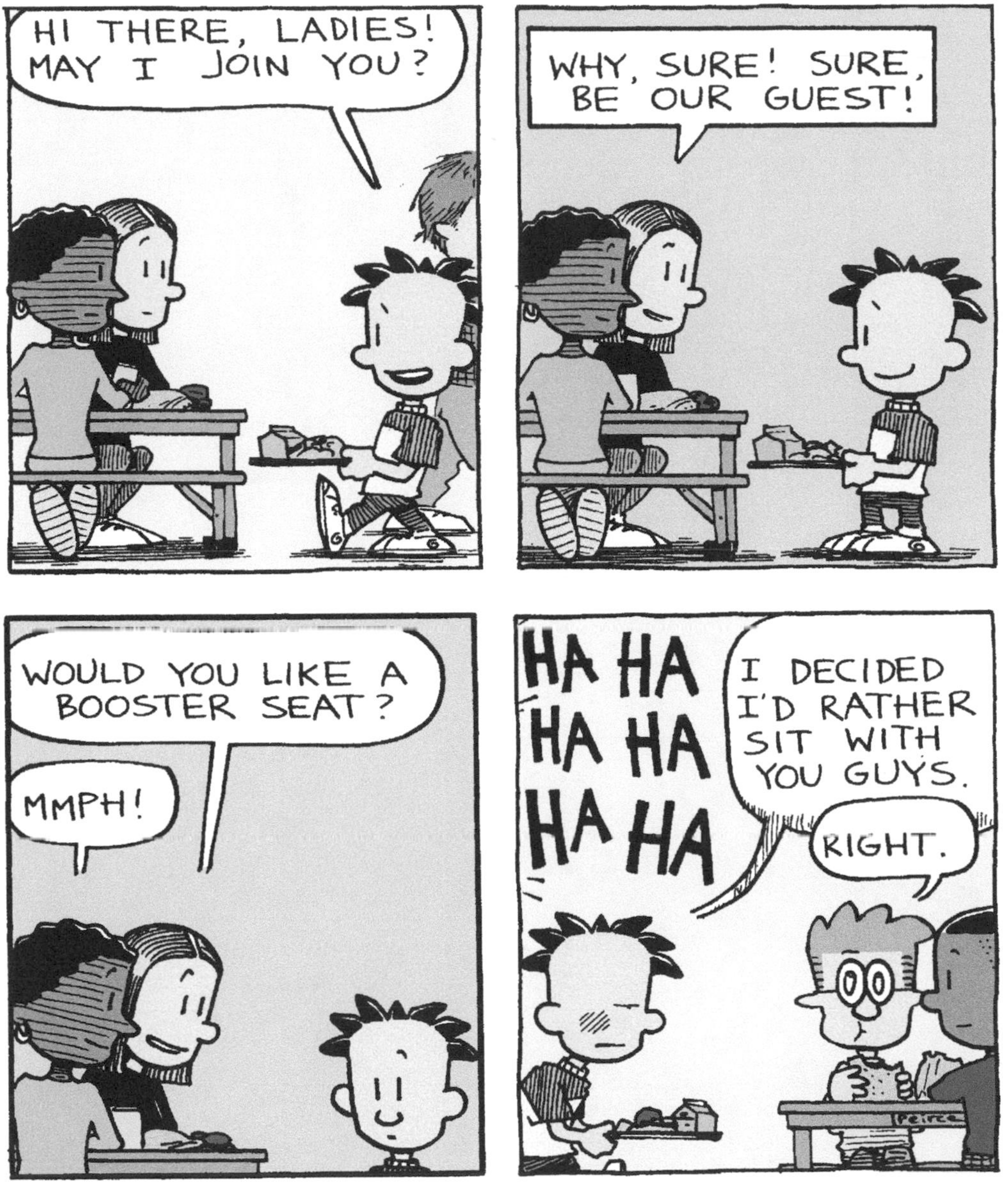
HI THERE, LADIES! MAY I JOIN YOU?
WHY, SURE! SURE, BE OUR GUEST!
WOULD YOU LIKE A BOOSTER SEAT?
MMPH!
HA HA HA HA HA HA
I DECIDED I'D RATHER SIT WITH YOU GUYS.
RIGHT.
Peirce

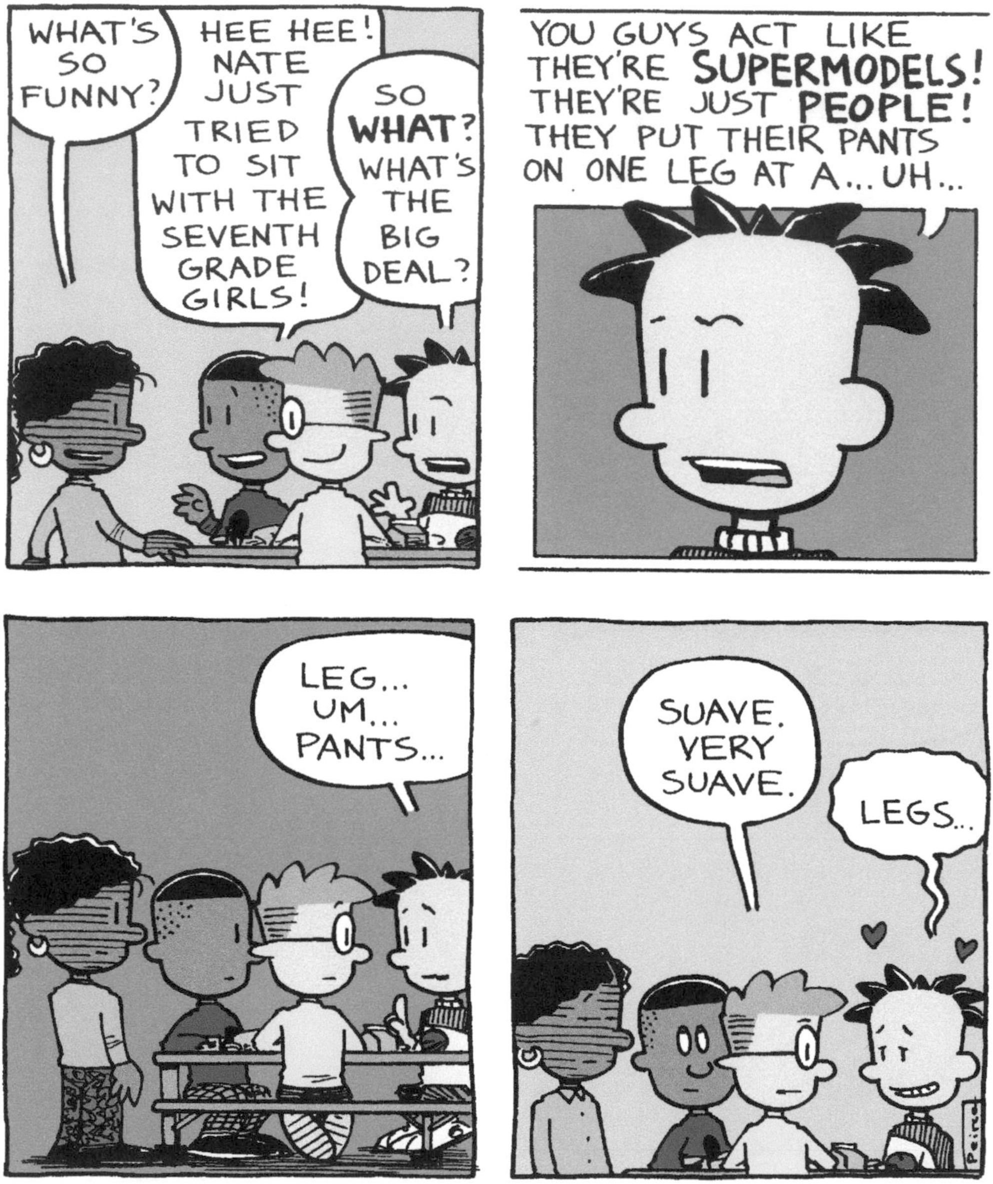
WHAT'S SO FUNNY?
HEE HEE! NATE JUST TRIED TO SIT WITH THE SEVENTH GRADE GIRLS!
SO WHAT? WHAT'S THE BIG DEAL?
YOU GUYS ACT LIKE THEY'RE SUPERMODELS! THEY'RE JUST PEOPLE! THEY PUT THEIR PANTS ON ONE LEG AT A... UH...
LEG... UM... PANTS...
SUAVE. VERY SUAVE.
LEGS...
Peirce

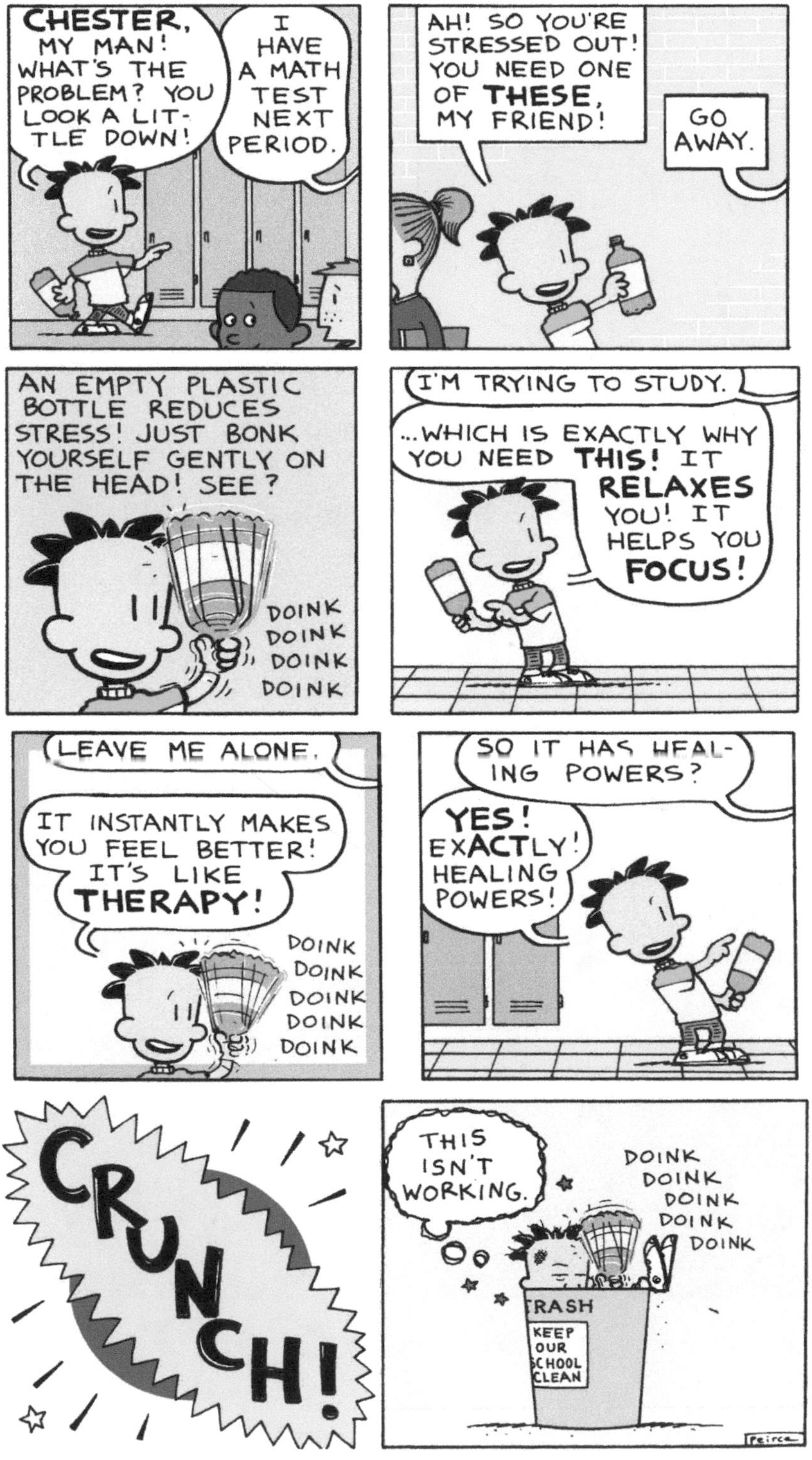
CHESTER, MY MAN! WHAT'S THE PROBLEM? YOU LOOK A LIT-TLE DOWN!
I HAVE A MATH TEST NEXT PERIOD.
AH! SO YOU'RE STRESSED OUT! YOU NEED ONE OF THESE, MY FRIEND!
GO AWAY.
AN EMPTY PLASTIC BOTTLE REDUCES STRESS! JUST BONK YOURSELF GENTLY ON THE HEAD! SEE?
DOINK DOINK DOINK DOINK
I'M TRYING TO STUDY.
...WHICH IS EXACTLY WHY YOU NEED THIS! IT RELAXES YOU! IT HELPS YOU FOCUS!
LEAVE ME ALONE.
IT INSTANTLY MAKES YOU FEEL BETTER! IT'S LIKE THERAPY!
DOINK DOINK DOINK DOINK DOINK
SO IT HAS HEAL-ING POWERS?
YES! EXACTLY! HEALING POWERS!
CRUNCH!
THIS ISN'T WORKING.
DOINK DOINK DOINK DOINK DOINK
TRASH
KEEP OUR SCHOOL CLEAN
Peirce

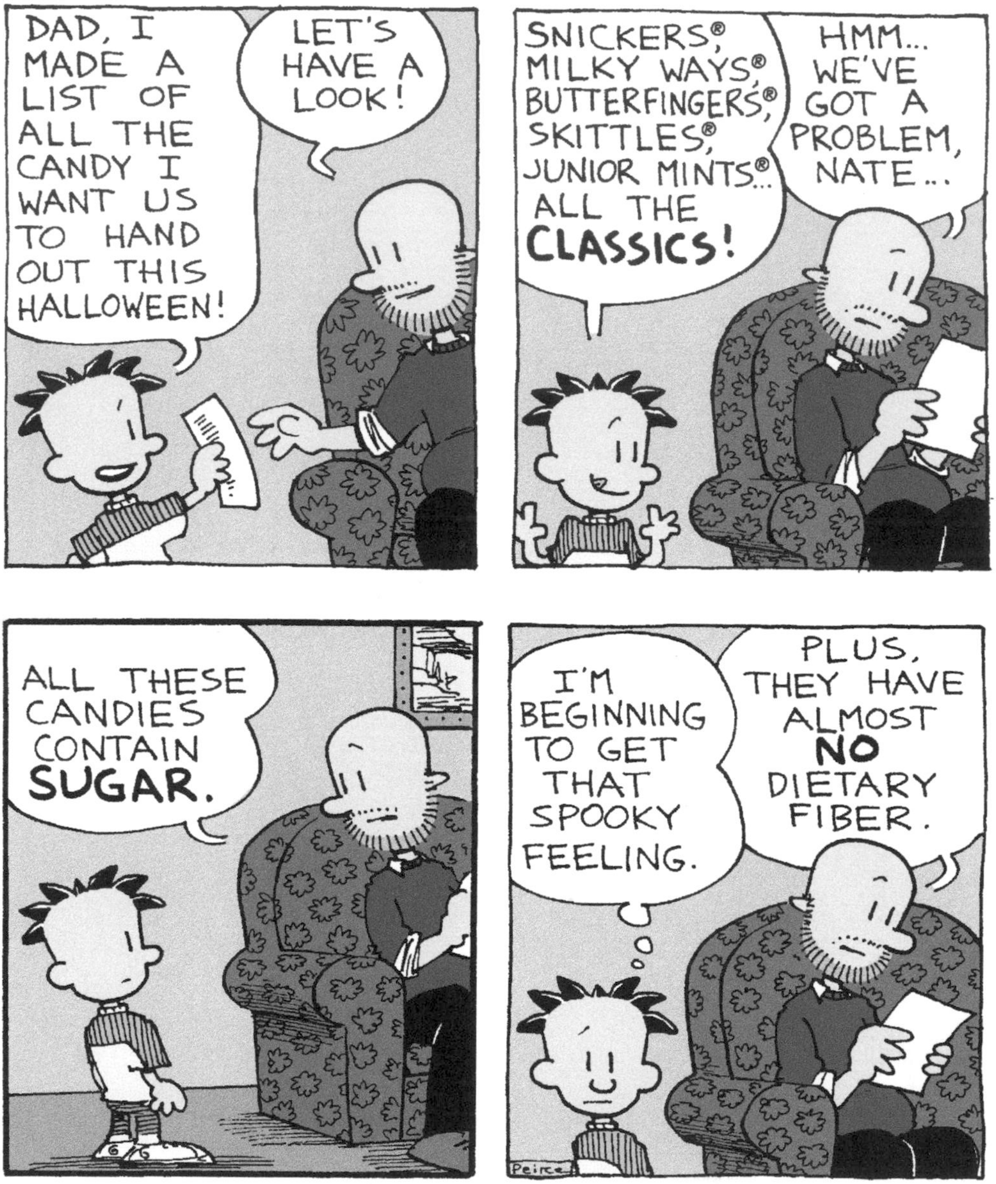
DAD, I MADE A LIST OF ALL THE CANDY I WANT US TO HAND OUT THIS HALLOWEEN!
LET'S HAVE A LOOK!
SNICKERS®, MILKY WAYS®, BUTTERFINGERS®, SKITTLES®, JUNIOR MINTS®... ALL THE **CLASSICS!**
HMM... WE'VE GOT A PROBLEM, NATE...
ALL THESE CANDIES CONTAIN **SUGAR**.
PLUS, THEY HAVE ALMOST **NO** DIETARY FIBER.
I'M BEGINNING TO GET THAT SPOOKY FEELING.
Peirce

YOU'RE BACK! DID YOU BUY OUR HALLOWEEN CANDY?
MISSION ACCOMPLISHED!
WHAT'D YOU GET?
HERE'S A HINT: **CANDY** MAY BE **DANDY**...
YES?... YES?
...BUT **SOY** IS A **JOY**!
NO!... NO!
IT'S TEMPTING, BUT NO NIBBLING 'TIL FRIDAY!
Peirce

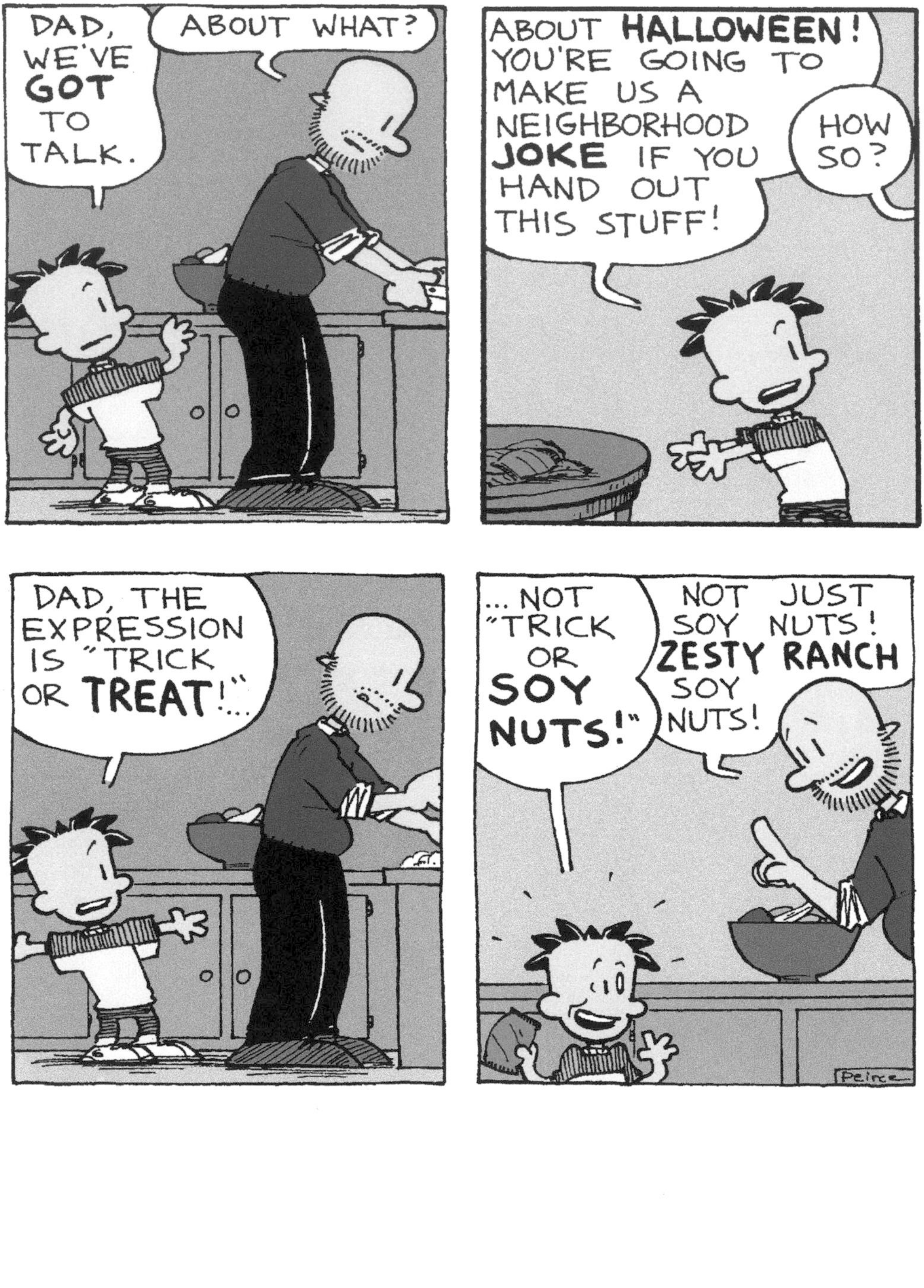
DAD, WE'VE **GOT** TO TALK.
ABOUT WHAT?
ABOUT **HALLOWEEN**! YOU'RE GOING TO MAKE US A NEIGHBORHOOD **JOKE** IF YOU HAND OUT THIS STUFF!
HOW SO?
DAD, THE EXPRESSION IS "TRICK OR **TREAT**!"...
..NOT "TRICK OR **SOY NUTS**!"
NOT JUST SOY NUTS! **ZESTY RANCH** SOY NUTS!
Peirce

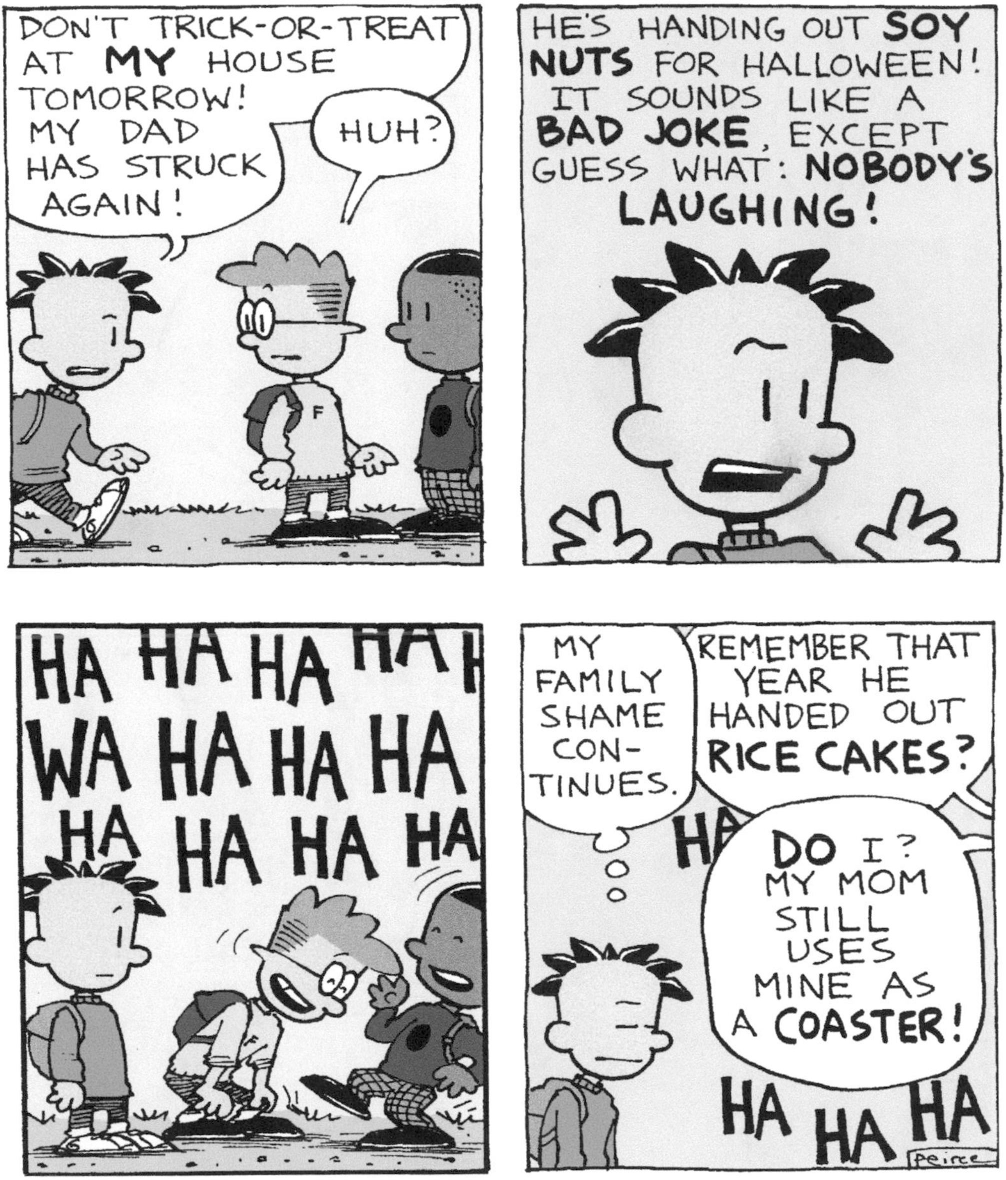
DON'T TRICK-OR-TREAT AT MY HOUSE TOMORROW! MY DAD HAS STRUCK AGAIN!
HUH?
HE'S HANDING OUT SOY NUTS FOR HALLOWEEN! IT SOUNDS LIKE A BAD JOKE, EXCEPT GUESS WHAT: NOBODY'S LAUGHING!
HA HA HA HA HA
WA HA HA HA
HA HA HA HA
MY FAMILY SHAME CON-TINUES.
REMEMBER THAT YEAR HE HANDED OUT RICE CAKES?
HA
DO I? MY MOM STILL USES MINE AS A COASTER!
HA HA HA
peirce

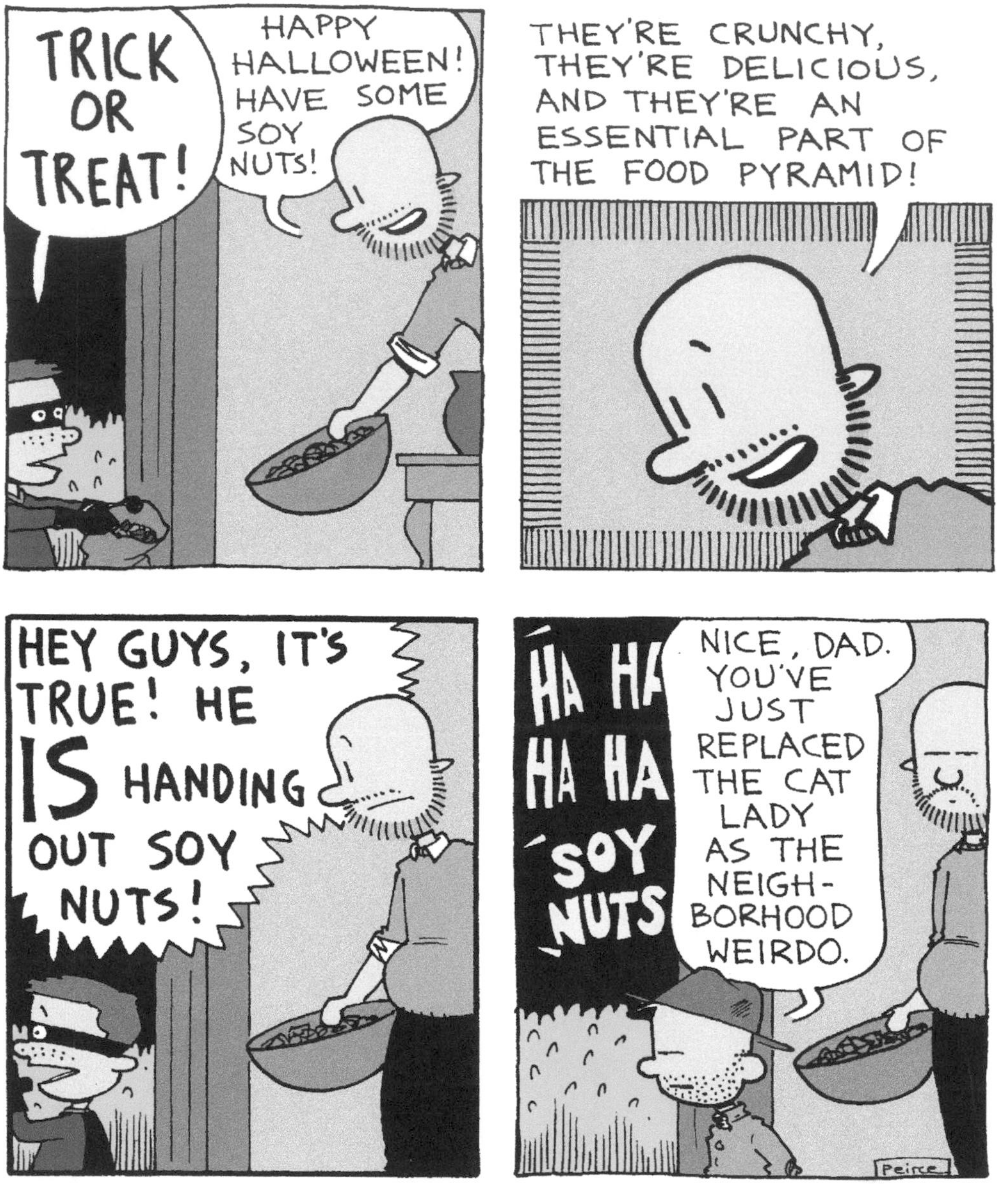
TRICK OR TREAT!
HAPPY HALLOWEEN! HAVE SOME SOY NUTS!
THEY'RE CRUNCHY, THEY'RE DELICIOUS, AND THEY'RE AN ESSENTIAL PART OF THE FOOD PYRAMID!
HEY GUYS, IT'S TRUE! HE IS HANDING OUT SOY NUTS!
HA HA HA HA
SOY NUTS
NICE, DAD. YOU'VE JUST REPLACED THE CAT LADY AS THE NEIGH-BORHOOD WEIRDO.
Peirce

I'M BACK.
LOOK AT THIS, NATE! THE BOWL IS ALMOST EMPTY!
THE BAGS OF SOY NUTS HAVE BEEN GOING LIKE HOTCAKES! KIDS CAN'T GET ENOUGH OF 'EM! AND DO YOU KNOW WHY?
WAP!
BECAUSE EVERY-BODY'S RUN OUT OF EGGS.
HEY! HAVE YOU EVEN TRIED THEM? THEY'RE ZESTY RANCH!
Peirce

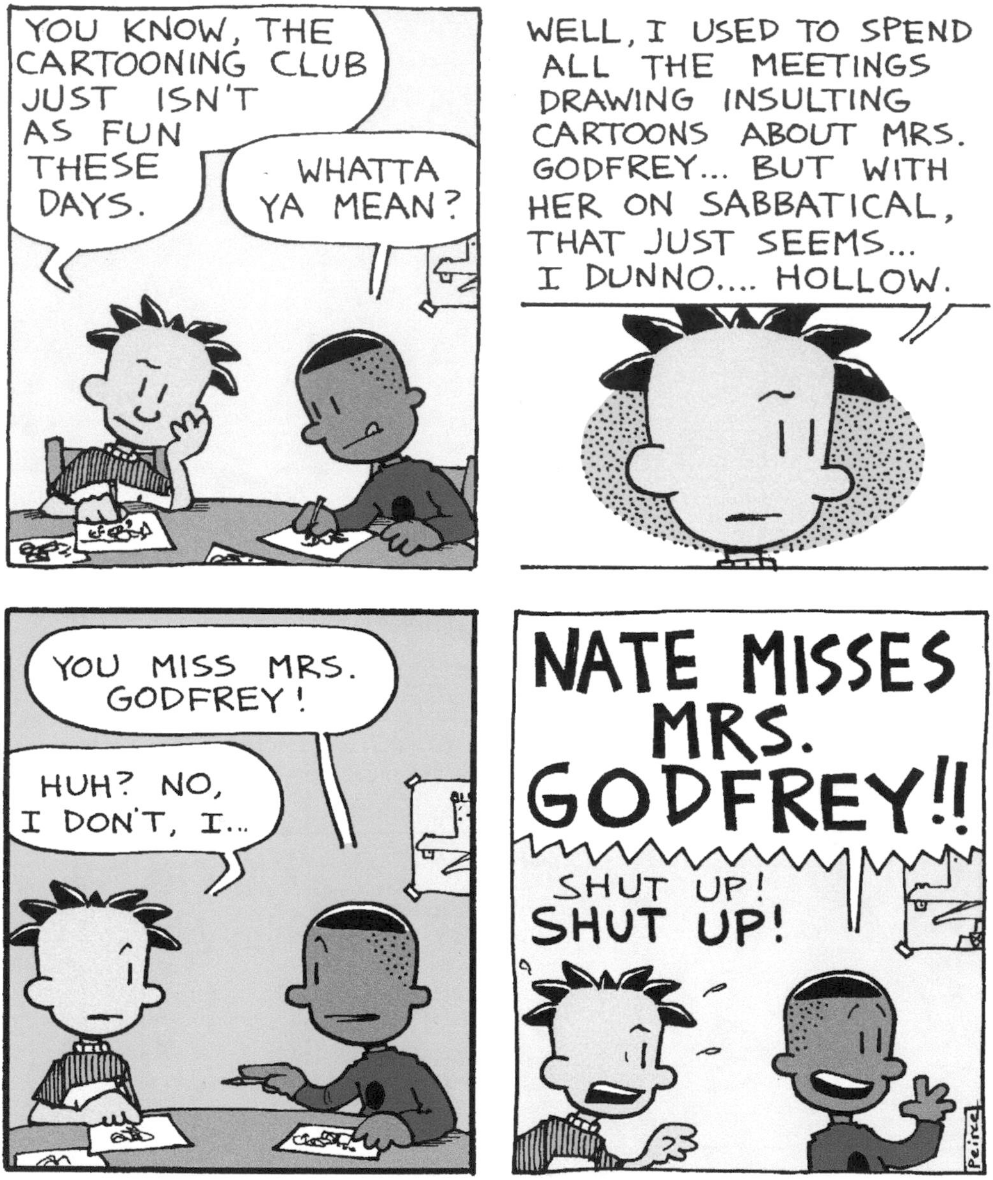
YOU KNOW, THE CARTOONING CLUB JUST ISN'T AS FUN THESE DAYS.
WHATTA YA MEAN?
WELL, I USED TO SPEND ALL THE MEETINGS DRAWING INSULTING CARTOONS ABOUT MRS. GODFREY... BUT WITH HER ON SABBATICAL, THAT JUST SEEMS... I DUNNO.... HOLLOW.
YOU MISS MRS. GODFREY!
HUH? NO, I DON'T, I...
NATE MISSES MRS. GODFREY!!
SHUT UP! SHUT UP!
Peirce

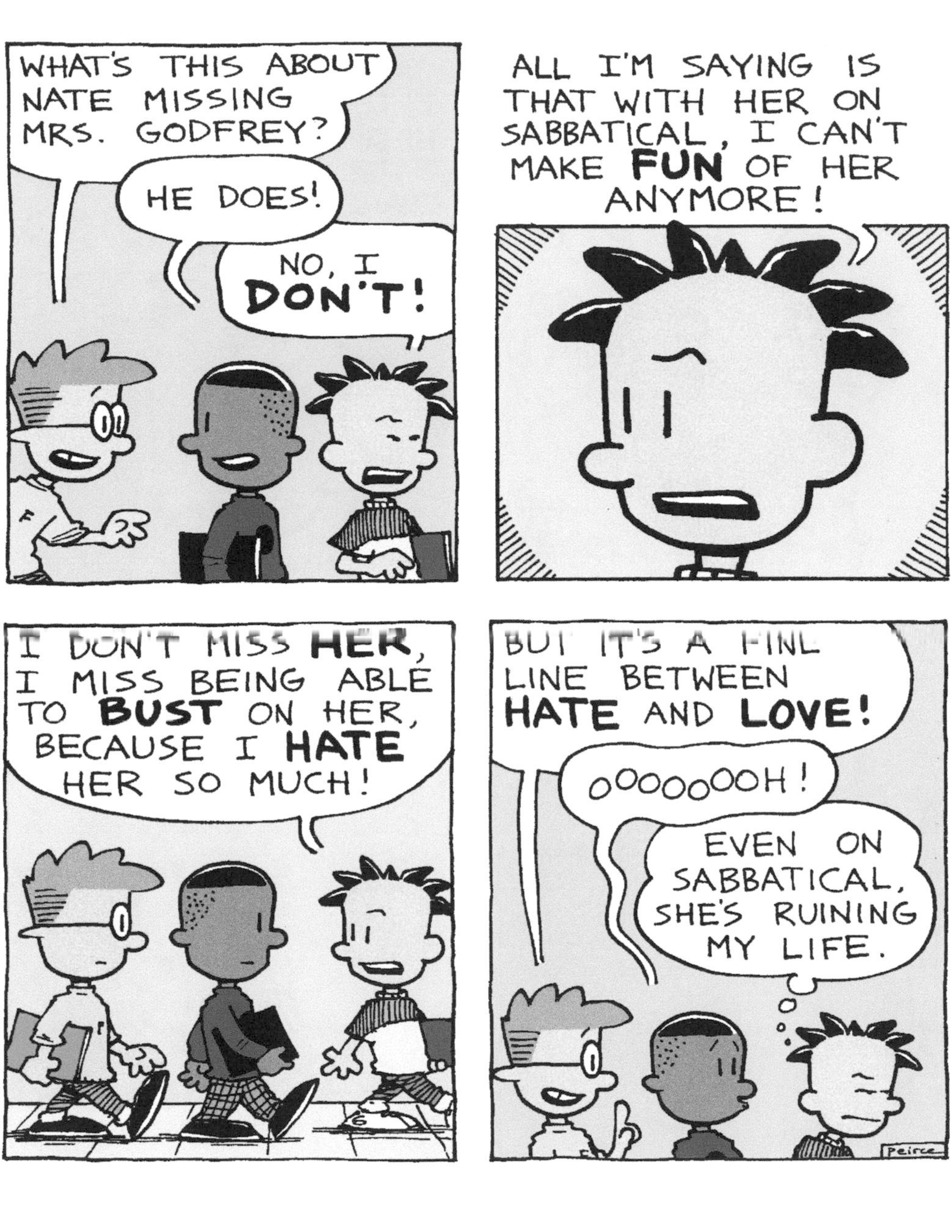
WHAT'S THIS ABOUT NATE MISSING MRS. GODFREY?
HE DOES!
NO, I DON'T!
ALL I'M SAYING IS THAT WITH HER ON SABBATICAL, I CAN'T MAKE FUN OF HER ANYMORE!
I DON'T MISS HER, I MISS BEING ABLE TO BUST ON HER, BECAUSE I HATE HER SO MUCH!
BUT IT'S A FINE LINE BETWEEN HATE AND LOVE!
OOOOOOOH!
EVEN ON SABBATICAL, SHE'S RUINING MY LIFE.
Peirce

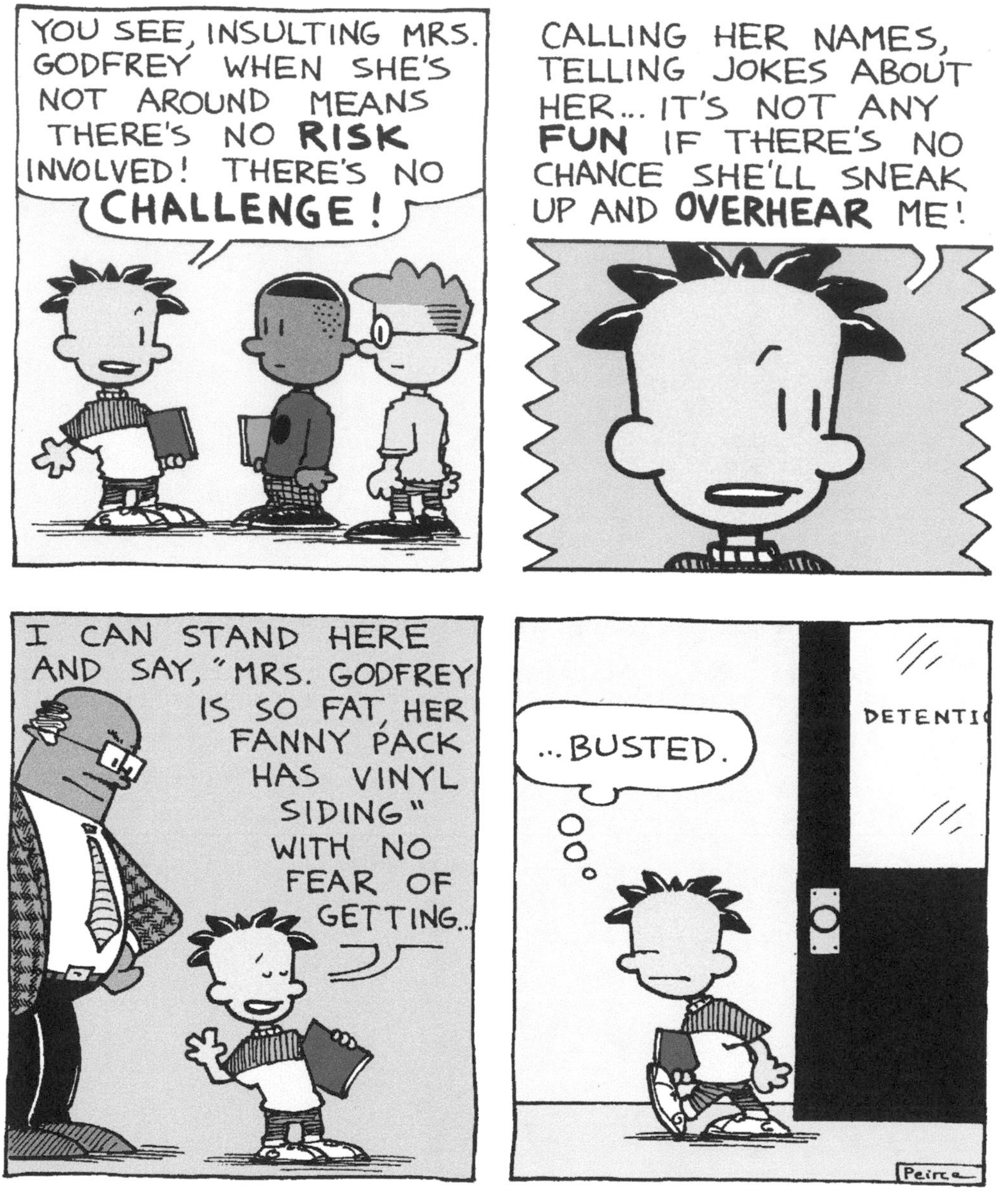
YOU SEE, INSULTING MRS. GODFREY WHEN SHE'S NOT AROUND MEANS THERE'S NO RISK INVOLVED! THERE'S NO CHALLENGE!
CALLING HER NAMES, TELLING JOKES ABOUT HER... IT'S NOT ANY FUN IF THERE'S NO CHANCE SHE'LL SNEAK UP AND OVERHEAR ME!
I CAN STAND HERE AND SAY, "MRS. GODFREY IS SO FAT, HER FANNY PACK HAS VINYL SIDING" WITH NO FEAR OF GETTING..
...BUSTED.
DETENTI
Peirce

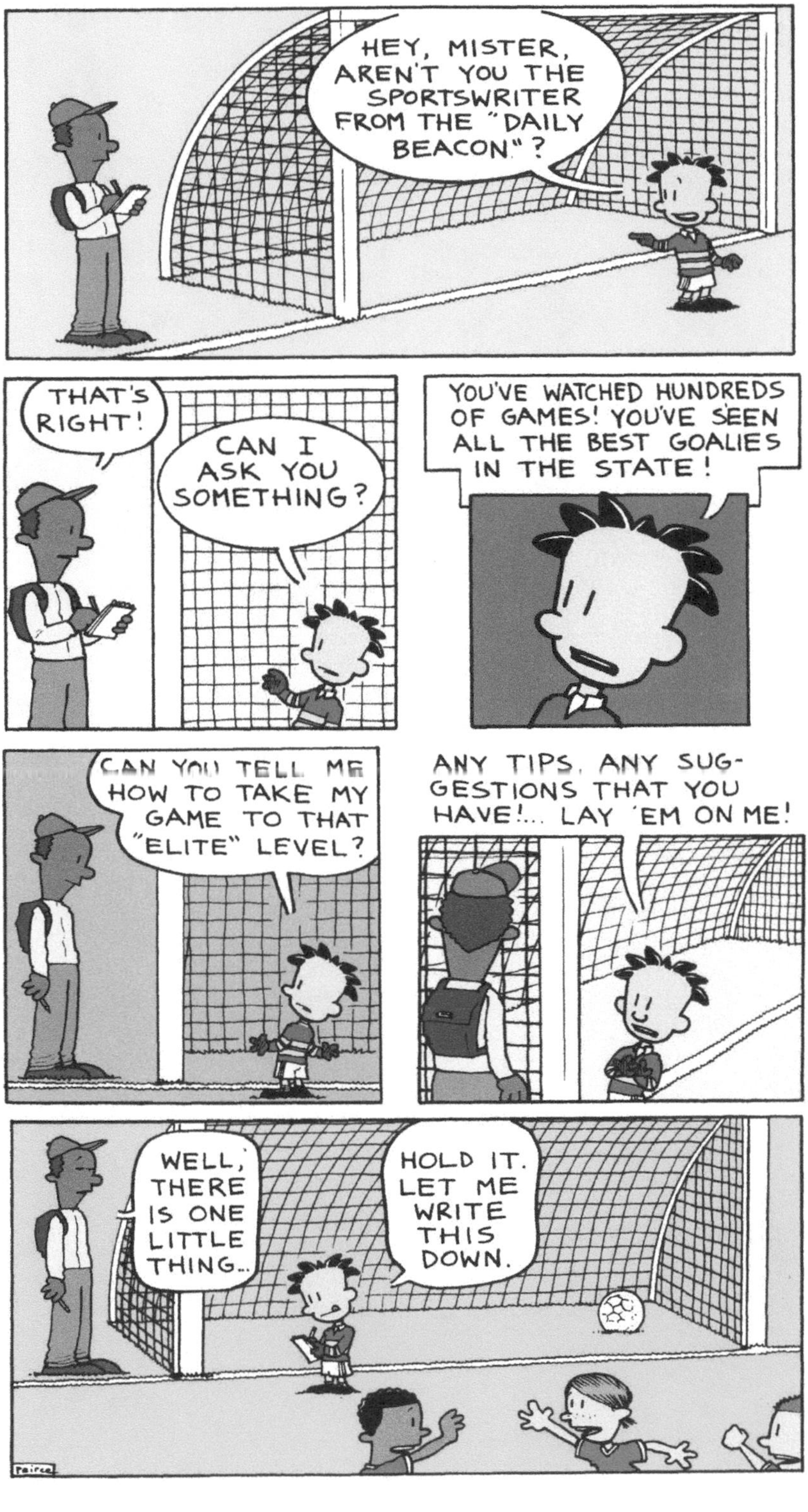
HEY, MISTER, AREN'T YOU THE SPORTSWRITER FROM THE "DAILY BEACON"?
THAT'S RIGHT!
CAN I ASK YOU SOMETHING?
YOU'VE WATCHED HUNDREDS OF GAMES! YOU'VE SEEN ALL THE BEST GOALIES IN THE STATE!
CAN YOU TELL ME HOW TO TAKE MY GAME TO THAT "ELITE" LEVEL?
ANY TIPS, ANY SUG- GESTIONS THAT YOU HAVE!... LAY 'EM ON ME!
WELL, THERE IS ONE LITTLE THING...
HOLD IT. LET ME WRITE THIS DOWN.
peirce

LADIES AND GENTS, I NEED A VOLUNTEER!
AH, JENNY! VERY GOOD!
NOW HOLD STILL! THIS WILL JUST TAKE A MOMENT!
ALL RIGHTEE! AS YOU CAN SEE, CLASS, JENNY HAS GIVEN ME A PIECE OF HER HAIR!
HEY, SWEETCAKES, CAN I HAVE A FEW STRANDS OF THAT FOR MY SCRAP-BOOK?
GO AWAY.
Peirce

ALL RIGHT, I'VE CAREFULLY PLACED THE GLASS SLIDE BENEATH THE LENS.
NATE, YOU'RE FIRST IN LINE! GO AHEAD AND TAKE A LOOK AT JENNY'S HAIR, MAGNIFIED FOUR HUNDRED TIMES!
DID YOU HEAR THAT, JENNY? FOUR HUNDRED TIMES!
I'M ABOUT TO GET UP CLOSE AND PERSONAL WITH YOUR DNA!
EW.
PEIRCE

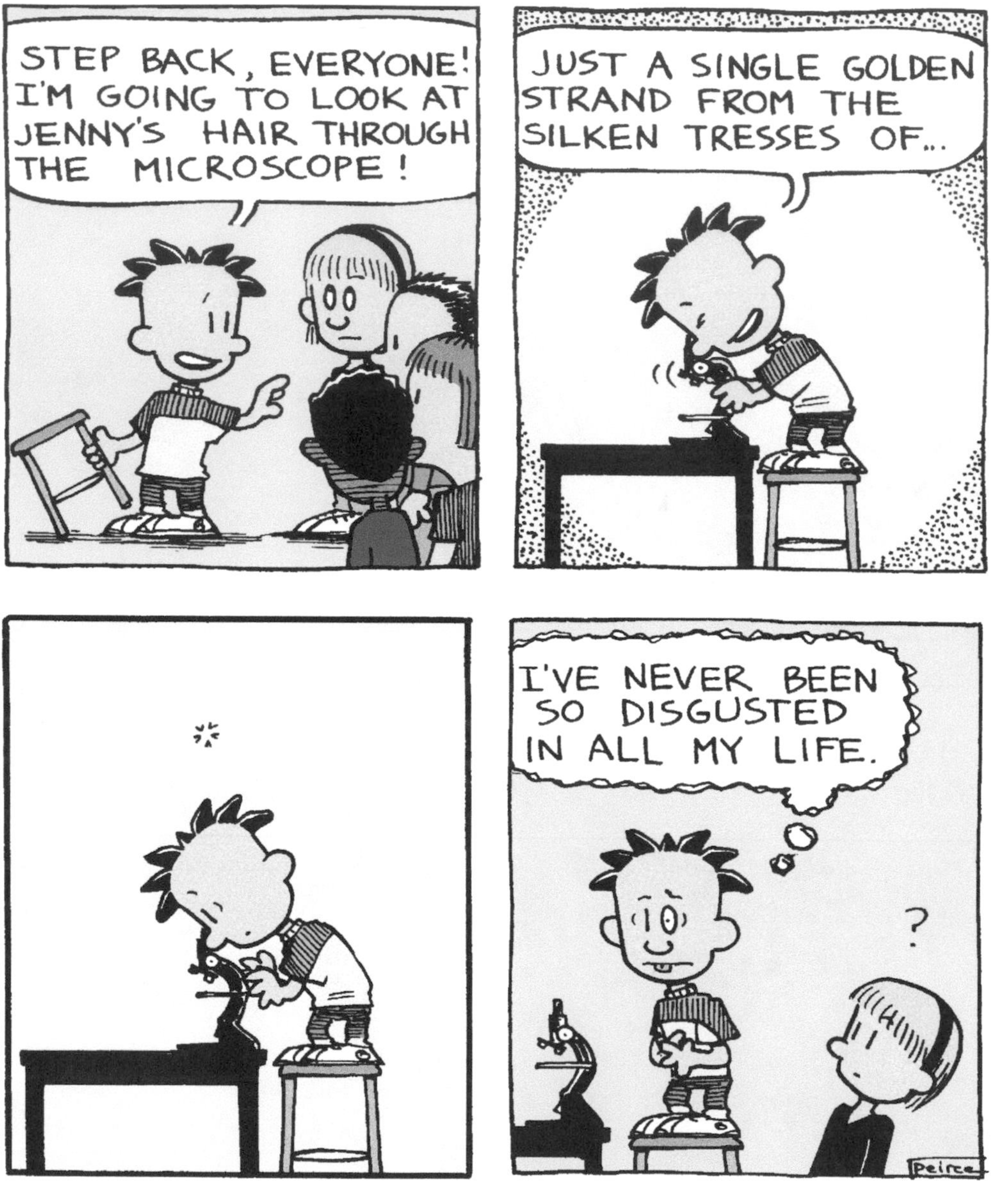
STEP BACK, EVERYONE! I'M GOING TO LOOK AT JENNY'S HAIR THROUGH THE MICROSCOPE!
JUST A SINGLE GOLDEN STRAND FROM THE SILKEN TRESSES OF...
I'VE NEVER BEEN SO DISGUSTED IN ALL MY LIFE.
?
Peirce

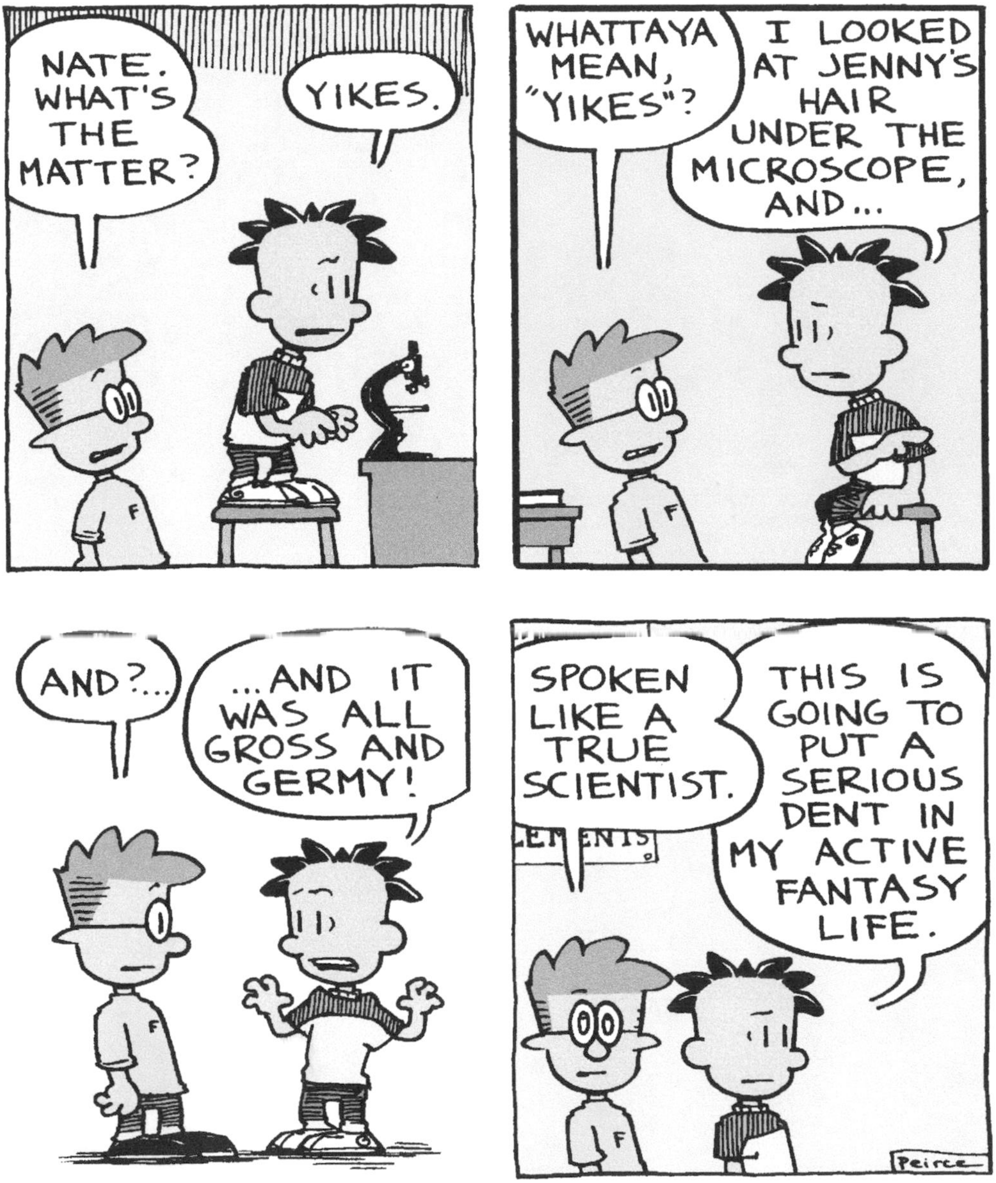
NATE. WHAT'S THE MATTER?
YIKES.
WHATTAYA MEAN, "YIKES"?
I LOOKED AT JENNY'S HAIR UNDER THE MICROSCOPE, AND...
AND?...
...AND IT WAS ALL GROSS AND GERMY!
SPOKEN LIKE A TRUE SCIENTIST.
THIS IS GOING TO PUT A SERIOUS DENT IN MY ACTIVE FANTASY LIFE.
Peirce

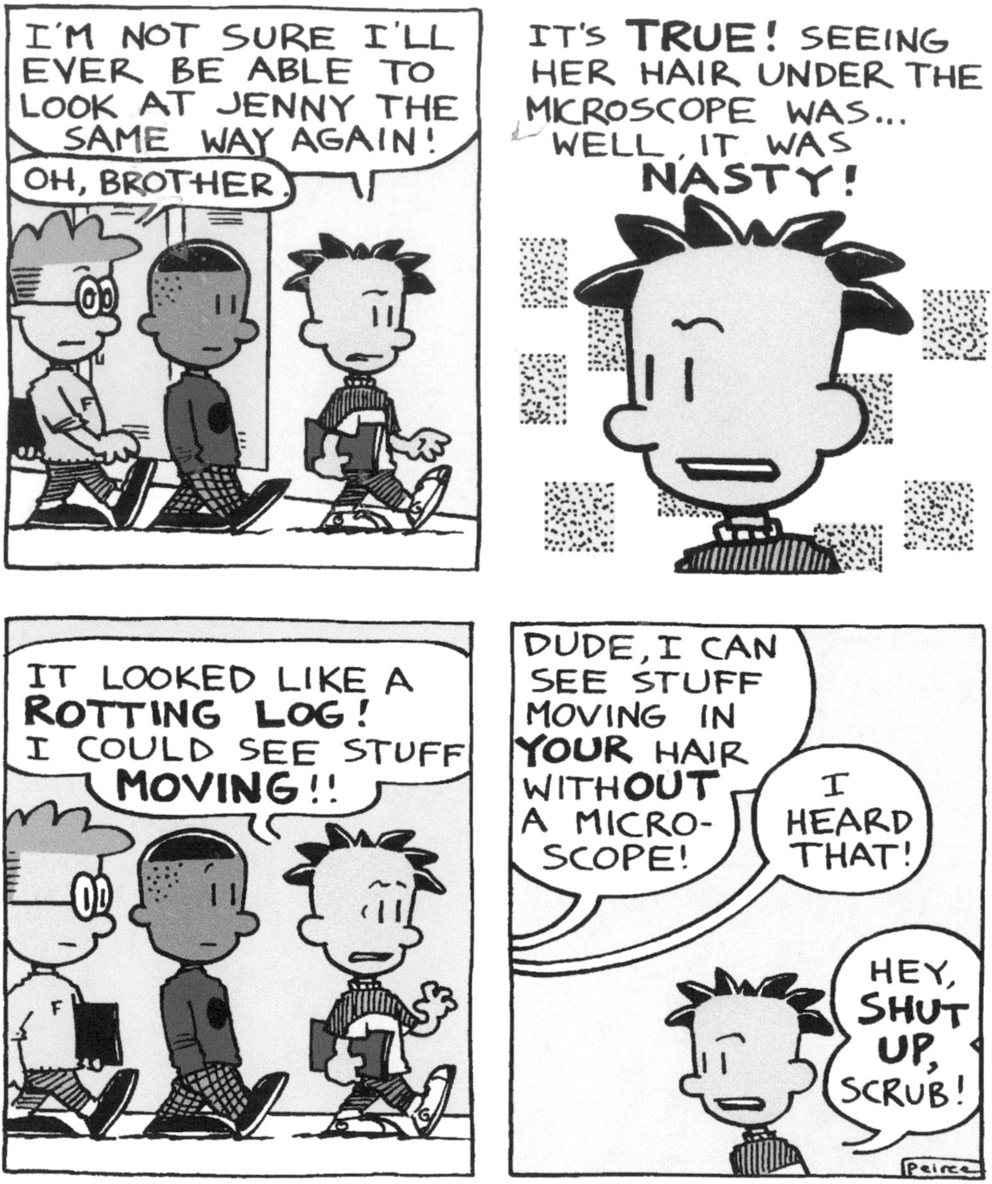
I'M NOT SURE I'LL EVER BE ABLE TO LOOK AT JENNY THE SAME WAY AGAIN!
OH, BROTHER.
IT'S TRUE! SEEING HER HAIR UNDER THE MICROSCOPE WAS... WELL, IT WAS NASTY!
IT LOOKED LIKE A ROTTING LOG! I COULD SEE STUFF MOVING!!
DUDE, I CAN SEE STUFF MOVING IN YOUR HAIR WITHOUT A MICRO-SCOPE!
I HEARD THAT!
HEY, SHUT UP, SCRUB!
Peirce

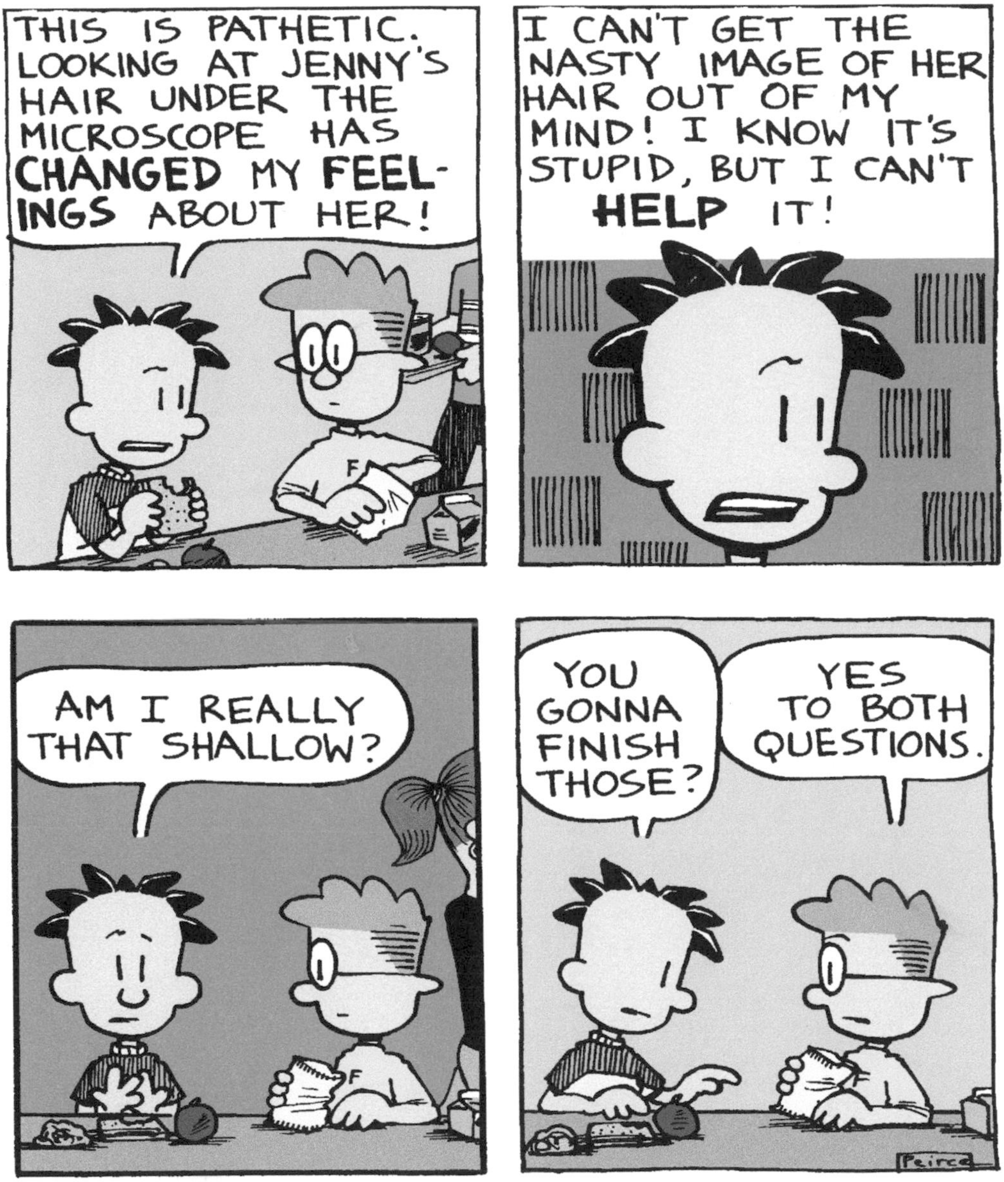
THIS IS PATHETIC. LOOKING AT JENNY'S HAIR UNDER THE MICROSCOPE HAS CHANGED MY FEELINGS ABOUT HER!
I CAN'T GET THE NASTY IMAGE OF HER HAIR OUT OF MY MIND! I KNOW IT'S STUPID, BUT I CAN'T HELP IT!
AM I REALLY THAT SHALLOW?
YOU GONNA FINISH THOSE?
YES TO BOTH QUESTIONS.
Peirce

IT'S A PROVEN FACT THAT YAWNING IS CONTAGIOUS!
HM.
IT'S TRUE! HERE, LOOK! I'LL YAWN, AND BY WATCHING ME YAWN, YOU'LL FEEL LIKE...
EEEYAWNNN!
HEY, NOT YET!
DID I HAVE A CHOICE?
Peirce

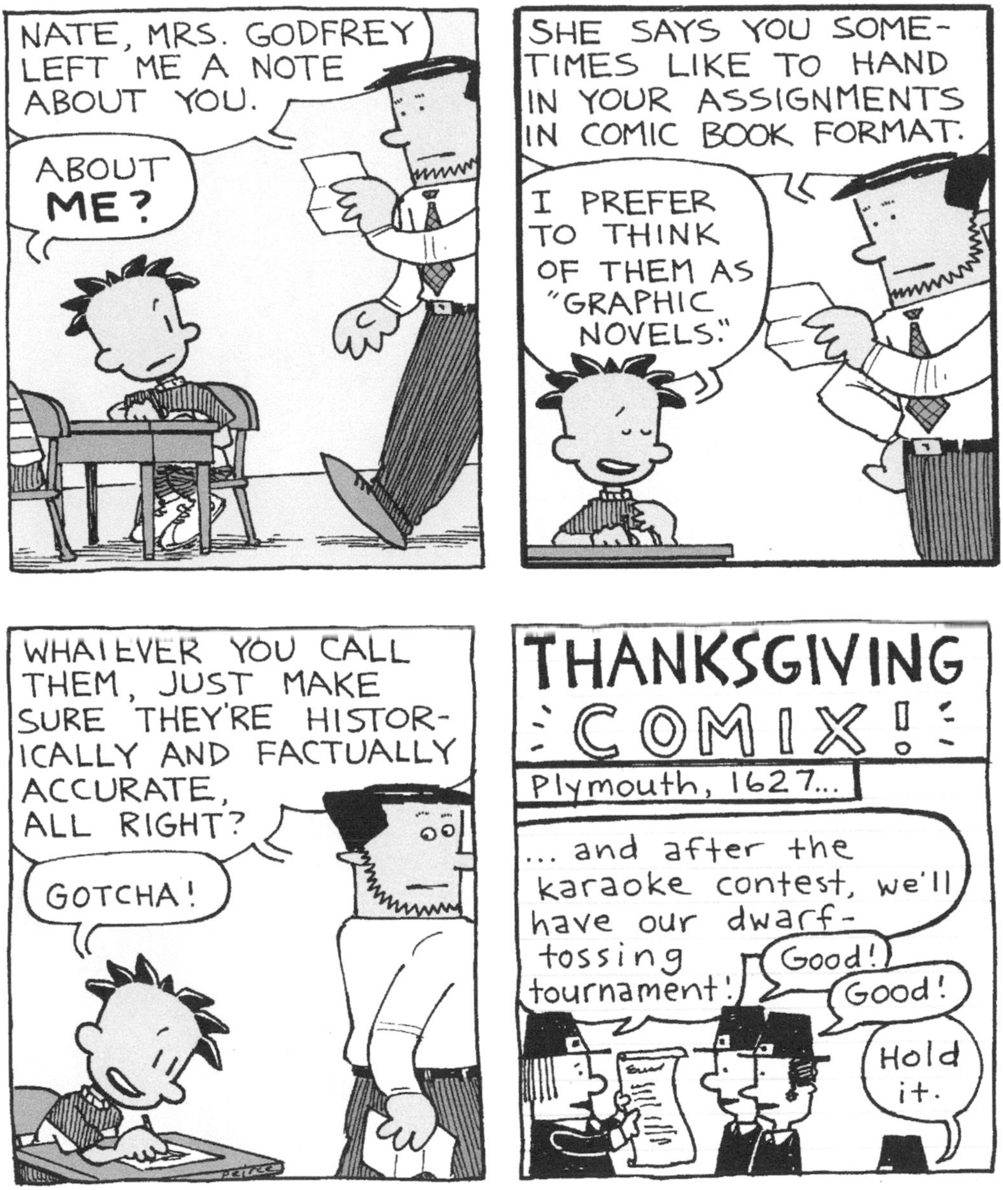
NATE, MRS. GODFREY LEFT ME A NOTE ABOUT YOU.
ABOUT ME?
SHE SAYS YOU SOMETIMES LIKE TO HAND IN YOUR ASSIGNMENTS IN COMIC BOOK FORMAT.
I PREFER TO THINK OF THEM AS "GRAPHIC NOVELS."
WHATEVER YOU CALL THEM, JUST MAKE SURE THEY'RE HISTORICALLY AND FACTUALLY ACCURATE, ALL RIGHT?
GOTCHA!
THANKSGIVING COMIX!
Plymouth, 1627...
... and after the karaoke contest, we'll have our dwarf-tossing tournament!
Good!
Good!
Hold it.

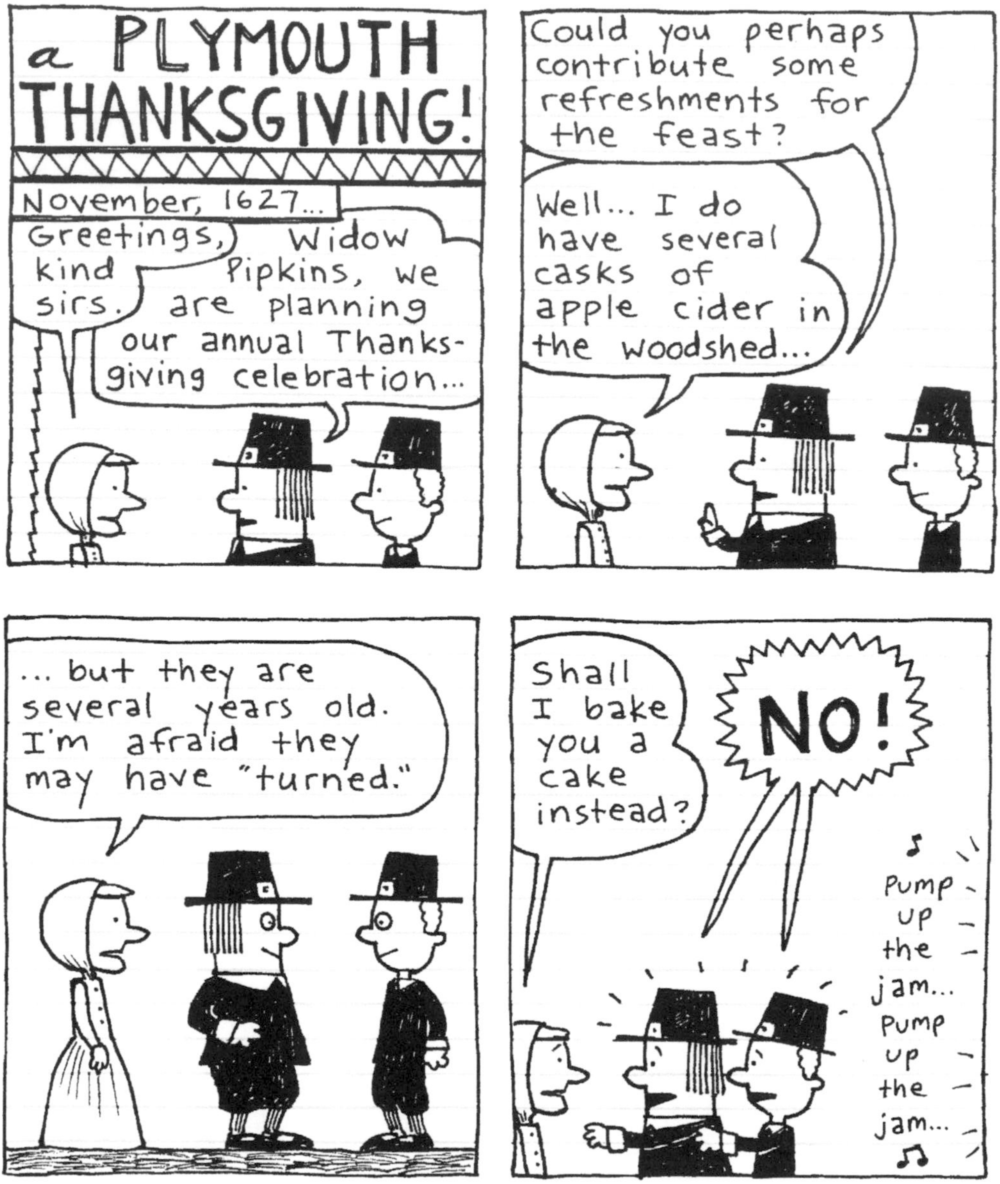
a PLYMOUTH THANKSGIVING!
November, 1627...
Greetings, kind sirs.
Widow Pipkins, we are planning our annual Thanksgiving celebration...
Could you perhaps contribute some refreshments for the feast?
Well... I do have several casks of apple cider in the woodshed...
... but they are several years old. I'm afraid they may have "turned."
Shall I bake you a cake instead?
NO!
Pump up the jam... Pump up the jam...

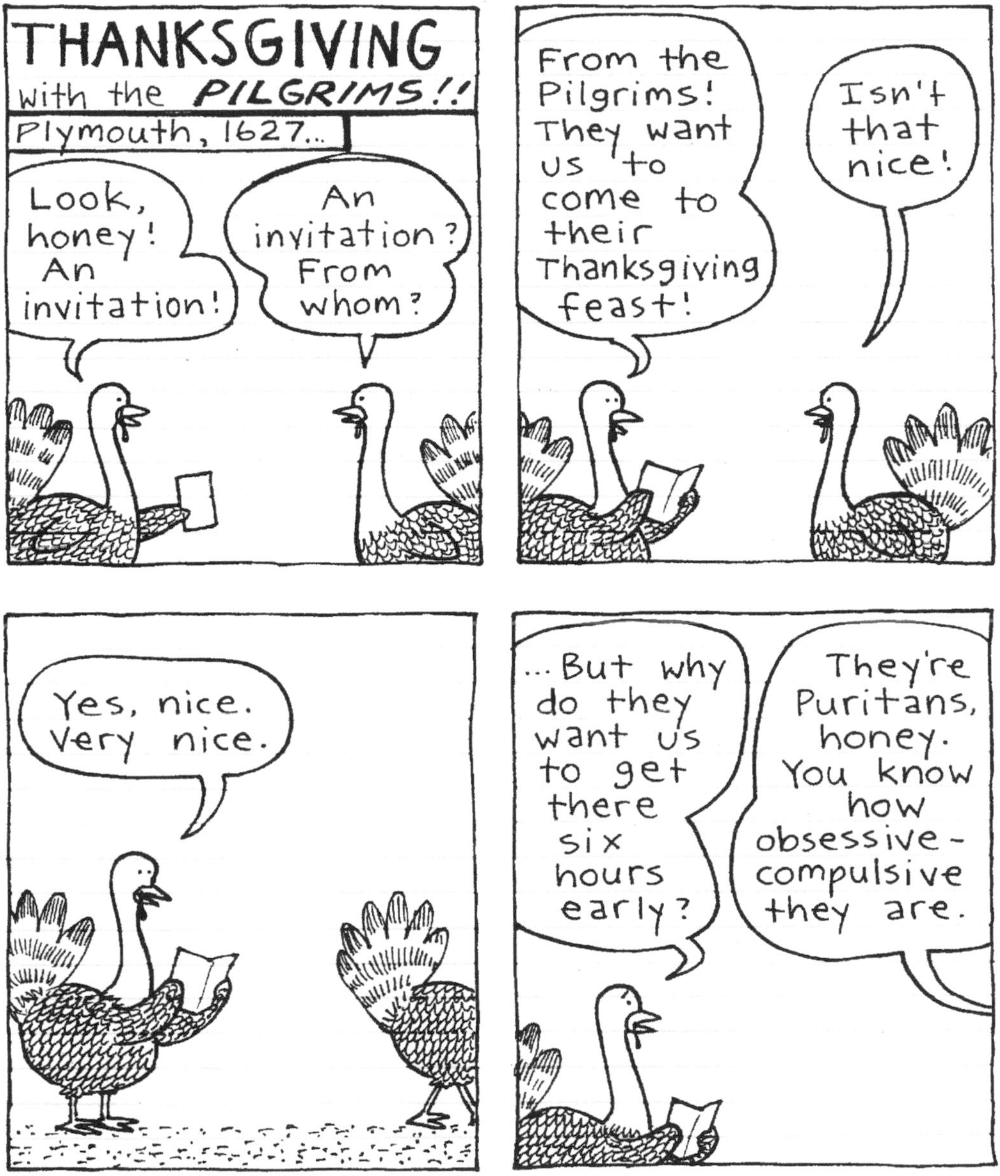
THANKSGIVING
with the PILGRIMS!!
Plymouth, 1627...
Look, honey! An invitation!
An invitation? From whom?
From the Pilgrims! They want us to come to their Thanksgiving feast!
Isn't that nice!
Yes, nice. Very nice.
...But why do they want us to get there six hours early?
They're Puritans, honey. You know how obsessive-compulsive they are.

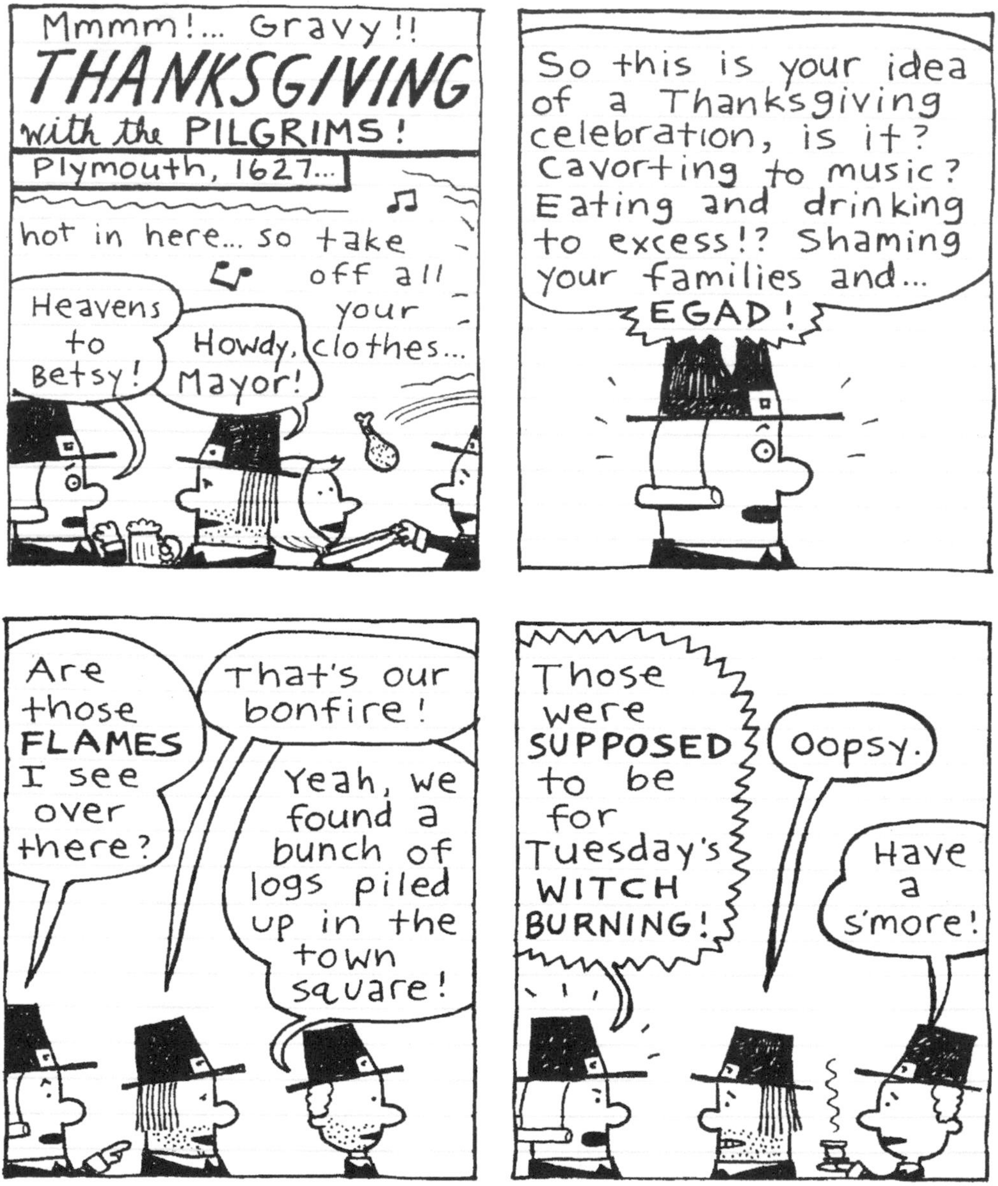
Mmmm!... Gravy!!
THANKSGIVING with the PILGRIMS!
Plymouth, 1627...
hot in here... so take off all your clothes...
Heavens to Betsy!
Howdy, Mayor!
So this is your idea of a Thanksgiving celebration, is it? Cavorting to music? Eating and drinking to excess!? Shaming your families and...
EGAD!
Are those FLAMES I see over there?
That's our bonfire!
Yeah, we found a bunch of logs piled up in the town square!
Those were SUPPOSED to be for Tuesday's WITCH BURNING!
Oopsy.
Have a s'more!

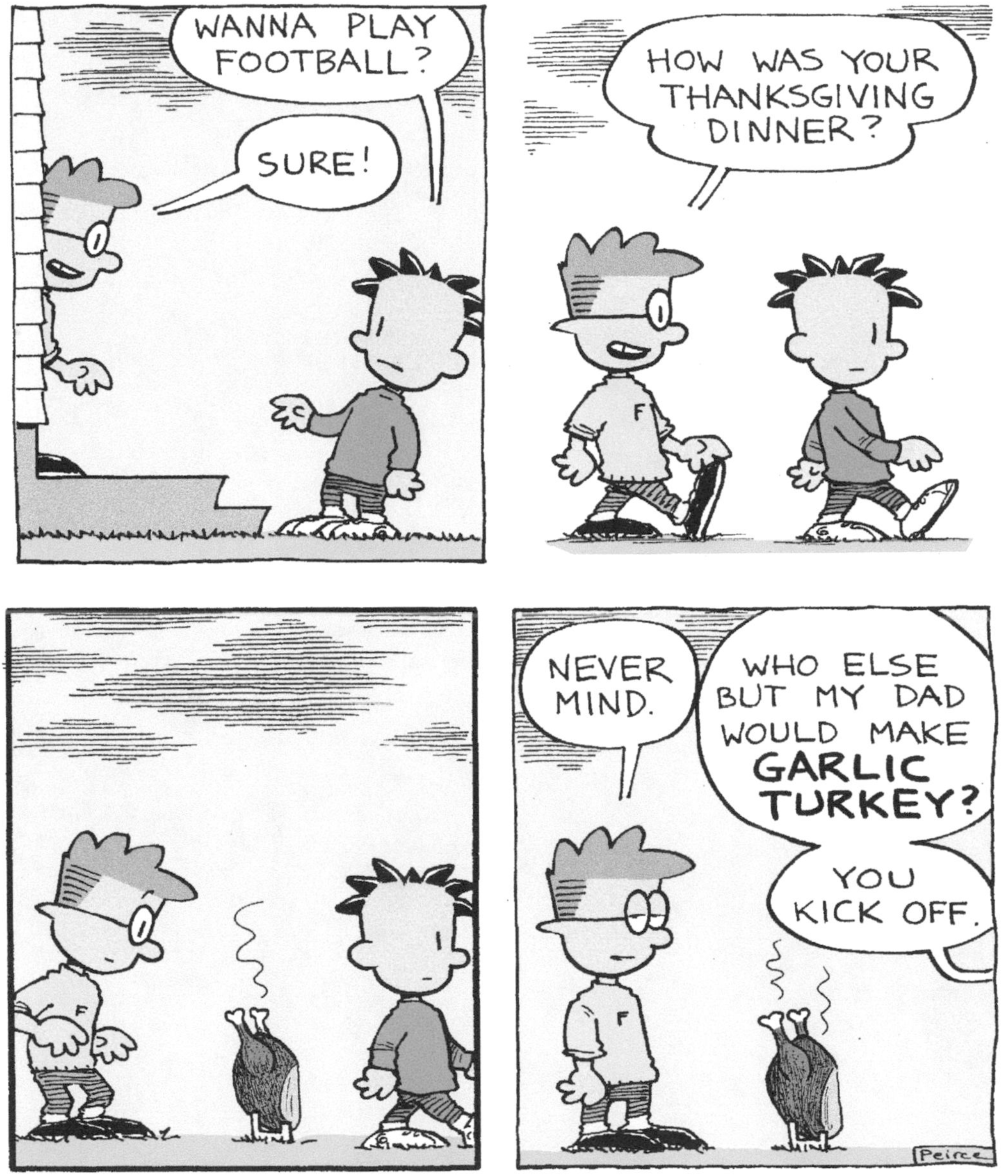
WANNA PLAY FOOTBALL?
SURE!
HOW WAS YOUR THANKSGIVING DINNER?
NEVER MIND.
WHO ELSE BUT MY DAD WOULD MAKE **GARLIC TURKEY?**
YOU KICK OFF.
Peirce

WHERE IS IT?
NATE! DID YOU FINISH OFF THE TURKEY?
WUMP!
LET ME REPHRASE THAT.
FUMBLE!
peirce

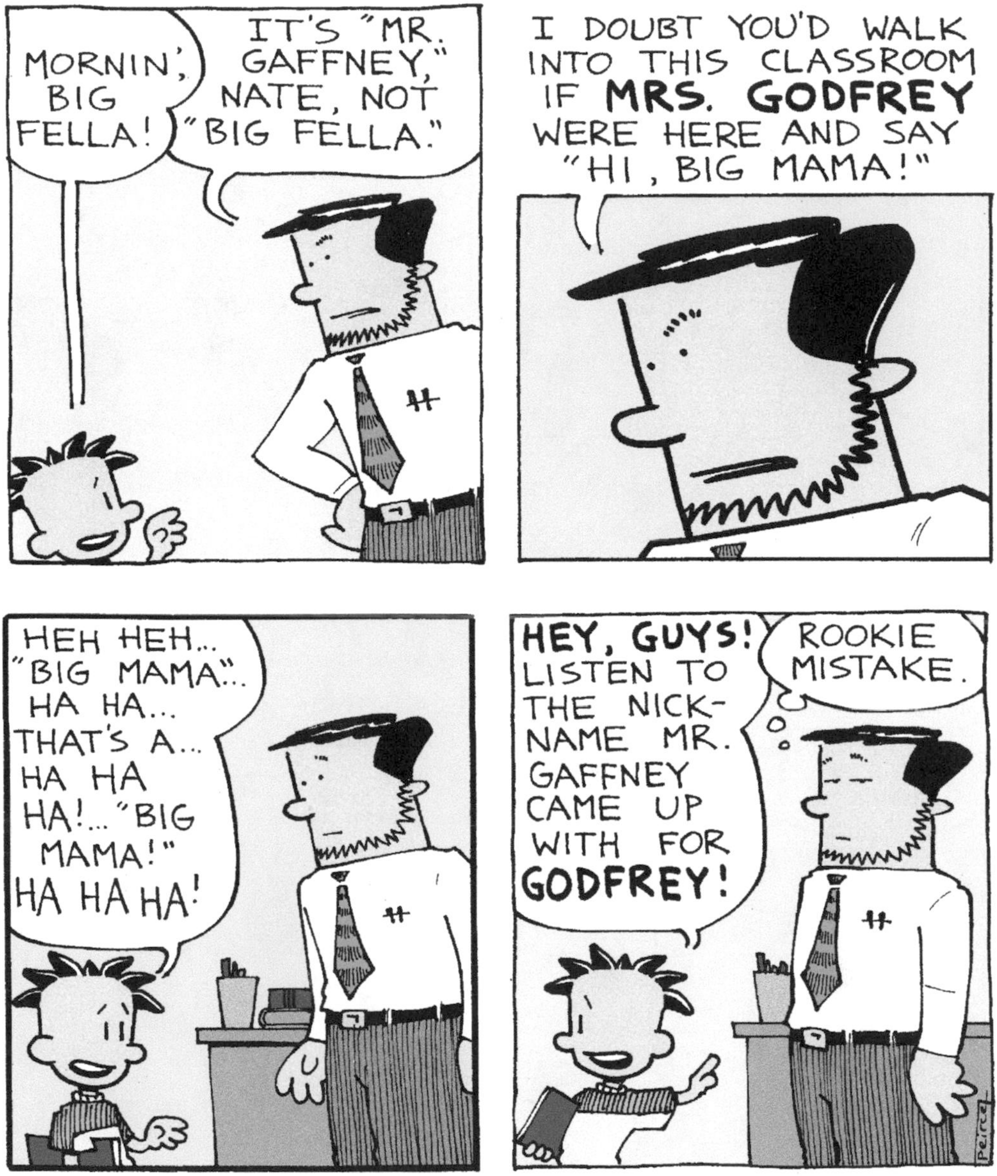
MORNIN', BIG FELLA!
IT'S "MR. GAFFNEY," NATE, NOT "BIG FELLA."
I DOUBT YOU'D WALK INTO THIS CLASSROOM IF MRS. GODFREY WERE HERE AND SAY "HI, BIG MAMA!"
HEH HEH... "BIG MAMA"... HA HA... THAT'S A... HA HA HA!... "BIG MAMA!" HA HA HA!
HEY, GUYS! LISTEN TO THE NICK-NAME MR. GAFFNEY CAME UP WITH FOR GODFREY!
ROOKIE MISTAKE.
peirce

HI, AL!

"HI, AL"?

IT'S YOUR NEW NICK-NAME, MR. GAFFNEY! WE CALL YOU AL G!

BUT... MY NAME'S NOT AL.

'COURSE IT ISN'T! "AL G." COMES FROM THE LETTERS A.L.G.!

A.L.G?

AMISH-LOOKING GUY!

MIGHT BE TIME TO LOSE THE BEARD.

YOU SEE, MR. GAFFNEY, THE FACT THAT THE STUDENTS HAVE GIVEN YOU A NICK-NAME MEANS YOU'VE MADE IT!
MADE IT?
YOU'RE NO LONGER THOUGHT OF AS A SUB! SUBS DON'T GET NICK-NAMES! BUT REAL TEACHERS DO!
ACCORDING TO WHOM?
ACCORDING TO ME! I'M THE COM-MISSIONER OF NICKNAMES!
A SELF-APPOINTED POST, I'M GUESSING.
HEEEEY! Q-TIP!
Peirce

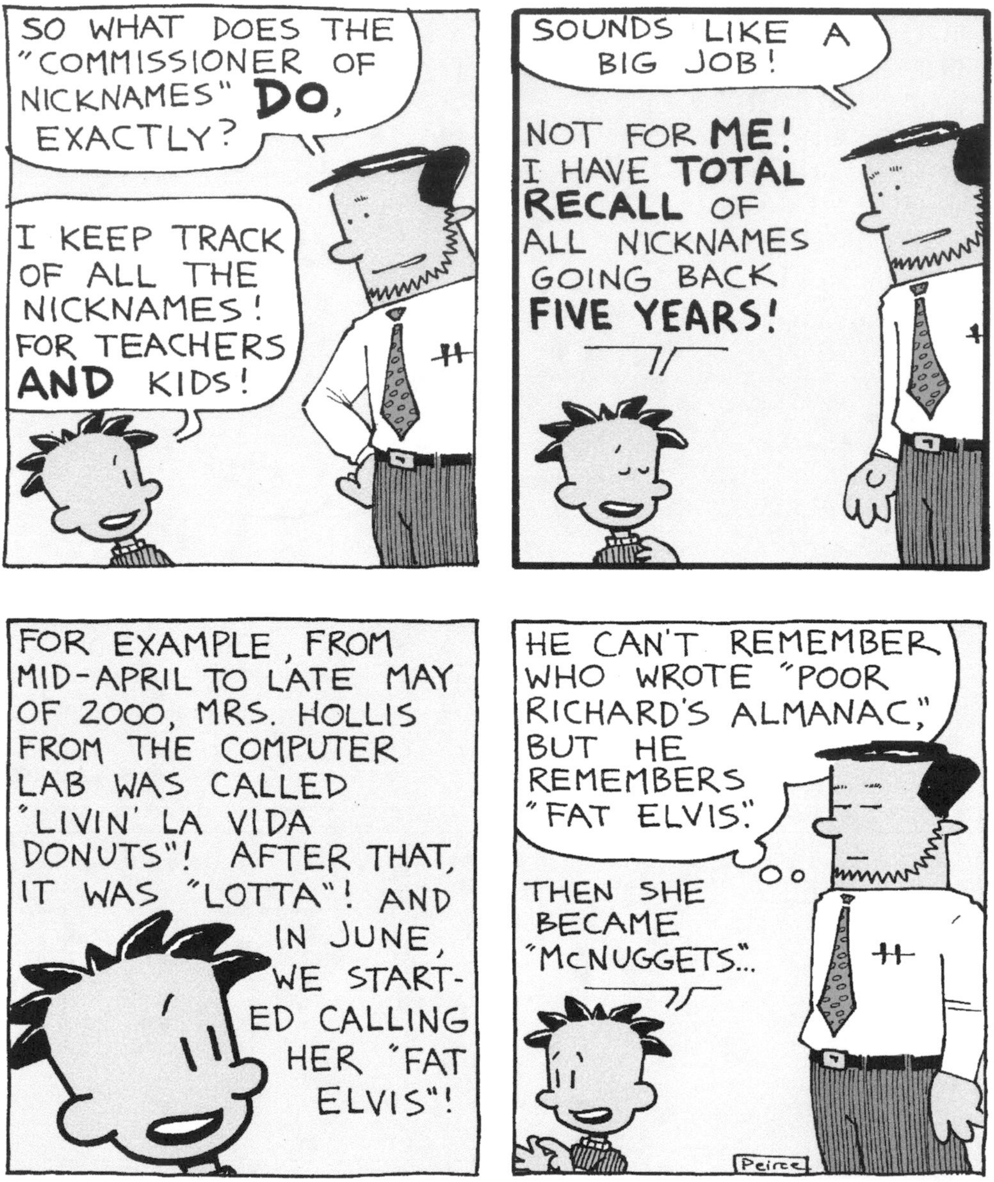

SO WHAT DOES THE "COMMISSIONER OF NICKNAMES" DO, EXACTLY?
I KEEP TRACK OF ALL THE NICKNAMES! FOR TEACHERS AND KIDS!
SOUNDS LIKE A BIG JOB!
NOT FOR ME! I HAVE TOTAL RECALL OF ALL NICKNAMES GOING BACK FIVE YEARS!
FOR EXAMPLE, FROM MID-APRIL TO LATE MAY OF 2000, MRS. HOLLIS FROM THE COMPUTER LAB WAS CALLED "LIVIN' LA VIDA DONUTS"! AFTER THAT, IT WAS "LOTTA"! AND IN JUNE, WE START-ED CALLING HER "FAT ELVIS"!
HE CAN'T REMEMBER WHO WROTE "POOR RICHARD'S ALMANAC," BUT HE REMEMBERS "FAT ELVIS."
THEN SHE BECAME "McNUGGETS."..
Peirce

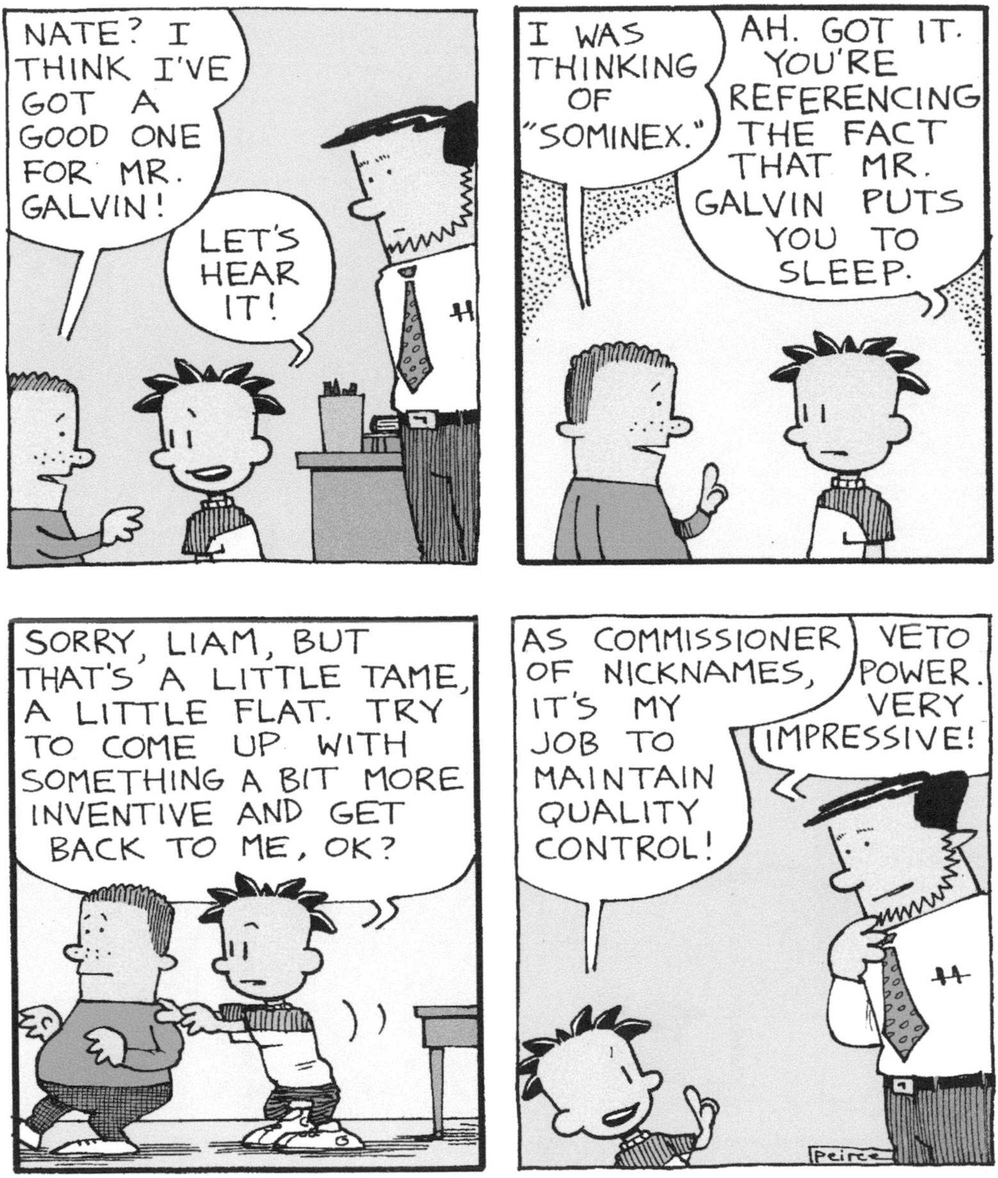
NATE? I THINK I'VE GOT A GOOD ONE FOR MR. GALVIN!
LET'S HEAR IT!
I WAS THINKING OF "SOMINEX."
AH. GOT IT. YOU'RE REFERENCING THE FACT THAT MR. GALVIN PUTS YOU TO SLEEP.
SORRY, LIAM, BUT THAT'S A LITTLE TAME, A LITTLE FLAT. TRY TO COME UP WITH SOMETHING A BIT MORE INVENTIVE AND GET BACK TO ME, OK?
AS COMMISSIONER OF NICKNAMES, IT'S MY JOB TO MAINTAIN QUALITY CONTROL!
VETO POWER. VERY IMPRESSIVE!
peirce

SO LONG, AL! SEE YOU TOMORROW!
NATE, I UNDERSTAND THAT YOU'VE GOT A NICKNAME FOR EVERYONE, BUT PLEASE... CALL ME MR. GAFFNEY.
MR. GAFFNEY
"AL." GOOD GRIEF.
I KIND OF LIKE THAT.
Peirce

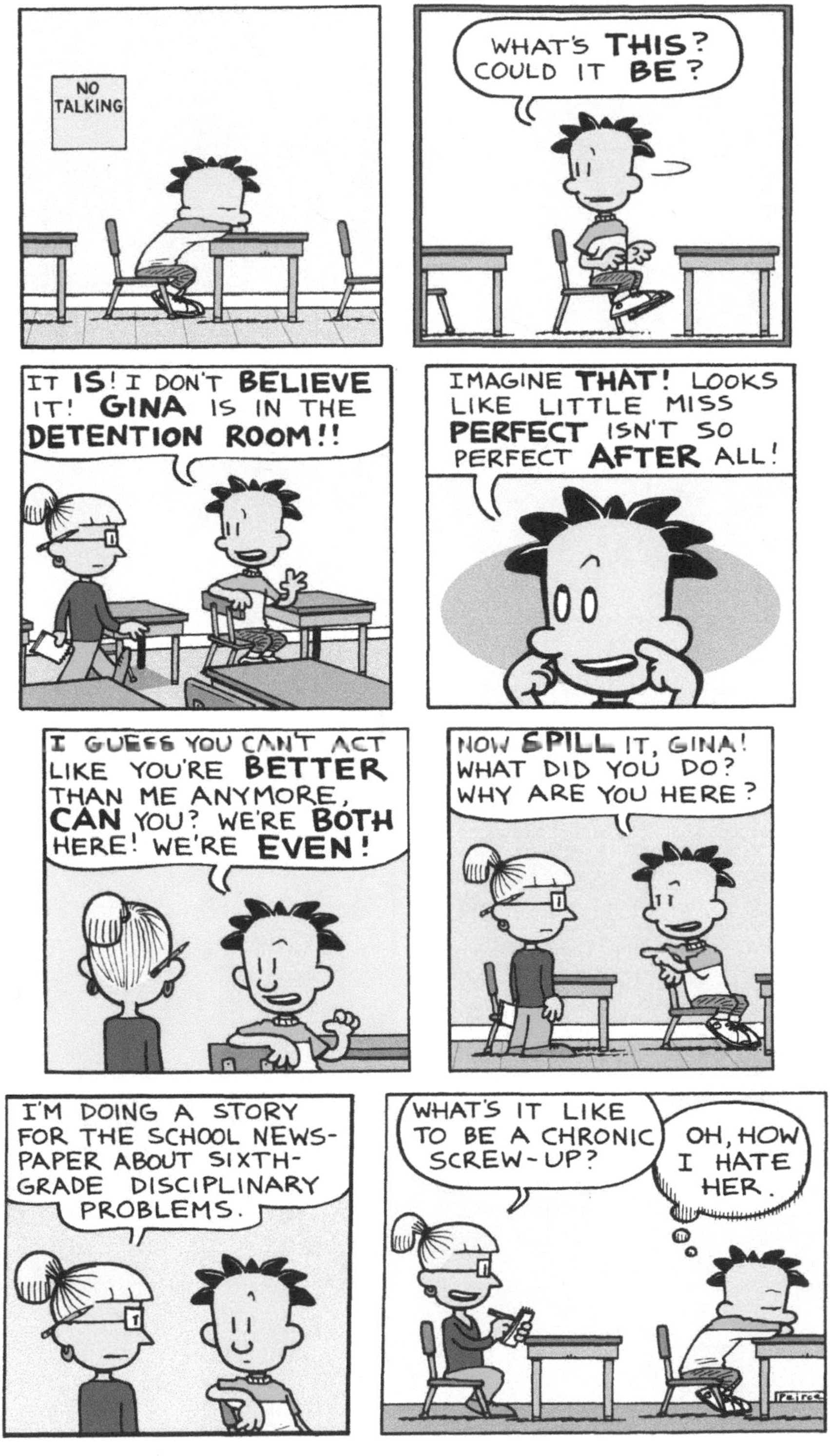
NO TALKING
WHAT'S THIS? COULD IT BE?
IT IS! I DON'T BELIEVE IT! GINA IS IN THE DETENTION ROOM!!
IMAGINE THAT! LOOKS LIKE LITTLE MISS PERFECT ISN'T SO PERFECT AFTER ALL!
I GUESS YOU CAN'T ACT LIKE YOU'RE BETTER THAN ME ANYMORE, CAN YOU? WE'RE BOTH HERE! WE'RE EVEN!
NOW SPILL IT, GINA! WHAT DID YOU DO? WHY ARE YOU HERE?
I'M DOING A STORY FOR THE SCHOOL NEWS-PAPER ABOUT SIXTH-GRADE DISCIPLINARY PROBLEMS.
WHAT'S IT LIKE TO BE A CHRONIC SCREW-UP?
OH, HOW I HATE HER.
PEIRCE

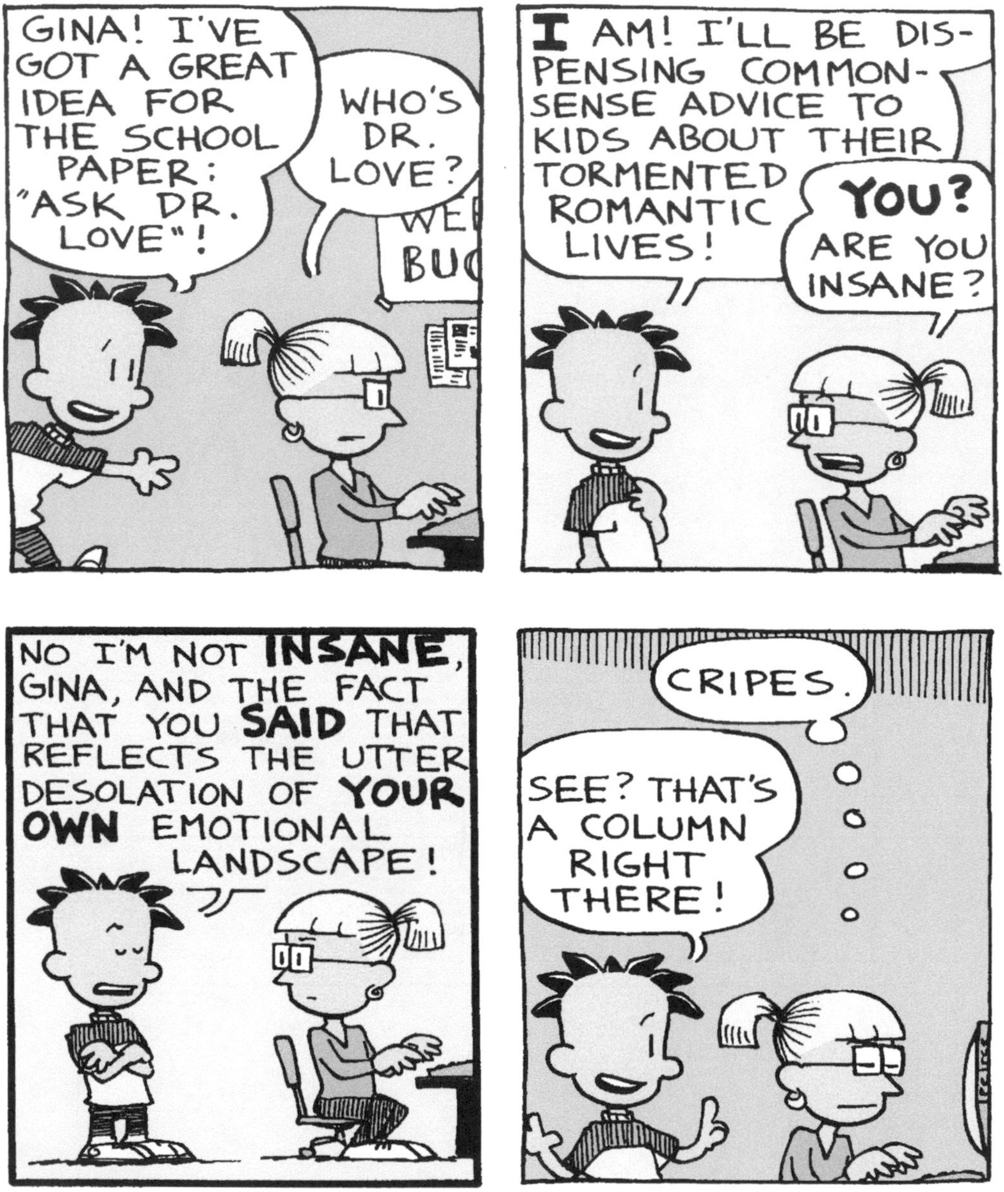
GINA! I'VE GOT A GREAT IDEA FOR THE SCHOOL PAPER: "ASK DR. LOVE"!
WHO'S DR. LOVE?
I AM! I'LL BE DISPENSING COMMON-SENSE ADVICE TO KIDS ABOUT THEIR TORMENTED ROMANTIC LIVES!
YOU? ARE YOU INSANE?
NO I'M NOT INSANE, GINA, AND THE FACT THAT YOU SAID THAT REFLECTS THE UTTER DESOLATION OF YOUR OWN EMOTIONAL LANDSCAPE!
CRIPES.
SEE? THAT'S A COLUMN RIGHT THERE!

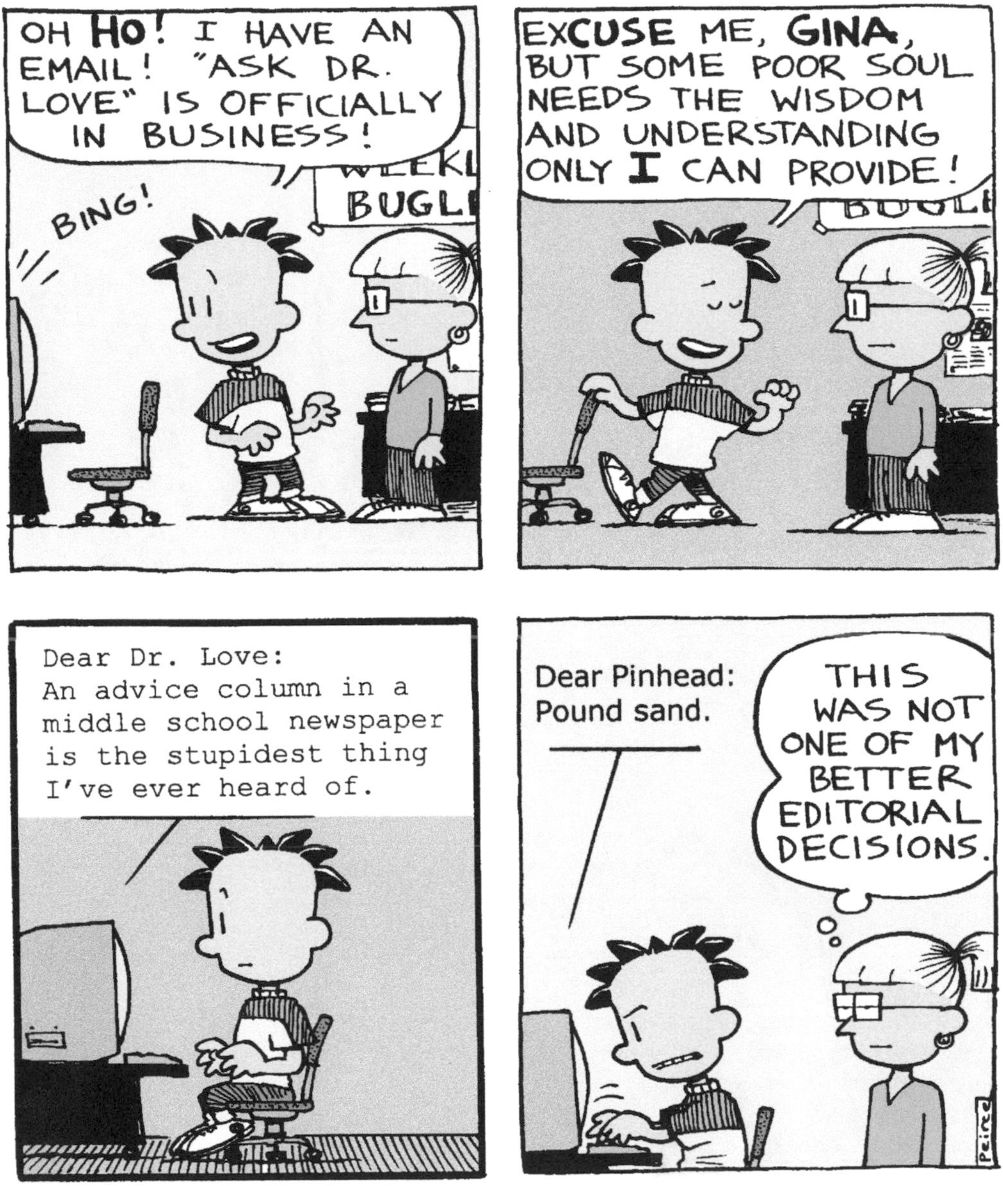
OH HO! I HAVE AN EMAIL! "ASK DR. LOVE" IS OFFICIALLY IN BUSINESS!
BING!
BUGL
EXCUSE ME, GINA, BUT SOME POOR SOUL NEEDS THE WISDOM AND UNDERSTANDING ONLY I CAN PROVIDE!
Dear Dr. Love:
An advice column in a middle school newspaper is the stupidest thing I've ever heard of.
Dear Pinhead:
Pound sand.
THIS WAS NOT ONE OF MY BETTER EDITORIAL DECISIONS.
Peirce

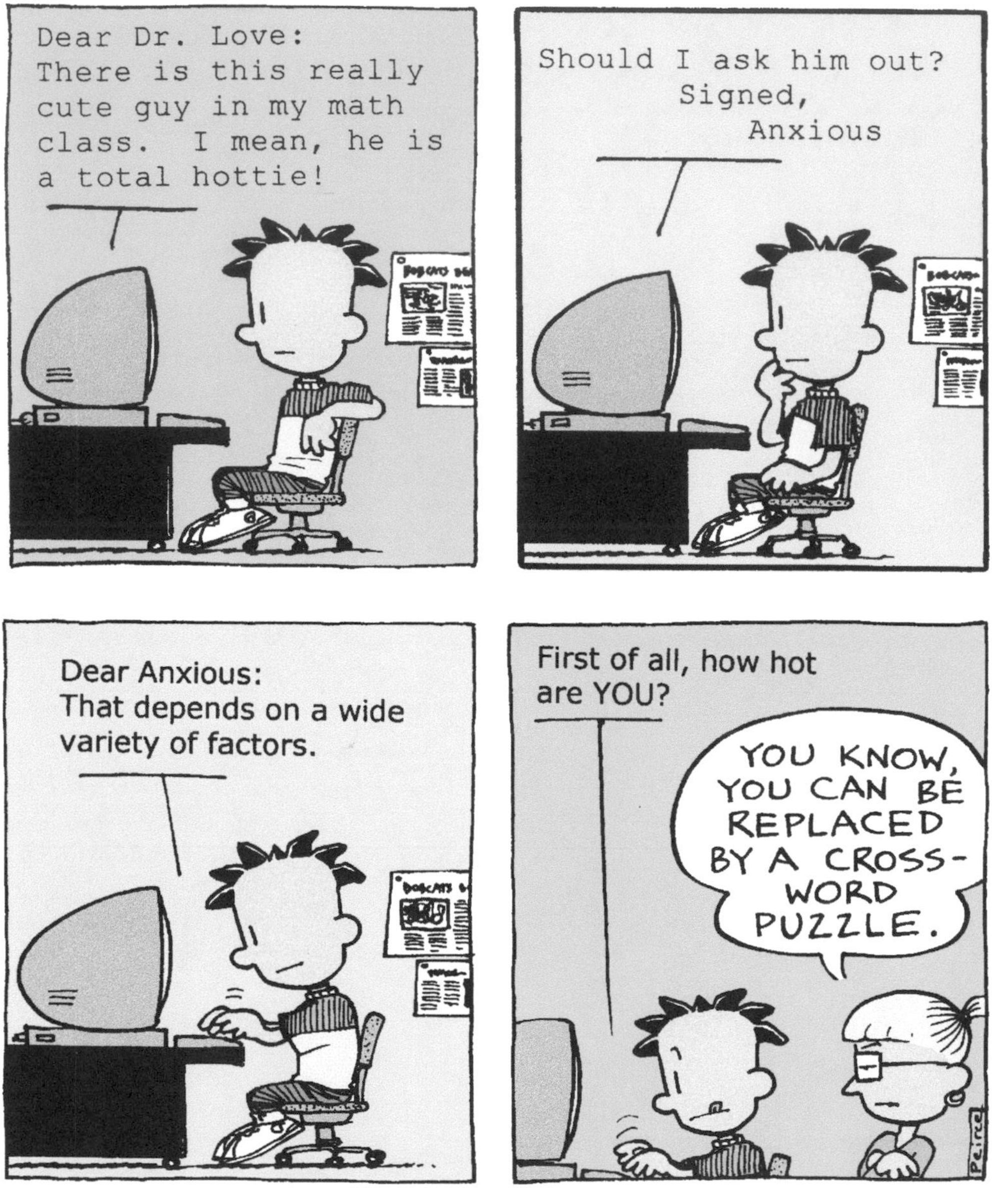
Dear Dr. Love:
There is this really cute guy in my math class. I mean, he is a total hottie!
Should I ask him out?
Signed,
Anxious
Dear Anxious:
That depends on a wide variety of factors.
First of all, how hot are YOU?
YOU KNOW, YOU CAN BE REPLACED BY A CROSS-WORD PUZZLE.
Peirce

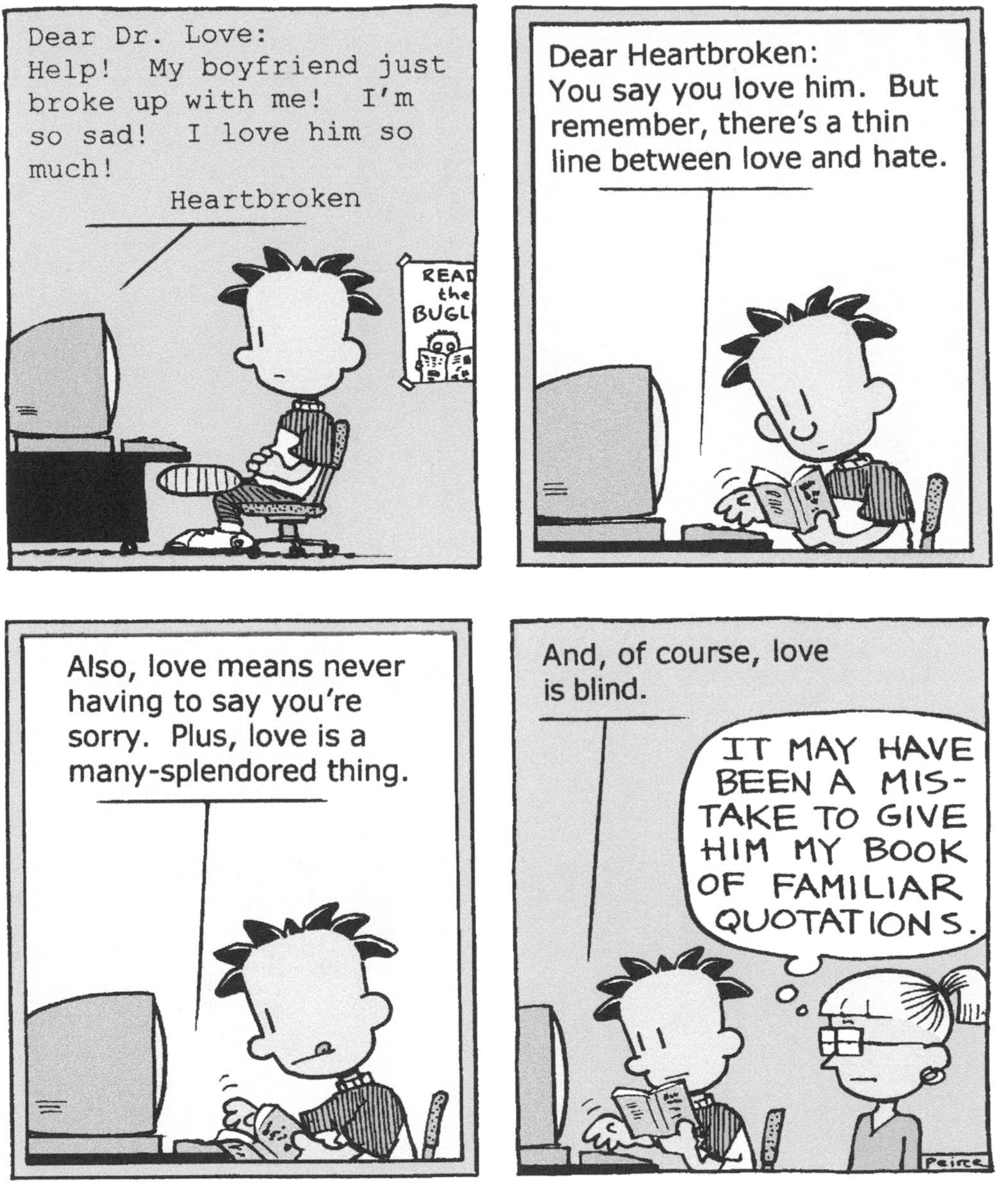

Dear Dr. Love:
Help! My boyfriend just broke up with me! I'm so sad! I love him so much!
Heartbroken
READ the BUGL
Dear Heartbroken:
You say you love him. But remember, there's a thin line between love and hate.
Also, love means never having to say you're sorry. Plus, love is a many-splendored thing.
And, of course, love is blind.
IT MAY HAVE BEEN A MISTAKE TO GIVE HIM MY BOOK OF FAMILIAR QUOTATIONS.
Peirce

Dear Dr. Love,
My girlfriend and I
really enjoy board games.
Every weekend she comes
over and we play Clue,
Monopoly, etc.

But lately it seems like
she is getting bored
with the same old games.
What should I do?
                Puzzled

Dear Puzzled:
Get a Life.

Or perhaps a
Yahtzee.

AND
PEOPLE
WONDER
WHY NEWS-
PAPERS
ARE IN
DECLINE.

222

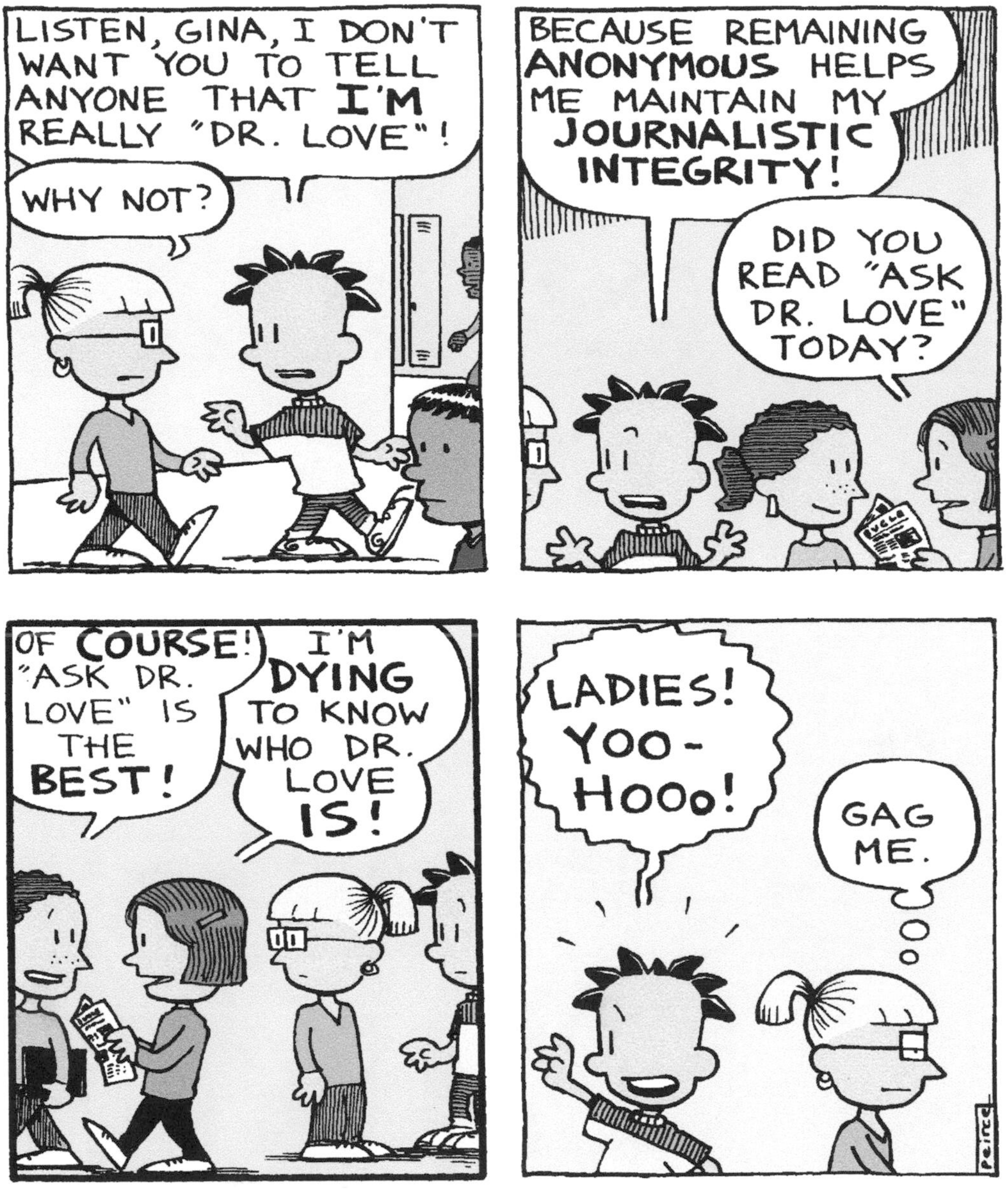
LISTEN, GINA, I DON'T WANT YOU TO TELL ANYONE THAT I'M REALLY "DR. LOVE"!
WHY NOT?
BECAUSE REMAINING ANONYMOUS HELPS ME MAINTAIN MY JOURNALISTIC INTEGRITY!
DID YOU READ "ASK DR. LOVE" TODAY?
OF COURSE! "ASK DR. LOVE" IS THE BEST!
I'M DYING TO KNOW WHO DR. LOVE IS!
LADIES! YOO-HOOoo!
GAG ME.
PEIRCE

Check out these and other books at ampkids.com

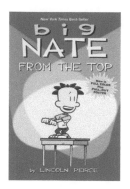

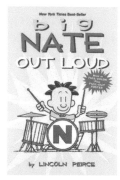

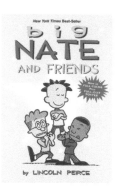

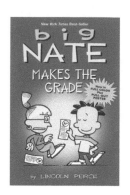

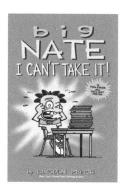

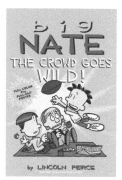

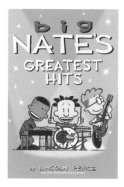

Also available:
Teaching and activity guides for each title.
AMP! Comics for Kids books make reading FUN!

CPSIA information can be obtained
at www.ICGtesting.com
Printed in the USA
LVHW071917130222
710754LV00039B/227